Veilfire

Sarah Finn

Published by Sarah Finn, 2024.

This is a work of fiction. Similarities to real people, places, or events are entirely coincidental.

VEILFIRE

First edition. November 9, 2024.

Copyright © 2024 Sarah Finn.

ISBN: 979-8227241061

Written by Sarah Finn.

Chapter 1: The Red District

He leans against a lamppost, utterly unfazed by the chaos around him. I can't help but notice his perfectly controlled stillness, like a predator biding its time. The crowd flows around him, giving him a wide berth, which only adds to his unsettling allure. No one here commands that kind of respect—except him. His gaze doesn't waver, like he's weighing me, measuring me against some unseen scale. He wears his confidence like armor, and it makes me itch to either challenge him or run as far as my legs can take me.

I try not to look back as I slide into a side alley, the damp bricks pressing in around me, narrowing my path to a single, lonely door at the end. The alley smells of rain and something metallic, like old blood and rusted iron. This is a place where people come to forget or be forgotten. The Guild's network thrives on places like this: grim, hidden nooks where whispers hold more value than coin, and the walls are thick with secrets nobody wants to know.

The Guild warned me about tonight. "Dangerous waters," they'd said. "Keep your head down, get the artifact, and get out." Simple instructions that somehow manage to feel impossible now that I'm here, especially with his face lingering in my mind. I shake it off. I can't let him, whoever he is, distract me. Focus is everything in my line of work, and distractions get you killed.

The door creaks open, and I step inside. The room is lit by a low, amber glow, flickering from a single bulb suspended from the ceiling, which casts ghostly shadows across the walls. I keep my hands steady as I scan the room, assessing the exits, the occupants—two men huddled in a corner, talking in low tones, a bartender polishing glasses with a damp rag, and an older woman nursing a drink, her gaze sharp and knowing. She notices me, her eyes narrowing just slightly before returning to her glass. Nothing here seems overtly threatening, but I know better than to let my guard down.

I step up to the bar, tapping the counter twice—a signal that means I'm here on business. The bartender raises an eyebrow, his face impassive, but he nods and disappears behind a curtain. A chill runs down my spine. This is the part I hate—the waiting. Every second feels like bait dangling from a hook, tempting fate. I glance over my shoulder, half expecting to see that intense stranger leaning in the doorway, watching me like a fox who knows exactly how the hunt will end. But the doorway is empty.

Moments later, the bartender reemerges with a small wooden box. He slides it across the counter to me without a word, and I can feel the weight of whatever's inside tugging at me even before I touch it. This is the artifact, all right—wrapped in spells so thick they nearly buzz. The Guild wasn't exaggerating when they said this was potent. I tuck it under my arm, nod to the bartender, and turn to leave.

That's when I feel it—a hand on my shoulder, firm and insistent. My heart stops. Slowly, I turn, and there he is, the man from the street, standing so close I can smell a hint of something dark and intoxicating on him, like leather and smoke. His hand lingers on my shoulder, his grip strong but not painful. He's not trying to hurt me. No, his touch is gentle, which somehow feels worse, more disconcerting.

"Leaving so soon?" His voice is smooth, just a touch amused, like this is all some elaborate game. I should shove him away, tell him to mind his own business, but something about his stare pins me in place, holds me there like a moth caught in a web. I force a smirk, trying to keep my cool.

"Didn't realize you were planning a welcoming committee," I reply, arching an eyebrow. His grin widens, flashing a hint of something dark and thrilling.

"You looked like you could use one," he says, his eyes flicking down to the box under my arm. "That's a dangerous trinket you've got there. You sure you know what to do with it?"

"Maybe I do," I shoot back, shrugging his hand off. I try to step away, but he blocks my path, one hand braced against the wall. He's close—too close. His gaze is sharp, challenging, and there's a glimmer of something in his eyes that feels dangerously close to admiration.

"Or maybe you're just a girl playing with fire," he murmurs, his voice low, dripping with dark amusement. "What's your name, anyway?"

I meet his gaze, my chin lifting defiantly. "What's yours?"

A slow, lazy grin spreads across his face, and he chuckles, shaking his head. "Ah, a mystery woman. I can respect that." He steps back, giving me space, but his eyes remain locked on me, as if he's memorizing every detail, every twitch, every flicker of emotion.

"Good luck with that artifact," he says, tipping an imaginary hat. "Just don't get yourself killed over it."

He walks away, his footsteps fading into the night, leaving me feeling strangely bereft. I'm not sure why, but part of me wishes he'd stayed, that he'd pressed a little harder. Instead, I'm left standing there, clutching the box and feeling the weight of his words settling in my chest. There's a warning there, a caution that I'd be foolish to ignore.

As I slip out into the cold, damp air, my mind races. The Red District has a way of getting under your skin, of making you question every choice, every instinct. I glance down at the box, feeling its pull once more, and a strange, exhilarating chill runs through me. This isn't over, not by a long shot.

The city swallows sound in strange ways, the hustle and hum of the Red District muting to a low, droning throb as I walk away. The air feels charged, thick with the murmur of secrets and half-kept promises. But his presence lingers, leaving a frisson of something—curiosity, wariness—buzzing in my chest. I know better than to look back, but the urge is there, persistent and tantalizing. What game was he playing? Or, more likely, what game did he think I was playing? I take a steadying breath and tighten my grip on the box, feeling its odd warmth seep through my coat. Every nerve is on edge. I have what I came for, and I can't afford to let anything jeopardize my exit.

A couple of blocks away, I duck into an alcove and take a moment to catch my breath, trying to still the strange fluttering in my chest. The box, which looks deceptively plain, pulses against my side, as if it has its own heartbeat. I haven't dared to open it yet, not with the Guild's warnings echoing in my mind. But its pull is undeniable, an invisible thread weaving itself through my skin, compelling me to understand it, to figure out what makes it so valuable.

I steady myself and step back into the crowded street, weaving through throngs of late-night revelers and vendors hawking oddities that glint and shimmer under the electric lights. As I move, I catch snippets of conversation: deals struck in harsh whispers, laughter so hollow it sounds like a cough, promises exchanged with no more weight than a puff of smoke. In the Red District, everything is currency, and trust is a rare commodity that fetches a high price. Not that I've ever wanted it—trusting people has never been high on my list of priorities. Still, tonight has rattled me more than I'd care to admit. I can still feel his eyes on me, that sly smirk flickering in the edges of my mind.

But there's no time to dwell. I need to get out of this part of town before the artifact decides to make itself known in a way I can't control. I pick up my pace, keeping my head low, feeling the weight of the night pressing in.

"Leaving without saying goodbye?"

His voice is casual, too casual, and I freeze mid-step. I turn slowly, forcing my face into a mask of indifference as I find him standing there, hands in his pockets, leaning just slightly in my direction. It's him. Somehow, he's managed to find me again, slipping through the streets as easily as shadows cling to the corners. My stomach twists, a slow, uneasy spiral. It takes everything in me not to let him see how much he's rattled me.

"Goodbye implies there was ever a hello," I reply, keeping my voice steady. His eyebrows lift, and he chuckles, the sound low and strangely warm despite the icy edge to his gaze. He steps closer, and I have to resist the urge to step back.

"You're funny," he says, as if he's sizing me up anew. "Though, I wouldn't be surprised if you haven't heard that much. Funny doesn't keep you alive in these parts."

I match his gaze, refusing to look away. "Maybe I don't have to be funny to stay alive. Maybe I'm just that good."

He smiles, a slow, almost reluctant curve of his lips, and for a moment, I catch something softer, more familiar in his eyes. But then, just as quickly, it's gone, replaced by a steely glint that makes my skin prickle.

"Good," he says softly, almost to himself. "I'd hate for this to be too easy."

The words hang between us, heavy and foreboding. He tilts his head, studying me with an intensity that makes me feel like a specimen under glass, like he's unraveling every layer I've carefully built around myself. But I don't flinch. I've played this game before, with men more dangerous than him. Or at least, that's what I tell myself.

"So, what now?" I say, keeping my tone light, as if I'm unbothered. "You've found me. Congratulations. Do you want a medal or just a pat on the back?"

He grins, but there's a hardness behind it. "I was hoping for a bit more than that, actually. Something tells me that box of yours might hold something worth my trouble."

My pulse spikes, but I force myself to keep calm. "Funny. I thought you'd be the type to value his trouble more highly."

"Oh, I do," he murmurs, and his voice drops, just enough to make the hairs on my arms rise. "Which is why I suggest you hand that over before things get... complicated."

I scoff, though I can feel my heart hammering in my chest. I'm in deep, but the Guild sent me for this job because they knew I could handle it. They trust me—or as much as the Guild trusts anyone—and I'm not about to let some smug stranger wrest it away with a cocky smile.

"Let me guess," I say, adopting a bored tone. "This is the part where you try to intimidate me, and I swoon helplessly in fear, maybe hand over the goods in some grand gesture of defeat?"

"Something like that," he says smoothly, but there's a flicker of genuine amusement in his eyes, as if he's impressed. "Though I'd hardly call it grand. I'm just here to make an offer."

"And if I'm not interested?"

"Then I'll just have to insist."

His hand moves, quick as lightning, but I'm faster. Before he can lay a finger on me, I twist, sliding out of his reach. He straightens, a dark light sparking in his eyes, and I realize I've surprised him. Good. Let him think I'm more than what I seem. In this line of work, it pays to have people underestimate you.

But before I can move again, he blocks my path, his expression hardening. There's a tension between us now, coiled and dangerous, and I can't deny the thrill of it, even if it's laced with the knowledge that this could end badly.

"Last chance," he says, his voice a low rumble. "Walk away now, leave that box, and I might just let you get on with your night."

I laugh, shaking my head. "Nice try. But I don't hand over priceless artifacts to strange men in alleys."

He sighs, a sound filled with mock exasperation, but I can see the challenge flicker to life in his gaze again. For a second, I think he's going to lunge, but then he pauses, tilting his head as if listening to something far off.

"Fine," he says, and the unexpected surrender catches me off guard. "But don't say I didn't warn you."

With one last, unreadable look, he steps back, melting into the shadows like he was never there. I exhale, the adrenaline draining from me in a dizzying rush. I don't know why he gave up so easily, but I don't waste time questioning it. I slip back into the street, the artifact tucked securely against me, my mind racing.

It's only as I make my way home, weaving through the darkened streets, that his final words echo in my mind, carrying a weight that feels ominous and undeniable.

The night clings to me like damp fog as I push forward, weaving through the shadows and keeping my grip tight on the box. I can still feel the stranger's gaze burning into my memory, his cryptic warning lingering like a bruise I can't quite shake. I know he's not gone for good—he doesn't seem like the type to let things go. And his retreat, if anything, only makes him more of a threat. People in the Red District rarely pull back unless they've got a plan, and something about him tells me he's always a few steps ahead.

My destination, an old Guild safehouse tucked behind an abandoned theater, looms in front of me. The building is silent, practically swallowed by ivy and grime, its once-grand façade cracked and crumbling like the rest of this forgotten part of town. Perfectly unassuming. As I slip through the side door, the silence amplifies, the faint hum of the artifact pressing against my ribs with an insistent energy. It's like it knows we're close to the Guild's warded space and wants out. Too bad it doesn't get a choice. Neither of us does.

Inside, the air is stale, thick with the scent of dust and damp wood. A few candles flicker in sconces along the hallway, their flames dim and wavering as if reluctant to burn. I pass a mirror with a spiderweb crack across it, and for a moment, the distorted reflection catches me off guard, casting an eerie, fractured version of myself back at me. It's unsettling, as if the mirror sees more than just the tired, wary face I wear on the outside.

In the next room, a familiar figure leans against the far wall, arms crossed. Felix, a senior Guild operative with an expression that could sour milk, looks up as I enter, his sharp eyes glinting with irritation.

"You're late," he says, his tone clipped, unimpressed. Felix doesn't believe in pleasantries; he's all business, every line in his face carved from years of hard deals and harder consequences. His gaze drops to the box under my arm, and a flicker of something close to relief crosses his face. "At least you've got it."

"Nice to see you too, Felix," I reply, keeping my tone light, but he's not biting. His expression remains stony, and he gestures impatiently for me to hand it over. I feel the box's warmth grow, almost resisting the motion as I pass it into his outstretched hands. He hesitates, his fingers hovering above the latch, a shadow of doubt creeping into his features.

"You didn't open it, did you?" His voice is low, just barely covering the concern creeping in.

"No," I say, a touch defensive. "I'm not stupid."

Felix gives a slight nod, but his gaze doesn't soften. He turns the box over in his hands, his expression growing darker as he examines the fine carvings and runes etched into the wood. There's something reverent, almost fearful in the way he holds it, and I can't help but feel a prickle of curiosity. I've handled dangerous artifacts for the Guild before, but nothing has ever felt quite like this. Even Felix, who's as tough as they come, seems rattled.

"What exactly is it?" I ask, breaking the silence, though I'm half sure he won't answer.

He looks up, his mouth twisting in a grim line. "It's better if you don't know. Just... leave the magic to those who understand it."

I roll my eyes, unable to help myself. "Oh, sure, because ignorance always makes things safer."

Felix's gaze sharpens. "In this case, yes. Don't think you're above the rules just because you're quick on your feet." He gives me a hard look, the kind that could strip paint off a wall. "Some things aren't meant to be messed with."

The weight in his tone kills any comeback I had ready, and for once, I decide to hold my tongue. Felix is many things—irritable, demanding, and as fun as a brick wall—but he's not prone to exaggeration. If he's telling me to leave it alone, there's probably a good reason.

He tucks the box under his arm, making his way toward the small, hidden vault behind a faded tapestry. I watch him slip the artifact inside, the sound of the lock clicking shut like a final heartbeat. Whatever is in that box is out of my hands now, and I try to convince myself that I don't care. It's Guild business, and that means it's no longer my concern. Still, a tendril of unease winds through me, and I can't shake the feeling that tonight's events have left an unseen thread pulling at me, tighter with each passing moment.

Felix turns back, his face softened just a fraction, which in his language is practically a hug. "Get some rest," he says. "And stay out of sight. There are eyes everywhere, and I don't want this job tracing back to us."

The words hang in the air, an implicit warning. I nod, mumbling a half-hearted goodnight as I make my way to the small, bare room I sometimes crash in when the Guild wants to keep me close. But sleep doesn't come easily. The stranger's warning circles my mind, repeating with an eerie persistence. His voice, that low, unsettling rumble, and the way he'd looked at me—like he already knew the end to a story I hadn't even started reading.

Just as I'm beginning to drift off, a faint sound cuts through the silence. I sit up, heart pounding, my hand instinctively reaching for the dagger tucked under my pillow. It's nothing... or so I think, until I hear it again—a whisper of movement outside my door, so soft it could be the wind, if only it weren't accompanied by the distinct sensation that I'm not alone.

I swing my legs over the edge of the cot, every nerve alight. The shadows seem to deepen around me, the air growing thicker, pressing in like a weight. Slowly, I stand, edging toward the door, my fingers wrapped tightly around the dagger's hilt. I can hear the faintest hum, a vibration that pulses through the floorboards, rising up through my feet.

Without warning, the door creaks open, and a figure steps into the room. My blood runs cold. It's him. The stranger, somehow slipping past every lock and ward to stand here, staring at me with that same challenging gaze, his smirk a slash of darkness against his face.

"What are you doing here?" My voice is barely more than a whisper, every word laced with accusation, even though I know the question is pointless. He isn't here to chat.

He takes a step closer, his expression darkening, and the room seems to contract, the walls pressing in tighter, the air electric with tension. "I warned you, didn't I?" he says, his voice soft, dangerous.

My grip tightens around the dagger, but he doesn't flinch. In fact, he almost looks amused.

"You're persistent," I manage, forcing the words out even as my pulse thunders in my ears.

He raises an eyebrow, his gaze never wavering. "Persistent? That's the polite word." His eyes drop to the dagger in my hand, his smirk widening. "You think that'll help you?"

"Try me," I say, hoping my voice sounds more confident than I feel. But he just laughs, low and unhurried, a sound that curls around me like smoke.

"Oh, I will," he replies, his tone laced with something chillingly calm. And as he steps forward, the room seems to spin, the shadows pulling in closer, swallowing us whole.

Chapter 2: Smoke and Mirrors

The door barely has time to shut before his presence is imprinted on the air, a slick oil stain of arrogance mixed with intrigue. Damian leans against the doorframe, one eyebrow raised as if he's appraising me, like he's sizing up an investment or evaluating a meal before deciding if it's worth the effort. His look is dark, his eyes as cold as midnight on the ocean, calculating, with a touch of humor that I'm sure is nothing more than a cover for the lurking ambition I can sense simmering just under the surface.

"So," he says, letting the word drip with an unsettling ease, "I'm guessing you're here for the same reason I am." His voice is smooth, that particular tone cultivated by people who know they're a little bit better at something than everyone else. He doesn't wait for my answer—of course he doesn't. Instead, he saunters into the room, hands in pockets, gaze casually flicking over the faded maps on the walls and the stacks of ancient tomes that look as though they'd crumble at a touch.

I resist the urge to clench my fists. "I'm here on my own business," I say, hoping my voice carries the right balance of disinterest and venom. There's no way I'll give him the satisfaction of knowing he's ruffled me. "Not that it's any of your concern."

He smirks, an infuriatingly smug little twist of his lips. "Oh, I think it is." He takes a step closer, close enough that I catch a faint, unsettling scent—something sharp and smoky, like embers from a fire. His eyes lock onto mine with unnerving intensity. "In fact, I think we're both after the same piece of...merchandise."

"Artifact," I correct him, and instantly regret it. I can practically hear his mind filing away the information, slotting it somewhere useful, like a tool he'll use against me later.

"Right," he says, drawing the word out. "Artifact." He leans back, crossing his arms with the kind of lazy ease that suggests he's completely at home here, even in enemy territory. "You know, it's funny. I expected someone a little more...intimidating. Aren't you supposed to be the best they've got?"

He's baiting me, but I don't bite. I've had enough experience with his type—smooth operators who believe their charm is both a sword and shield. "I could say the same about you," I reply, letting the words slide off my tongue with a lightness I don't feel. "But then again, I don't make a habit of underestimating my opponents."

"Opponents," he echoes, tilting his head slightly. His gaze sharpens, just a flash of something colder, harder. "Is that what we are? Funny, I was thinking 'rivals' had a nicer ring to it."

I don't blink, don't let his words settle in. Rivals, obstacles, opponents—it's all the same. He's in my way, and he's got to go, one way or another. "Look," I say, letting my tone sharpen, "whatever you think you're doing here, it's not going to work. I don't lose."

His grin is wolfish. "Neither do I."

There's a thick silence between us, one that thrums with barely contained tension, and it takes all my self-control not to shatter it with some scathing remark. I can practically feel the heat of his gaze lingering on me, and part of me—a very foolish part—almost wonders what he's thinking. But I banish that thought as quickly as it comes. Curiosity is a luxury I can't afford.

"Well, may the best thief win," I say, forcing a smile that doesn't reach my eyes.

He gives me a mock bow, one that's more sardonic than sincere. "Don't worry. I intend to." And with that, he turns on his heel and heads for the door, throwing a final, infuriating wink over his shoulder. "See you around, sweetheart."

I clench my teeth so hard I can feel the ache. "Sweetheart," I mutter under my breath, practically tasting the venom in the word as I watch him disappear. It's ridiculous, the way he's gotten under my skin already. People like Damian—cocky, relentless, maddeningly self-assured—are usually a quick blip on my radar, a passing irritation that's easily swept aside. But there's something about him that's different, something darker and deeper that makes him feel like a threat I can't just ignore.

For a moment, I let myself sink into the frustration, savor the way it tightens in my chest. But then, with a deep breath, I shake it off. He's just another competitor, another obstacle. And if he thinks he's going to outsmart me, he's in for a surprise.

The door closes, and I'm left alone with the faint scent of smoke lingering in the air. I take a moment to gather my thoughts, running through everything I know about Damian's faction. Ruthless, resourceful, and undeniably effective, they're known for handling "problems" in ways that leave little room for error—or mercy. If he's here, it's because he's the best they've got, and that means he's going to be trouble.

I glance at the maps, my fingers tracing over the worn parchment, feeling the weight of years and secrets embedded in every line. I can't afford to let him get the upper hand. Not when I'm so close. The artifact's location is still a mystery, but I've pieced together enough clues to have a decent head start. I know he'll be on my tail, but that doesn't worry me as much as it should. In fact, a small part of me almost welcomes the challenge.

A smirk tugs at my lips. Let him chase me. Let him try to keep up.

The moment the door clicks shut behind him, I feel the chill settle back into the room, like a draft sneaking through cracks in a forgotten house. Damian's presence lingers, but I refuse to let it cloud my thoughts. He's a distraction, nothing more—a dark, tempting shadow that's wormed its way into my mind. As much as I'd like to spend a few seconds replaying his infuriating smirk, I've got work to do. I focus instead on the maps, following the tangled lines of rivers and mountains with my finger, tracing a path that's taken me months to piece together. Somewhere in the grid of ancient routes and cryptic notes lies the artifact's location, the final prize in a hunt that's cost me sleep, friendships, and more close calls than I care to remember. There's something undeniably alluring about it—a fragment of power, a relic from a time when people feared what they couldn't understand. And as much as I want to get my hands on it before Damian, I know that it isn't just a prize to me. It's a ticket to something more, a key to a door that's always been locked. But I'm not foolish enough to say that out loud, even in the privacy of my own head. Desires like that are dangerous, especially when you've got rivals like Damian.

There's a knock on the door, sharp and quick. I freeze, instinct prickling. Friends don't knock, and enemies don't wait for permission to come in. I let my hand hover over the dagger at my waist, ready to pull it free in a second if necessary.

The door swings open, and Ava slips in, moving with that quiet efficiency she's honed from years of running scams. Her gaze sweeps over the room, taking in the maps, the dusty relics, and the faint smell of smoke Damian left behind. She raises an eyebrow, her lips twitching in that sly, knowing way of hers.

"So," she says, crossing her arms, "I take it the infamous Damian paid a visit?"

I roll my eyes, but there's no use denying it. Ava reads people like other people read books—one look, and she knows more about you than you'd care to admit. "Yes," I reply, my voice deliberately flat. "He was here, full of charm and his usual brand of smug confidence."

Ava snorts. "He's as charming as a snake and twice as slippery. You know he's only here because he knows you're close. You might as well have sent him an engraved invitation."

I grit my teeth. "Believe me, I don't need reminding. But I can handle him." I shove the maps into a pile, more aggressively than necessary, trying to shake off the way his voice still lingers in my mind, like a song you can't quite forget.

Ava's expression softens, her gaze shifting from teasing to something closer to concern. "I know you can handle him. But remember, he's not the only one you're up against. Half the city's whispering about the artifact now. Word's gotten out."

The implications of her words settle over me like a heavy fog. "If that's true," I say slowly, "then it's only a matter of time before more of his kind show up. And they won't be as polite."

"Polite?" Ava laughs, a dry, humorless sound. "Damian's only polite when he's trying to distract you. Don't forget that. And don't let your guard down. Not even for a second."

I let her words sink in. It's not the first time I've faced competition, but Damian has a way of complicating things, of making them messier than they need to be. The last thing I need is to fall for whatever game he's playing. I've worked too hard to get this far, to gather every clue, every scrap of information, while staying one step ahead of everyone else. But with Damian here, I can feel the pressure building, a silent ticking clock I can't ignore.

Ava gives me a long, measured look, then sighs. "Look, you don't have to do this alone. I know you don't trust anyone, but I'm not just anyone."

I look at her, really look at her. She's one of the few people who knows why this matters to me, who's seen the things I've had to do, the things I've given up to be here. If anyone understands, it's Ava.

"I know," I say softly, my voice almost a whisper. "And believe me, I appreciate it. But I have to finish this on my own."

Ava's eyes flicker with something like disappointment, but she doesn't push. Instead, she reaches out, gives my shoulder a quick squeeze, and then steps back, her expression hardening into something more businesslike. "Just remember—don't get caught up in whatever Damian's selling. He's good, but he's also predictable.

He'll play the game, act like he's letting you win, just so he can swoop in at the last minute and take it all."

I give her a grim smile. "Believe me, I've met his kind before."

She nods, but there's a glimmer of doubt in her eyes. "I hope so. Just don't let him turn your strength into a weakness."

With that, she slips out of the room, leaving me alone again with the maps and the silence. I trace my finger over the intricate lines once more, letting the details absorb me, hoping they'll drown out the memory of his smirk, the glint in his eye that spoke of secrets I'm almost afraid to uncover.

The night stretches long and quiet, and when I finally slip out of the room, the city is cloaked in darkness, the streets empty and shrouded in mist. I move like a shadow, hugging the narrow alleys, every step measured, every glance calculated. I know Damian's somewhere out here, lurking in the shadows, watching, waiting. He's like a phantom that refuses to be shaken, a specter who haunts my every move.

I reach the edge of the city, where the buildings give way to wild, tangled woods, and I pause, glancing back one last time. I feel his presence behind me, a whisper on the wind, a flicker in the dark. For a moment, a chill runs down my spine, but I shake it off. He might think he's got the upper hand, but he's about to find out just how wrong he is.

As I slip into the forest, the trees close around me, their shadows long and twisted in the moonlight. I move quickly, silently, each step carrying me closer to the artifact and the answers I've been seeking for so long. I know Damian's somewhere behind me, but I don't look back. He might think he's clever, but he hasn't seen what I'm capable of.

And as the night deepens, the hunt begins in earnest, with only the faint whisper of leaves to witness our silent race.

The moonlight barely filters through the dense canopy of trees, casting eerie shadows on the forest floor, turning every twisted branch into a clawed hand reaching out of the earth. The air is thick, damp with the smell of moss and decay, the silence broken only by the soft crunch of leaves under my boots. My senses are on edge, every nerve sharpened to a point as I listen for any sound that doesn't belong. He's out here, somewhere, pacing through the same tangled shadows, his presence like a ghost in the back of my mind.

A part of me wishes he'd just show himself. It would be easier that way, simpler. But Damian isn't one for simplicity; he thrives on the game, the thrill of pushing boundaries, of circling closer and closer until you realize he's been watching you all along. And despite myself, I can't help but feel that familiar pull, a magnetic force I should have the good sense to resist. I've spent my life avoiding people like him—dangerous, calculating, the kind who wrap you up in a game only they know the rules to. And yet here I am, in the dead of night, chasing the same trail as if I'm just another piece in his game.

The path narrows, winding deeper into the forest, the air growing colder with every step. I pause, my eyes catching on a glint of something in the dirt—a thin, broken chain, half-buried in the mud. I crouch, brushing away the dirt, feeling a slight twinge of satisfaction. He'd passed through here, maybe hours before, leaving behind the smallest clue. A faint thrill spikes in my chest, and I push it down. This isn't a victory, not yet. He's good, but so am I.

The forest is thick with memories, whispers of past hunts, and I can feel the weight of every chase, every risk I've taken to get this far. The artifact is close—I know it, can almost feel its pull like a heartbeat in the earth beneath me. I move forward, each step careful, calculated. And then, just as I reach a clearing, the silence is broken by a low chuckle from the shadows.

"So, you do know how to follow a trail," Damian's voice drawls, smooth and mocking, like he's been waiting for this moment. He steps out from behind a tree, his figure shrouded in shadow, yet every inch of him radiating that insufferable confidence. "I was beginning to wonder if you'd lost your touch."

I don't flinch, don't let the satisfaction on his face get to me. "I could say the same thing about you. I thought you'd be halfway to the artifact by now, not lingering around like you're waiting for applause."

He smirks, crossing his arms, his gaze sweeping over me with an infuriating slowness. "What can I say? The company's better than expected."

A laugh bubbles up in me, short and sharp. "Well, I hate to disappoint, but I'm not here to entertain you."

"No?" he says, tilting his head in that way that makes him look more predatory than playful. "Because from where I'm standing, it looks like you've been enjoying this game as much as I have."

I feel a flicker of annoyance, hot and irrational, because he's right, and I hate it. "Game? I think you're confusing a competition with a game. One of us is going to win, and one of us isn't."

"And you think you know who's going to come out on top?" He raises an eyebrow, his tone teasing, but there's something harder lurking in his eyes. "I'll admit, it's been a while since I've had a worthy opponent."

"I'm touched," I say dryly. "But flattery isn't going to slow me down."

He steps closer, close enough that I can see the slight curve of his mouth, the gleam in his eyes that's half-amused, half-challenging. "Wouldn't dream of it. But maybe you should consider that slowing down isn't always a bad thing. Sometimes, patience is just as effective as speed."

I roll my eyes, resisting the urge to shove past him. "Are you really giving me life advice right now?"

"Consider it...a courtesy." He grins, a dangerous glint flashing across his face. "After all, once I have the artifact, I'd hate for you to feel like you didn't get your chance."

I take a step forward, refusing to let him dominate the space between us. "I'll get my chance, don't worry. But I don't need any courtesy from you."

He doesn't move, doesn't flinch. His gaze remains locked on mine, intense, probing, as if he's searching for something I'm not ready to give. And then, in a low, almost conspiratorial tone, he says, "Tell me something. Why are you really here? What is it you're so desperate to find?"

The question catches me off guard, hitting closer to home than I'd like. I recover quickly, my voice steady, controlled. "I think you know as well as I do. We're both here for the same reason."

"Maybe," he replies, his tone softening, almost contemplative. "But I don't think that's the whole story."

A muscle in my jaw tightens, but I keep my expression impassive. "Believe what you want, Damian. Just stay out of my way."

He studies me for a long moment, and there's a flicker of something in his gaze, something I can't quite name. It almost feels like he's seeing through me, past the walls I've carefully built, past the defenses I've spent years perfecting. I hate how easily he gets under my skin, how quickly he turns my resolve into something brittle, breakable.

Finally, he steps back, his expression shifting, the mask of casual arrogance slipping back into place. "Fine. Have it your way," he says, his voice light, dismissive. But there's an edge to his words, a quiet warning I can't ignore. "Just remember—I don't lose. Not even to someone as...persistent as you."

He turns, disappearing into the shadows before I can respond, leaving me alone in the clearing, his words hanging in the air like smoke. For a long moment, I stand there, letting the silence close in around me, my heart pounding harder than it should. I've spent years chasing artifacts, uncovering secrets, facing down rivals, but nothing has ever felt quite like this. There's a part of me that wants to go after him, to follow the path he's carved through the trees, to prove that I'm not as shaken as he thinks.

But instead, I turn back to the trail, my gaze fixed on the path ahead. I won't let him distract me, not now, not when I'm so close. Every instinct tells me he's lurking somewhere nearby, watching, waiting, but I refuse to let that stop me.

And just as I reach the edge of the clearing, a sharp snap echoes through the trees, a branch breaking somewhere behind me. I freeze, my hand reaching instinctively for my dagger, my senses flaring to life. I strain to listen, to make out any sound beyond the whisper of leaves, the rustle of distant creatures.

Then, a figure steps out from the shadows, tall and unrecognizable, their face hidden beneath a hood, their stance unmistakably hostile.

The blade gleams in their hand, catching the thin sliver of moonlight. I feel the chill of danger coil around me, tightening with every second. My grip tightens on my dagger, heart pounding as I brace myself.

I take a breath, steadying myself, eyes locked on the figure before me. Then, they lunge.

Chapter 3: The Hunter and the Fox

The city hums under a thin mist tonight, a faint glow of neon and streetlight casting the damp streets in a soft, eerie glow. It's the kind of night that wraps its cold fingers around your neck, sends you scurrying home early, or if you're unlucky, keeps you looking over your shoulder. And tonight, I'm both of those things—scurrying and unlucky, apparently.

I've made it back to my building without running into trouble, but something feels off. The street is too empty, the silence too loud. When I reach my door, I fumble with my keys, hyper-aware of the shadows shifting around me. That's when I see him, a silhouette leaning casually against the lamppost at the far end of the block. His stance is relaxed, but there's an undeniable alertness to him, like a lion playing the part of a housecat. Damian. Of course. Who else would follow me home just to lean against a lamppost and wait?

I want to ignore him. My mind's screaming at me to get inside, lock the door, and draw the blinds. But instead, my hand slips from the door handle, and I turn to face him, defiance burning low in my gut. I can't let him see any weakness, any hint that his presence rattles me. He takes that as his cue, pushing off the lamppost and sauntering over with a slow, deliberate grace that says he knows exactly what he's doing to my pulse rate.

When he's close enough for me to smell the faint trace of smoke and leather clinging to him, he stops, tilting his head with a wry smile that, infuriatingly, doesn't reach his eyes. "Is this how you greet all your admirers?" he asks, voice dripping with that smooth, infuriating charm.

"Admirers? Is that what we're calling stalkers these days?" I quip back, lifting my chin in a show of bravado I'm not sure I feel. His smile only widens, a glint of amusement sparking in those dark eyes.

"Call it whatever you like. I'm here because I couldn't resist a little midnight chat," he says, and there's a subtle shift in his tone, a challenge lingering just beneath the surface. "You and I, we seem to keep crossing paths. I figured it was time to call a truce. Or at least clear the air."

My eyebrows shoot up in mock surprise. "A truce? I'm not the one who's been lurking in the shadows outside someone else's apartment."

He laughs, a low, throaty sound that sends a shiver down my spine, and for a moment, he looks almost disarmed. Almost. "Touché. But I think we both know you haven't exactly been playing it safe either. You're... an enigma," he says, searching my face with that unsettling gaze that makes me feel as though he's dissecting my very thoughts.

"What can I say? It's a gift." I give him a lopsided smile, attempting to keep my tone light, but I know he can sense the underlying tension.

He steps closer, just enough that I can see the faintest scar slicing across his eyebrow, a hidden flaw in his otherwise perfect mask. And the proximity is unsettling—too close for someone I've been telling myself is the enemy, but too intoxicating to resist. I swallow, fighting the urge to lean into that dangerous energy he seems to exude. It's like standing on the edge of a cliff, the thrill of the drop pulling you closer.

"You don't strike me as the kind of woman who trusts easily," he murmurs, voice dropping just enough to make me wonder if I should step back.

"Trust is overrated," I reply, my words a little sharper than intended, but I need him to see that I'm not some doe-eyed damsel, wide-eyed and innocent. I've played this game too many times. And yet, the nagging curiosity tugs at me, an insistent whisper at the back of my mind that I can't quite shake.

Damian studies me in silence, his eyes narrowing slightly as if he's weighing my response, considering what to do next. Then, in a swift, unexpected move, he pulls out a small, battered notebook from his coat pocket and extends it to me. I glance at it, uncertain. His expression is unreadable, a mask of calm that only heightens my suspicion.

"What's this?" I ask, my voice steady, though my fingers betray me, trembling slightly as I reach for it.

"A truce. Sort of," he says, and his eyes flicker with something I can't place. "It's a list of everything I know about you, things I've found out—whether by accident or... not. If we're going to keep circling each other, we might as well do it with all the cards on the table."

I hesitate, flipping through the pages. My name, my favorite drink, even the route I take to work each morning—all laid out in a neat, meticulous scrawl that makes my stomach clench. The sheer invasion of it, the fact that he knows so much without my having given him a single piece of myself, sends a chill down my spine.

"How thoughtful of you," I manage, a bitter edge creeping into my voice. "But you're right—I don't trust easily. And this... this doesn't exactly scream 'truce.'"

He watches me closely, his gaze softer now, almost contemplative. "You've got every reason not to trust me," he says quietly, and for the first time, there's something raw in his tone, something almost vulnerable. "But you're wrong about one thing."

"Oh, am I?" I challenge, raising an eyebrow.

"Yes. You're not just the fox, you're the hunter too. And that's why I'm here. Because I can't quite figure you out. You're... unexpected."

I want to scoff, to laugh off his words like they're nothing more than a line, another clever manipulation in a string of endless deceptions. But there's an honesty there, a crack in his armor that catches me off guard. And just like that, the roles blur, the lines between hunter and prey dissolving as we stand there, locked in a silent understanding neither of us can quite name.

I swallow, feeling the weight of his gaze, the depth of his words, like a subtle shift in the air between us. Part of me wants to turn and leave, to close the door and never look back. But the other part, the part that's been dancing on the edge of danger since the night we met, feels drawn in, compelled by the challenge he offers, by the possibility that maybe, just maybe, we're more alike than I want to admit.

And so, without a word, I step back, clutching his notebook, and slip into my apartment, my heart racing, my mind a whirl of questions. Just as I close the door, I catch a glimpse of his shadow retreating down the street, and a strange, unbidden thought tugs at the corners of my mind: maybe, in a city full of ghosts, Damian is the only one who really sees me.

The quiet of my apartment offers little relief from the tension still thrumming beneath my skin. Damian's notebook sits on the coffee table, taunting me from its spot under the lamp's soft glow. I stare at it for a long moment, as if expecting it to come alive and spill his secrets, his reasons for shadowing me, his motives cloaked in mystery and an odd, unsettling attraction. I know I should open it, thumb through those pages filled with the careful observations of a man who clearly makes it his business to know everything. And yet, I hesitate.

Instead, I busy myself with the small tasks of unwinding: slipping off my shoes, hanging up my coat, pouring myself a glass of wine. The usual rituals feel hollow tonight, more like the motions of someone pretending to have a normal life rather than living it. I take a sip, watching the wine catch the light, deep red and smooth, something to distract me from the small notebook just an arm's length away.

Eventually, curiosity wins out, and I sink into my worn-out couch, my fingers resting on the cover. The edges are frayed, the leather worn and softened by years of handling. It feels odd, holding a part of him in my hands, a record of the ways he's studied me, scrutinized my life with the kind of precision that makes me feel both flattered and violated. I tell myself it's only fair; after all, I've been keeping tabs on him too, haven't I? But this is different. This is too close, too intimate.

When I finally open the cover, I'm greeted by a neat, almost clinical script—his handwriting as precise as the man himself. Each page is filled with details about me, my routines, my favorite haunts, even the coffee shop I frequent on Thursday mornings. There's an odd comfort in seeing myself reduced to bullet points, my life dissected and catalogued with such detached efficiency. But then, halfway through the page, the notes change. They become less clinical, more personal, as if he's stopped observing from a distance and started looking closer, seeing things that only someone who's genuinely curious would notice. He's written about the way I laugh when I think no one's listening, the way I fidget with my ring when I'm nervous, the way my eyes light up when I talk about my work. It's unsettling, almost like he's looked straight into my soul and written down everything he's seen.

I close the notebook abruptly, setting it down as though it might burn me. I feel exposed, laid bare under the gaze of someone who, by all accounts, should be nothing more than a fleeting encounter, a face in the crowd. But there's no denying it—Damian has become more than that. He's a question that refuses to be answered, a mystery that gnaws at me, demanding my attention. And for reasons I can't quite fathom, I want to know more, want to unravel the layers he so carefully hides behind that charming, enigmatic smile.

A knock on the door jolts me out of my thoughts, sending a jolt of adrenaline through me. I'm half-expecting him to be on the other side, standing there with that maddening smile, as if he's fully aware of the effect he has on me. But when I open the door, it's not Damian. It's Mrs. Ellis, my elderly neighbor from down the hall, clutching a tin of cookies and wearing the kind of hopeful expression that makes it impossible to turn her away.

"I baked too many again," she says, offering the tin with a warm smile. "Thought you might like some."

I accept the tin with a grateful nod, inviting her in out of habit. Mrs. Ellis has been bringing me cookies since I moved in, convinced I need some motherly attention. She settles on the couch, her sharp eyes sweeping over my small apartment, her gaze landing on the notebook I'd left open in my haste. I see her eyes narrow slightly, and I brace myself for questions. She's nosy, but it's the kind of nosiness that comes from genuine care, a trait I've come to appreciate in her own way.

"What's this?" she asks, pointing to the notebook with a curious frown.

"Oh, just some work stuff," I lie smoothly, sliding it out of her view. "Nothing too interesting."

She doesn't buy it, of course. Mrs. Ellis has a way of seeing through my excuses, a trait that's both endearing and infuriating. But to my relief, she lets it slide, settling back with a sigh as she adjusts her glasses.

"You know," she begins, her tone taking on that familiar note of gentle reproach, "you're too young to be cooped up here alone all the time. A pretty girl like you should be out, meeting people, having fun."

I bite back a smile, feeling the familiar tug of warmth that her concern brings. "I have plenty of fun, Mrs. Ellis. Just last week, I went to the grocery store twice in one day."

She rolls her eyes, giving me a look that's equal parts exasperation and fondness. "That's not what I meant, and you know it. You should be meeting someone. A nice young man, maybe."

Her words settle over me, carrying a strange sense of irony, given my current situation. I think of Damian, of his intense gaze and the way he lingers on the edges of my life, a shadow that refuses to be ignored. I wonder what Mrs. Ellis would think of him, this mysterious figure who seems to embody every warning she's ever given me about bad boys and troublemakers.

"Maybe someday," I reply with a noncommittal shrug, trying to deflect her attention. But the truth gnaws at me, the realization that I am more alone than I'd like to admit. For all my bravado, for all the walls I've built around myself, there's a part of me that longs for connection, for someone to see me the way Damian seems to—flaws and all.

Mrs. Ellis watches me with a knowing smile, her eyes softening. "You deserve to be happy, dear," she says, patting my hand with a warmth that seeps into me, a reminder that there's kindness in this world, even amidst the shadows. "Don't forget that."

Her words linger long after she's gone, echoing in the quiet of my apartment as I sit alone, the tin of cookies untouched beside me. I think about Damian's notebook, the strange, unsettling intimacy of his observations, the way he's captured pieces of me that I didn't even realize were visible. It's a strange, bittersweet feeling, knowing that someone sees you, truly sees you, even if their motives are shrouded in mystery.

As I finally settle into bed, the city's quiet hum filling the air, I realize that Mrs. Ellis is right. I do deserve happiness, even if I don't quite know what that looks like yet. And maybe, just maybe, there's something worth exploring in this strange connection with Damian, something that goes beyond the game of cat and mouse we've been playing.

Sleep is elusive, slipping through my fingers like water no matter how tightly I try to hold on. I toss and turn, the memory of Damian's face hovering in the darkness like a specter I can't shake. Every time I close my eyes, I see the glint in his gaze, that sly, knowing smile as if he's already a few steps ahead, watching as I stumble to keep up. I finally give up on sleep and lie staring at the ceiling, wondering what strange game I've let myself get caught up in.

The city outside is still, save for the occasional honk or rumble of a late-night bus. It's the kind of quiet that feels fragile, a moment of calm that could shatter at the slightest disturbance. And as if on cue, my phone vibrates on the nightstand, slicing through the silence like a knife. I reach for it, blinking against the glare of the screen, heart thudding as I see a single text message. From an unknown number, of course, but the words are unmistakable.

Meet me on the rooftop. Now.

No signature, no clue as to who it's from, but I don't need one. I know. Damian has a way of making his presence felt, even through something as impersonal as a text. There's no reason I should go. Every rational part of me screams to ignore it, to stay here in the safety of my apartment and pretend I never saw it. But my feet move before my mind can catch up, and soon I'm pulling on my jacket and making my way to the stairwell, pulse quickening with each step.

The rooftop is colder than I expected, the wind biting against my skin as I step out into the open air. The city stretches out before me, a sea of lights blinking against the inky black, a reminder of how small I am in the grand scheme of things. And yet, at this moment, the world feels shrunken down to this rooftop, this meeting, this undeniable pull that keeps dragging me toward him no matter how hard I try to resist.

He's already there, of course, leaning against the low wall at the edge of the roof, his silhouette cutting a sharp line against the skyline. He doesn't turn as I approach, but I can feel his awareness, that sixth sense of his kicking in as I get closer. I stop a few feet away, arms crossed over my chest, trying to look casual, though I doubt I'm fooling him.

"Couldn't resist, could you?" he asks, his voice smooth and quiet, carrying over the wind. There's a smirk in his tone that makes me want to both laugh and shove him off the edge—though only one of those options would likely end well for me.

"You texted me in the middle of the night to meet you on a rooftop," I reply, letting a hint of exasperation slip into my voice. "So no, apparently not. But I'm starting to think my curiosity is going to get me killed."

He turns then, his gaze catching mine with an intensity that makes my breath hitch. "Maybe," he says softly, his face only partially visible in the faint glow from a nearby building. "But wouldn't it be worse to die bored?"

There it is again—that maddening charm, that wry twist of humor that makes it impossible to stay angry at him for long. I roll my eyes, fighting the urge to smile. "You really think highly of yourself, don't you?"

He grins, an unabashed, almost boyish grin that does nothing to ease my nerves. "Only because you're here. If you'd ignored me, I might have to start doubting myself."

I shake my head, taking a step closer, studying him in the dim light. "You're playing at something, Damian. I just can't figure out what it is."

He holds my gaze, his expression shifting, growing serious in a way that sends a chill through me. "Maybe I'm just trying to keep you out of trouble."

I laugh, a harsh sound that echoes off the empty rooftops around us. "You don't exactly strike me as the knight-in-shining-armor type."

His jaw tightens, a shadow crossing his face that's gone almost as soon as it appears. "Maybe not," he admits, his voice low, rough.

"But you're in over your head, whether you realize it or not. There are people watching you—people who won't play nice just because you have a quick wit and a charming smile."

I raise an eyebrow, refusing to let his warning rattle me. "I think I can handle myself."

"Maybe. But not against them." He steps closer, his presence pressing in on me, filling the space between us with a tension that's both exhilarating and terrifying. "They know who you are, where you go, who you talk to. And they don't have a soft spot for clever foxes."

The words hang heavy in the air, thick with a meaning I can't quite decipher. I want to brush it off, to tell him he's being melodramatic, but something in his gaze stops me. There's a hardness there, an edge I've never seen before, as if he's trying to tell me something without saying it outright.

"Why are you telling me this?" I ask, my voice barely above a whisper.

For a moment, he doesn't answer, his gaze flicking away to the city stretched out beneath us. When he finally speaks, his voice is softer, almost vulnerable, a side of him I'd never thought I'd see. "Because I don't want to see you get hurt."

The admission catches me off guard, and I feel a strange, unwelcome warmth settle in my chest, a flicker of something I don't dare name. It would be easy to laugh it off, to make a joke and keep things light, but I find myself unable to look away, caught in the intensity of his gaze.

"Then help me," I say quietly, surprising even myself with the words. "If you know so much about what's going on, then tell me. Show me who these people are."

For a long moment, he's silent, his face a mask of careful neutrality, but I can see the conflict in his eyes. Finally, he lets out a slow breath, nodding almost imperceptibly. "Fine," he says, his voice barely audible over the wind. "But you're not going to like it."

Before I can respond, he reaches into his coat and pulls out a small, silver key, placing it in my hand with a deliberate slowness that makes my heart pound. His fingers linger on mine, the warmth of his touch grounding me, tethering me to this moment.

"Tomorrow night. Midnight," he says, his gaze never leaving mine. "There's a door, two blocks over, behind the old warehouse. This key opens it. Go inside, and you'll find what you're looking for."

I swallow, my fingers curling around the key, feeling the weight of it settle in my palm like a promise, or perhaps a curse. I don't know whether to thank him or throw it back in his face, but the choice is taken from me when he turns and disappears into the shadows without another word, leaving me alone on the rooftop with nothing but the cold night air and the faint metallic taste of fear lingering on my tongue.

Chapter 4: The Unbreakable Pact

Damian has that infuriating sort of confidence that slides into a room ahead of him, wrapping itself around every innocent bystander before he's even opened his mouth. It's not arrogance—no, arrogance is brash and obvious. Damian's confidence is quiet, wrapped in the sleek fabric of custom-tailored suits and glances that linger just a fraction too long, leaving their mark. If he knows I'm already at the meeting point, he doesn't show it. Instead, he saunters in, late by exactly five minutes, as if every second were a gift he alone was generous enough to bestow. He pauses just inside the door, his gaze sweeping over me like he's taking inventory of a particularly stubborn stain on an otherwise pristine carpet. The corner of his mouth tilts up, not a smile, but close enough to one that it makes my fingers itch to wipe it away.

"Nice of you to join us," I say, tapping my wrist where a watch would be if I could actually afford one that wasn't purely decorative.

"Patience, darling," he purrs, the word dripping with so much patronizing charm that I briefly fantasize about hitting him with something heavy. "A minute late is fashionable; five is character."

I resist the urge to roll my eyes. Barely. "If that's your idea of character, it explains why you work alone."

"Well," he says, sauntering closer, "until now."

Our arrangement, sanctioned with all the reverence and formality of a marriage contract, mandates that we work together on retrieving the artifact. An unbreakable pact, they called it, one bound by the Guild's ironclad rules. They didn't even pretend that it was for our safety. This is all about leverage, a forced alliance of necessity that has nothing to do with trust. I wonder if Damian even understands the concept.

The map they provided is spread out on the table between us, detailing the terrain we'll have to cross and the route we'll need to take. It's marked with ominous little symbols—dangerous creatures, treacherous cliffs, the sort of obstacles that make normal people reconsider their life choices. But we're not normal people. Or at least, we pretend we're not.

"Don't think this is some bonding experience," I say, tracing the map with my fingertip, stopping at the spot marked as our destination. "We're here to get the job done, not trade life stories."

"Oh, I wouldn't dream of prying into your tragic backstory," he replies with mock solemnity. "You'd probably charge me for the privilege."

Ignoring him, I pull out a small leather-bound journal from my satchel and flip it open to a page filled with hastily scribbled notes and sketches. "There's a patrol here," I say, pointing to a narrow ravine that slices through the eastern part of the map. "They change shifts every six hours, but there's a blind spot near the cliff edge that could give us just enough cover."

Damian leans over the table, his shoulder almost brushing mine. I'm immediately aware of his cologne, dark and smoky with a hint of something sharp underneath, like citrus on the edge of a blade. It's distracting in a way that feels deliberately crafted, like he's chosen every detail of himself to catch people off guard. I hate that it's working.

"Efficient," he murmurs, glancing at my notes. "I knew the Guild wouldn't send me someone completely useless."

"Keep underestimating me," I say, flashing a saccharine smile. "It'll make things so much easier."

He raises an eyebrow. "Oh, I don't underestimate you. I just don't trust you. Big difference."

"Trust is a luxury neither of us can afford," I reply smoothly, closing the journal with a sharp snap. "So here's the deal: we stick to the plan, we watch each other's backs as required, and once we've secured the artifact, we go back to pretending the other doesn't exist."

He smirks, as though the prospect genuinely amuses him. "Agreed, though I'll admit, I'm not used to ignoring people who find me this charming."

I don't dignify that with a response. Instead, I shove the journal back into my bag and double-check my weapons. A sleek dagger, a set of smoke bombs, and a small vial of poison, just in case things go sideways. Damian watches me, a glint of intrigue in his eye, but says nothing. He's probably got his own arsenal hidden somewhere beneath that smug exterior, something equally polished and expensive. We're both armed to the teeth, each ready to defend ourselves at a moment's notice. Trust, as we established, is nowhere on the table.

We head out into the night, the forest stretching around us in shadowed layers, silent but for the crunch of leaves beneath our boots. The moon hangs low, casting everything in an eerie silver light. Damian moves with surprising stealth for someone who has "public nuisance" written all over him. He glides between the trees with practiced ease, as though he's made his home in the darkness. I can't deny he's good at what he does, and that's the part that makes him dangerous. You can't predict someone who's as confident in chaos as they are in control.

As we approach the ravine, a flicker of movement catches my eye. I grab Damian's arm, pulling him behind a thick tree trunk just as a patrol passes by, their torches casting long shadows that stretch and shift with the breeze. We wait, breath held, watching as they disappear into the night. I realize only after they've gone that my hand is still on his arm. The fabric of his sleeve is cool beneath my fingers, soft but hiding something solid underneath. I release him, but not before I catch a ghost of a smile tugging at the corner of his mouth.

"Enjoying yourself?" he whispers.

"Focus," I snap, more to steady myself than anything else.

We slip past the patrol's line, using the cover of the cliffs to mask our approach. The path narrows as we go, forcing us closer together. I can feel the warmth of him beside me, hear his steady, measured breathing. For a second, it feels like the world has shrunk to just this—a narrow trail, a shared goal, and a tension that crackles between us, waiting for one wrong move to set it off.

At the edge of the ravine, the artifact lies hidden in a cavern marked by ancient symbols etched into the rock, symbols I've studied and researched until they felt as familiar as my own name. I feel a surge of anticipation, a thrill that I won't admit to Damian. This is what I've been working for, every grueling moment, every sacrifice.

But as we step inside, Damian's fingers brush mine, just barely, and it hits me that maybe there's more danger in this partnership than I realized. Not from the artifact, or the traps, or the patrols. But from him. And, as much as I hate to admit it, from me.

Damian's footsteps echo beside mine, his every move infuriatingly controlled. I sense him studying me out of the corner of his eye, as if he's sizing up a puzzle missing half its pieces. I imagine I'm giving him nothing—stone-faced and steely-eyed, the textbook definition of unruffled. Or at least, that's what I tell myself. But his gaze lingers a beat too long, enough that I feel the heat of it, and I have to remind myself to look away, to resist matching his intensity.

We navigate deeper into the cavern, the ancient etchings on the walls illuminated only by the flickering glow of Damian's flashlight. The symbols are hypnotic, swirling in patterns that seem to dance in the shadowy light. There's a strange hum in the air, an energy I can feel all the way down to my bones, buzzing with a potent kind of magic that feels both ancient and dangerous.

"Feel that?" Damian's voice is low, almost reverent. For a moment, he almost sounds sincere.

"It's hard not to," I reply, running my fingers lightly over one of the symbols. The stone is cool, but there's a pulse beneath it, as if the entire cavern is alive. I pull my hand back, unnerved but intrigued. There's something about this place that feels like it's watching us, waiting.

Damian steps closer, his shoulder brushing mine, and I catch his scent again—dark, smoky, with a sharp undertone that makes my skin prickle. It's infuriating, the way he manages to invade every one of my senses, as if he's deliberately woven himself into the very fabric of this mission. He leans in, just slightly, close enough that his breath brushes my cheek as he speaks.

"Careful," he murmurs, his voice laced with that infuriating mixture of charm and caution. "These symbols aren't just decoration. They're traps. Touch the wrong one, and this place will swallow you whole."

"Oh, don't worry," I reply, plastering on a smirk that I hope looks more confident than I feel. "I know exactly what I'm doing."

"Do you?" His gaze is piercing, challenging, as if daring me to prove myself. He doesn't pull back, his eyes locked on mine with a kind of intensity that's almost unnerving. "Because I don't have time to babysit someone who's in over their head."

"I don't need you to babysit me," I snap, the words sharper than I intended. "And if you're so concerned, feel free to turn back. I'm sure I'll manage just fine on my own."

"Oh, I'm sure you would," he replies, the hint of a smirk tugging at his lips. "But where's the fun in that?"

He steps back, giving me just enough space to breathe again, though the tension between us doesn't dissipate. If anything, it sharpens, taut and electric, crackling in the air around us. I force myself to focus on the task at hand, reminding myself why I'm here.

I didn't come this far to get distracted by a cocky smirk and a pair of too-sharp eyes.

We continue deeper into the cavern, navigating around jagged rocks and narrow ledges. The air grows colder, thick with the scent of damp earth and something else—something metallic and ancient that lingers at the back of my throat. Damian is silent beside me, his gaze scanning the shadows with a practiced wariness. I can tell he's tense, every line of his body coiled and ready, like a predator waiting to strike. It's strange, seeing him like this, stripped of his usual smugness. There's a ruthlessness to him now, something raw and dangerous that makes my heart race.

Suddenly, a sound echoes through the cavern—a low, rumbling growl that sends a shiver down my spine. I freeze, instinctively reaching for my dagger, my eyes darting around the dimly lit space. The growl grows louder, reverberating off the walls, and I feel Damian tense beside me.

"Do you see it?" I whisper, my voice barely audible over the sound.

He nods, his gaze fixed on a shadow at the far end of the cavern. Slowly, he raises his flashlight, illuminating a creature lurking in the darkness. It's massive, its body covered in scales that glint in the faint light, its eyes glowing with a feral intensity. It watches us, its lips pulled back in a snarl that reveals rows of razor-sharp teeth. I can feel its gaze, piercing and hungry, and I know we've stumbled into something far more dangerous than either of us anticipated.

"Don't move," Damian whispers, his hand brushing mine as he reaches for his own weapon. "It's sensing movement. We need to be smart about this."

"Smart?" I hiss back, clutching my dagger with a grip so tight it's almost painful. "We need to be gone, Damian. Now."

But he's already stepping forward, his movements slow and deliberate, his gaze locked on the creature. There's a confidence in his posture, an assurance that I envy, and for a moment, I wonder if he actually believes he can control this situation. He glances back at me, his expression unreadable.

"Trust me," he says, his voice low but steady.

I open my mouth to argue, to tell him he's insane, but something in his eyes stops me. Against all logic, against every instinct screaming at me to run, I nod. I don't trust him—not really—but right now, he's all I've got.

He takes another step forward, his gaze never leaving the creature, his body radiating a calm I can only dream of. I follow his lead, moving slowly, carefully, every muscle in my body tense with anticipation. The creature watches us, its eyes narrowing, its growl deepening, but it doesn't attack. Not yet.

Damian raises his hand, holding it out as if he's trying to communicate with the creature. I have no idea what he's doing, but there's a strange kind of reverence in his expression, a quiet respect that feels oddly out of place. It's almost as if he's trying to negotiate with it, to find some unspoken understanding. And, somehow, it seems to work. The creature's growl softens, its body relaxing ever so slightly, and for a brief, breathless moment, I think we might actually make it out of this alive.

But then, without warning, something shifts. A stone crumbles beneath my foot, echoing through the cavern like a gunshot, and the creature's eyes snap to me, its body tensing in an instant. It lunges, faster than I thought possible, its claws flashing in the dim light.

I throw myself to the side, narrowly avoiding its attack, my heart pounding as I scramble to my feet. Damian is beside me in a heartbeat, his hand closing around my arm as he pulls me back, his face grim.

"Run," he says, his voice barely more than a whisper.

And this time, I don't argue. We sprint through the cavern, the creature's snarls echoing behind us, its footsteps pounding against the stone as it chases us. My lungs burn, my legs screaming with every step, but I don't stop. I can't stop. Not now.

We burst out of the cavern, the cool night air hitting me like a slap, and we don't slow until we're well away from the entrance, hidden in the shadows of the trees. Only then do I allow myself to breathe, collapsing against a tree, my chest heaving as I try to catch my breath.

Damian stands beside me, equally winded but with a strange, exhilarated grin on his face, as if he's just come back from the best thrill of his life. I shake my head, both irritated and amused despite myself.

"You're insane," I manage to say between gasps.

"Perhaps," he replies, still grinning. "But admit it—you love it."

We're deep in the forest, the moonlight trickling through the trees in broken shards that paint our skin in silver. Damian still wears that ridiculous, exhilarated grin, and I half expect him to let out a victory cry. I lean against the trunk of a tree, catching my breath and trying to ignore the lingering shivers that chase over my skin. It's too easy to imagine that creature's hot breath on my neck, those razor-sharp claws flashing toward me. The thrill of it still lingers, and I despise myself a little for the way it makes me feel alive.

"Admit it," Damian says, leaning in close enough that I catch a fresh whiff of his cologne, crisp and somehow aggravatingly inviting. "You got a rush from it. You liked that little dance with death."

"Speak for yourself," I scoff, though he's not entirely wrong. "There's a fine line between thrill-seeking and self-destructive tendencies, you know."

"And I have perfect balance," he quips, stepping back with an exaggerated bow, as though he's some sort of court jester instead of the infuriating, competent rogue the Guild insists on binding me to. He gestures down the path we're meant to take, a dark, narrow trail that snakes between the trees and disappears into more shadow. "Ladies first."

I roll my eyes, but my feet start moving, a small part of me savoring the silence around us, the pulse of adrenaline still thrumming just beneath the surface. I don't look back to see if Damian follows; I know he's there, his footsteps nearly silent as he moves with the smooth, predatory grace of someone who's spent his life in shadow.

We walk in silence, and for a brief, deceptive moment, it almost feels peaceful. The air is thick with the scent of damp earth and pine, cool and sharp in my lungs. There's an eerie beauty to this forest, a stillness that feels heavy with secrets. But I remind myself that beauty often comes at a price, and in our line of work, that price is usually blood.

"Do you think they're watching us?" I murmur, breaking the silence, unable to shake the feeling that something's lurking in the darkness, just out of sight. I'm not talking about the Guild or the rival faction we're working against. I'm talking about something older, something that doesn't adhere to the rules of any organization.

"Who knows?" Damian replies with a shrug, his tone maddeningly carefree. "Maybe they are. Maybe they're just curious, seeing as we've already left quite the impression on their doorstep."

"It's unsettling," I admit, my voice softer, my gaze fixed ahead as I try to ignore the weight of his eyes on me. "Not knowing who—or what—could be watching."

"Ah, but that's what makes it interesting, isn't it?" he says, his voice taking on a darker edge, a note of something I can't quite place. "The unknown. The danger. It's what keeps us coming back for more."

I shake my head, refusing to give him the satisfaction of a response. If there's one thing I've learned about Damian, it's that he thrives on reaction. Silence, I've found, is the best way to keep him at bay—if only a little.

The trail curves, leading us toward a small, moss-covered bridge that spans a narrow ravine. The water below rushes in a steady, relentless current, the sound oddly soothing in the stillness of the night. But as we approach, something shifts. A flicker of movement catches my eye, a shadow darting across the trees on the other side of the bridge.

I stop, holding up a hand to signal Damian. He halts immediately, his expression sharpening, the teasing glint in his eyes vanishing in an instant. He follows my gaze, his body tensing as he scans the darkness.

"Did you see that?" I whisper, my fingers tightening around the hilt of my dagger.

"Yes," he replies, his voice low and steady. "Something's out there."

We stand there, side by side, our eyes locked on the darkness beyond the bridge, waiting. The silence stretches, thick and heavy, broken only by the rush of water below us. I feel my pulse quicken, my senses heightening, every sound amplified, every shadow suddenly suspect. And then, just as I'm beginning to think it was a trick of the light, the figure emerges.

It steps into the moonlight, a tall, hooded figure draped in dark robes that blend seamlessly with the shadows. Its face is obscured, but there's an undeniable aura of power radiating from it, an otherworldly energy that prickles over my skin like static electricity.

Damian shifts beside me, his hand moving to his weapon, though he doesn't draw it. Not yet. We both know better than to make the first move.

"Who are you?" I call out, my voice steady despite the knot of tension coiling in my stomach.

The figure doesn't respond. Instead, it lifts a hand, a slow, deliberate movement that sends a ripple of unease through me. I grip my dagger tighter, ready for anything, but what happens next is beyond anything I could have anticipated.

The air around us seems to thicken, the temperature dropping until I can see my breath misting in front of me. A chill settles over the clearing, the kind that sinks deep into your bones and refuses to let go. I glance at Damian, and for the first time since I met him, he looks genuinely unnerved.

The figure tilts its head, as though studying us, and then it speaks, its voice a low, echoing whisper that seems to come from everywhere and nowhere at once.

"Your journey ends here."

The words hang in the air, heavy and final, and I feel a shiver run down my spine. I glance at Damian, his jaw clenched, his eyes narrowed as he meets the figure's gaze with a defiance that borders on reckless. But I can see the fear there, too, a flicker of doubt that mirrors my own.

"What do you want?" Damian demands, his voice laced with a bravado that sounds almost convincing.

The figure is silent for a long, agonizing moment, and then it extends its hand, palm up, as though offering something. But when I look closer, I realize there's nothing there—only an empty hand, open and waiting.

"You seek the artifact," the figure says, its voice softer now, almost gentle. "But it will cost you more than you are willing to pay."

I swallow, feeling the weight of its words settle over me like a shroud. There's a part of me that wants to turn back, to leave this place and forget this mission, forget the Guild, forget Damian and his infuriating grin. But I know that's not an option. Not anymore.

"We're not here for bargains," I say, forcing the words past the tightness in my throat. "We're here to complete a mission."

The figure lets out a soft, chilling laugh, a sound that echoes through the clearing like the rustle of dead leaves. "Ah, but you misunderstand. The bargain has already been made. And the price..." It pauses, as though savoring the moment. "...will be your loyalty."

I feel a jolt of shock, my mind racing as I try to process its words. Loyalty—to whom? To what? I glance at Damian, but his expression is unreadable, his gaze fixed on the figure with a mixture of defiance and suspicion.

"What do you mean?" he demands, his voice low and dangerous.

The figure only smiles, a slow, twisted smile that sends a fresh wave of unease skittering through me. It lowers its hand, stepping back into the shadows, its form gradually dissolving into the darkness.

"Choose wisely," it says, its voice fading as it vanishes. "For once the pact is made, there is no turning back."

And then, in an instant, it's gone, leaving us standing alone in the clearing, the silence pressing down around us like a weight. Damian meets my gaze, his expression a mixture of determination and something darker, something that looks almost like fear.

"What now?" he asks, his voice barely more than a whisper.

I swallow, the enormity of our situation settling over me like a storm cloud. "Now," I say, my voice steady but laced with a fear I can't hide, "we decide how much we're willing to sacrifice."

And as the words leave my lips, a distant rumble echoes through the forest, growing louder with each passing second, until it feels like the very ground beneath us is trembling, as though warning us of what's to come.

Chapter 5: The Garden of Hidden Shadows

The garden feels alive, but not in a way that welcomes. The leaves shiver without wind, casting faint shadows across Damian's back as he strides confidently ahead. I, on the other hand, am as jumpy as a hare in a hawk's shadow, trying to step as lightly as possible, careful not to disturb the thorny tendrils that stretch and twist from every corner, as though reaching for us. The air is thick with the scent of wet earth and decayed blossoms, oddly sweet yet pungent enough to stick in my throat.

Damian, of course, doesn't hesitate. His boots crunch over the gravel path, the sound like small bones snapping underfoot. I wonder how he does it—keep his head high, shoulders squared, as though there's nothing in the world that could frighten him. He's a fortress with iron walls, that one. If I'm honest with myself, I almost envy his lack of fear. Almost.

"Keep up," he calls over his shoulder, his voice barely a whisper, yet loud enough to cut through the quiet.

I quicken my pace, my fingers brushing the cool hilt of the dagger strapped to my side. A comfort, though it probably wouldn't do much against spirits, if the legends are true. But I can't help the way I cling to it, as if steel could somehow anchor me in this place that feels more like a dream—or a nightmare.

We press on, winding deeper into the garden. Ancient statues, their faces smudged with moss, watch us from beneath the shadows of towering trees. I catch glimpses of their chipped features—an empty-eyed cherub here, a solemn-faced woman there—each one a little more unsettling than the last. They seem to follow us with their hollow stares, as if warning us away from something hidden just beyond the next turn.

I can't resist breaking the silence. "Who even knew this place existed?" My voice sounds small, swallowed up by the shadows.

Damian doesn't look back, but there's a slight pause in his step, just enough for me to notice. "People forget," he says. "The city's built on layers. The old gets buried under the new, until it's nothing but a story passed around like an old wives' tale. But just because something's hidden doesn't mean it's gone."

I chew on that thought, my eyes darting from one twisted tree to the next. There's a weight to this place, a history that feels tangible, like the garden is holding onto secrets older than both of us combined. For a brief moment, I imagine that if I were to reach out, I might pull back a piece of someone else's memory—frayed and ghostly, but real.

We reach a clearing, and there, in the center, stands a massive, ancient oak, its trunk split down the middle as if struck by lightning ages ago. Despite its scarred appearance, it's thriving, thick branches stretching out to form a canopy that blocks even the moonlight. At the base of the tree, nestled in the crook of its roots, is a stone bench, half-buried in moss.

Damian stops, tilting his head as if he's listening to something I can't hear. His hand rests on the hilt of his sword, fingers tapping out a slow, rhythmic beat. It's the only sign of nerves I've seen from him all night, and it's enough to set my heart racing.

"What is it?" I ask, keeping my voice low.

He shakes his head. "Probably nothing. Just... stay close."

It's strange, hearing him say that, as if I'm someone who needs protecting. But I don't argue. Instead, I take a step closer, so close that I can see the way his jaw tenses, the muscle twitching as he scans the shadows. And for the first time, I realize he might actually be afraid—though he'd sooner cut off his own hand than admit it.

A sudden rustling comes from behind us, the sound sharp and out of place in the stillness. I spin around, hand on my dagger, but there's nothing there—just the same winding path, the same statues watching with empty eyes.

"Did you hear that?" My voice comes out steadier than I feel.

Damian's eyes narrow. "We're not alone."

The words send a shiver down my spine. I want to laugh it off, make some smart comment about ghosts, but I can't bring myself to do it. Not here. Not when there's something distinctly wrong about this place, something that seems to pulse and shift with every heartbeat.

We stand in silence, straining to hear any other sounds. But the garden has returned to its eerie quiet, as if whatever moved in the shadows has decided to bide its time. I'm not sure if that's comforting or terrifying.

"Come on," Damian says finally, his voice low and rough. "We're almost there."

Almost where? I want to ask, but the look in his eyes stops me. There's a grim determination there, a stubborn refusal to turn back, even when common sense would scream otherwise. It's reckless, maybe even suicidal, but I know there's no talking him out of it.

So, I follow him, feeling the garden close in around us as we leave the clearing behind. The path narrows, branches clawing at our clothes, our skin, as though the garden itself is trying to keep us here. Damian marches on, his jaw set, while I stumble after him, trying to ignore the prickling sensation at the back of my neck.

Just when I'm certain we're lost, we emerge into another clearing, this one smaller and more intimate. In the center is a pool, its surface black and still, like a piece of polished obsidian. Moonlight filters through the trees, casting a faint glow over the water. I catch a glimpse of my own reflection, pale and wide-eyed, before Damian steps up beside me.

He stares into the pool, his face unreadable. "They say this place shows you what you need to see," he murmurs, almost to himself.

I raise an eyebrow. "Need, or want?"

He shrugs, a flicker of something—regret, maybe?—passing over his face. "Sometimes, they're the same thing."

Before I can ask what he means, he steps forward, peering into the water as though expecting it to reveal some great truth. For a heartbeat, the world holds its breath. Then, just as suddenly, the surface ripples, and I feel a chill run through me as shadows start to shift and dance across the water.

I don't know what he sees, but judging by the haunted look in his eyes, it's nothing good.

I stand by the edge of the pool, watching Damian as he stares into it, his shoulders tense, his eyes locked on something only he can see. Whatever it is, it has him rooted there, like his boots have grown roots of their own. I half expect to see some eerie image surface, maybe a skeletal face peering back at him. But the water remains murky, betraying nothing but the occasional ripple as if something far beneath the surface is breathing.

I shift my weight, crossing my arms and tapping my fingers in a quick rhythm, an old habit I can never quite break when tension coils in my chest. The silence feels thick, oppressive, as if the garden itself is holding its breath, waiting for us to make a move. My gaze drifts from Damian to the trees circling the clearing. I swear I see one of the shadows shift, slinking back behind a branch as if caught in the act. I bite my lip to keep from saying anything, not wanting to startle Damian from whatever trance he's in—or to let on that I might be seeing things that aren't there.

Finally, he tears his gaze from the pool and turns to me, his expression carefully blank, but his jaw tight, as though he's holding back words that would rather leap out.

I lift an eyebrow, hoping to lighten the mood. "See anything worth sharing? Or are you just admiring your reflection?"

He almost smiles—a brief, reluctant twitch at the corner of his mouth. "If I was admiring my reflection, I'd be here all night."

"Humility looks good on you." I smirk, feeling some of the tension ease between us, though my pulse is still racing. "But seriously, what did you see?"

He lets out a sigh, rubbing the back of his neck as though shaking off some unseen weight. "Nothing worth mentioning," he says, though his tone suggests otherwise. "Just... memories, maybe." He glances back at the pool, his brow furrowed, as if reconsidering. "This place plays tricks, or so they say. It dredges up what's buried."

"Sounds like a cheap parlor trick," I scoff, though even I can hear the waver in my voice. I can feel the garden's eyes on us—or whatever passes for eyes in a place like this. Every rustle of leaves, every shadow stretching across the path, feels deliberate, like we're trespassers in a place that's long forgotten the warmth of human company.

He shakes his head, fixing me with a look that's unsettlingly serious. "Don't mock it. This place... it's powerful. You'd be wise to respect that."

I roll my eyes, more out of habit than any real bravado. "Powerful, maybe, but I'm not about to let a few garden ghouls mess with my head. I'm made of sterner stuff."

"Are you, now?" he murmurs, his gaze searching, as if daring me to prove it.

I feel a prickle of irritation but bite back a retort, focusing instead on the uneasy energy winding its way through the trees around us. Part of me wants to argue, to remind him that I can hold my own as well as he can, but the quiet intensity in his expression makes me pause. It's like he's testing me, waiting for something—though I'm not quite sure what.

Just as I'm about to break the silence with a snappy comeback, a soft, chilling whisper snakes through the air. It's barely more than a breath, faint and distant, but it sends a shiver down my spine. My hand tightens instinctively on the hilt of my dagger, and Damian's head snaps up, his eyes scanning the shadows.

"Did you hear that?" I whisper, the words slipping out before I can stop them.

He nods, his expression turning grim. "We're not alone."

The whispered words come again, closer this time, though still indistinct, like fragments of a conversation we're not meant to overhear. I strain to make sense of it, but the voices slip through my mind like water through a sieve, leaving only a hollow unease in their wake.

Damian motions for me to follow, his movements slow and deliberate. We inch our way around the edge of the pool, careful not to disturb the stillness any more than necessary. Every step feels heavier than the last, as though the garden itself is pulling us down, trying to keep us tethered here. My heart pounds in my chest, each beat echoing in my ears like a drum.

The whispers grow louder, overlapping and intertwining until they're a constant murmur that seems to seep into my bones. I catch bits and pieces—a name here, a sigh there—but nothing concrete. Just disjointed fragments, as if the garden is trying to tell us something but can't quite find the words.

"Why are we here, really?" I murmur, glancing sideways at Damian. It's a question I probably should have asked earlier, but in the quiet, haunted depths of this garden, it feels urgent, pressing.

He hesitates, his gaze flicking back to the path behind us. "We're looking for something... or rather, someone," he says slowly, as though weighing each word. "Someone who vanished here years ago. People come into this place and don't always come back."

His answer sends a chill down my spine. I knew we weren't here for a casual stroll, but I hadn't realized just how dangerous our mission might be. I swallow, forcing myself to keep my voice steady. "And you think they're still here?"

He gives a slight nod. "That's the hope. Or at least, some trace of them. The garden... it has a way of holding onto things. People, memories... maybe even a way out, if you know where to look."

A flicker of dread coils in my stomach, but I force a smile, hoping to mask my unease. "So, we're ghost hunters now? I didn't exactly pack for that."

Damian's expression softens, a hint of amusement breaking through his serious demeanor. "Consider it an adventure," he says, though there's a sadness in his eyes that belies his words.

Adventure or not, every fiber of my being is telling me to turn and run, to leave this haunted place and never look back. But there's something about the look in Damian's eyes—a mixture of hope and regret—that keeps me rooted here, unwilling to abandon him to the shadows.

Just then, a sudden gust of wind sweeps through the clearing, rustling the leaves and sending a cascade of dried petals spiraling through the air. It carries with it a faint, haunting melody, so soft I can barely hear it over the pounding of my heart. But it's enough to stop us in our tracks, both of us standing still as statues, listening.

The melody is eerie, lilting, and strangely beautiful, like a lullaby sung by someone who's forgotten the words. It fades in and out, as though carried by the wind itself, and for a moment, I feel an inexplicable sense of longing—a deep ache that I can't quite explain.

Damian reaches out, his hand hovering near mine. "Are you ready?" he asks, his voice low, as if afraid to disturb the fragile stillness around us.

I nod, though I'm not entirely sure what I'm agreeing to. There's a tension in the air, a sense of something unseen waiting just beyond the shadows, and I can feel the garden's gaze on us, watching, judging.

Without another word, we step forward, leaving the pool and its haunting reflections behind, and make our way deeper into the heart of the garden.

The path winds narrower, twisting between gnarled roots that claw their way up from the soil like skeletal hands. Branches weave a thick canopy above us, blocking out what little moonlight we had left, so we're left navigating in near darkness. I can hear Damian's steady breathing beside me, and somehow that small, simple sound is grounding. I focus on it, letting it drown out the creeping sense of unease prickling at the back of my mind.

We reach a fork in the path, where a pair of statues stands on either side. They're worn and moss-covered, but their expressions are unmistakably sinister, frozen in a twisted grimace that almost seems to sneer at our intrusion. Damian pauses, his gaze darting from one path to the other, as if weighing some invisible scale.

"So," I say, keeping my voice light, "left or right? Or do we flip a coin and hope for the best?"

"Funny," he murmurs, his eyes never leaving the statues. "This isn't a place for hoping."

It's not the answer I wanted, but I stay quiet, letting him think. There's something in his face—a flicker of doubt, maybe—that makes me want to reach out, say something comforting, anything that might lighten the shadows gathering around us. But before I can find the words, he steps forward, choosing the path on the right, his expression hardening with a resolve that I can't help but admire.

We move in silence, each step measured, careful. The ground beneath us is uneven, riddled with roots and stones that trip me up more than once. Damian's hand reaches back instinctively, steadying me without a word, his grip warm and reassuring. For a moment, I almost forget where we are, almost forget the foreboding press of the darkness, and feel only the solid weight of his hand holding me steady.

But then I see it—a shadow shifting just out of the corner of my eye. I freeze, my heart leaping into my throat as I scan the darkness, straining to make out any sign of movement. It's gone in an instant, but the sense of unease lingers, a chill that seeps into my bones.

"What?" Damian's voice is low, urgent.

I shake my head, forcing a weak smile. "Probably just my imagination." But even as I say it, I don't quite believe it. I can feel something—watching, waiting.

He frowns but says nothing, though his hand doesn't leave mine as we move forward. The path takes a sudden dip, leading us down into a hollow where the air feels denser, laced with a damp, earthy scent that clings to my skin. And then I see it, through a break in the trees ahead—a faint light, barely more than a glimmer, like the last ember of a dying fire.

Damian tenses beside me, his hand tightening around mine. "Stay close," he murmurs, though I have no intention of wandering off.

We inch closer, our footsteps muffled by the thick layer of moss blanketing the ground. As we near the source of the light, I realize it's not fire at all—it's a glow, an eerie, unnatural radiance that seeps from the cracks of an ancient stone altar nestled between the roots of a massive tree. Symbols are carved into the stone, worn and faded, but their meaning is clear enough: this is a place of power, a place where rituals were once performed. The air hums with an energy that feels both foreign and familiar, a low, thrumming pulse that seems to vibrate through the ground beneath my feet.

I glance at Damian, his face cast in shadow, his eyes locked on the altar with a look that borders on reverence—or maybe dread. I can't tell, and I'm not sure I want to.

"What is this?" I whisper, though I don't expect an answer.

But he gives one, his voice barely more than a breath. "An anchor. A tether to something... beyond." He hesitates, his gaze flicking to me, as though gauging how much to reveal. "Some say it's a gateway, a bridge between worlds. If there's any chance of finding what we came for, it's here."

I feel a shiver creep down my spine, the weight of his words settling like a stone in my stomach. A gateway. The idea feels absurd, like something out of a fairy tale. And yet, standing here in this ancient, forgotten garden, it somehow doesn't feel impossible. The air is thick with an energy that defies logic, a presence that seems to press against my skin, wrapping around me like a second, colder skin.

Before I can process any of it, a low, mournful sound drifts through the trees. It's barely a whisper, but it's enough to make every hair on my arms stand on end. I glance at Damian, and I can see that he's heard it too, his face tight with a tension that mirrors my own.

Then, without warning, a figure emerges from the shadows, stepping into the pale glow of the altar. I suck in a breath, instinctively reaching for my dagger, though I'm not sure it would do me any good here.

The figure is tall and gaunt, draped in a cloak that seems to shift and shimmer, blending with the darkness around them. Their face is obscured by a hood, but I catch a glimpse of eyes that gleam like polished stones, reflecting the eerie light from the altar.

Damian steps forward, his stance wary but unyielding. "Who are you?"

The figure tilts their head, a slow, deliberate movement that sends another shiver down my spine. "A keeper of memories," they say, their voice low and hollow, echoing through the clearing like a distant bell. "I am bound to this place, as are the memories of all who have come before you."

I feel a tightening in my chest, a weight pressing down on me, as if the garden itself is bearing witness to this moment. Damian holds his ground, his gaze steady, but I can see the flicker of uncertainty in his eyes.

"We're looking for someone," he says, his voice firm, though there's an edge to it, a hint of desperation that he can't quite hide. "Someone who disappeared here, years ago."

The figure's eyes narrow, glinting with something that might be amusement—or pity. "Many have come seeking the lost," they murmur, "but few find what they are looking for. The garden does not give up its secrets easily."

The words hang in the air, heavy with a finality that sends a jolt of fear through me. I swallow, forcing myself to speak, though my voice comes out barely more than a whisper. "Is there a way out?"

The figure's gaze shifts to me, and for a moment, I feel as though they're seeing straight through me, peeling back every layer, every secret I've ever tried to hide. "The way out is the same as the way in," they say, their voice soft, almost kind. "But be warned: those who leave are never the same as those who enter."

I don't know what to say, but I feel Damian's hand tighten around mine, a silent reassurance, though I can feel the tension radiating from him. He's as shaken as I am, though he hides it better.

The figure steps back, melting into the shadows, their form dissolving like mist. The light from the altar dims, fading until it's nothing more than a faint glow, barely enough to see by.

Damian lets out a breath, his grip on my hand loosening. "Are you ready?" he asks, his voice low, almost a whisper.

I nod, though the truth is, I'm not sure I am. There's a sense of finality here, a feeling that once we leave, there's no going back. But I push the thought aside, forcing myself to focus on the task at hand.

Just as we turn to leave, a sudden, sharp crack echoes through the clearing, a sound like splintering wood. I spin around, my heart pounding, but there's nothing there—only the empty altar, and the faint, lingering glow that seems to pulse, like a heartbeat.

And then, without warning, the ground beneath us shifts, the earth trembling as a deep, rumbling sound rises from the depths below. The garden seems to come alive around us, the trees swaying, their branches reaching out as though trying to pull us back, hold us here.

Damian grabs my arm, his eyes wide with a fear I've never seen before. "Run," he says, his voice urgent, desperate.

But before I can take a step, the ground gives way beneath us, and we're falling into darkness.

Chapter 6: A Dance with Darkness

The moonlight cascades through a lattice of ancient oaks, painting fractured light across the path where Damian and I stand. We're deep enough into the garden that it feels we've stepped out of the world entirely, into some hidden universe caught between reality and the flickering light of fireflies. There's a richness to the air, a damp, earthy scent mingled with the sweetness of night-blooming jasmine, the kind of smell that clings to your skin long after you've left. Damian's voice—low, a little hoarse, like he's unused to talking for this long—draws me back from my thoughts.

"My mother," he says finally, the words dragging out as if from some deep cavern, "was an actress. Or rather, she wanted to be." There's a subtle bitterness in his tone, laced with something softer, something like regret. "She spent years performing in dusty theaters, playing the parts of someone else's dream. I think she believed one day she'd wake up famous." His laugh is soft, almost inaudible, but it hits me like a wave. "But she never did. Woke up famous, I mean. She just woke up."

I study his face, trying to catch the flickers of emotion he hides so well. In the dim light, his features look sharper, carved from shadows and secrets. He's letting me in, piece by reluctant piece, and the feeling is dizzying. It's like watching a fortress slowly crumble, stone by stone, revealing a glimpse of something fragile beneath.

"What about you?" His eyes flicker up to meet mine, and there's something in his gaze that feels like a challenge and an invitation, all at once.

I swallow, feeling a pang of hesitation rise in my throat. I've spent so long keeping my walls up, deflecting questions with half-truths and easy smiles. But here, in this quiet, hidden place, under the spell of Damian's voice and the steady pulse of the night, I feel myself slipping.

"My father was a painter," I begin, the words strange and heavy on my tongue. I can't remember the last time I talked about him. "Not a very good one, if I'm being honest. He had the soul of an artist but the talent of an amateur. He'd spend hours trying to capture some image in his head, only to end up with a mess of colors that barely resembled anything." I laugh, a little too loudly, and it echoes in the night. "But he loved it. And maybe that's what mattered most."

Damian's gaze softens, and there's something unreadable in his expression, a glint of something raw and unguarded. For a moment, he doesn't say anything, just watches me with an intensity that makes my pulse race. His silence is a question, an invitation to say more, to dig deeper. But I'm not sure I can.

"I think I was his favorite canvas," I add finally, my voice a whisper. "He liked the idea of shaping me, molding me into his vision. It's why I left." The words slip out before I can stop them, and I feel a sharp pang of vulnerability. I've never admitted that to anyone—not even to myself, not really.

We fall silent, the weight of our confessions hanging in the air between us. Somewhere in the distance, an owl hoots, a low, mournful sound that echoes through the trees. Damian shifts, his hand brushing against mine, and I feel a jolt, like a spark igniting in the dark. His touch is warm, grounding, pulling me back from the edge of whatever precipice I've found myself on.

"I don't think he deserved you," Damian murmurs, his voice a mix of conviction and something else, something darker. "No one should have the right to shape you, to turn you into something you're not."

I feel a strange, bittersweet pang at his words, like a wound being exposed to the air for the first time. I want to laugh it off, to make some flippant remark and deflect the tenderness in his voice, but I can't bring myself to. Instead, I let the silence settle between us, thick and heavy, filled with the things we're both too afraid to say.

And then, as if sensing my thoughts, Damian steps closer, his fingers brushing against my cheek, a touch so soft it feels like a dream. "You don't have to pretend with me," he whispers, his voice barely audible over the rustling leaves. "Not here. Not now."

For a heartbeat, I think about pulling away, about putting up my walls and shutting him out. But something in his gaze holds me captive, something raw and vulnerable and achingly real. So instead, I close my eyes, letting myself lean into his touch, letting myself feel.

In that moment, it's as if the entire world has faded away, leaving only the two of us, caught in a fragile, beautiful moment that feels as fleeting as the fireflies dancing in the darkness. His hand moves from my cheek to my jaw, his thumb grazing my skin, and I feel a shiver run down my spine. There's something almost dangerous about his touch, something that makes me feel alive in a way I can't explain.

But just as quickly as it began, the moment is shattered. A twig snaps somewhere in the distance, followed by a low, guttural growl that sends a chill down my spine. Damian tenses, his hand dropping from my face as he scans the shadows, his body taut with a sudden, fierce protectiveness.

I feel a flicker of fear, sharp and unexpected, but Damian's presence beside me is like an anchor, grounding me. He glances at me, his expression hard, his eyes dark and intense. "Stay close," he whispers, his voice a low, urgent command. "I won't let anything happen to you."

His words send a thrill through me, mingling with the fear in a way that's both exhilarating and terrifying. I nod, my heart pounding as we move forward, deeper into the shadows, leaving the comfort of the moonlight behind.

We move as one, our footsteps silent, our breaths shallow as we navigate the winding paths of the garden. The growling sound echoes again, closer this time, and I feel a surge of adrenaline, a wild, desperate urge to run. But Damian's hand tightens on mine, steadying me, and I force myself to stay calm, to trust him.

For a heartbeat, I glance up at him, and in the darkness, his eyes meet mine, filled with a fierce, unyielding determination. And in that moment, I know, without a doubt, that he would fight to protect me, that he would face whatever dangers lie ahead without a second thought. The thought fills me with a strange, aching sense of belonging, of safety, and I find myself gripping his hand tighter, refusing to let go.

The air feels sharper now, carrying a faint chill that prickles at my skin, heightening my senses in a way that borders on exhilarating. The garden looms around us, a strange and shifting maze of shadows and whispers. I can't shake the feeling that it's not just Damian and me moving through this space but something ancient and unseen, watching us as we weave further into the thick, moonlit greenery.

Damian's face is etched with a focus that I've only seen once before, back when he fixed that door hinge in my apartment as though it held the mysteries of the universe. But now, he's not fussing over hardware; he's watching the trees, listening for something that I can't quite catch. Every so often, his hand finds mine in a firm, protective grip, steadying me when I stumble over an unseen root or when the path narrows, and branches close in overhead.

"So, you were telling me about your father," he says, his voice softer now, as though he's as wary of disturbing the silence as I am. There's a flicker of interest in his gaze, something that feels oddly like concern—or curiosity, perhaps, though with Damian, it's hard to tell.

"He painted strange things, really," I say, my voice a little too loud, startling even myself. "Most people paint flowers or the sea, or at least something recognizable. But my father... he painted shadows." The words feel heavier than I intended, slipping out as if they'd been waiting for this moment. "Dark things, twisted shapes. I think he thought they were beautiful. I tried to see it, too, but they always made me uneasy."

Damian pauses, his gaze holding mine in the moonlight. "Maybe he was seeing something that others couldn't. Something real." His tone is so matter-of-fact that it takes me aback.

"Are you implying that my father saw ghosts?" I tease, though my heart thuds faster at the suggestion. There's a weight in the garden tonight that makes even the most absurd ideas feel plausible.

Damian smirks, but it's tinged with a seriousness that makes me uneasy. "I wouldn't put it past him. Art like that... it comes from somewhere. Or something."

There's a sudden rustle behind us, and I jump, my grip tightening on Damian's hand. He tenses, his eyes narrowing as he scans the shadows. For a heartbeat, I think he might let go of my hand and stride off into the dark, ready to confront whatever it is. But instead, he pulls me closer, his body a shield between me and the shifting leaves.

"I'll admit," I murmur, trying to ignore the way my pulse races at the nearness of him, "I'm not exactly sure if you're the bravest person I've ever met, or just incredibly reckless."

He chuckles softly, the sound rolling through the quiet night. "And you're what? Pure caution and sensibility?"

I roll my eyes, though there's a grin tugging at my lips. "Of course. Just ask my landlord."

Damian's laugh is full and real, breaking the tension, and I find myself relaxing, if only a little. But just as the warmth settles, something else shifts in the garden, a shiver of movement in the corner of my eye. I don't know if it's the night or my own imagination, but I can't shake the feeling that we're not alone, that something lingers just beyond the edges of our vision.

I glance at Damian, my voice dropping to a whisper. "Did you... see that?"

He follows my gaze, his face hardening, and for a moment, I think he might say no, might brush it off. But instead, he nods, his eyes scanning the darkness with a wary, calculating intensity that sends a chill down my spine.

"There's been... something," he says, his voice barely audible, "following me for a while now. I thought it might have left by now. But maybe it's just gotten better at hiding." His tone is almost too casual, and I can tell it's an effort to keep it that way.

"Better at hiding? Damian, what exactly have you gotten yourself into?" I demand, unable to mask the worry in my voice.

He gives a slight shake of his head, as if to brush the question aside, but there's a flash of something raw in his expression. "Let's just say there are certain things I've had to keep in the dark. They prefer shadows, after all."

A surge of frustration rises in me. "You know, it'd be nice if you could occasionally speak in plain English. Prefer shadows? What does that even mean?"

"Would you believe me if I told you?" His voice is rough, tinged with something that borders on resignation.

I hesitate, searching his face, but there's no answer there, only more questions, more shadows. And despite everything in me that wants to stay safe, to stay far away from whatever mess Damian has wrapped himself in, there's another part—a small, reckless part—that can't look away.

"I guess there's only one way to find out," I say finally, hoping my voice sounds braver than I feel.

A slow smile creeps onto his face, softening the tension in his eyes. "I knew there was a reason I liked you."

It's such an absurd thing to say, given the situation, that I find myself laughing, the sound breaking through the lingering tension in the air. Damian laughs too, a real, unguarded laugh that feels like a rare and precious thing. But our laughter fades quickly, replaced by the quiet weight of the night and the strange, shifting presence that seems to surround us.

He takes my hand, his grip firmer this time, and together, we press forward, moving deeper into the garden. The path narrows, winding through a cluster of towering hedges that seem to close in on us, casting long, twisting shadows across the ground. Each step feels heavier, as if the ground itself is reluctant to let us go.

"You're going to think I'm crazy," Damian says suddenly, his voice a low murmur, "but sometimes I feel like the darkness here is alive. Like it has a mind of its own."

For a moment, I want to brush it off, to tell him that he's being ridiculous. But something about the way he says it—the raw vulnerability in his voice, the unspoken fear in his gaze—stops me. I squeeze his hand, a silent reassurance.

"You're not crazy," I say, my voice steadier than I feel. "If you think it's real, then maybe it is."

We move in silence, the weight of my words hanging between us. But the quiet doesn't last long. Somewhere in the shadows, a low, echoing growl reverberates through the night, sending a fresh wave of fear coursing through me. Damian tenses, his hand tightening around mine, and for a split second, I think he might run.

But instead, he stands his ground, his gaze fierce and unwavering. "Whatever happens," he murmurs, his voice low and fierce, "I'm not letting you go."

And in that moment, I know, deep in my bones, that whatever shadows lie ahead, whatever secrets Damian has yet to reveal, I'm in this with him.

The garden's maze-like paths grow narrower, twisting in unexpected directions that have me turning back over my shoulder, certain we're being followed. My skin prickles as I half-expect to see a shadow slinking in the dimness, some elusive creature darting behind the hedges, leaving only the faintest trace of its presence. I glance at Damian, who moves forward with an uncanny steadiness, his hand in mine an anchor pulling me through this strange, dreamlike labyrinth.

"You act like you've done this before," I say, keeping my voice low, almost as if speaking too loudly would awaken the dark that hovers around us.

Damian glances at me, his face shadowed but his eyes sharp. "You get used to certain things," he murmurs. "You start to see the world differently."

"Differently, like expecting a monster around every corner?" I try to keep my tone light, but there's an edge to my words, a sharpness I can't hide.

"Something like that." He's too casual, but I catch the tightness in his jaw, the way his eyes flicker into the darkness, his shoulders tense. He's scared, but he hides it well. And for some reason, that terrifies me more than anything else.

Just as I'm about to press him, there's a sudden, eerie silence. The night sounds—crickets, the whisper of leaves, the distant hum of the city—vanish, leaving only a hollow stillness that feels unnatural. It's as if the entire garden is holding its breath, waiting.

"Did you hear that?" I whisper, though I'm not even sure what I'm listening for.

Damian's hand tightens on mine, pulling me close, his breath warm against my ear. "Stay with me," he murmurs, his voice low and fierce. "No matter what happens, don't let go."

I nod, my heart racing, each beat echoing in my ears. For a moment, everything feels surreal, the world blurred at the edges, Damian's face the only clear thing in my vision. But then, just as quickly as the silence fell, a soft sound breaks it—a faint rustle, almost too quiet to hear, but unmistakably close.

We freeze, both of us straining to catch another sound, another hint of movement. But the garden remains still, the air heavy with a tension that's almost tangible. And then, without warning, something darts through the shadows, a dark figure moving too quickly to identify. I catch a flash of eyes—sharp, feral, glinting in the moonlight—and my heart skips, a surge of adrenaline flooding my veins.

"What was that?" My voice is barely more than a whisper, but Damian's hand steadies me, his grip grounding me in the face of this unknown threat.

"Probably not the kind of thing we want to meet," he mutters, his voice tense but calm. "Come on. Slowly."

He leads me forward, each step careful, deliberate, as though one wrong move might trigger whatever it is lurking in the shadows. The path ahead winds sharply, and I feel a strange, almost electric energy in the air, as if the very garden itself is alive, aware of our presence. The hairs on the back of my neck stand up, and I have to resist the urge to turn and run.

Then, out of the silence, a low growl reverberates through the air, a sound so deep and guttural it sends a chill straight to my bones. Damian pulls me close, his body between me and the direction of the sound, his stance protective, ready. The growl grows louder, a menacing rumble that seems to come from all around us, as if the garden itself is growling.

My voice catches, panic rising in my throat. "Damian, what is that?"

He doesn't answer, his focus locked on the shadows. But I see a flicker of something in his expression, a glint of fear that he tries to mask, though he's failing miserably. His hand shifts, reaching behind him to pull something out of his jacket—a knife, its blade gleaming faintly in the moonlight.

"Just in case," he says, his voice steady, though there's an edge to it that makes my stomach clench.

"Just in case what?" I ask, though I'm not sure I want to know the answer.

He glances at me, his face softened for a brief, fleeting moment. "In case running isn't an option."

The words hang between us, stark and final, and I feel a fresh wave of fear washing over me. But before I can say anything, the growling stops, replaced by an eerie silence, thicker and more oppressive than before. We wait, our breaths shallow, listening to the stillness, waiting for whatever comes next.

And then, in the blink of an eye, it lunges—a massive, shadowy creature, its body a blur of darkness, its eyes fierce and unblinking. Damian shoves me aside, his movement swift and instinctive, and I stumble backward, barely catching myself as he faces the creature head-on.

The thing circles him, its movements fluid and unnatural, like it's made of smoke and shadows rather than flesh and blood. Damian's knife glints as he holds it steady, his gaze fixed, unyielding, but there's an edge of desperation in his stance, a tension that tells me he knows he's outmatched.

"Stay back!" he shouts, his voice raw, filled with an intensity I've never heard before. But I can't move, can't tear my eyes away from the sight in front of me.

The creature lunges again, its form twisting, elongating in the air, and Damian moves to meet it, his knife flashing as he strikes. The blade makes contact, but instead of drawing blood, it slices through the creature like it's nothing more than mist, its form scattering and reforming in the blink of an eye.

"Damian!" My voice breaks, filled with fear, desperation, and something else, something I can't name. He glances at me, his face pale, his expression a mixture of anger and fear and something heartbreakingly vulnerable.

"It's not... solid," he says, almost to himself, as though he's realizing it for the first time. "It's not—"

But he doesn't get to finish. The creature moves faster this time, lunging at him with a ferocity that leaves no room for defense. Damian barely manages to dodge, his body twisting out of the way, but it's not enough. The creature's shadowy form wraps around him, its dark tendrils clinging to his arms, his chest, binding him in a grip that looks both deadly and surreal.

"Let him go!" I scream, the words ripping out of me, my voice trembling with fear and fury. I lunge forward, driven by an impulse I can't explain, my hands reaching for Damian, trying to pull him free. But as my fingers brush his, I feel an icy chill, a strange, numbing sensation that spreads through me, stealing my breath, my strength.

"Don't..." he gasps, his voice weak, strained. "Get... away."

But I can't. I can't leave him, can't turn back, can't let this strange, terrible darkness take him. I tighten my grip on his hand, fighting against the cold, against the fear, against everything that tells me to run.

And then, just as suddenly as it began, the darkness shifts, its grip loosening, as if startled. Damian's fingers tighten around mine, his gaze meeting mine, fierce and unyielding. But in his eyes, I see something else—something terrifying, something I can't understand.

And then, without warning, the world around us shatters, plunging us into an abyss of blinding light and deafening sound, and I feel myself falling, Damian's hand slipping from mine as everything fades into chaos.

Chapter 7: The Blood Moon's Warning

There's an eerie glow cast by the Blood Moon, the kind of light that seems to drink color from everything beneath it, leeching vibrancy until even my skin feels like a strange, washed-out ghost of itself. A rust-red halo circles the moon, twisting the stars around it into unnatural shapes. I almost swear they're blinking in some coded rhythm, like some otherworldly Morse code, if only I could understand. It sets my nerves humming. Tonight feels different, and the artifact—I feel its weight humming beneath my shirt—leads us here like some kind of celestial map. I can feel it in my bones: something's about to happen.

Beside me, Damian's gaze is locked on the sky, his jaw clenched, eyes narrowed. He's wary, but that's nothing new. Damian practically invented wary. Every muscle in his body is pulled taut, a coiled spring that looks ready to snap, ready to fight. He hasn't spoken since we crossed into the clearing. His silence grates against me; it's both a comfort and an irritation. That's the strange thing about Damian—he's this brooding presence you'd think you'd want to avoid, but the quiet intensity pulls you in, like a dangerous flame that promises warmth but warns of burns.

A twig snaps to our left, and the sound is too sharp, too deliberate. I don't even need to look at Damian; I know he heard it too, and I know what it means. We're not alone. I slip my hand down to the hilt of my dagger, the artifact's weight cold against my chest, almost vibrating with something like a heartbeat. My own pulse picks up to match it, quick and skittering as a wild animal's.

A figure emerges from the shadows, then another, and another until they're everywhere, a silent crowd closing in with military precision. They're dressed head-to-toe in dark cloaks that ripple like liquid when they move, blurring the lines between flesh and shadow. They circle us, a living snare tightening with each second. I cast a glance at Damian, catching the quick flicker of his eyes. He's scanning, calculating, searching for an opening. But there's none.

"We're surrounded," I murmur, low and quick, not so much a warning as a confirmation of the obvious.

Damian grunts, his hand twitching near his own weapon. "Brilliant observation, truly. Care to tell me anything I don't already know?"

He's insufferable, really. But there's something grounding in his sarcasm, a bizarre kind of normalcy in his jabs that keeps me from spiraling. He shifts his stance slightly, shoulders braced, giving off this silent signal: Get ready.

The leader of our new friends steps forward, a man with a face so sharp it looks like it was carved from granite. His eyes catch the glow of the Blood Moon, making them look red and feral, a pair of polished garnets embedded in stone. He tilts his head, studying us with a curious sort of amusement.

"So, you two are the ones foolish enough to meddle with things best left buried," he drawls, his voice smooth as silk and twice as dangerous. There's a lilt in his tone that suggests he's already decided we're defeated, like he's watching a foregone conclusion play out.

"We've got the whole burying things part handled," I say, lifting my dagger a fraction. "Why don't you and your friends do the same?"

Damian rolls his eyes beside me. "Really? Now's the time for sass?"

The leader smirks, as if he finds our little exchange charming in its own doomed way. Then, with a flick of his wrist, his followers launch forward, and we're swallowed by a wave of blackened shadows.

The fight is swift, brutal, a chaotic dance of blades and grunts and near-misses. Damian and I move in a rhythm we barely knew we had, his left covering my right, my back shielding his. His sword cleaves through the air, swift arcs of silver that gleam in the Blood Moon's light, while I'm all quick stabs and narrow dodges, fighting like a cornered animal. There's no finesse to it, no elegance—just survival. It's rough and messy, but it works.

Then I hear a sharp intake of breath, and out of the corner of my eye, I see Damian stagger. One of them got a lucky strike, a blade cutting deep across his shoulder. Blood blooms immediately, dark and spreading, and he stumbles. Without thinking, I lunge forward, putting myself between him and the shadows circling closer.

"Move," he snarls, but the pain in his voice robs the command of its usual bite.

"Shut up and let me protect you for once," I snap back, kicking one of the cloaked figures hard enough to send them sprawling.

We manage, somehow, to fight our way through. Our attackers seem to realize they won't take us as easily as they'd hoped, and they begin to retreat, melting back into the shadows, leaving the clearing as empty as if they'd never been there. But the damage is done. Damian's breathing is ragged, each inhale a wince, and the blood stains his shirt a dark, unsettling crimson.

I crouch beside him, my fingers working to tear a strip of cloth to bind the wound. He watches me, a strange, searching look in his eyes as I work. The silence stretches between us, thick with unspoken words, questions neither of us are quite brave enough to ask. I risk a glance up, catching the flicker of something soft in his gaze, something hesitant and unguarded.

"Thank you," he murmurs finally, almost grudgingly, as if the words were wrestled out of him.

"Try not to sound so enthusiastic," I reply, tightening the makeshift bandage. He winces, and I stifle a smirk. "Just returning the favor. Now we're even."

There's a beat of quiet, then he chuckles, a sound so rare it catches me off guard. I look at him, eyebrow raised, and he shrugs, the motion a little stiff. "Even? You've got a long way to go before we're even, princess."

"Princess? I don't think so," I scoff, though the nickname holds a strange, warm weight in the night air. I don't let it show.

The Blood Moon casts its light over us, bathing Damian's face in that eerie crimson glow, highlighting the edges of his sharp jaw, the deep cut of his cheekbones, and the faint, crooked smile that lingers as he watches me. It's a look I can't quite decipher—part respect, part something else, something far too complicated to unpack here in the middle of nowhere with blood on our hands and enemies waiting in the shadows.

In that moment, beneath the ominous gaze of the Blood Moon, an unspoken agreement passes between us. Trust—fragile, tentative, but real.

I glance over at Damian, who's still watching me with that same intensity, his face set in an unreadable expression as I press down on the makeshift bandage. The silence is thick, charged, and I can't tell if it's the lingering adrenaline or something else that has my heart hammering against my ribs. The shadows have retreated, but I can still feel their presence, like a promise whispered in the dark, waiting.

"You're too quiet," I say, breaking the stillness. "It's creepy."

He lets out a low chuckle, though it quickly fades into a grimace as pain shoots through his shoulder. "Well, excuse me if bleeding out makes me less chatty."

I roll my eyes, but there's a warmth behind it. "Always the martyr."

"You'd miss me if I were gone."

It's a statement, not a question, and that irks me more than it should. He's smug, even now, and maybe he's right, but I'll be damned if I admit it. "I'd miss the silence, that's for sure."

He quirks a brow, that same wry smile flickering on his lips. "Funny. The silence seems to bother you just fine."

I mutter under my breath, feigning irritation as I pull another strip of cloth tight around his shoulder. His skin is pale beneath the blood, a stark contrast against the inky black of his shirt. The blood's dried, crusting along the edges of his wound, and he winces as I tighten the knot. "There. That'll hold for now."

He tests the binding, flexing his arm just enough to feel the pull of the bandage. "You've done this before."

"Once or twice." I glance away, not really wanting to get into the specifics of how many times I've had to patch myself up. Or others. It's a skill, and like most useful things, it's been learned the hard way.

"Who taught you?" he asks, and the question is so simple, so unexpectedly genuine, it catches me off guard.

"Life, I guess." I shrug, and there's a pause, heavy with things neither of us will say. He watches me for a beat longer than comfortable, then nods, as if that answer was enough.

Before I can feel too unsettled, a low hum fills the air, vibrating through the ground beneath us. It's a warning, an unnatural pulse that feels like it's coming from the very heart of the forest. Damian stiffens, his gaze snapping to the trees. The eerie crimson light of the Blood Moon casts long, twisting shadows between the trunks, and there's something different in the air—a chill that creeps into my bones, a pressure that makes me feel like something's watching us, weighing and waiting.

"I thought they left," I whisper, more to myself than him.

Damian's hand drifts to his sword. "They did. But we didn't."

A shiver runs down my spine. I'd wanted to believe we were safe for the night, that the shadows had slinked back to whatever corner of darkness they'd crawled out of. But the forest feels alive now, shifting around us, and I know that whatever trap we walked into isn't done with us yet. Damian catches my eye, his expression sober.

"We need to move," he says, his tone leaving no room for argument. He rises slowly, his movements stiff, and for once, he doesn't try to hide the pain. There's a vulnerability to him now, an unguarded moment that flickers and fades as he straightens, shoulders squared, his focus sharp.

"We're in no condition to run into another ambush," I say, weighing my options. We could stay, try to wait it out. Or we could risk it, push through the trees and hope we find a way out before whatever's out there finds us.

He glances back, his mouth set in a hard line. "Waiting isn't going to make them go away."

I hate that he's right. I hate it more that he knows he's right. With a grudging nod, I take a step forward, and he falls into step beside me, his presence a steady, silent force beside me as we navigate through the darkened woods. The trees loom overhead, their branches twisted and reaching like skeletal fingers, casting strange, fractured patterns of light and shadow across the ground. The only sound is the crunch of leaves beneath our feet, the occasional whisper of wind through the trees, and the quiet, ragged rhythm of Damian's breathing.

Every now and then, I steal a glance at him, watching the way he moves with that same determined grace, even wounded. There's a part of me that wants to ask him why he does it, why he keeps pushing, why he doesn't just stop and let someone else carry the weight for once. But I don't. Because maybe that's something I'd rather not know.

A low rumble echoes through the trees, and the ground trembles beneath us, a warning that comes too late. Without thinking, I grab Damian's arm, dragging him down as a massive root bursts up from the earth, twisting and coiling like a serpent before crashing down where we'd just been standing. I barely have time to process it before another root rises up, splitting the ground with a thunderous crack, sending splinters of wood and rock flying.

Damian pulls me to my feet, his hand gripping mine as he leads us into a sprint, dodging the roots that rise up in our path, each one closer than the last. The forest has come alive, the trees shifting and writhing, as if the very ground is trying to swallow us whole. I don't know if it's the artifact, or the Blood Moon, or some dark magic set loose in the night, but whatever it is, it's angry.

"Keep moving!" Damian shouts, his voice barely audible over the roar of the earth tearing itself apart beneath us. He pulls me forward, his grip steady, unyielding, as we weave through the trees, ducking and dodging, our breaths coming in ragged gasps.

I can feel the energy building around us, a raw, electric charge that prickles against my skin, tightening the air with the promise of something terrible. My heart pounds, a frantic rhythm that echoes the pulsing beat of the earth. My lungs burn, my legs ache, but I don't dare stop, not when each step could mean the difference between escape and being buried alive.

Just when I think we can't run any further, the trees open up, revealing a small clearing bathed in the ominous glow of the Blood Moon. Damian stumbles, his strength flagging, and I catch him, pulling him upright as we stagger into the open space. The silence that follows is sudden, absolute, a vacuum that makes the ringing in my ears feel like a scream.

We collapse to the ground, gasping for breath, our backs pressed against each other as we scan the tree line, waiting, watching. The shadows dance along the edges, shifting and restless, but they don't cross into the clearing. It's as if some invisible barrier holds them back, keeping them at bay.

For a long moment, we sit there, catching our breath, the weight of our near escape settling over us. I feel Damian's hand brush against mine, a fleeting, almost accidental touch that lingers in the charged silence. I don't pull away.

"You don't have to... stay close," he says, his voice low, barely more than a whisper, but there's a softness to it, an unspoken gratitude.

"Maybe I like the company," I reply, forcing a lightness I don't feel.

His lips twitch in a faint smile, but there's something in his eyes that stays with me, something that feels like a promise neither of us is ready to make. The Blood Moon hangs heavy above us, watching, waiting, and I can't shake the feeling that this night has changed something between us, something fragile and dangerous and very, very real.

Damian's breathing steadies as the night deepens around us, the crimson hue of the Blood Moon casting a haunting glow over the clearing. Shadows dance at the edge, twisting like things alive, though they never breach the invisible barrier that keeps us safe. I can feel the weight of the artifact beneath my shirt, pulsing faintly against my chest as if reminding me of its presence. I want to yank it off, throw it as far as I can, but that's the problem with cursed things—they cling to you, like guilt or a bad memory.

Damian shifts beside me, wincing slightly. "You're staring a hole through that artifact. Something you want to tell me about it?"

My hand instinctively moves to cover the metal through my shirt. "I don't trust it. Or whoever decided we should carry it across enemy territory without a decent plan."

He raises an eyebrow, his mouth curving into that infuriating half-smile. "Plans are just guesses we pretend are set in stone. We've made it this far on a little luck and a lot of improv."

"A stellar recipe for survival," I mutter, giving him a sidelong glance. "You sure you're all right? You look like you're about to pass out."

He rolls his eyes, but it doesn't hide the pallor beneath the dried blood. "Not that delicate, believe it or not. Besides," he adds, his gaze shifting to the dark woods, "we have bigger problems than a scratch."

His words settle like a stone in my stomach, and I scan the trees, where shapes twist and undulate like shadows with minds of their own. The faint rustling in the distance sounds suspiciously like whispers, a constant murmur that threads through the silence, rising and falling in a rhythm that feels far too alive. I can't shake the feeling that we're being watched—not by the usual spies or scouts, but by something ancient, something that doesn't belong in any world I know.

I lean toward Damian, lowering my voice. "If you've got any genius ideas, now's the time."

He doesn't respond immediately, his eyes narrowing as he studies the perimeter. "This clearing—we're here for a reason," he says slowly, like he's piecing together a puzzle. "The artifact, the Blood Moon... They're tied somehow. Whoever set this up wanted us here, in this exact spot."

"So we're bait?"

"Seems that way." He sighs, as if that was the only logical outcome.

My stomach twists. "Brilliant. That's just what I was hoping for."

"Relax. Bait isn't always meant to be caught. Sometimes it's just meant to lure out the bigger fish." He smirks, though the glint in his eye betrays a flicker of uncertainty.

The faint hum from before grows louder, and suddenly, the artifact beneath my shirt grows warm, its steady beat accelerating, syncing with my heartbeat until they're a rapid, insistent rhythm. I clutch it, feeling the metal heat against my skin, and Damian's gaze flicks down to my hand, his eyes widening.

"You feel that too?" I ask, barely above a whisper.

He nods, a muscle in his jaw clenching. "Something's coming. Or maybe it's already here."

The clearing grows deathly still, and then, from the shadows, a figure steps forward, draped in dark robes that swirl around them like smoke. Their face is hidden beneath a hood, but I can feel their gaze piercing through, burning with a strange, otherworldly light. They stand at the edge of the clearing, silent, unmoving, like a statue come to life.

Damian's hand inches toward his sword, but I stop him with a touch. "Wait. Let's see what they want."

The figure raises a hand, and a soft, lilting voice drifts through the night air. "You carry something that does not belong to you."

The words are spoken in a tone so calm it's almost hypnotic, but there's an edge to them, a warning that prickles across my skin. I tighten my grip on the artifact, the weight of it suddenly feeling unbearable.

"Last I checked, it doesn't belong to you either," I say, my voice sharper than I intended. "Who are you, anyway?"

The figure tilts their head, the hood slipping back just enough to reveal a glimpse of pale skin and dark, calculating eyes. "Names are for those who have yet to be forgotten," they say, a cryptic smile tugging at their lips. "I am beyond such trivialities."

Damian scoffs under his breath. "Great, a cryptic ghost with a superiority complex. Just what we need."

The figure's gaze snaps to him, and though their expression remains neutral, I sense a flicker of irritation. "You jest, but you carry power you do not understand. Power that others would kill to possess."

My fingers tighten around the artifact, and it pulses in response, a warning—or maybe a promise. "Why do you want it?" I ask, forcing my voice to stay steady.

"Because it is not yours to keep," the figure replies, each word a carefully sharpened blade. "The Blood Moon has called me forth to restore balance. And to do so, I must take back what belongs to the night."

Damian steps forward, his stance protective. "Well, that's a problem. Because as long as we're breathing, you're not getting anywhere near it."

The figure laughs, a low, chilling sound that seems to echo in the stillness. "Brave words, but empty. You cannot stop what has already begun." They raise their hand, and the ground beneath us trembles, a deep rumble that feels like the heartbeat of the earth itself.

I glance at Damian, and for the first time, I see a flicker of genuine fear in his eyes. "Run?" I suggest, my voice barely a whisper.

"Run," he agrees, and we bolt, our footsteps pounding against the earth as the clearing erupts in a frenzy of roots and vines, twisting and coiling, reaching for us like hungry hands. The figure watches, unmoving, their dark eyes glinting with satisfaction.

We race through the forest, dodging branches and leaping over roots that seem to rise out of nowhere, trying to trip us, ensnare us, pull us down into the waiting earth. The artifact burns hotter with each step, like it's fighting against me, trying to pull me back toward that shadowed figure. My lungs burn, my legs ache, but I don't dare stop, not when I can still feel their gaze piercing through the trees, a cold, relentless presence that feels like it's breathing down my neck.

"Faster!" Damian shouts, grabbing my arm and pulling me forward as a root snaps up from the ground, missing my ankle by inches. The forest twists and shifts around us, a labyrinth of shadows and shifting light, each step more disorienting than the last.

Just when I think we're safe, the artifact jerks violently against my chest, a sudden, searing pain radiating through my body. I stumble, gasping, and Damian's grip slips from my hand. The world blurs, a dizzying rush of crimson and black, and I feel myself falling, spiraling down into an endless darkness.

My vision clears just in time to see Damian reaching for me, his eyes wide with terror, but it's too late. A hand—a shadowy, clawed hand—emerges from the darkness, gripping the artifact through my shirt, its touch cold and searing all at once.

The figure's voice echoes in my mind, a whisper that chills me to the bone. "Balance will be restored."

And then, with a final, brutal tug, I'm pulled into the shadows, the world around me disappearing in a rush of silence and darkness.

Chapter 8: Wounded Hearts and Whispered Secrets

The wind outside is relentless, its icy fingers clawing at the thin walls of our makeshift shelter, filling the room with an eerie hum. Damian winces with every gust, his fingers wrapped tightly around his side, where blood still seeps through the thin cloth I'd hastily pressed there. I keep my face blank, refusing to let him see my worry. Weakness was never tolerated in my world; you either survived or you were forgotten. But watching Damian, so formidable and unyielding under the sun, now brought to his knees by a wound and bad luck, something stirs. It's infuriating, the way my chest tightens seeing him in pain.

"Does it hurt?" I ask, my voice cooler than I feel. I pretend to busy myself with gathering supplies, though we both know I've collected every last thing this ramshackle space has to offer.

"Only when I breathe," he replies, attempting a smirk that quickly turns into a grimace. He's trying to keep up the bravado, to pretend that a little blood and broken bones aren't more than a minor inconvenience. But the way his lips pale, the trembling in his fingers as he releases his grip—it tells another story.

I shake my head and move closer, shoving my pride and whatever lingering animosity I might have down where it belongs. "Let me look at it," I demand, without room for refusal. To my surprise, he doesn't fight me. Damian lets his hand fall to the side, and his head drops back against the cold wall, eyes shut, surrendering to the agony for the first time. It's like watching a lion finally lie down, too tired to fight the inevitable.

I peel back the cloth slowly, wincing at the jagged wound beneath. It's deep, messy, the kind of injury you don't walk away from easily. "You need a doctor," I mutter, though it's not as if there's one waiting just down the road. We're miles away from anything resembling civilization, both hiding from people who'd sooner see us dead than breathing.

"No doctor." His eyes flash open, piercing me with that steel gaze that once made me hate him. Made me think him unbreakable. "Just... do what you can."

I clench my jaw, annoyed at the command, even now, as if he's still the one calling the shots. "Lucky for you, I was raised by someone who believed in rough remedies." I rummage through my pack, pulling out an ancient bottle of whiskey and a fraying needle, blunt but better than nothing. His eyes narrow at the sight.

"Can't say I'm feeling lucky right now," he murmurs, though there's a faint glimmer of amusement behind the pain.

"Then you're finally catching on." I try to keep my tone light, but it's hard when his breathing grows ragged, and I know the whiskey isn't going to make this any easier for him. "Drink this." I press the bottle to his lips, and he drinks, the liquid barely washing down his throat before he's coughing and swearing under his breath. He tosses his head back, and for a moment, I catch a flicker of something else there. Something... vulnerable. There's a crack in his armor, one I hadn't realized could even exist.

He mutters something incoherent as I begin to stitch, his eyes unfocused, a far-off look crossing his face. It's strange, seeing him like this, so human and fragile. This is Damian, the man who's dodged bullets and betrayed allies, who once swore he'd sooner rot than share his secrets with anyone. And yet, here he is, reduced to bleeding and breathing, stripped of all pretenses. I feel a pang of guilt—or something resembling guilt—pricking the edges of my chest.

In the silence that follows, I surprise myself by asking, "How did you end up here? I mean, really here." His eyes flicker, but he says nothing. I push the needle through another layer of torn skin and feel him flinch, though he tries to hide it. "It's not like you don't owe me answers," I add, feigning nonchalance, "after dragging me into this mess."

For a long moment, he doesn't answer, staring off into the distance, his gaze hardening into something unreadable. Just as I'm about to drop it, let the moment dissolve, he speaks. "There was... someone once," he says, so quietly I almost miss it. His voice is raw, brittle, like he's pulling words from a place he'd sealed away long ago. "We were... partners, in every sense of the word. She was my everything."

I pause, my hand hovering over his wound, feeling an unexpected ache twist inside me. I hadn't known there was anyone else. The Damian I knew was as solitary as a wolf, unyielding and self-contained. He must see my expression because he lets out a humorless laugh.

"Surprised? Don't be. It was a lifetime ago." He takes a shallow breath, his eyes clouding with memories. "We had plans—escape from all of this, find some place where no one knew our names or our faces." A bitter smile touches his lips, one that barely reaches his eyes. "But life doesn't work that way, does it?"

I don't reply, partly because I don't know what to say, and partly because I'm terrified of where this conversation could lead. I've spent so long building walls, convincing myself that I didn't care about anyone or anything. And here he is, breaking down his own defenses, and somehow, piece by piece, pulling mine down with them.

"I lost her," he whispers, his voice barely a breath, but it echoes in the quiet room. "Because of this life. Because of me." He looks up, and for once, he doesn't look at me with that fierce, challenging glare. Instead, there's a softness there, a regret I didn't think he was capable of.

"Damian..." My voice falters, caught somewhere between anger and compassion. I finish the last stitch, my hands suddenly trembling. This is the last thing I'd expected, and yet, here we are, two broken souls in a world that's forced us to be harder than we were ever meant to be.

He doesn't say anything else, just leans his head back and closes his eyes, the weight of his confession settling like dust in the air. And as I sit there, my hand lingering against his shoulder, I wonder how much longer I can keep pretending that I don't care.

The silence stretches, pressing against us like the frayed walls of the shelter. Damian's eyes remain closed, but I feel his awareness. Every breath he takes, ragged and shallow, feels like a shared heartbeat in the tense quiet. It's almost maddening, this suspended moment, as if the world outside—our factions, our pasts—has fallen away, leaving just us in the shadows of each other's broken histories.

My gaze drifts, following the lines of his face, noting the smudges of exhaustion and the stubble casting his jaw in sharp relief. There's something about the vulnerability clinging to him now, like an aftertaste, that leaves me unbalanced. I've always known Damian as a ruthless survivor, someone I would never dare to trust. And yet, here we are, our bodies bruised and minds tangled in a war neither of us asked for.

"Stop looking at me like that," he murmurs, eyes still closed, though a ghost of a smile hovers around his lips.

I jolt, my cheeks warming, more annoyed than embarrassed. "Like what?" I ask, feigning indifference, though the lie barely holds in my voice. I sit back, wrapping my arms around myself as if I could build my own shield to match his.

"Like I'm some tragic hero," he says, a glint of humor finally surfacing in his tone. "It doesn't suit you."

"Tragic hero?" I scoff, raising a brow. "You're giving yourself way too much credit. More like stubborn fool with a martyr complex."

His laugh is weak but real, and for a fleeting second, it transforms his face into something softer, almost gentle. It's a dangerous expression, one that teases the possibility of a version of him I could let in. A version I could imagine somewhere other than this hollowed-out room, beyond the life we're trapped in. But that's a lie too tempting to believe in.

"Martyr complex," he repeats, and there's a note in his voice that makes me wonder if he's half-proud of the title. "Maybe so. Or maybe I'm just holding on to whatever scraps of dignity I have left."

"Dignity? Is that what this is?" I wave a hand around, gesturing to the torn walls, the grimy floor, and the faint scent of whiskey still lingering in the air. "Look around. I think we're both fresh out of dignity."

He opens his eyes, and they catch mine in a way that feels like he's sifting through every thought I've hidden, every doubt I've tried to ignore. It's disarming, that gaze, as if he sees past all the armor I thought was impenetrable. He's done it before, I realize, broken through my defenses with that quiet intensity, but this time I feel it hitting somewhere that matters.

"You're right," he says softly, and there's a strange, bitter honesty in his voice. "We've lost more than dignity. We've lost the right to look at ourselves in the mirror and see someone whole."

I swallow hard, the weight of his words pulling at my chest. He's not just talking about himself; he's talking about me too, about the things I've buried, the choices I've made that haunt me in the dark when no one else is watching. I look away, hating the way his words carve into me, how they make me want to dig up the pieces of myself I'd rather leave forgotten.

"Stop it," I snap, more harshly than I intended. "Don't act like you know me. We're just here because we're both too stubborn to die."

There's a long silence, and for a moment, I wonder if I've gone too far, if I've shattered the fragile truce we've formed. But then he leans back, his head resting against the wall, and a small, resigned smile curls at his lips.

"You're right," he murmurs, and there's a softness to his voice that catches me off guard. "We're here because we're stubborn. But that doesn't mean I don't see you."

The words slip into the silence like a thread pulling tight, winding around the spaces between us, connecting in ways I hadn't asked for. He's right. He does see me, and that's the worst part. The realization feels like an ache, something deep and unyielding. Because as much as I hate it, I realize I see him too. Beyond the hardened exterior, beyond the broken edges and scars he tries so hard to hide, I see the parts of him that mirror my own.

The wind rattles the windows, shaking me from the intensity of the moment, and I focus on something safer, anything to keep my thoughts from spiraling. "You think you're some kind of tortured poet now?" I ask, forcing a smirk to my lips. "Just because you've got a couple scars and a sob story?"

He chuckles, the sound warm and unexpected. "If I'm a poet, then you're a comedian. Who knew you had jokes?"

A laugh slips from me before I can stop it, and for the first time in what feels like ages, the weight between us lightens. It's a fragile reprieve, one that I know can't last, but for a moment, it feels real. Like maybe, just maybe, we're more than the people our factions want us to be.

But then the reality of our situation rushes back in, cold and unyielding, settling over us like a heavy blanket. I pull my knees to my chest, leaning back against the wall, staring at the cracked ceiling as if it could offer some kind of answer.

"Do you ever think about leaving?" I ask quietly, the words slipping out before I can second-guess them. "Just... walking away. Starting over somewhere no one knows us."

The silence stretches, and for a moment, I think he won't answer. But then he sighs, the sound heavy with unspoken regrets. "Every day," he says, so softly I almost miss it. "But there's no running from this life. Not really. You can try, but it follows you. It catches up eventually."

I close my eyes, letting his words sink in. He's right, of course. I've seen enough to know that escape is an illusion, that the past clings to you like a shadow, no matter how far you run. But a part of me wants to believe, just for a moment, that there's something beyond this, something more than hiding in abandoned rooms and patching up wounds that never really heal.

"Guess we're both just fools, then," I murmur, my voice barely a whisper.

He doesn't answer, but I feel his gaze, the quiet understanding that passes between us. We're both trapped, caught in a world that's stolen too much, and yet here we are, clinging to each other's presence like it's the only solid ground in a sea of shifting loyalties.

The silence stretches again, thicker this time, but not uncomfortable. It feels like an agreement, an unspoken promise that, for now, we're in this together. The wind howls outside, the walls shake, but inside, in this small, fleeting moment, there's a strange sense of peace. And maybe that's enough. For now.

The quiet becomes a presence of its own, thick and dense, settling around us like smoke. Damian's breathing has grown even, his eyes shut again, and I wonder if he's finally drifted off. Outside, the wind moans through the crevices of the walls, making me feel as though the world itself is groaning under the weight of everything we've left undone, every battle waiting for us once we step outside. But here, in this strange stillness, there's a raw honesty that feels harder to face than any enemy.

I know I should be checking our supplies, calculating our next move. Instead, I'm studying the faint crease in Damian's brow, the tension still etched into his features even in sleep. His hand rests loosely at his side, fingers twitching every so often as if holding on to something unseen. I reach out, hesitating just above his hand, unsure why I'm even tempted to touch him. My fingertips brush against his, and a sudden surge of warmth courses through me, unexpected and undeniable.

"You're going soft on me," he murmurs, his eyes flickering open, and I realize he's been awake this whole time, watching me with that half-smirk playing on his lips.

I pull my hand back, folding my arms over my chest defensively. "Don't flatter yourself. I was just checking if you were still breathing."

"Right," he says, still smirking. "You're a real saint, watching over me like that."

I roll my eyes, but there's a flicker of something else in his gaze, something vulnerable lurking beneath his usual bravado. It catches me off guard, and for a moment, I feel the tug of an unspoken question hovering between us, one that neither of us is brave enough to ask.

"Why are you really here?" I blurt out, unable to hold back any longer. "Why did you stay, Damian? You had a thousand chances to walk away. Why didn't you?"

He hesitates, his gaze shifting, and I wonder if he's about to dodge the question, throw up one of those smirking deflections he's so skilled at. But instead, he sighs, running a hand through his hair, the movement surprisingly weary.

"Maybe I got tired of running," he says, his voice low. "Maybe I wanted... I don't know, a reason to stop."

I don't breathe. I can't. His words hang in the air, a confession wrapped in shadows. I don't know what I expected him to say, but it wasn't that. The idea that someone like Damian—someone who'd made survival his religion—would consider staying for anything other than obligation or necessity seems impossible. But here he is, looking at me with a vulnerability that makes my heart pound, a glimmer of something more than just survival in his gaze.

"You don't get to say things like that," I murmur, trying to keep my voice steady, though I know he can hear the tremor in it. "Not when we're..." I trail off, the weight of our reality settling between us like an invisible barrier.

He leans closer, his gaze piercing, as if daring me to look away. "Not when we're what?" he asks, and there's a challenge in his voice, a silent demand that I meet him halfway.

I feel my resolve crumbling, the walls I've spent so long building cracking under the intensity of his stare. I want to tell him to stop, to leave me alone with my guarded heart and carefully constructed detachment. But there's a part of me—a part I didn't realize existed—that wants to lean into him, to let him see the fragments of myself I've hidden from everyone, including myself.

"We're on opposite sides, Damian," I say, my voice barely more than a whisper. "Our lives don't fit together. Not here. Not anywhere."

He sighs, leaning back, and the look in his eyes is almost resigned, as if he's heard those words before and knows them to be true. But then he shakes his head, a hint of defiance sparking in his gaze.

"Maybe that's what they want us to believe," he says quietly, his voice edged with something fierce. "Maybe they've fed us lies so we'll keep tearing each other apart. So we'll never realize that we're just pawns in their game."

There's a dangerous logic to his words, one that sends a shiver down my spine. I've spent so long fighting, so long hating the people on the other side of the lines drawn for us, that I've never stopped to question if any of it was real. If maybe, just maybe, we're all trapped in a cage we can't see.

"What are you saying?" I ask, a note of fear creeping into my voice.

He looks at me, his gaze steady, unwavering. "I'm saying that maybe there's a way out. A way to end this war, to break the cycle."

The enormity of his words leaves me breathless. I want to argue, to dismiss his words as foolishness, but there's a part of me that wants to believe him. A part of me that's tired of fighting, tired of watching people I care about disappear into the void of war. And yet, the risk, the cost—it's almost too much to bear.

"And what if you're wrong?" I ask, my voice barely a whisper.

He reaches out, his fingers brushing against mine, grounding me in the present, in the quiet intimacy of this moment. "Then we'll go down together," he says, his voice steady, resolute. "But at least we'll be fighting for something real."

His words ignite something within me, a spark of hope I didn't realize I'd lost. The walls around us feel less like barriers and more like witnesses to a decision that could change everything. But before I can respond, before I can let myself believe in the possibility he's offering, a noise shatters the silence—a faint creak, followed by the sound of footsteps just beyond the door.

My heart pounds, every nerve on high alert. Damian's hand tightens around mine, a silent promise, as he shifts, readying himself. There's no time for words, no time to consider what this means. All that matters now is survival.

The footsteps grow louder, closer, and I feel my pulse racing, my thoughts spiraling as I brace myself for what's coming. I can see the tension in Damian's stance, the way his gaze sharpens, assessing every sound, every shadow outside. It's as if the entire world has narrowed to this moment, to the heartbeat of anticipation that fills the air.

I reach for my weapon, every sense on high alert, but there's a part of me that can't shake the feeling that this is more than just another enemy, more than another obstacle to overcome. The footsteps stop, hovering right outside the door, and for a brief, agonizing moment, there's only silence.

Then, with a sudden, forceful crash, the door bursts open, and the figure standing on the threshold isn't who I expected.

Chapter 9: Shadows of the Past

The room was cloaked in shadows, the dim light casting long fingers across the walls as if it, too, held secrets it couldn't quite confess. Damian stood across from me, watching with that unnerving intensity of his, his gaze slipping through all my defenses like a thief. It was that look—something bordering on tender, yet underlined by sharp curiosity—that always made my skin prickle, like I was being seen in a way I hadn't allowed anyone in years.

His hand hovered, the space between us heavy with unspoken words. I could tell he sensed the storm roiling beneath my calm exterior. Most people took my silence as indifference or coldness, but Damian had always been unnervingly perceptive, unearthing emotions I'd tucked away, hidden even from myself. He wasn't supposed to care. We weren't supposed to be anything more than cautious allies on our best days, reluctant enemies on our worst. Yet here we were, standing too close, our breaths mingling in the quiet space of my tiny apartment.

I averted my gaze, focusing on the half-empty glass on the table beside me, my fingers tracing the delicate rim. My heart thudded with a stubborn rhythm, and my mind battled itself, fragments of a past I'd tried to bury slipping through the cracks. I wanted to keep it hidden—no, I needed to keep it hidden. That part of my life was gone, severed cleanly like a severed limb. Or so I'd thought.

"Lena," Damian's voice was low, the syllables roughened by concern or maybe frustration; I wasn't sure. "Whatever it is you're hiding, you don't have to keep it from me."

The way he said it, simple, unadorned by dramatics, almost made me laugh. What he didn't know—what he couldn't know—was that my secrets weren't something you could just lay bare under the dim glow of a single bulb, sandwiched between coffee cups and lingering tension. There were parts of me that had sharp edges, broken glass embedded in places no one else could see. And if he tried to touch them, he'd bleed.

But the problem was, he was right. The weight of what I carried was becoming too much, creeping into every moment of my life, filling the silence with shadows of things I'd rather forget. The problem with keeping the past in the past is that it has a nasty habit of sneaking back into the present, demanding attention at the worst possible times. Like now.

I pressed my lips together, weighing my next words carefully. The air between us felt charged, like static before a storm, and I was painfully aware of how close he was, how easily I could just step forward, let his hand close around mine, and find comfort in that single, foolishly dangerous gesture.

"You wouldn't understand," I finally whispered, hoping to push him away with those words, to make him recoil, or better yet, turn around and walk right out the door.

"Try me," he said, his voice steady, his gaze unwavering. There was no sarcasm, no sneer, no hint of the hardened facade he usually wore around me. Just that raw, sincere determination that made my chest ache in ways I didn't like to think about.

I sighed, knowing I was probably about to regret this. There were only so many times a person could skirt around the truth before it grew teeth and bit back. "You remember that story in the papers a few years ago? The one about the missing girl, found months later, only to disappear again?" My voice barely held, wobbling between brittle and defeated.

Recognition flickered in his eyes. I could tell he was piecing it together, running through his memory of headlines, scandalous murmurs, whispered stories that had slipped into obscurity before anyone could know the real details. It hadn't even been a story long enough to matter. Just another tragedy in a city brimming with them, another name reduced to ink on a page. But to me, it was more than a headline; it was my life—a life I'd shoved down and buried as deeply as possible.

"I'm her," I said, the words coming out like a confession, slipping from my lips before I could snatch them back. "Or I was. Until I found a way out."

Damian's eyes didn't widen in shock, nor did he step back or frown in confusion. Instead, he reached for me, his hand finally finding mine, his fingers warm and grounding. The air felt thin, like we were standing on the edge of something monumental, a cliff with no bottom, and I had just taken the first step off it.

His thumb traced a soothing arc along my knuckles, and despite every instinct telling me to pull away, I stayed rooted in place, as if his touch alone could keep the shadows from closing in around me. There was no judgment in his eyes, no flicker of pity or disdain, just a steady acceptance that both reassured and terrified me.

"Why didn't you tell me sooner?" he asked, his voice so quiet it felt like a whisper meant only for me.

"Because it doesn't matter," I lied, forcing my voice to sound firm, as if I could make it true. "Because I walked away from that life, and I'm not going back."

He tilted his head, a faint smirk tugging at the corner of his mouth. "Lena, you don't get to decide when the past is done with you. It's clear as day that it's not done with you."

I pulled my hand away, a small flare of irritation spiking through the murk of my vulnerability. "And what would you know about it?"

"More than you think," he replied, with a tone so loaded, so shadowed by something I couldn't quite name, that it froze my retort on my tongue.

He moved closer, his gaze intent, as if he were peeling back layers I hadn't realized I still wore. "We're not so different, you and I," he said softly, his voice barely above a murmur. "I know what it's like to carry scars, Lena. And I know what it's like to keep people at arm's length because of them."

I hated that he was right, hated the empathy in his eyes and the way it made me feel so naked, so uncomfortably seen. But maybe, just maybe, he was someone who could carry the weight with me—if I dared to let him. And maybe, for the first time, it wouldn't feel like carrying it alone.

Damian's gaze held mine, steady and unrelenting, the kind of look that seemed to strip away every careful layer I'd built around myself. He hadn't moved since my confession, hadn't even flinched, as if my broken past was merely another piece of the puzzle he'd already begun to piece together. It was infuriating, his calm acceptance of everything I'd just spilled, as though he knew from the beginning that I was keeping parts of myself hidden in shadowed corners, too afraid to shine a light on them.

For a long, charged moment, we just stood there, breathing in sync, our silence punctuated by the hum of the world outside. I could hear the faint murmur of voices from the street below, the sporadic honk of a car horn, the city's indifferent rhythm beating on, oblivious to the precariousness of this moment. It was strange to think that the world carried on so casually while mine felt like it had been flung into some fragile orbit, vulnerable and ready to shatter.

"You know," he began, his voice low, almost conspiratorial, "for someone who seems to hate revealing things, you sure know how to drop a bombshell."

I snorted, the sound surprising even myself. Leave it to Damian to throw humor at the rawest parts of me, to poke at my exposed nerve endings until they stung just a little less. "What, you thought I was going to lead with my deepest, darkest secrets over coffee? Not exactly first-date material."

He raised an eyebrow, his lips curving in a faint, wry smile. "So you're admitting this is a date?"

My pulse did a small, traitorous leap, and I felt a prickle of heat creep up my neck. "Only if you're counting impromptu therapy sessions as date material now."

"Well, it's cheaper than a therapist," he shot back, his eyes gleaming with that same mischievous spark that always seemed to catch me off guard. It was remarkable how he could make the heaviness of my confession feel lighter, like he was taking some of the weight off my shoulders with just a glance, a grin. And before I knew it, I was smiling back, the corners of my mouth twitching in a way that felt like an unexpected relief.

"Now that you mention it," I said, shifting to lean back against the arm of my couch, "maybe I should start charging. I have a lot more baggage where that came from."

"Trust me," he replied, leaning in just enough to close the distance between us, his hand bracing against the wall beside me, "I think I can keep up."

His presence, close and unwavering, felt like both a challenge and a promise. He wasn't backing away; if anything, he seemed to be stepping deeper into the murky waters of my past, as if he wanted to dive headfirst into the mess I'd spent years keeping at bay. It terrified me, how willing he was to be part of this, even if he didn't fully understand the shadows that clung to me. And maybe, in that terrifying possibility, there was a glimmer of hope—hope that, for once, I didn't have to go through this alone.

Still, old habits die hard. My defenses went up like an automatic reflex, my shoulders pulling back, my gaze hardening as if to deflect the sympathy I saw gathering in his eyes. "Don't get any ideas about playing hero," I warned, my tone sharper than I intended. "I'm not some damsel in distress."

"Who said anything about heroes?" he countered, his smile fading into something more serious, more weighted. "I just think you deserve a little backup. You've been carrying this alone for too long, Lena. You don't have to anymore."

A part of me wanted to scoff, to brush him off with some dismissive quip, but his words struck a chord, vibrating through me with a truth I hadn't been ready to acknowledge. I had been alone. For so long, I'd convinced myself that isolation was a shield, that by keeping people at arm's length, I was protecting myself from the inevitable disappointments, betrayals. But Damian was proving harder to push away, slipping past every carefully constructed wall I'd erected around myself.

And in that moment, with his eyes locked on mine, the distance between us shrinking by the second, I realized he wasn't just offering his support. He was asking me to trust him—to let him into a part of my life that had been off-limits to everyone else.

With a slow exhale, I let my gaze drift past him, fixing on a point just over his shoulder. "I'm not good at... this," I admitted, the words scraping against my pride. "Letting people in. Trusting. It's not exactly my strong suit."

He didn't move, his silence gentle but firm, as if he knew that sometimes words were best left unsaid. Instead, his hand reached out, a subtle, hesitant gesture, as though he was giving me the option to pull away if I wanted to. But I didn't. Instead, my hand found his, my fingers curling around his as if seeking an anchor in the storm that had been brewing within me for too long.

"What happened to you wasn't your fault," he said quietly, his voice a murmur that seemed to settle into the cracks of my guarded heart. "And it doesn't define you, Lena. You're stronger than whatever tried to break you. I see that. I've always seen that."

The simplicity of his words, the quiet conviction behind them, threatened to unravel me. Here I was, tangled in the mistakes and betrayals of a life I'd left behind, unable to forgive myself for things I couldn't change. But Damian... he didn't see me as some broken relic of my past. He saw me, all of me, even the parts I was still learning to reclaim.

"I don't know why you're even here," I muttered, half-embarrassed, half-grateful, the vulnerability raw and unfamiliar on my tongue. "You could have just walked away, kept your life uncomplicated."

He chuckled, a soft, rumbling sound that melted the tension strung taut between us. "If I wanted uncomplicated, I wouldn't be here with you," he replied, his eyes crinkling at the corners. "Something tells me we're both a little too stubborn for that."

Before I could respond, he leaned forward, his forehead resting against mine, a small, grounding gesture that felt like a promise in and of itself. There was a quiet strength in the way he held me there, not demanding, not forcing, just waiting, patient and unwavering, as if he understood that I needed time, that I needed space to find my footing.

And in that moment, with the warmth of his breath mingling with mine, his hand a reassuring weight in my own, I felt something shift within me—a small, tentative step toward trust, toward a future where I wasn't defined by the shadows of my past. A future where, maybe, I could let someone else carry the weight with me, even if it terrified me to let go.

I closed my eyes, breathing him in, his scent mingling with the heady thrill of newfound possibility. Maybe, just maybe, I didn't have to keep fighting alone. Maybe letting him in wasn't a weakness after all, but the first true act of strength. And for the first time, as I leaned into the comfort he offered, I thought that perhaps, I could finally start to believe in something—someone—beyond the walls I'd built.

The air between us is taut, charged with words unsaid and questions unanswered. Damian's hand lingers just above mine, suspended as if he's weighing the risks of touch, of comfort. His expression is unreadable, guarded in that way I've come to know too well, a mask he slips on whenever he's cornered. And yet, for all his enigmatic tendencies, his gaze is earnest, piercing in its intensity. I've seen that look before in fleeting moments, a glimpse of something softer lurking behind his tough exterior—a vulnerability he keeps as locked away as I do my own secrets.

I take a sharp breath, considering my options, feeling the old panic flutter in my chest. If I tell him, everything shifts. This thin, fragile line we've been toeing between rivalry and...whatever this is...would snap, and we'd fall one way or the other. And if I don't tell him? Well, he'd leave eventually. People always do. Secrets like mine don't stay buried. They seep, leaking through the cracks, and when they're finally unearthed, they bring everything crashing down.

Damian clears his throat, the sound snapping me out of my thoughts. "You're a thousand miles away right now," he murmurs, his voice low, almost reluctant, like he hates asking but can't help himself. "And I can't decide if you're thinking about running away from me or telling me the truth."

It's a subtle challenge, and he's watching me closely, waiting to see if I'll rise to meet it or sidestep, like I always do. I can't decide if he's bluffing, trying to call me out, or if he actually wants the truth. Part of me wishes he didn't care enough to ask, that he'd let me maintain my safe distance, let me keep my barriers up. But another part—the part that's been quietly yearning for something, anything real—is screaming at me to let him in.

"I—" The words die in my throat, hesitant, and his gaze sharpens, catching on the stutter like a wolf scenting weakness.

"Just say it," he urges, a bit too forcefully, and there's a flicker of frustration in his eyes, mingling with something like...hope? "Whatever it is you're afraid of, I'm not going anywhere."

"Damian," I start, but his name feels strange on my lips, too intimate, too vulnerable. My pulse thrums as I search for the right words, but they seem to slip away the closer I get. I've been carrying this weight alone for so long that the idea of sharing it feels foreign, almost wrong. But his gaze holds mine steady, grounding me in a way I didn't think possible.

"There are things...things I don't talk about," I say finally, my voice barely above a whisper. "Things that I thought I could outrun, but it turns out, some shadows are faster than others."

For a beat, he doesn't respond, just watches me with an intensity that almost makes me wish I could shrink away. But then he nods, a barely perceptible dip of his head that somehow feels like an agreement, an acknowledgment. He's not pressing, not demanding—just waiting, like he knows there's a storm brewing inside me and he's willing to stand there in the rain.

The words start spilling out before I can stop them, a torrent of confessions I've buried for too long. I tell him about the betrayal that nearly broke me, about the love I once thought was real and the lie it turned out to be. I tell him about the way it hollowed me out, left me raw and jaded, convinced that trust was a luxury I couldn't afford.

Damian listens, silent and still, his expression unreadable. But there's a tension in his posture, a barely restrained anger that I realize isn't directed at me but at the people who hurt me. It's a strange, unfamiliar comfort, knowing he's angry on my behalf, that he feels something about my past beyond judgment or pity.

When I finally fall silent, my throat is raw, and there's a heavy, hollow ache in my chest, as if I've just cut out a piece of myself and handed it to him. I wait for his reaction, bracing for whatever judgment might come next. But Damian just leans back, his gaze steady, unflinching.

"You know," he says, his voice soft but tinged with that wry edge I've come to expect, "you're not the only one with skeletons in the closet."

It's not a revelation—of course, he has his own demons; everyone does. But there's something in the way he says it, an invitation wrapped in a challenge, as if he's daring me to ask, to dig deeper into his darkness now that I've shared mine.

I raise an eyebrow, my lips quirking despite myself. "Oh? Let me guess—yours come in the form of bad business deals and broken hearts left in your wake?"

He chuckles, a low, almost bitter sound, and for a moment, I see something flicker in his eyes, something that looks suspiciously like regret. "Something like that," he murmurs, his gaze drifting away, lost in some memory I can't reach. "But it's a bit more complicated than that."

I tilt my head, curiosity piqued. He's always been a puzzle, and now, with my own secrets laid bare, I can't resist the urge to press, to see what lies beneath the layers he keeps so carefully constructed. "Try me," I challenge, my voice daring, pushing him the way he pushed me.

For a moment, he hesitates, his fingers tapping a slow rhythm against the table as he considers his words. And then he looks up, his gaze sharp and unguarded, like he's bracing himself for impact.

"My past," he starts, his voice low, almost a whisper, "isn't as clean as you might think. There are people who would prefer if I disappeared, people who would rather see me fall than succeed." He pauses, the weight of his words hanging heavy between us. "And they're not the kind who take no for an answer."

The revelation hits me like a punch to the gut, and suddenly, everything feels different. The casual rivalry we've shared, the push and pull of our relationship—it all seems insignificant in the face of this new, dangerous reality. I can feel my heart pounding, a mix of fear and exhilaration thrumming through my veins as I realize just how much I still don't know about him.

"What does that mean?" I ask, my voice barely above a whisper, but he only gives me a grim smile, one that sends a chill down my spine.

"It means," he replies, his voice steady but tinged with a hint of resignation, "that getting close to me might be the most dangerous thing you've ever done."

Before I can respond, there's a sudden, sharp knock on the door, a sound that shatters the fragile tension between us. Damian's expression shifts instantly, his gaze snapping to the door, his body tensing in a way that sends a jolt of alarm racing through me. I can see the change in him, a hardened, wary edge that wasn't there a moment ago, as if he's preparing for a fight.

"Stay here," he murmurs, his voice barely audible, and then, without waiting for a response, he moves toward the door, his steps slow and deliberate, like a predator stalking its prey.

I watch him go, my heart in my throat, and a thousand questions racing through my mind. And as the door swings open, revealing a shadowed figure on the other side, I feel a chill creep down my spine, a sense that everything I thought I knew is about to be turned upside down.

Chapter 10: Secrets in the Rain

Damian shifts his weight, favoring his good leg, and I notice the telltale tightening of his jaw. He's trying to hide the pain, to keep up this stoic facade, but I can see right through him. It's strange—after everything, every dark alley we've skulked down, every lie we've told, there's still this small corner of my heart that aches for him. And that's the problem, isn't it? I didn't sign up for feelings, didn't intend to care this much. Especially not about him.

The rain hasn't let up. It slams against the buildings, drumming on the tin roofs and washing the streets clean, as if it could somehow cleanse this city of its secrets. The thunder echoes through the empty alleys, and the sky is a deep, bruised shade of gray, the kind that sinks into your bones and stays there. It's a fitting backdrop for what we're about to do, and for what I might have to confess before the night's through.

A figure appears at the end of the street, cloaked and silent, moving with an easy confidence that immediately puts me on edge. Damian stiffens beside me, his gaze sharpening. His hand twitches toward his concealed weapon—a comforting weight against his hip, but something I've only ever seen him reach for in the most dire situations. This isn't exactly what I'd call dire, but then again, when you're dealing with people like us, every encounter has the potential to go sideways.

"Remember, we're here for information," I whisper, my words just loud enough to cut through the pattering rain. "No heroics."

He raises an eyebrow, a sardonic smile creeping onto his face. "Since when have I ever been the heroic type?"

"Just making sure," I murmur, a touch of sarcasm slipping into my tone. "I wouldn't want you doing something noble on my behalf. I wouldn't know what to do with myself."

The figure draws closer, and now I can make out the details—a gaunt face partially obscured by a wide-brimmed hat, eyes that gleam like two chips of obsidian, flickering from Damian to me and back again, assessing. It's eerie, really, the way he looks at us, like he's already pieced together every skeleton in our closets, every shadowy detail we've tried to bury. I force myself to hold his gaze, refusing to let him see any cracks.

"Ms. Hart," he greets, voice smooth and practiced, like an actor taking his mark. He doesn't bother with Damian's name, barely even glances his way. All his attention is fixed on me, and it sets my nerves on edge.

"We've come a long way," I say, keeping my tone neutral. "I trust you've brought what we agreed on?"

The man nods, reaching into his coat with a deliberate slowness, and pulls out a small, weathered notebook. It's battered and frayed at the edges, as though it's been tossed in and out of a hundred pockets, maybe even fought over a time or two. The sight of it makes my heart kick against my ribs. If this holds even a fraction of the secrets we're after, it could blow everything wide open. But trust isn't something we're rich in these days, and I can't afford to take anything at face value.

"Show it to me," I demand, holding out my hand. He hesitates for a fraction of a second, and that's all I need to know this man doesn't give anything freely. I glance at Damian, who's watching him like a hawk, every muscle coiled and ready to strike if necessary.

The man hands it over reluctantly, and I take it, feeling the worn leather beneath my fingers. There's an electricity in the air, an unspoken threat, as if one wrong move could spark a chain reaction. I open the notebook, skimming the contents, the rain-damp pages crinkling under my touch. Names, dates, transactions—all scrawled in a careful, meticulous hand. But as I read, a sick realization begins to settle in my stomach.

These aren't just any names. They're people I know. People I trusted. People who... well, people who probably never trusted me much in return, but still. Seeing their names here, knowing they're involved in something even darker than I anticipated, sends a chill down my spine.

Damian leans in, his breath warm against my ear, and mutters, "Something wrong?"

I snap the notebook shut, tucking it into my coat pocket. "Nothing that won't keep," I say, my voice betraying none of the turmoil churning inside me.

The man watches me with an unsettling smile, like he's enjoying this little dance, savoring every step. "Satisfied?" he asks, voice dripping with mockery.

"Ecstatic," I reply dryly, crossing my arms. "But don't mistake this for the end. If this turns out to be a dud..."

He cuts me off, a glint of amusement in his eyes. "Oh, Ms. Hart, I think you'll find my information is always reliable. The real question is, are you ready to face the consequences of knowing it?"

It's a warning, veiled but unmistakable, and as he slips back into the shadows, I feel the weight of his words settling around me like chains. Damian is silent beside me, and I know he's itching to ask what I saw in that notebook, to pull the truth from me no matter the cost. But this is one burden I'm not ready to share, not with him, not yet.

As we turn to leave, the rain seems to grow colder, each drop a shard of ice slicing through the night. Damian's hand finds mine, a surprising gesture, but I let him hold it. It's strange, comforting in a way I didn't expect, and I realize, maybe for the first time, just how dangerous this thing between us has become.

"You're awfully quiet," he says after a moment, his voice low, a little teasing, as if he's trying to lure a smile from me. "Should I be worried?"

"You should always be worried," I retort, trying to mask the tremor in my voice with a hint of humor. "Especially when I'm around."

He chuckles, the sound warm and rich against the cold night. "Good thing I like a little danger."

I glance up at him, rain trickling down his face, darkening his hair, softening his edges. There's a vulnerability there, a flicker of something I don't quite understand but find myself wanting to. Maybe he sees the same in me, because his expression shifts, and I feel the pull between us intensify, charged and heavy, as if even the storm can't wash away what's brewing between us.

But as much as I want to close the gap, to lean into whatever this is, I can't. Not with the truth I now carry like a curse. So I pull away, letting the cold settle between us, a silent reminder of the secrets that still stand in our way.

I don't know what possesses me to reach out just then, but my fingers find Damian's, and for a second, he lets me hold his hand. His skin is cold and rough, and I can feel the pulse in his wrist, steady and strong beneath the surface. I tell myself it's just the rain, the darkness, the threat of danger lurking in every shadow that makes me want to draw close to him. It's just the absurdity of this entire night, and yet the weight of his hand in mine feels more grounding than anything I've known in years.

He glances down at our entwined fingers, eyebrow lifting slightly, a small smirk tugging at the corner of his mouth. "Didn't know you were the hand-holding type."

"Temporary lapse," I mutter, pulling my hand back, though a part of me misses the warmth as soon as I let go. "Don't get used to it."

He chuckles, low and quiet, a sound that cuts through the rain like a spark. It's a little ridiculous, how easily he can get under my skin with that lazy, careless confidence of his. But maybe that's exactly why I keep my distance, why I've learned to keep myself wrapped in layers, only letting people close enough to see what I want them to see. Even Damian, who's pried open more than a few of those layers with a skill that surprises me as much as it infuriates me.

We head down a narrow alley that looks more like a dark river now, with rainwater pooling around our ankles. The smell of damp stone and earth fills my nose, and every step echoes against the walls, reminding me just how alone we are here. In the distance, a stray cat yowls, and I can almost convince myself it's the city itself, howling at us for disturbing its peace.

"So," Damian says, keeping his voice low, "are you planning on telling me what's really in that notebook, or should I start guessing?"

I stiffen, my grip tightening around the worn leather cover hidden in my coat pocket. His eyes are on me, sharp and probing, and I can tell he's not going to let this go easily. Damian doesn't do half-measures. He's the kind of man who doesn't believe in holding back, not when there's something he wants to know.

"It's not that simple," I reply, hedging. "There are people's lives involved. People who trusted me once."

He lets out a short, humorless laugh. "Trust is a flimsy thing to be worrying about now, don't you think? You've seen what this world is like. Nobody here survives by being innocent, or by playing nice."

The words sting more than I'd like to admit, and I clench my jaw, trying to swallow down the mix of guilt and defiance rising up in my throat. He's not wrong. Innocence is a luxury neither of us can afford, and if I wanted to play nice, I wouldn't be standing here in the rain, with a notebook full of secrets that could ruin lives. And yet, something inside me resists Damian's blunt pragmatism. There's a part of me that still wants to believe in something softer, something untouched by all this.

"You really don't get it," I say, looking away, focusing on the rain streaming down the cracked stone walls. "This isn't just business for me. These names... they're people I grew up with. People who looked out for me when nobody else did."

Damian's face softens, just a fraction, but it's enough to make my pulse quicken. He leans in, his voice dropping to a near whisper, barely audible over the rain. "Then why are you doing this? Why are you here with me, risking everything?"

I hesitate, the words lodged in my throat. The truth is a twisted, tangled mess, one I'm not sure I can even explain to myself, let alone to him. But there's something about the way he's looking at me, with that strange mix of curiosity and understanding, that makes me want to try.

"I don't know," I finally admit, surprised at how raw my voice sounds. "Maybe because I'm tired of running. Tired of pretending I don't care."

He studies me for a moment, his eyes dark and unreadable. Then, to my surprise, he reaches out and tucks a damp strand of hair behind my ear, his fingers lingering just long enough to send a shiver down my spine. "Join the club," he says, his voice rough around the edges, almost tender. It's as if, in that brief moment, he's letting down his guard, just a sliver, letting me see the man behind the mask.

But before I can respond, a sudden noise cuts through the silence—a metallic clatter, followed by the sound of hurried footsteps splashing through the rain. Damian's hand drops instantly, and his face hardens, every muscle going tense. Instinctively, I reach for my own weapon, heart pounding as I scan the darkness, trying to make out the figure now looming at the end of the alley.

It's a woman, her face obscured by a hood, but I can see the flash of something metallic in her hand. She steps closer, her movements quick and deliberate, and I recognize her immediately. Eliza. She was one of my contacts, someone I'd trusted once, back when I still believed in loyalty and honor among thieves. But the cold, steely look in her eyes now tells me she's not here to catch up on old times.

"You have something that belongs to me," she says, her voice sharp as a blade, cutting through the rain-soaked air. "Hand it over, and maybe I won't kill you right here."

Damian shifts, positioning himself between us, and I can feel the tension radiating off him. He doesn't know who she is, but he's not about to let his guard down, not when there's a threat in front of him. I almost want to laugh at the irony—two people willing to kill for a notebook that I'm not even sure I want to hold onto anymore.

"Eliza," I say, my voice calm but edged with steel, "last I checked, you didn't own me. Or my choices. You want what I have? Then you'll have to take it."

Her eyes narrow, and she lets out a dry, humorless laugh. "Oh, I don't have to take anything. I've got my own insurance policy." She reaches into her coat and pulls out a small device, holding it up so we can both see it. "One call, and every name in that book goes public. Every dirty little secret, every lie you thought you buried—it's all one press away."

The threat is as clear as it is devastating. She has leverage, and she knows it. I feel a surge of anger rising in my chest, a fierce, protective instinct kicking in. These names, these people—they may have their flaws, but they don't deserve to be exposed, not like this. I glance at Damian, who's watching me intently, waiting for my next move.

He gives me a barely perceptible nod, a silent assurance that he's with me, whatever I decide. It's a dangerous alliance, one that feels as fragile as glass, but in this moment, it's all I have. And I realize, with a clarity that's as unsettling as it is empowering, that I'm not about to let Eliza or anyone else take that away from me. Not now. Not ever.

"Go ahead," I say, my voice steady, daring. "Make the call."

Eliza's eyes gleam, a twisted satisfaction creeping into her smirk. She holds her finger over the device like a king about to give a fatal nod to the executioner. "You think I'm bluffing?" Her voice is soft, almost amused. "I don't make idle threats, darling. I'd hate for all those people's secrets to scatter into the wind... or rain, as it were."

Damian shifts, a flicker of tension in his stance. He's watching her, eyes narrowed, sizing her up like a cat about to pounce. But I know his mind is churning. He knows that whatever Eliza has on that device could spell disaster, for me, for him, for people he doesn't even know. I feel his gaze flick over to me, his silent question clear as day. What's the plan?

A thousand thoughts race through my mind. The rational part of me screams that I should just give her what she wants, that the risk is too high. But there's something that digs in, a stubbornness that refuses to yield. Eliza's threats have pushed me to the edge, and though it terrifies me, a strange calm settles over me too.

"Do it then," I say, the words cool, almost indifferent. I force a shrug that feels casual enough, but my heart is hammering, beating so hard it's a wonder she can't hear it. "Ruin them all. See what it gets you."

Eliza's finger hovers over the device, her smirk faltering. It's subtle, but I see it—the faintest flicker of uncertainty in her eyes. "You're bluffing," she says, but her voice wavers, just a fraction. "You wouldn't let all those people burn."

"Wouldn't I?" I challenge, raising my chin. "Maybe I'm a little tired of protecting people who wouldn't lift a finger for me. Maybe I'm just as ruthless as you think."

Her hesitation is almost imperceptible, but Damian picks up on it too. He edges forward, silent as a shadow, his steps unhurried but deliberate. He's close now, within reach, and his fingers brush mine, an unspoken pact passing between us. He's waiting for my cue, ready to act in an instant.

But then, as if sensing his intent, Eliza straightens, her hand tightening around the device. Her gaze darts to him, sharp and wary. "Ah, no heroics, Damian," she warns. "One wrong move, and this little box sings, and every name in that book will become the city's latest scandal. And you know they'll come after you, too. Are you ready for that?"

He smiles, slow and infuriatingly calm. "Funny thing, Eliza. I've never been one to worry about consequences. You should know that by now."

The rain continues its relentless downpour, and we stand there, locked in a deadly stalemate. Eliza's face is a mix of defiance and caution, but I can see the faintest crack in her facade. She didn't expect us to call her bluff, and now she's teetering, caught between her threats and her own doubts. But then, she does something I hadn't anticipated—she takes a step back, her eyes shifting from me to Damian, calculating, weighing the odds.

And then, just as I start to think she might actually back down, she smiles—a slow, venomous smile that makes my blood run cold. "You've made your choice," she says softly, her fingers poised over the device.

Without warning, she presses a button, and a loud beep fills the air. My heart plummets as a message lights up on her screen, a notification that sends her face twisting with malicious delight.

"It's done," she says, her voice triumphant. "I've just sent the information. Every dirty secret, every name... gone. Delivered. Enjoy watching it all burn."

My stomach twists, dread crashing over me like the relentless rain. She's won. Every scrap of leverage we had, every carefully guarded secret—it's all out there now, in the hands of people who'll use it to tear down lives.

For a moment, we stand frozen, the weight of her victory settling over us. Damian's face is unreadable, but I know he's thinking the same thing I am: we're too late. We've lost everything. But then, a strange look flickers in his eyes, something almost like relief.

"Eliza," he says, his voice dangerously soft, "you should really double-check who you're sending your messages to."

Her eyes narrow. "What are you talking about?"

With a slow, deliberate motion, he pulls out his phone and shows her the screen. It's open to a message thread—her message thread. And there, sitting at the top, is the very notification she sent just seconds ago. I stare at it, my mind racing to piece it together, and then it hits me.

Somehow, Damian managed to intercept the transmission. He must have rerouted her device, forcing it to send the information to his phone instead. I can barely contain my shock, and I know Eliza is just as stunned, though she hides it behind a mask of fury. Her face twists in anger, her eyes flashing with rage as she realizes the trap she walked right into.

"You think this little trick will save you?" she hisses, her voice shaking. "I still have the original files. And believe me, I won't hesitate to send them again."

Damian doesn't flinch. "Do it," he replies, his tone cold, almost mocking. "We'll just intercept them again. Keep playing, Eliza, but know that every move you make, we're two steps ahead."

Her hands tremble, and for the first time, I see fear flicker in her eyes. She knows she's been cornered, her every advantage slipping through her fingers like sand. And though I know this is far from over, a spark of hope ignites within me. We might have a chance, a small sliver of a chance, to come out of this intact.

But Eliza's not done yet. With a growl of frustration, she lunges forward, her arm swinging out in a vicious arc. I barely have time to react before she's on me, her nails digging into my shoulder as she tries to wrestle the notebook from my grasp. Pain flares through me, and I struggle to hold on, to keep her from tearing away the one piece of leverage we still have.

Damian moves to intervene, but Eliza kicks out, her foot connecting with his injured leg, and he staggers, his face twisting in pain. The sight of him stumbling fuels my desperation, and I twist, using every ounce of strength I have to shove her back. She stumbles, her grip loosening just enough for me to break free.

But before I can catch my breath, she's back on her feet, her gaze wild, feral. "This isn't over," she snarls, her voice venomous. "You think you've won? You have no idea what you're up against."

With a final, furious glare, she whirls around and vanishes into the rain, her figure disappearing into the shadows. For a few moments, all I can do is stand there, breathing heavily, the adrenaline still pulsing through my veins.

Damian straightens, wincing as he puts weight on his injured leg. He glances at me, a faint smile tugging at his lips. "Not exactly how I pictured tonight going," he says, his voice laced with a weary humor.

I shake my head, unable to help the small, incredulous laugh that escapes me. "Tell me about it."

But even as the tension eases, a sense of dread lingers. Eliza may have been thwarted for now, but I know she won't give up so easily. And as I look at Damian, his face shadowed and unreadable, a new realization dawns. Whatever comes next, we're deeper in this than I'd ever planned, and there's no way to turn back now.

In the distance, thunder rumbles, a low, ominous warning that seems to echo my own fears. And as the rain continues to fall, I can't shake the feeling that we're standing on the edge of something dark and dangerous, a storm that's only just begun.

Chapter 11: The Gilded Mask

The first thing that strikes me about the woman is how her voice carries across the vast hall, though she's barely above a whisper. It sounds like someone has layered music beneath her words, a strange, haunting melody that wraps around the syllables, coaxing each one to land perfectly in my ears. She's tall, draped in a deep emerald cloak that shimmers like river water under the light, and her face is hidden by a mask that gleams in the dim glow of the lanterns. It covers her entire face, intricately carved gold etched with delicate whorls that catch the light and seem to pulse with every breath she takes. Somehow, that gilded mask, hiding every hint of expression, tells me she knows more about us than I'd ever like a stranger to know.

Damian, to his credit, stands as still as a statue beside me. He's tense—I can feel it in the way his fingers twitch just slightly near his dagger. He's poised for a fight, but there's a flicker in his eyes, an unmistakable uncertainty. This isn't the contact we were supposed to meet, not even close. Our intel pointed to a local man who'd worked for years as a messenger in this region, an unremarkable man in worn-out boots who'd sooner spit in a noble's face than wear a mask as ornate as this. And yet, here she is, our unexpected herald draped in mystery, her presence too grand, too... otherworldly.

"The artifact you seek is bound by old magic," she says, her voice dipping into something almost reverent, as if she's telling us a secret meant only for the dead. "Older than anything you've faced, older than the cities your forefathers built on these bones." She pauses, letting her words sink in, and I feel a chill crawl up my spine, the kind that prickles at your skin like the sting of nettles. "It twists the souls of those who seek it, binds them to itself until there's nothing left of the person they once were. Not even the strongest can resist its lure."

Damian clears his throat, his voice sharper than I'd expected. "We're well aware of the dangers," he says, though the flicker of doubt in his eyes betrays him. "We didn't come here without preparation."

She tilts her head, and for a moment, I catch the gleam of her eyes through the narrow slits of her mask. Dark eyes, glinting with a knowledge that makes me feel young and foolish. "No one is ever prepared, young ones," she says with a strange, melancholy sigh. "Not for what you are about to face."

"Listen," I say, trying to keep my voice steady, trying not to let her get under my skin with her riddles and ghost stories. "If you're here to help us, we'll take any information you've got. If not, then spare us the theatrics and let us get on with it." I didn't expect my voice to sound as confrontational as it does, and even Damian shoots me a sideways glance, an eyebrow raised.

The woman doesn't flinch. If anything, her mask seems to brighten, the lines of gold catching a strange, inner light as if it's absorbing my defiance and wearing it like a second skin. "You have spirit," she murmurs, almost to herself, and something about her tone makes me bristle. I feel as if she's watching me, judging me, seeing parts of myself that I'd prefer to keep locked away. "But spirit alone won't be enough. The two of you... You will find yourselves tested, in ways you cannot begin to imagine."

Her words hang in the air like a curse, each one sinking into the silence between us. Damian shifts beside me, his jaw set tight, but there's a shadow in his eyes, a fear I haven't seen before. And maybe I'm feeling it too, deep down, though I'm not about to let her see it.

"Tested?" I ask, forcing a scoff, trying to laugh in the face of this ominous warning. "Is that all you've got? A vague prophecy? I think we'll take our chances."

She pauses, and for the briefest moment, I swear her shoulders sag, just a little, as if the weight of her own words is too much even for her. "You may find yourselves wishing you hadn't," she says softly, almost too soft for me to hear, before she turns away, her cloak billowing like a dark storm around her. The sound of her footsteps fades into the shadows, leaving us alone with nothing but the echoes of her warning.

I let out a breath I hadn't realized I was holding, my chest tight as I look over at Damian. He's staring at the spot where she disappeared, a crease etched between his brows, his fingers flexing and curling by his side as if he's still ready to reach for his weapon.

"Well," I say, keeping my voice low even though we're alone. "That was... not exactly reassuring."

He turns to me, his eyes shadowed, the usual spark dulled by something else, something darker. "Do you think she was serious?"

"What, you mean all that talk about our souls being twisted? Ancient magic? Look, Damian, I think she was just trying to scare us off. Probably hoping we'll turn tail and leave before we get too close." I try to keep my tone light, brushing off the eerie sensation lingering in the pit of my stomach. But as the words leave my mouth, I can't shake the feeling that I'm only trying to convince myself.

Damian doesn't respond, his gaze still lost in thought, his shoulders tense beneath his cloak. Finally, he lets out a long breath, glancing at me with a weary half-smile that does nothing to hide the anxiety etched in the lines of his face. "You know, for once, I wouldn't mind if we did turn tail. Just this once."

I roll my eyes, nudging him lightly with my elbow. "Where's your sense of adventure? Besides, we've come this far. I don't know about you, but I'm not about to let some masked woman scare me off." It's a bold statement, but my voice wavers, just slightly, betraying the gnawing doubt clawing at the back of my mind.

He laughs, a rough, humorless sound. "I swear, if we make it out of this alive, you owe me a drink. And I'm talking the good stuff, not whatever swill you usually bring around."

"Oh, please," I say, grateful for the return of his usual dry humor. "Like you'd know the good stuff if it slapped you in the face."

For a moment, the tension breaks, the weight of the woman's warning easing just enough for us to catch our breath. But as we start walking again, her words echo in my mind, a haunting refrain that settles like a dark cloud over my heart. The path ahead suddenly seems longer, the shadows darker, as if the very air has taken on her warning, whispering of danger yet to come. And for the first time, I wonder if Damian's right—if maybe we're not ready for what lies ahead.

The woman's warning lingers in the dim air long after she's gone, like a whisper that just won't leave. Damian is still staring off into the shadows where she disappeared, his jaw clenched and fists curling and uncurling by his sides. I wonder if he can hear the same unnerving echo in his head that I do, that haunting layer of melody in her voice, as if she'd come straight from some otherworldly place to haunt us.

Finally, he breaks the silence, but his voice is low, as if he's still trying to shake off her ghost. "If we're smart, we'll turn back."

"Turn back?" I let out a sharp laugh that sounds far braver than I feel. "Damian, when have we ever done anything smart?"

He cuts a look at me, a half-smile tugging at the corner of his mouth. "You're right. I'd almost forgotten the time you thought challenging those bandits to a drinking contest was a good strategy."

"That was absolutely strategic," I say, grinning. "They didn't know what hit them. And you're forgetting I won."

"Yes, by a miracle," he mutters, though his eyes are a little brighter now, his shoulders relaxing just the slightest bit. "But this... This isn't the same, and you know it." His gaze sharpens, fixing on me with an intensity I'm not used to from him. "I'm serious. That woman—whatever she was—didn't show up just to scare us for fun. There's something wrong with this job. Maybe we should just let it go."

I scoff, not quite able to shake the uneasy thrill that's wormed its way into my chest. "Let it go? You and I both know we didn't come all this way to turn around at the first sign of trouble. Besides, we're this close." I hold up my thumb and forefinger, pinching the air as if I could almost feel the artifact's power humming between them. "We can't stop now."

He lets out a long, heavy sigh, rubbing a hand over his face. "Of course you'd say that. You were always the one dragging us into these things."

"Oh, so it's my fault now, is it?" I cross my arms, feigning offense. "If I remember correctly, you were the one who insisted we take this job. And now you're the one getting cold feet?"

He snorts, giving me an exasperated look. "I'm not getting cold feet. I'm just trying to keep us both alive. Not that you've ever made that easy."

I can't help but grin, though the grin is tinged with a strange sort of nervousness, an energy buzzing just beneath my skin. "Well, lucky for you, I have no intention of getting us killed. This is just another challenge. We've faced worse."

Damian doesn't answer, his expression shadowed, unreadable. It's a rare look for him, and it makes my stomach twist in a way that I don't want to examine too closely. He's usually the calm one, the voice of reason. And for a second, I wonder if maybe he's right—maybe I'm pushing us toward something we're not ready to face.

But then I remember the artifact, the promise of adventure, the thrill that had pulled me into this life in the first place. And I know I won't walk away, not when I can feel the pull of the unknown calling to me like a magnet. Damian may be hesitant, but he won't leave me behind. He never has.

I shrug, forcing a casualness I don't quite feel. "Fine. But if you're that worried, maybe you can come up with a foolproof plan. I know you like a challenge."

He raises an eyebrow, the corner of his mouth quirking up into a reluctant smile. "Oh, I've got plenty of plans. Just none that involve tangling with ancient magic."

"Well, guess you'll have to improvise," I say, trying to lighten the mood.

For a moment, he almost looks like he's going to argue, but then he just shakes his head, muttering something under his breath that sounds suspiciously like, I'm going to regret this.

We fall into step beside each other, moving through the narrow corridors of the ancient, half-ruined temple that's supposedly hiding the artifact we've been searching for. The walls loom on either side of us, etched with faded symbols that seem to pulse in the shadows, as if they're alive. The silence is thick, oppressive, broken only by the soft scuff of our boots against the stone.

There's a strange energy in the air, something that prickles at the edges of my awareness, like an itch I can't quite scratch. I can feel the weight of the place pressing down on us, like we've stepped into a story that's been waiting centuries to be told. The woman's warning echoes in my mind, but I shove it aside, focusing instead on the thrill of discovery, the sense of danger humming beneath my skin.

And then, as we turn a corner, something flickers at the edge of my vision—a glint of gold, a flash of movement. I whip around, heart pounding, but there's nothing there. Just shadows, stretching long and dark across the stones.

Damian stops beside me, his hand instinctively going to the hilt of his dagger. "What is it?"

"I thought..." I trail off, feeling ridiculous. But the chill at the back of my neck hasn't faded. "I thought I saw something."

He frowns, his eyes scanning the shadows. "Let's keep moving," he says, his voice low, tense. "We're close. I can feel it."

We move forward, and the tension between us seems to thicken, growing heavier with every step. The air is thick, almost stifling, and I can feel the weight of the temple pressing down on us, as if the walls themselves are watching, waiting.

And then, suddenly, we're there—standing in front of an archway that leads into a vast, echoing chamber. The room is bathed in an eerie, golden light, illuminating the massive stone pedestal in the center, where a single, gleaming object rests. The artifact.

It's smaller than I expected, almost delicate, its surface etched with intricate patterns that seem to shift and twist as I look at them, like a puzzle just out of reach. There's a strange energy radiating from it, a pull that makes my heart race, a whisper at the edge of my mind that calls to me, beckons me forward.

But as I step closer, a hand catches my arm, pulling me back. I glance up to see Damian's face, his expression shadowed, his grip tight.

"Wait," he says, his voice barely a whisper. "We don't know what it'll do if we touch it."

I feel a flash of irritation, a stubborn thrill that refuses to be tempered by caution. "Isn't that what we came here for? We can't just leave it."

He shakes his head, his eyes dark, intense. "I don't like this. That woman... She warned us."

I can feel his hesitation, his fear, but the call of the artifact is too strong, too alluring to ignore. I gently pull my arm from his grip, stepping forward, drawn by something I can't explain, a need that goes beyond logic, beyond reason.

"Just trust me," I say softly, glancing back at him with a half-smile that I hope is more confident than I feel.

For a moment, he just watches me, his expression unreadable, and then he lets out a long, defeated sigh, his shoulders sagging as he nods.

I step forward, my heart pounding, the thrill of discovery pulsing through me. And as I reach out to touch the artifact, the world seems to hold its breath, the silence thick and expectant, like the pause before a storm.

The moment my fingers brush against its surface, a jolt of energy races through me, sharp and electric, searing through my veins like fire. I gasp, my vision blurring, the world tilting around me as a thousand voices seem to whisper in my mind, their words tangled and chaotic, like fragments of a broken song.

And then, just as suddenly, everything goes silent.

The silence after I touch the artifact feels like a living thing—thick, watchful, as if the very air has eyes on me, holding its breath to see what I'll do next. The jolt that shot up my arm when my fingers grazed the surface still tingles in my veins, electric, relentless. I feel rooted to the spot, unable to pull away, my fingertips brushing over the intricate symbols etched into the metal. They seem to pulse under my touch, each swirl and line alive, twisting in patterns that I can't quite understand but feel like they're burrowing into me, binding me to something deeper.

Damian hisses my name behind me, sharp and urgent, but his voice sounds far away, muted against the artifact's strange pull. A shiver crawls down my spine, but I don't step back; I can't. It's as though the artifact itself has snared me, like invisible chains latching onto something inside me. Every sense is heightened—each heartbeat loud in my ears, each breath harsh against the quiet.

A strange light shimmers from the artifact, faint but growing, filling the room with an eerie glow. The symbols on its surface begin to shift, rearranging themselves under my fingers, forming words I can almost read. I feel a thrill of something—curiosity, maybe, or a reckless excitement—but it's tainted by a deep, creeping unease that I can't ignore.

Damian's hand closes around my wrist, tugging me back with a strength that makes me stumble. I snap back to myself, blinking as the room rushes back into focus. The artifact's glow fades instantly, as though it was only a mirage, a trick of my imagination.

"What the hell were you thinking?" Damian's voice is a low, furious whisper, his fingers still tight around my wrist. He looks at me like I've lost my mind—and maybe I have, because even now, part of me wants to reach out, to touch the artifact again, to understand what it's hiding from me.

"I don't know," I say, my voice barely more than a breath. "It felt like... It was calling to me."

"Calling to you?" He gives me a look that's equal parts exasperation and fear. "This is exactly what she warned us about! And you just... you just went ahead and touched it?" He lets go of my wrist, running a hand through his hair. "If you want to throw yourself into some ancient curse, fine. But don't drag me along for the ride."

The words sting, more than I'd like to admit. I open my mouth to snap back, to defend myself, but something in his expression stops me. I can see the worry behind the frustration, the tension in his jaw, the way his hand hovers near his dagger as if he's ready to defend me against whatever force he thinks I might have just unleashed.

"I'm sorry," I say, surprising even myself. "I didn't mean to..." My words trail off as I glance back at the artifact, its surface dull and lifeless now, as if it's hiding its secrets again.

"Let's just get this over with," Damian mutters, his gaze flicking from the artifact to the dark corners of the room, his posture tense, alert. "Take it, and let's get out of here."

I nod, feeling a strange heaviness settle over me as I step forward again. This time, Damian stays close, his presence steadying me, grounding me. I reach out, wrapping my fingers around the artifact's cool surface, and lift it carefully from the pedestal. It's lighter than I expected, almost weightless, and yet it feels like it's pressing down on me, its energy thrumming through my skin.

The moment it leaves the pedestal, a low rumble echoes through the chamber, like a deep, ancient growl. Dust sifts down from the ceiling, and the walls seem to shudder, as if the temple itself is waking up, angry at our intrusion.

"Move!" Damian's voice is sharp, urgent, and he grabs my arm, pulling me toward the exit just as the ground beneath us begins to tremble.

We sprint through the narrow corridors, the artifact clutched tightly in my hands, its strange warmth seeping into my skin. The temple seems to come alive around us, the walls closing in, shadows lengthening, twisting into shapes that feel almost human. I swear I can hear whispers, faint and ghostly, growing louder with each step.

We burst into the open air, the cool night breeze hitting my face like a shock. I gulp down a breath, my heart pounding as I glance back at the temple, half-expecting to see it crumbling behind us. But it stands as it was, silent, ominous, the entrance gaping like a dark mouth.

"Are you all right?" Damian's voice is tense, his gaze fixed on me, scanning for any sign that the artifact has done something to me, changed me somehow.

I nod, though I can still feel the strange pull of the artifact in my hands, as if it's whispering secrets that I'm not yet ready to understand. "I'm fine," I say, my voice steadier than I feel.

Damian eyes me for a long moment, his expression unreadable. "You know, there's a difference between bravery and recklessness," he says finally, his tone gentler than before. "You can't just—"

But before he can finish, a flicker of movement catches my eye, and I turn just in time to see a shadow detach itself from the trees at the edge of the clearing. It's a figure, tall and cloaked, a gleam of gold catching the moonlight. I recognize the mask before I even see her face.

She steps forward, her movements smooth and fluid, as if she's gliding over the ground. Her eyes glint from behind the mask, sharp and assessing, and I feel a chill run through me, sharper than the night air.

"So," she says, her voice carrying that same eerie, musical echo that makes the hairs on my arms stand up. "You've ignored my warning."

Damian steps in front of me, his stance protective, his hand hovering near his weapon. "We got what we came for. If you're here to stop us—"

She laughs, a sound that's cold and humorless, cutting through the night like a blade. "Stop you? Oh, no. It's far too late for that." Her gaze shifts to me, piercing, as if she's looking straight into my soul. "The artifact is yours now. But be warned—it is bound to you as much as you are bound to it. You cannot simply walk away."

I swallow, tightening my grip on the artifact, feeling its strange pulse thrumming through my fingers. "What do you mean?"

She tilts her head, a slow, deliberate movement that makes my skin prickle. "You'll find out soon enough. The artifact will reveal its true nature in time, and when it does..." She trails off, a cold smile curving beneath the edge of her mask. "Well, let's hope you're strong enough to survive it."

With that, she turns, her cloak sweeping around her like a shadow, and disappears into the trees, leaving nothing but silence in her wake. I stand there, frozen, the weight of her words pressing down on me like a stone. Damian watches her go, his expression grim, his hand still resting protectively at his side.

After a long moment, he turns to me, his face hard, his eyes dark with something I can't quite read. "What have you done?"

I don't have an answer. The artifact feels heavier in my hands, its surface cold and unyielding, and I feel a strange sense of dread settling in my chest. I glance down at it, at the intricate patterns that seem to shift and twist under the moonlight, and a chill runs through me as I realize the truth.

I'm bound to it now, in ways I don't yet understand. And whatever secrets it holds, whatever power it hides, I know that this is only the beginning.

Chapter 12: The Beast in the Ruins

The ruins are everywhere, towering heaps of stone and twisted metal, cloaked in moss and draped in a green so deep it feels more alive than anything breathing. My boots crunch over broken shards of glass, scattered like old stars fallen from some sky no one's seen in ages. Vines creep up around fractured columns, their stone chipped and faded, telling tales of some ancient glory long past. Even the air here feels dense, weighed down with secrets waiting to be exhaled, secrets left behind by people who vanished into dust while no one was looking.

I glance at Damian, who moves beside me with a kind of languid grace that shouldn't fit in a place like this, his dark cloak catching the occasional stray glimmer of daylight as if it's got a mind of its own. He's quiet, his eyes flicking back and forth, scanning the rubble, the shadows, and every conceivable place something could hide. I've learned that he doesn't speak unless he has to, like he's rationing his words for some later date, and yet every silence of his is filled with a weight that speaks louder than anything he might say.

A low, grumbling sound begins to stir, like the earth itself is gritting its teeth. I freeze, hand instinctively reaching for the dagger strapped to my side, and catch Damian's quick, knowing glance. He raises one finger to his lips—a signal to stay quiet, to listen, to stay alive.

It's then I see it, emerging from the darkened archway of what once might have been a grand hall. A beast. If I hadn't seen it with my own eyes, I might have thought someone had stitched it together from nightmares and abandoned it here to rot. The creature is massive, its body armored with thick, bone-plated scales that catch the faintest trickle of sunlight filtering through the broken walls. Its eyes, gleaming like molten gold, hold a dark, insidious intelligence, and when it steps forward, the ground trembles under its weight.

Razor-sharp claws scrape against the stone with a sound that sends chills skittering up my spine.

My heart lurches. Damian's already moving, his posture calm, deadly, as he steps into the beast's line of sight. Every nerve in my body screams at me to run, to flee this thing that has no right to exist outside a nightmare. But Damian's hand catches my wrist, his touch grounding, steadying. "Together," he murmurs, his voice like iron, unbreakable.

In a heartbeat, it charges, and the world tilts sideways as I dodge to the right, feeling the rush of air as one of its massive claws sweeps past my head, close enough to feel its heat. I dart around, catching a glimpse of Damian as he moves, a flash of steel in his hand. He's quick, a dance of fluid strength, his blade slicing through the air, deflecting a swipe from the beast that could have easily torn him apart. And suddenly, it's just us and this creature, locked in a rhythm of dodging and striking, parrying and retreating, a brutal waltz where one wrong step means death.

The beast snarls, a deep, guttural sound that reverberates in my chest, shaking me to my bones. I grit my teeth and lunge forward, slicing my dagger down its side. The blade barely scratches its hide, but it's enough to catch its attention, to give Damian a second to close in. He moves like he's done this before, as if he knows exactly where to strike, where the armor's weak, where its defenses fail. His knife finds a chink just below its jaw, and with a ferocious cry, he drives it in deep.

The beast lets out a hideous scream, thrashing wildly. I stumble backward, barely catching myself as I brace for the inevitable retaliation. But Damian's already there, ducking low, twisting his blade with a precision that's almost graceful, his every movement calculated, deliberate. With a final, agonized growl, the beast staggers, its enormous body sinking to the ground with a heavy, echoing thud.

My breaths come in quick, shallow gasps, a mixture of adrenaline and relief that makes my head spin. Damian wipes his blade on the edge of his cloak, glancing over at me with an expression that's more relief than triumph. "You good?" he asks, and for a moment, there's a flicker of something close to concern in his eyes.

I nod, feeling a strange sense of exhilaration mingled with exhaustion. My whole body feels electric, like I've just touched something wild and untamed. "That... was not what I signed up for," I say, though my voice shakes just enough to betray me. I try to muster a smirk, something to cover the raw fear still clawing its way up my throat.

"Really?" His eyebrow quirks up, amused. "Thought you came along for all the thrilling, life-threatening adventures."

I scoff, rolling my eyes. "Sure, that's me. Just a girl looking for a monstrous thrill."

His gaze lingers on me, his mouth curving into a smirk that somehow feels warmer than it has any right to in the aftermath of a battle. "Well, if you're still in one piece after that, maybe you're cut out for this more than you think."

I feel myself softening, some small part of me letting go of the fear I've held tight to since we stepped into this forgotten ruin. But then I catch sight of the beast's golden eyes, now dull and empty, staring up at nothing, and the moment of levity fades. There's something about those eyes that feels hauntingly familiar, as if they belonged to someone or something that understood more than it could ever say. And for a second, I wonder if we really were the heroes here, or if we just destroyed the last remnant of something that once had a story of its own.

Damian sheaths his blade and nods toward the darkened hallway ahead. "Come on," he says, his voice softer, more measured. "If this place is guarded by something like that, it means there's something here worth finding."

I take a deep breath, letting his words settle. There's a strange thrill in the idea, a tugging curiosity that pulls me forward despite the dangers. And with one last glance at the ruins around us, at the shadows that hide untold mysteries, I follow Damian into the depths, ready to face whatever else this place has in store.

As we slip through the crumbling stone archway deeper into the ruins, the air shifts, growing colder, sharper. It's as if the beast's death stirred something in the walls around us, a memory of a time when these halls thrummed with life. The silence is thick, but it's not empty; there's something watchful about it, something waiting. Damian doesn't seem fazed, his stride as steady as ever, his hand resting loosely on the hilt of his blade, but I can feel the tension coiling in my own muscles, a readiness to spring at the first sign of trouble.

He pauses by an old stone slab that juts out from the wall, inspecting a series of strange markings carved into its surface. His fingers trace the symbols with a familiarity that suggests he understands more than he lets on. I lean in, squinting at the odd shapes, but they're unfamiliar, a language from another world—or another time.

"You know what this says?" I ask, trying to sound casual, like it doesn't bother me that he knows things I don't.

He doesn't look at me, but I can see the faintest twitch at the corner of his mouth, a smirk he's trying to hide. "Bits and pieces. It's... a warning, of sorts. Something about a 'bound guardian' and a 'door to the beyond.'"

My eyebrows shoot up. "A bound guardian? Is that what we just fought back there?"

"Possibly." He shrugs, still studying the symbols, but there's a new tension in his jaw. "Or it could be something else entirely. These ruins are full of surprises."

The way he says it makes me wonder if he knows more about these ruins than he's letting on, but I don't push it. There's something almost comforting about the mystery with Damian; it's like every answer he gives just leads to more questions, and somehow that makes everything feel less terrifying. Like the unknown is a game we're playing, one he's better at, sure, but one I might be able to catch up on if I keep my wits about me.

We move on, our footsteps echoing against the stone walls as we navigate a twisting series of narrow passageways. The deeper we go, the darker it becomes, and the shadows seem to cling to us, reaching out like bony fingers. I swear I catch glimpses of movement from the corner of my eye, but every time I turn, there's nothing there. Just shadows, flickering and wavering in the dim light.

At one point, Damian stops abruptly, his hand shooting out to stop me from walking forward. I'm about to ask why when he points down. There, half-buried in the dust and rubble, is a fine thread, barely visible, stretching across the width of the corridor.

"Tripwire," he murmurs, crouching down to examine it more closely.

My heart skips a beat. "Who sets a trap in a place like this?"

"The same kind of people who'd leave a monster to guard it," he replies, his voice soft but with an edge that sends a shiver down my spine.

Carefully, he disarms the trap, his fingers deftly maneuvering the wire until it's harmlessly coiled in his hand. It's a skill he clearly knows well, and I can't help but wonder just how many traps he's had to disarm in his life, how many more he's walked straight into without flinching. He straightens, and his gaze meets mine, a flicker of something unreadable in his eyes.

"Stay close," he says, a touch of warmth in his voice. "There might be more."

I swallow and nod, my hand brushing the cool stone wall as we continue. The tension in the air is palpable now, like we're creeping through the belly of some ancient beast that could wake up at any moment. Damian seems to sense it too; he's moving more carefully, his steps lighter, his hand never straying far from his blade.

Eventually, we reach a large chamber, and the sight takes my breath away. It's a vast, domed hall, the ceiling stretching so high above us it vanishes into shadow. Massive pillars line the walls, each one carved with intricate designs that twist and coil, creating patterns so dizzyingly complex I can't look at them for too long. In the center of the room stands a large, ornately decorated door, its surface inlaid with shimmering stones and symbols that glint in the dim light.

Damian approaches it slowly, and I follow, my eyes tracing the strange symbols that spiral across the door. They pulse faintly, as if alive, as if they're aware of our presence. It's beautiful, in a way that feels otherworldly and dangerous, and I can feel a pull, a tugging sensation in my chest, drawing me closer to it.

I reach out, my fingers hovering just above the surface, but before I can touch it, Damian's hand clamps around my wrist, pulling me back.

"Don't," he says, his tone sharper than I've ever heard it.

I blink, startled by the intensity in his gaze. "What is it?"

"This door isn't... ordinary." He's still gripping my wrist, his expression unreadable, but there's something almost protective in the way he holds me back. "If you touch it without knowing what you're doing, you might not come back from it."

His words send a chill through me, but there's a spark of frustration too, the sting of feeling like I'm being treated as some helpless tag-along. I shake off his grip, folding my arms defiantly.

"And you know how to open it, do you?"

A flicker of something crosses his face—hesitation, maybe, or a hint of guilt. "I know enough to be careful," he says quietly. "There's a reason doors like this are guarded."

For a moment, I just stand there, staring at him, wondering who he really is, what he's seen that's left him so haunted. But then he shifts, the familiar smirk returning, though it doesn't quite reach his eyes.

"Besides, where's the fun if you just dive headfirst into every enchanted doorway?"

I can't help but laugh, despite myself, the sound echoing oddly in the vast, empty chamber. "Oh, and here I thought I was supposed to be the reckless one."

We stand in silence for a moment, side by side, gazing at the door. I can feel its pull, like a whisper just at the edge of hearing, calling to something deep inside me. And I can tell Damian feels it too; there's a tension in his stance, a reluctance that tells me he's just as curious, just as drawn to it as I am. But there's something else too—a fear, buried so deep I can only sense it in the way he holds himself, as if he's ready to bolt at any moment.

Finally, he turns to me, his gaze steady. "We don't have to go through it," he says, his voice softer, almost gentle. "We could turn back. Leave whatever's behind that door where it belongs."

But I know I can't. Something inside me is screaming to know, to see what lies on the other side, to unravel the mystery that's been haunting us since we set foot in these ruins. I meet his gaze, holding it with a resolve I didn't know I had.

"We came this far," I say, my voice steadier than I feel. "And besides... I don't think either of us is very good at walking away from a mystery."

Damian sighs, a resigned smile tugging at his lips. "Fine. But if something tries to eat us on the other side, just remember: this was your idea."

And with that, we step toward the door, bracing ourselves for whatever lies beyond.

Damian places his hands on the door, his fingers resting lightly against the cold, intricate designs, and I can tell he's bracing himself for something. He glances at me, giving me one last chance to back out, but I set my jaw, meeting his gaze with a stubborn tilt of my chin. If I'm anything, I'm stubborn, and I'm not about to let some ominous door full of ancient symbols get the better of me. He nods, almost approvingly, then takes a steadying breath and pushes.

The door swings open with a deep, groaning creak that reverberates through the air, echoing down the dark corridors behind us. Beyond it lies a vast chamber, dimly lit by a strange, ethereal glow that seems to come from nowhere and everywhere all at once. The walls are covered in more of the intricate carvings, the kind that twist and writhe in the dim light, like they're trying to shift and rearrange themselves when you're not looking.

I step inside, my heart hammering against my ribs, the air thick with a scent I can't quite place—something ancient and earthy, like wet stone and burnt wood. Damian follows, his movements careful, his gaze sharp as he surveys the room. Every muscle in his body is tense, coiled, like he's waiting for something to lunge out of the darkness. I get the feeling he's right to be cautious.

In the center of the room stands a raised platform, and on it, an object that takes my breath away. It's a large, intricately designed chest, covered in more of those strange symbols, but unlike the rest of the carvings, these seem to glow faintly, as if they hold some kind of power within them. I approach slowly, my curiosity outweighing my better judgment, and I can feel the energy radiating off of it, humming just beneath the surface.

"Careful," Damian warns, his voice low. "Things like this usually come with a price."

"Funny, coming from you," I murmur, unable to tear my eyes away from the chest. There's something about it, something that calls to me, like it's meant for me and no one else. It's an absurd thought, and yet, here I am, my fingers itching to open it, to see what lies inside.

"Do you even know what's in there?" he asks, his voice slicing through the haze of my fascination.

"No," I admit, glancing at him. "But that's the point, isn't it?"

He doesn't answer, just watches as I reach out, my fingers brushing against the cool, engraved metal. The symbols pulse beneath my touch, and a shiver runs through me, a strange feeling of being watched, of something ancient and powerful stirring just beyond my reach. I lift the lid, half expecting it to explode or release some curse, but it opens smoothly, silently, revealing a strange, dark stone nestled within, its surface as smooth as glass and as black as night.

The moment I touch it, a surge of energy floods through me, sharp and biting, like ice running through my veins. My vision blurs, and for a moment, I see images flickering in my mind—glimpses of places I've never been, people I've never met. A city made of glass towers under a sky filled with stars, a river of fire winding through a dark forest, a face, familiar yet unrecognizable, staring back at me with eyes that are hauntingly like my own.

I stagger back, clutching the stone in my hand, my breathing shallow. Damian is by my side in an instant, his hand on my arm, grounding me, steadying me. "What happened?" he asks, his voice laced with concern, though he tries to hide it behind a mask of indifference.

"I... I saw something," I manage, still reeling from the intensity of the vision. "I don't know what it was, but it felt real. Like a memory, only... not mine."

His gaze sharpens, his expression unreadable. "That stone. It's a conduit."

"A conduit?" I echo, turning the stone over in my hand. It's warm now, almost pulsing with an energy of its own, like a heartbeat. "A conduit to what?"

"To whatever it's bound to," he says, his tone grim. "And if what you saw was real, then it's bound to something powerful, something that wants you to know it exists."

I swallow, a chill running down my spine. The idea of being connected to something I don't understand, something beyond my control, is both thrilling and terrifying. I want to throw the stone back into the chest, slam the lid shut, and walk away, but I can't. I'm drawn to it, to whatever secrets it holds, to the mystery that's woven itself around me like a net I can't escape.

"What do we do?" I ask, my voice barely more than a whisper.

Damian studies me for a long moment, his gaze intense, searching. "We leave. Now. Before whatever's bound to that stone decides to come looking for it."

A part of me wants to argue, to say that we should stay, that we should try to understand what this place is, what it means, but the look in his eyes stops me. There's a fear there, raw and unguarded, and it strikes me that this might be the first time I've seen him afraid of something he can't simply fight or outwit.

But before we can move, a low rumbling fills the room, a deep, resonant sound that seems to come from the very walls themselves. The carvings on the stone chest begin to glow brighter, pulsing in time with the rumbling, and the ground beneath our feet starts to tremble.

"What did you do?" Damian snaps, his voice sharp with urgency.

"I didn't do anything!" I retort, clutching the stone tightly in my hand, as if it's the only thing anchoring me in the chaos around us. The air grows thick, heavy with an energy that crackles and hums, and I can feel it pressing down on me, filling my lungs, making it hard to breathe.

The door we came through slams shut, the sound echoing through the chamber like a gunshot. I whirl around, panic clawing at my chest. We're trapped, sealed inside this room with whatever ancient power I've just awakened.

Damian steps in front of me, his stance protective, his hand gripping his blade. "Stay close," he mutters, his eyes scanning the room, his body tensed for a fight. "If something comes through that door, we face it together."

But before I can respond, the floor beneath us begins to shift, the stones moving and sliding like pieces of a puzzle, forming a circular pattern around the chest. The air hums with an intensity that makes my skin prickle, and I can feel the stone in my hand growing hotter, the energy within it building, coiling, like it's waiting for something, for some final release.

Then, just as suddenly as it began, the rumbling stops. The silence that follows is thick, suffocating, like the room is holding its breath, waiting.

And then I see it—a shadow, darker than the deepest black, taking shape at the far end of the chamber. It's not a creature, not like the beast we fought earlier. It's something else, something less solid, more fluid, shifting and twisting, its form barely distinguishable from the darkness around it. But I can feel its gaze on me, cold and piercing, and I know, with a certainty that chills me to the bone, that it's here for the stone.

I take a step back, my heart racing, my hand tightening around the conduit, its heat searing against my palm. Damian stands beside me, his expression hard, his blade raised, but even he looks shaken, his confidence fraying at the edges.

The shadow moves closer, and I can feel its power pressing down on me, suffocating, consuming. I glance at Damian, my voice barely a whisper.

"What do we do now?"

But he doesn't answer. His gaze is fixed on the shadow, his jaw clenched, and I can see the same fear in his eyes that I feel rising in my own chest. We are outmatched, trapped, with nowhere to run.

And the shadow, with an agonizing slowness, stretches out a hand.

Chapter 13: The Whispered Betrayal

The dim, flickering light from the dying campfire casts strange shadows over Damian's face, accentuating the hard angles of his jaw and the hollow depths of his eyes. He sits across from me, silent, his gaze trained somewhere far beyond our makeshift camp, as though the crumbling world around us were of little consequence. And maybe to him, it is. Maybe it's all just a stage, and he, its reluctant actor. I study him, searching for some hint of the warmth he used to show, but his expression has turned as impenetrable as stone. It's like I'm staring into a stranger.

"Damian," I start, the name scraping against my throat. "What's going on with you?"

His eyes flicker toward me briefly, almost reluctantly, before they settle on the dark line of trees beyond. He doesn't answer. The silence stretches, thick and uncomfortable, and I find myself grasping at words, anything to break through the walls he's erected overnight.

"We're supposed to be a team," I say, my voice more pleading than I'd intended. "You can't just...shut me out like this. Not now, not when we're so close."

He tenses, jaw clenched, hands curling into fists by his side. But still, he says nothing. I feel the heat rising in my face, anger mixing with the icy fingers of doubt clawing at my chest.

I push, my voice sharpening. "Are you even listening to me?"

At last, he looks at me fully, his eyes cold, unreadable. The man I'd trusted, the man I'd counted on, is nowhere to be seen. It's as if I'm staring into the face of a stranger, and in that moment, an unsettling realization begins to worm its way into my mind. He has secrets—dark, hidden truths that he's been guarding fiercely, keeping me in the dark while I've bared my soul.

"Maybe you should stop asking questions you don't want the answers to," he says finally, his voice low, calculated. "There's an edge to it that I haven't heard before, a biting quality that sends chills down my spine.

"I deserve answers, Damian," I counter, refusing to let him see the fear gnawing at my insides. "Whatever you're hiding, it's affecting the mission. It's affecting us."

He chuckles, a mirthless sound, and leans forward, his gaze boring into me with an intensity that feels almost cruel. "Us?" he repeats, as though the very concept were laughable. "You really think there's an 'us,' don't you? You think this is all about trust and camaraderie?"

My heart sinks, his words slicing through me with precision. "What are you saying?"

His smile is a thin, twisted thing. "Maybe it's time you woke up, realized that the world isn't the grand stage for noble causes you seem to think it is."

I swallow hard, struggling to keep my voice steady. "So, what? You're admitting it, then? You've been...using me?"

His silence answers louder than any confession. Betrayal lodges itself in my chest, sharp and unyielding, and I hate how vulnerable I feel, sitting here in the open with my heart on display, while he's wrapped himself in layers of secrecy and deception.

"I trusted you," I whisper, more to myself than to him. It's a painful admission, and I can see a flicker of something in his eyes—regret, maybe? Or perhaps just a momentary weakness. Whatever it is, it vanishes as quickly as it came.

"Trust is a luxury," he replies, his tone hard, dismissive. "And one you should have learned not to indulge in by now."

I shake my head, refusing to accept the indifference in his voice. "You don't mean that."

He shrugs, leaning back, his posture relaxed, as though this entire conversation is nothing more than a mildly interesting diversion. "Maybe I do."

The weight of his words presses down on me, filling the space between us with an almost suffocating tension. I want to scream, to demand answers, but a part of me is terrified of what I might hear. And in that moment, I realize just how little I know about this man I thought I trusted. He's kept me at arm's length, always deflecting, always sidestepping my questions. I'd convinced myself it was because he was broken, haunted by some past trauma he couldn't yet share. But now, the truth feels far more sinister.

"Damian, I need to know," I say, my voice barely more than a whisper. "Why are you really here? What is it you want?"

He looks away, and for a brief, agonizing moment, I see something close to guilt flicker across his face. But then, it's gone, replaced by that same steely detachment.

"You wouldn't understand," he mutters.

"Try me."

For a moment, he just stares at me, his gaze piercing, as though he's assessing whether I'm worth the effort. Then, finally, he leans forward, his voice dropping to a conspiratorial whisper.

"The artifact... It's not what you think it is. It's not some key to salvation or a means to save the world." He pauses, watching me carefully, gauging my reaction. "It's a weapon. And whoever controls it controls everything."

His words hang in the air, heavy, suffocating. I can feel my pulse quicken, a sense of dread settling in the pit of my stomach. "But we're supposed to be protecting it. We're supposed to be making sure it doesn't fall into the wrong hands."

A cruel smile twists his lips. "And who decides whose hands are the 'right' ones? You? Me?"

I feel the floor of my world crack, shattering into pieces that I can't put back together. Everything I've believed in, everything I've fought for, feels like a lie. And I can see it now—the calculated manipulation in his every word, every action. He's been using me, positioning me like a piece on a chessboard, moving me wherever he needs to achieve his goal.

"But...why?" My voice sounds small, pathetic, even to my own ears.

"Because power," he says simply, his tone chillingly pragmatic, "is the only thing worth fighting for."

His answer leaves me breathless, a mix of fury and despair swirling inside me. I want to scream, to cry, to lash out at him, but I know that none of it will change anything. He's made his choice, and now I'm left standing on the edge, teetering between betrayal and the terrifying reality of what lies ahead. And in that moment, I realize that the Damian I thought I knew—the man I thought I could trust—never truly existed.

The silence between us stretches longer than the shadow of the mountains that loom ominously behind. Damian's face remains an unreadable mask, and I can't shake the feeling that every answer he might give is already hidden beneath layers of secrets I'll never untangle. I force myself to meet his eyes, to stare down that unflinching gaze and act as if his last words haven't carved me up inside.

"Power, huh?" I say, with a bitterness that surprises even me. "Is that really what you're after? A weapon and a throne?"

He tilts his head, lips quirking into a mockery of a smile. "You think I'm aiming too low? Should I be aspiring for more?"

"Maybe you should start by explaining why you let me think we were working toward the same goal," I snap. "Why you let me—" I stop myself, horrified at how close I am to admitting that I might've felt something for him. I clear my throat, tamping down the heat that rushes to my cheeks. "Why you let me trust you."

Damian lets out a dry laugh, a hollow sound that echoes into the night. "I didn't ask for your trust," he says coldly. "In fact, I told you right from the beginning that this was dangerous, that getting too close would be a mistake. If you chose to ignore that warning, then the blame isn't on me."

I grit my teeth, folding my arms tightly across my chest. I want to scream, to shake him and demand an apology, an explanation, something more than this infuriating indifference. But I know better than to expect anything from him now. His walls are back up, higher and thicker than ever, and I doubt even a wrecking ball could tear them down.

"Fine," I say, my voice tight. "Maybe you didn't ask for my trust, but you certainly did everything you could to win it. I don't know what game you're playing, Damian, but I'm not about to let you win."

He shrugs, entirely unbothered, and I want to scream. "That's your choice," he says mildly, as though we're discussing the weather. "But I don't have time for your moral grandstanding. We both have a job to do, and I suggest you remember that."

There's a coldness in his voice that makes my skin crawl, and I realize, with a jolt of horror, that the man sitting across from me is a stranger. The Damian I thought I knew is gone, replaced by this callous, calculating figure who doesn't care about anything but his own goals.

A sick feeling twists in my stomach, and I force myself to look away, unwilling to let him see how much his words have hurt me. I can't show weakness, not now. Not when I'm already questioning every decision I've made, every moment I've spent with him.

After a few moments, I rise to my feet, brushing the dust from my hands. "Then I suppose we should get moving," I say, my voice cold and distant. "The sooner we finish this, the sooner I can be rid of you."

He raises an eyebrow, his expression a mixture of amusement and disdain. "Funny, I was just thinking the same thing."

Without another word, I turn and start walking, my footsteps echoing in the quiet night. I can hear Damian following behind me, his presence a heavy, unwelcome weight on my shoulders. I don't look back, don't give him the satisfaction of knowing how much his betrayal has shaken me. I've already given him too much of myself, and I won't give him any more.

The path ahead is dark and treacherous, but I force myself to keep moving, to put one foot in front of the other. I can't afford to stop now, can't afford to let my emotions get in the way. There's too much at stake, too many lives depending on me.

As we walk, the silence between us stretches, thick and suffocating. Every now and then, I steal a glance over my shoulder, watching Damian out of the corner of my eye. He's still there, a shadowy figure moving in step with me, his face unreadable in the darkness. But I can feel his gaze on me, feel the weight of his presence pressing down on me like a physical burden.

The night grows colder, the air thick with the scent of damp earth and rotting leaves. I shiver, wrapping my arms around myself as I press on, determined to put as much distance between us as possible. But no matter how fast I walk, Damian remains close behind, a constant, unyielding presence that I can't escape.

Finally, unable to take the silence any longer, I stop and turn to face him. "Why did you come here?" I demand, my voice barely more than a whisper. "Why did you agree to help me if you never intended to see this through?"

He stares at me for a long moment, his expression unreadable. Then, slowly, he steps forward, closing the distance between us until we're almost touching. I can feel his breath on my face, warm and steady, and for a moment, I'm frozen, caught in the intensity of his gaze.

"Maybe I wanted to see if you were really as foolish as everyone said," he says softly, his voice laced with a cruel sort of amusement. "Or maybe I just enjoy watching people learn the hard way."

His words hit me like a slap, and I stumble back, my heart pounding with a mixture of anger and betrayal. "You're despicable," I hiss, my hands curling into fists. "You think you're so clever, so untouchable. But you're nothing more than a coward, hiding behind your lies and manipulation."

He shrugs, entirely unfazed by my outburst. "If that's what helps you sleep at night, by all means, go on believing it. But we both know that, in the end, you'll do whatever it takes to finish this. Just like me."

I grit my teeth, swallowing down the fury that threatens to consume me. I won't give him the satisfaction of knowing how deeply he's hurt me, won't let him see the cracks he's left in my armor. I'm stronger than that. I have to be.

Taking a deep breath, I turn and start walking again, forcing myself to ignore the sound of his footsteps behind me. The path ahead is dark and uncertain, but I'm determined to see it through, no matter the cost.

As we move deeper into the night, I find myself wondering if I'll ever be able to trust anyone again, if the scars Damian has left will ever truly heal. But I push those thoughts aside, focusing on the road ahead, on the mission that still lies before me.

And in that moment, I make a silent vow to myself: I will survive this. I will finish what I started, no matter who stands in my way.

The dawn creeps in sluggishly, casting a weak glow over the camp. Sleep eludes me, which is hardly surprising, considering that every attempt to close my eyes brings an unwelcome reel of memories. Damian's voice, laced with that maddening apathy, plays over and over, twisting through the stillness of my mind. I'm left lying in the brittle morning chill, trying to piece together how I ended up here—tangled in schemes and alliances I never intended to forge.

Eventually, I push myself up, brushing the dry, gritty earth from my arms. Damian is already awake, leaning against a weathered boulder a few paces away. His expression is as distant as ever, his gaze somewhere just beyond me, and I wonder, not for the first time, what he's actually thinking beneath that mask of his. The light plays over his face, harsh and unforgiving, accentuating the angles that make him look all the more unyielding.

"Couldn't sleep?" he asks, his voice as smooth and cool as ever. There's no trace of concern in it, only the slightest hint of forced civility, as though he's merely observing a shift in the weather.

"Shocking, I know," I reply, brushing off the edge in his tone. I won't give him the satisfaction of knowing how thoroughly he's disrupted my peace. "Let's just get this over with. I don't want to be stuck out here any longer than I have to be."

"Right." He pushes off the boulder, slipping back into that infuriatingly casual demeanor of his, as though he has all the time in the world. I turn and start moving before he can catch up. If he insists on keeping his secrets, then I'll keep my distance.

The forest thickens around us, branches twisting overhead and weaving a lattice of shadows across our path. Damian falls into step beside me, though he's careful to leave a respectable distance between us. I'm not sure if it's intentional or just his usual indifference, but I'm grateful either way. I can't think straight with him so close.

We move in silence for what feels like hours, the only sound the steady crunch of our boots against the forest floor. Occasionally, a bird will flutter overhead, its wings a brief flash of color in the monochrome dawn, but otherwise, everything remains eerily quiet. The silence between us grows heavier, thickening with each step, and I begin to wonder if he'll say anything at all.

Finally, Damian clears his throat, breaking the quiet. "You know, you're awfully prickly for someone who's supposedly on a mission for the greater good," he says, his tone lightly mocking.

I stop, turning to face him, arms crossed. "And you're awfully smug for someone whose only loyalty is to himself."

He shrugs, unfazed by my words. "Self-preservation isn't exactly a crime, you know. I've just learned to prioritize it."

"Funny. I could've sworn you once believed in something more." I watch him carefully, hoping for even the smallest crack in his defenses, some hint of the man I thought he was.

But he only laughs, a dry, humorless sound. "Belief is a luxury. One I can't afford."

I shake my head, frustration bubbling over. "You don't even try, do you? To be decent, to care about anything or anyone beyond yourself. It's all just a game to you, isn't it?"

He studies me, his gaze unwavering. "Is that what you think? That I don't care?" There's a strange edge to his voice, something almost vulnerable, but it vanishes as quickly as it appeared.

"Yes," I reply, my tone harsh, unrelenting. "I think you'd sacrifice anyone if it meant achieving your goals. You'd use anyone without a second thought."

There's a long pause, the tension between us thickening, and I half-expect him to deny it, to offer some glimmer of the person I once trusted. But instead, he just nods, as if agreeing with me.

"Maybe you're right," he says quietly, his gaze drifting past me to some distant point in the trees. "But we all have our parts to play. Don't we?"

I feel a chill crawl up my spine, but I refuse to back down. "Some of us didn't sign up to be pawns," I shoot back. "Some of us still have a conscience."

His lips twist into a bitter smile. "Then you're in the wrong line of work."

There's nothing left to say after that, no words that could bridge the chasm between us. I turn and keep walking, the path winding deeper into the forest. Damian falls silent, his presence little more than a shadow trailing behind me, and I can feel the weight of his gaze on my back, watching, waiting.

The trees close in around us, the air growing cooler and heavier with each step, and a faint prickling sensation starts at the base of my neck. Something isn't right. I glance over my shoulder, but there's nothing—just Damian's inscrutable expression and the endless stretch of forest behind him. I turn back to the path, my senses on high alert.

We're close now, nearing the place where the artifact is supposed to be hidden, and I can feel the energy in the air shift, thickening, humming with a strange, unfamiliar force. I reach for the map, smoothing it out and checking our position, but my hands tremble, making it difficult to focus. I don't dare let Damian see my unease, but I know he's watching, taking in every detail, every weakness.

Finally, I spot the entrance—an ancient stone archway covered in vines, barely visible through the dense undergrowth. My heart pounds as I step forward, brushing the vines aside and revealing the worn, faded symbols carved into the stone.

"This is it," I murmur, more to myself than to him.

Damian steps up beside me, his gaze fixed on the archway. For a brief moment, I catch a flicker of something in his eyes—awe, maybe, or perhaps something darker. But then it's gone, replaced by that familiar, guarded expression.

"Are you ready?" he asks, his tone deceptively casual.

I swallow hard, forcing myself to nod. "Yes."

But as we step through the archway, a cold wind sweeps through, chilling me to the bone. The light dims, and the path ahead twists and turns, the shadows growing deeper, darker, as if the forest itself is alive, watching, waiting. A faint whisper echoes through the air, too soft to make out, and I feel a shiver run down my spine.

Damian is right beside me, his gaze sharp, alert, and for the first time, I see a hint of tension in his posture, a subtle shift that tells me he's not as unaffected as he pretends to be. I feel a surge of satisfaction, but it's short-lived, replaced by a creeping sense of dread.

Something is wrong. The air grows heavier, the shadows closing in, and I can feel an unseen presence pressing down on us, watching from the depths of the forest. I open my mouth to say something, to warn him, but the words catch in my throat, silenced by a sudden, overwhelming sense of danger.

And then, without warning, the ground beneath us shifts, a low rumble that vibrates through my bones. The earth cracks, and I stumble, barely managing to catch myself. Damian reaches for me, his hand closing around my arm, his grip surprisingly strong, and for a brief, fleeting moment, I feel a strange sense of security.

But then, the rumbling intensifies, the ground splitting open, and I look up just in time to see a figure emerging from the shadows—a figure cloaked in darkness, its eyes glinting with a cold, malevolent light.

I freeze, my heart pounding, and I realize, with a sickening certainty, that we're not alone.

Chapter 14: The Lake of Reflections

The air was thick with an evening mist, curling off the lake's surface like secrets exhaled. I'd slipped away from Damian, needing distance from his calculating gaze, that smirk he wore as if he held every answer and I held nothing but questions. This lake—I hadn't meant to find it. I'd stumbled upon it, hidden among a bramble of trees so tightly packed they might as well have been guardians of some otherworldly portal. It was still. Not serene, no, but the kind of stillness that was heavy with anticipation. As if it knew me.

I crouched at the water's edge, and what I saw nearly had me tumbling backward. There, reflected in the glassy surface, were not just my eyes, but a thousand variations of them. The face staring back at me was mine, but distorted. Younger, angrier. Weaker. Stronger. All the versions of me I'd hidden away or tried to become. They stared up, accusing, their mouths twisted into mirthless smiles or pressed into solemn lines. A lump rose in my throat, and I tasted the bitterness of things I thought I'd buried long ago.

But here they were—memories, jagged and incomplete, flickering across the water like vignettes of my own private failings. I saw my first betrayal, the friend who'd whispered secrets of mine to others like they were currency. I could still feel the sting of that moment, the quiet humiliation of realizing I'd been too trusting, too open. And then there was the second one, the betrayal I'd tried to bury deeper. My fault, maybe, for seeing goodness where there was none. His face surfaced in the water, too, and I couldn't help but scoff at my own naivety.

But what frightened me most was not the faces of people who'd wronged me—it was my own face, in all the shapes it had taken over the years. That version of me, looking back with fierce determination in her eyes, daring me to sink or swim. Another me, lips pale with fear, pleading to be saved from the choices I'd already made. I felt the urge to shatter that reflection, to rip myself away from the strange allure of the water, but I stayed rooted there, mesmerized by a twisted fascination with my own pain.

The wind shifted, cold and smelling faintly of smoke, and I knew without looking that Damian had come up behind me. Even when he was silent, he had a way of pressing his presence onto the scene like a brand. I didn't turn to face him. I couldn't yet. My gaze was locked on the lake, and it felt like it held some dark spell over me.

"Interesting place to go wandering alone," he murmured, his voice just a ripple in the eerie quiet. I sensed rather than saw him crouch beside me, the casual ease he exuded contrasting sharply with the tension humming through me. He reached down and swirled his hand through the water, and my reflection shattered into fragments, like glass thrown against stone.

"What do you see?" he asked, voice laced with that maddening curiosity, like he knew the answer and was just testing me. He always looked at me like that—as if I were an experiment, a puzzle he could decode if he only tried hard enough.

"Nothing," I replied flatly, pulling my gaze from the lake. I turned to look at him, forcing every ounce of anger and bitterness into my expression. "Nothing that concerns you." My voice came out stronger than I'd expected, tinged with a defiance I hadn't known I still possessed.

His eyes met mine, a glint of amusement playing at the edges of his mouth. "Right. Just a little soul-searching by the lake. With shadows that look a lot like regrets. But you're right," he shrugged, the smirk falling into something almost sincere, "not my business, unless you want it to be."

I could have spat back a retort, something cutting to send him back where he came from, but something held me there. A hint of vulnerability flickered across his face, just long enough to make me wonder if I'd imagined it. It wasn't often that Damian showed anything other than calculated nonchalance, but in that moment, I almost believed he might understand. Almost.

"Fine," I muttered, lowering my gaze back to the lake, though I refused to meet the haunted reflection staring up. "It's just... people. Choices I made. Things that still cut."

I expected him to make some flippant comment, but instead he was quiet, watching me with a sharpness that bordered on intensity. "Do you ever think," he began, voice low and more serious than I'd ever heard, "that maybe those cuts are supposed to heal wrong? Not neatly. Maybe that's the point."

I felt the absurd urge to laugh, half at the irony of getting philosophical advice from him of all people, and half because I knew he was right. I glanced sideways at him, and he was still watching me, expression unreadable.

"It's hard to explain," I admitted, my voice barely a whisper now. "It's not that I wanted things to go perfectly. It's just... there's a part of me that doesn't know how to let go of what could have been. What should have been."

Damian's eyes softened, and for a brief, dangerous moment, I thought he might say something kind. But then he shook his head, as if shaking off some invisible chain. "Regrets are funny things," he said. "They're like thorns—you keep them close to remind yourself not to fall for the same tricks. Only problem is, you end up bleeding every time you think about them."

The way he said it, it was as if he spoke from some deep, well-hidden part of himself. I knew better than to ask, to probe into places he guarded so carefully. So I just nodded, feeling a strange understanding pass between us, something fragile yet oddly binding.

We sat there in silence, side by side on the cold ground, staring out over the lake that seemed to hold both of our secrets. The mist curled and twisted, drawing the darkness closer around us, and for once, it didn't feel stifling. It felt like a cloak, a shroud that allowed me, however briefly, to sit with the pieces of myself I'd tried so hard to forget.

When I finally pulled myself to my feet, I looked at Damian and, for the first time, didn't see him as an enemy or a puzzle. He was just... there, and so was I.

The silence stretched between us, thick enough to taste. Damian's gaze never left me, and the weight of it seemed to press into my chest, making it hard to breathe. For someone who thrived on charm and bravado, he had an uncanny ability to turn utterly silent, holding his thoughts close like cards he refused to play. Maybe that's what unnerved me most about him—the way he was as unreadable as the lake, a dark mirror that offered no answers, only reflections that hinted at secrets just out of reach.

I shifted my weight, forcing myself to break eye contact. My fingers felt cold, almost numb, and I clenched them into fists, grounding myself with the bite of my nails against my palms. "Why are you here, really?" The question slipped out before I could stop it. It was blunt, maybe even a little cruel, but I was too raw to care. I had spent too long trying to make sense of him, to sift through his half-truths and evasions. If he was going to keep lurking on the edges of my life, I wanted to know why.

He looked at me, his mouth curving up in the faintest hint of a smile, but his eyes remained distant, almost guarded. "You know why," he replied, his tone infuriatingly calm. He didn't elaborate, and I found myself gritting my teeth, resisting the urge to shake the answer out of him.

"Do I?" I shot back, my voice sharper than I'd intended. "Because from where I'm standing, all I see is someone who keeps showing up uninvited, then disappearing without a word. Like you're some sort of ghost who only haunts me when it's convenient."

His jaw tensed, and for a moment, I thought he might actually answer me, give me something real. But then he just shrugged, as if brushing off my words like they meant nothing. "Maybe I am a ghost," he said softly, his gaze drifting toward the lake. The water had grown darker in the waning light, its surface barely visible through the shroud of mist that clung to the air. "Or maybe," he added, a hint of bitterness in his voice, "you just keep looking for answers where there aren't any."

His words struck a nerve, and I felt a flash of anger flare up in my chest. I wanted to tell him he was wrong, that I didn't need his answers, that I didn't need him. But even as the thoughts formed, I knew they weren't true. I was drawn to him, inexplicably and relentlessly, and it infuriated me.

"You're impossible," I muttered, turning away from him. I couldn't stand the way he looked at me, like he could see through every layer of armor I'd wrapped myself in, right down to the fears and doubts I tried to hide even from myself.

Damian didn't respond, and the silence settled around us again, thick and uncomfortable. I could feel him watching me, his gaze heavy with something I couldn't quite name. And then, just as I thought I couldn't stand another second of it, he spoke, his voice low and surprisingly gentle.

"You think I don't see it, don't you?" he murmured, his words barely more than a whisper. "The way you carry all that weight, all those memories you keep trying to outrun. You think I don't notice, but I do."

I froze, his words hitting me like a punch to the gut. I wanted to deny it, to laugh it off, but I couldn't. He was right, and the truth of it was almost unbearable. I had spent so long trying to bury those memories, to keep them locked away where they couldn't hurt me. But somehow, Damian had seen through it all, had seen me in a way no one else ever had.

"Why does it matter to you?" My voice came out shaky, barely more than a whisper. I hated how vulnerable I sounded, but I couldn't help it. Damian had stripped away my defenses with just a few words, leaving me exposed and raw.

He looked at me, his expression softening in a way that made my heart ache. "Because I know what it's like to carry ghosts," he said quietly, his gaze never leaving mine. "I know what it's like to live with the shadows of the past, to feel like you'll never escape them."

The honesty in his voice startled me. I had always thought of Damian as someone who wore his scars lightly, who hid his pain behind a mask of confidence and charm. But now, in the dim light by the lake, I saw something deeper in his eyes—a vulnerability I hadn't noticed before, or maybe one he hadn't wanted me to see.

We stood there in silence, the weight of his words settling between us like a third presence, a shared understanding that neither of us had expected. For the first time, I felt a glimmer of empathy for him, a recognition of the pain he carried beneath his carefully constructed facade.

But just as quickly as the moment appeared, it was gone. Damian straightened, his expression hardening as he pulled himself back behind his walls. I could almost see the shift, like a door slamming shut, and the sudden distance between us was jarring.

He cleared his throat, his tone brisk and businesslike. "Anyway, we should probably get going. It's getting late, and I doubt you want to be out here in the dark."

I nodded, struggling to mask the disappointment that tightened in my chest. I didn't know what I'd been hoping for, but it wasn't this. I had wanted more, something real, something that didn't feel like it was slipping through my fingers the moment I reached for it. But I should have known better than to expect that from Damian.

We started walking back, the silence between us heavier than before. I kept my gaze fixed on the path ahead, refusing to look at him, to let him see the hurt I knew was written all over my face. I didn't want him to know how much his sudden withdrawal had affected me, how much I had let myself hope, even for a moment, that he might be willing to let me in.

But then, just as we reached the edge of the clearing, Damian stopped, his hand reaching out to gently touch my arm. I turned to face him, my heart pounding as I searched his eyes for some hint of what he was thinking.

He hesitated, his fingers brushing against my skin, a touch so light it was almost imperceptible. And then, in a voice so soft I barely heard it, he whispered, "For what it's worth, you're not alone in this."

Before I could respond, he pulled away, his expression shuttered, and he turned to lead the way back down the path. I followed in silence, my mind racing, the echo of his words lingering like a haunting melody in the back of my mind.

We walked side by side, our footsteps muffled by the damp earth, but the distance between us felt wider than ever. I wanted to reach out, to say something, anything that might bridge the gap, but I didn't. Instead, I kept my silence, the weight of unspoken words pressing down on me with every step.

And as we walked away from the lake, I couldn't shake the feeling that something fundamental had shifted between us, something that couldn't be undone.

The path back through the trees was barely a trail, more a suggestion than a route. Branches clawed at my sleeves, scratching thin red lines along my skin as I struggled to keep up with Damian, who walked with the kind of ease that made it clear he had no trouble leaving people behind. Each step felt heavier than the last, the silence between us practically humming with things unsaid. I knew I should let the moment pass, should swallow whatever simmering emotions were twisting in my chest, but I couldn't help myself.

I picked up my pace until I was walking beside him, close enough that I could feel the warmth radiating off him even in the damp chill of the forest. I waited for him to look at me, to give me something more than his usual mask of indifference, but his gaze stayed fixed on the darkening path ahead, his expression inscrutable. My throat tightened, and the words tumbled out before I could stop them.

"Why do you keep doing that?" I asked, my voice sharper than I intended. "Why do you keep pretending you don't care?"

Damian's head jerked toward me, his eyes narrowing. "Pretending?" he repeated, the word dripping with something like mockery, but not quite. "I think you're reading a bit much into things. Maybe I just have better things to care about."

I clenched my fists, resisting the urge to shake him. "Right," I said, my voice laced with sarcasm. "Because you just happened to show up here. Because you just happened to drag me halfway through this forest. You want me to believe that's all some big coincidence?"

He stopped, turning to face me fully, his gaze piercing in the fading light. "Maybe it is. Or maybe," he continued, a trace of something dangerous flickering in his eyes, "you want it to mean more than it does."

My heart pounded, and I forced myself to hold his gaze, even though the weight of it felt almost unbearable. "Maybe I just want the truth," I shot back. "Is that too much to ask?"

He laughed, a bitter, humorless sound that made my stomach twist. "Truth," he muttered, as if the very idea were a joke. "You think you want the truth, but the truth isn't what you think it is. It never is."

I opened my mouth to argue, but before I could say a word, a sudden noise echoed through the trees, a soft rustling that sent a chill skittering down my spine. Damian's expression shifted instantly, his body tensing, his gaze darting toward the shadows. The change in him was so swift, so complete, that it made my heart race. One moment he'd been the aloof, impenetrable Damian, and now he was something else entirely, his attention focused and razor-sharp.

"What was that?" I whispered, my voice barely more than a breath.

He held up a hand, silencing me with a quick, urgent look. "Stay here," he whispered, his tone leaving no room for argument.

"Stay here?" I repeated, incredulous. "Are you kidding me? I'm not staying here alone."

His jaw clenched, and for a second, I thought he might actually argue. But then, as if realizing the futility of it, he nodded. "Fine," he said, his voice taut. "But stay close, and be quiet."

I swallowed, nodding as I edged closer to him, every nerve in my body on high alert. The air felt thick, charged with an energy that was both thrilling and terrifying, and I could feel my heart pounding in my chest as we crept forward, moving as silently as we could through the undergrowth.

The noise came again, louder this time—a soft, shuffling sound, like something moving through the leaves. I glanced at Damian, but his expression gave nothing away. His attention was entirely focused on the shadows ahead, his body tense and poised, as if ready for whatever might come next.

We moved forward, our steps slow and careful, the silence around us growing heavier with each passing second. And then, just as we reached the edge of a small clearing, we saw it—a figure standing in the shadows, half-hidden by the trees. The figure was tall, their face obscured, and something about the way they stood, so still and silent, made my skin prickle with unease.

Damian's hand shot out, grabbing my arm and pulling me back, his grip tight and unyielding. "Don't move," he whispered, his voice barely more than a breath.

I nodded, my throat dry, my pulse racing as I stared at the figure, trying to make sense of what I was seeing. There was something familiar about them, something that tugged at the edges of my memory, but I couldn't quite place it. And then, as if sensing our presence, the figure turned, their gaze locking onto ours with an intensity that made my blood run cold.

"Damian," I whispered, my voice trembling. "Who is that?"

He didn't answer, his eyes fixed on the figure, his expression unreadable. And then, just as suddenly as they had appeared, the figure stepped back into the shadows, disappearing from view.

I let out a shaky breath, my heart pounding as I turned to Damian, searching his face for any hint of explanation. But he was already moving, his grip on my arm pulling me forward, his pace urgent and unrelenting.

"Come on," he said, his voice low and tense. "We need to go. Now."

I stumbled after him, struggling to keep up as he led me deeper into the forest, away from the clearing, away from whatever—or whoever—we had just seen. My mind raced, a thousand questions spinning through my head, but I knew better than to ask them now. Damian's expression was set, his focus unyielding, and I could tell that whatever he'd seen back there had rattled him in a way I'd never seen before.

We moved in silence, our footsteps muffled by the damp earth, and the further we got from the clearing, the heavier the air felt, as if some unseen force were pressing down on us. I could feel Damian's tension, the way his shoulders were rigid, his movements sharper than usual, and it sent a chill down my spine.

Finally, when we'd put what felt like a safe distance between us and the clearing, Damian slowed, releasing his grip on my arm. I stopped, catching my breath as I looked at him, my mind still racing with questions I didn't know how to ask.

"Who was that?" I managed, my voice barely more than a whisper.

He glanced at me, his expression dark and unreadable. For a moment, I thought he might actually answer me, but then he shook his head, his jaw tight. "It doesn't matter," he said, his tone clipped. "All you need to know is that we can't go back there."

"Can't go back?" I repeated, my voice tinged with disbelief. "Damian, what's going on? Why were they looking at us like that?"

His gaze shifted, his eyes distant, as if he were seeing something I couldn't. "There are things you don't understand," he said quietly, almost to himself. "Things I never wanted you to be part of."

The words sent a chill down my spine, and I took a step back, suddenly feeling like I was standing on the edge of a precipice. "What things, Damian? What aren't you telling me?"

He looked at me, his expression taut, and for the first time, I saw a flicker of something close to fear in his eyes. "Trust me," he said, his voice barely more than a whisper. "It's better if you don't know."

Before I could respond, a distant rustling sounded behind us, louder this time, closer. I felt the hair on the back of my neck stand on end, and I turned, my heart pounding as I searched the shadows for any sign of movement.

But the forest was empty, silent. Too silent.

And then, in the stillness, I heard it—a low, menacing whisper that seemed to come from all around us, wrapping around us like a shroud.

"Run," Damian said, his voice tight with urgency. "Now."

Chapter 15: The Veil of Lies

The city loomed ahead like a storm waiting to break, its iron-and-glass towers gleaming in the twilight, casting long shadows over the narrow streets below. The Guild's headquarters lay at its heart, a labyrinth of steely corridors and hidden agendas, where every whisper held a thousand lies and even the walls seemed to listen. Damian and I had been summoned back, told that the Guild required our "loyalty." As if we hadn't proven it enough already.

As we approached the gates, the usual scowling guards flanked us, their gazes cutting through us like knives, and I could almost hear their unspoken accusations. Their suspicion was so thick it hung in the air, pressing down like smoke. They didn't bother to hide their disdain—apparently, we'd been marked as untrustworthy, maybe even expendable. It wasn't the first time I'd felt like prey in the jaws of the Guild, but the weight of it settled heavier this time, laced with something more insidious. Something personal.

When we reached the inner chambers, the air grew colder, the walls closer. I couldn't help but think of how many people had been swallowed by this place, all of them either dead or loyal to the Guild in ways that hollowed them out from the inside. We were led to a stark room, where a long table gleamed under the overhead lights. Across from us sat the Guildmaster, eyes sharp and lips curled in a faint smile that didn't reach her eyes. Her gaze flicked over me and landed on Damian, the look in her eyes both calculating and dangerous.

"Loyalty," she began, voice smooth as silk and sharp as glass, "is a precious commodity. And it's come to our attention that you two may be lacking in it." She leaned back, fingers tapping rhythmically on the table as if counting down the seconds before something snapped. "We require proof. And that proof will not come easy."

Damian's hand was steady at his side, though his jaw was clenched so tight I could see the pulse ticking in his neck. He kept his gaze level, defiant even, while I tried to match his calm. But the Guildmaster had a way of slicing through even the toughest armor, like a predator scenting weakness. She smiled, a cruel twist of her lips, as if savoring our tension.

"You'll need to decide," she continued, each word precise, deliberate. "One of you must betray the other. In fact, we insist upon it."

My heart kicked in my chest, an instinctual flare of fear and fury mixing like poison in my veins. The Guildmaster watched us both, her eyes flickering with satisfaction. Damian's eyes found mine, and for a moment, everything else fell away. His hand tightened around mine—a barely perceptible squeeze, but it was enough to tether me, to remind me that we were still here, together.

I wanted to believe he wouldn't turn on me. But there was a part of me—small, traitorous—that wondered. This wasn't just survival anymore; it was survival with a knife edge of paranoia. The Guild had laid their trap well. They knew the human heart's weakest points, its bruises and fractures. And now, they were leaning into them.

The silence stretched, thick as fog. The Guildmaster watched with keen interest, the room shrinking under her gaze. When Damian spoke, his voice was low, a rough edge to it. "You want us to betray each other," he said slowly, his tone betraying nothing, "but that's where you're wrong. We're not your pawns to turn against each other. Not today."

He took my hand in his, a motion that was as much defiance as it was a promise. The Guildmaster's gaze sharpened, and I saw her fingers twitch as though tempted to clap, as if we'd amused her with some childish rebellion. But then her expression hardened, and the room crackled with tension so fierce it was almost visible. She leaned forward, her face inches from ours, her voice low and venomous.

"Together, then?" she asked, almost pitying. "A foolish choice. But don't say I didn't give you an opportunity."

That was all the warning we got.

The guards lunged forward, metal glinting, and the air filled with the scrape of blades and the clash of fists meeting flesh. Damian and I moved as one, our reflexes honed from years of facing down enemies, but this was different. These were no mere thugs; they were the Guild's finest, handpicked for the precision and ruthlessness they brought to their work. We ducked, twisted, lashed out with everything we had, our bodies a frantic blur of movement, fighting not only to survive but to deny the Guild their twisted satisfaction.

A fist glanced off my cheekbone, and I saw stars, but Damian was there, pulling me to my feet before I could stumble. He threw a swift, brutal kick, knocking a guard back, then turned to me, his breath ragged, eyes blazing. "You good?" he shouted over the chaos.

"Never better," I panted, forcing a smile that was more teeth than anything. I didn't have time to say more before another guard lunged, his blade flashing, and I barely dodged the strike aimed at my throat. The fight spun into a dizzying rhythm, a dance that was as deadly as it was desperate.

Finally, the last guard fell, and the room was eerily silent. Damian's arm was bleeding, and I could feel a bruise blooming along my jaw, but we were standing. For now, that was enough. I glanced up at him, breath catching at the fierce look in his eyes. There was something raw in his gaze, something that made my chest ache with an intensity I couldn't quite name.

The Guildmaster had vanished. Clever, really. We hadn't even noticed her slipping away in the chaos, a true snake in the grass. But this victory, if we could even call it that, felt hollow. We hadn't bested the Guild—we'd merely bought ourselves a temporary reprieve, a thin slice of freedom that could crumble any second. But as Damian took my hand once more, his grip as steady as steel, a thread of hope curled through me, fragile but undeniable.

In that moment, I understood: we weren't just fighting the Guild or the endless games they played with our lives. We were fighting for each other, for the bond we'd forged in the fire of survival, a bond that defied every rule they tried to bind us with. And maybe, just maybe, that would be enough.

We slipped out of the Guild's headquarters like shadows, ducking down alleys and weaving through narrow streets. The city hummed around us, a cacophony of voices and neon signs flashing in the dusk, but I barely heard it. My senses were dulled, too focused on the sting of fresh bruises, the burn in my lungs, and the pulse of Damian's hand still tightly wrapped around mine. I could feel the weight of his grip, warm and steady, and I hated how much I leaned into it, like it was the only thing anchoring me.

"You're still bleeding," I muttered, glancing at the slash across his forearm. The crimson had spread, soaking through the fabric of his sleeve, yet he held my gaze with an unbothered look that was almost infuriating.

"I'll survive," he said, flashing a lopsided grin that was all teeth and no warmth. "Can't get rid of me that easily, you know."

I rolled my eyes, more out of habit than irritation, but I couldn't deny the knot of anxiety tightening in my chest. The Guild didn't just let people walk away. This was a temporary escape, a stay of execution at best, and deep down, we both knew it.

"Don't flatter yourself," I said, my voice dry. "I'm only keeping you around because you make a decent human shield."

Damian chuckled, low and rough, the sound vibrating in the small space between us. "Happy to serve." His tone was teasing, but there was something darker beneath it, a note of resignation that echoed my own. We were free for now, but the Guild had long arms and an even longer memory. We wouldn't stay free for long.

We moved in silence, slipping through the backstreets and keeping our heads down. The city was a labyrinth, one we'd mapped out in our bones, but tonight, it felt unfamiliar, every corner a potential trap, every shadow concealing another threat. It didn't help that I could feel the weight of Damian's gaze on me, sharp and assessing, as if he was studying me, memorizing every flicker of emotion on my face.

"You don't trust me," he said, breaking the silence, his tone strangely matter-of-fact.

I shot him a sidelong glance, surprised by his bluntness. "And you trust me?" I countered, a bitter edge creeping into my voice.

He didn't answer right away, just kept his eyes forward, his jaw tight. When he finally spoke, his voice was low, almost pained. "I don't trust anyone. But I want to trust you."

It was a confession, one that left me momentarily speechless. There were walls around Damian, walls he rarely let anyone past, and the fact that he was even admitting this much was more than I'd expected. I felt the strange urge to reach out, to tell him I wanted to trust him too, but the words tangled in my throat, refusing to come out.

Instead, I cleared my throat, forcing myself to keep walking, to focus on the flickering neon signs ahead. "Wanting to trust someone and actually trusting them are two different things," I said, my voice softer than I intended. "I'd say we're both a little short on the latter."

He gave a soft, humorless laugh. "Fair enough."

We reached the edge of the district, slipping into a rundown alley lined with dilapidated buildings and flickering street lamps casting pale, sickly light over the cracked pavement. This was a part of the city where people kept their heads down and didn't ask questions—a place where even the Guild rarely bothered to look. Here, we could catch our breath, regroup, figure out what came next.

Damian found a crumbling stone ledge and sat down, pulling his sleeve back to inspect his wound. It was a nasty cut, deep and jagged, but he didn't flinch as he poked at it, his expression almost bored. I grimaced, rummaging through my bag for the small first-aid kit I'd stashed there weeks ago. With a muttered curse, I kneeled beside him, pulling out gauze and antiseptic.

"Hold still," I ordered, my tone brisk.

He raised an eyebrow, lips quirking into that infuriating smirk of his. "Bossy, aren't we?"

"Shut up," I muttered, dabbing antiseptic onto his wound with far less gentleness than necessary. He hissed but didn't pull away, his gaze flickering to my face as I worked.

The silence between us thickened, weighed down by things unspoken, by the memory of that brutal ultimatum the Guild had forced on us. Betrayal was their currency, and they'd wanted to see us splinter, to plant seeds of doubt and watch us tear each other apart. But we hadn't given them the satisfaction. At least, not yet.

"Why didn't you?" His voice was barely a whisper, a question laced with tension.

I paused, my hands hovering over his wound, feeling the weight of his gaze. "Didn't I what?"

"Turn on me," he said, his eyes dark, searching. "You could have. The Guild gave you an out, and you... didn't take it."

I swallowed, the question twisting something inside me. "You think I'd just throw you to the wolves to save my own skin?" My voice came out harsher than I intended, more vulnerable, but I didn't care. I needed him to understand that whatever he thought of me, I wasn't that kind of person.

His gaze softened, and he shook his head, almost regretful. "No. I don't think you would. But the Guild... they have a way of twisting people. Making them forget who they are."

I wrapped the bandage around his arm, my fingers moving with a mechanical precision, but my thoughts were spinning. He was right—the Guild took people, broke them, molded them into tools, stripped them of anything that made them human. And yet, here we were, somehow clinging to the scraps of ourselves, refusing to let them dictate our choices.

When I finished bandaging his arm, I looked up, meeting his gaze. There was a question there, a vulnerability that he rarely showed, and it made my breath catch. "I won't turn on you, Damian," I said quietly. "Not now. Not ever."

For a moment, he just looked at me, something unreadable flickering in his eyes. Then he gave a slow nod, his lips quirking into a faint, almost reluctant smile. "Guess we're stuck with each other, then."

A laugh escaped me, a quiet, surprised sound that cut through the tension. "Guess we are."

We sat there in the alley, the city buzzing around us, a fragile truce settling between us. The Guild was still out there, watching, waiting, but for the first time, I felt something like hope, small and stubborn, taking root. Whatever lay ahead, we would face it together. And maybe—just maybe—that would be enough.

The city pulsed around us, a heart beating with secrets and dangers that waited, just beneath the surface, like hungry sharks circling in dark waters. We found ourselves on the edge of the sprawling district known for its secrets, its whispered transactions and hidden doors that led into places no one dared to speak of. The air here was thick, a heady blend of damp stone, old leather, and a lingering scent of smoke that clung to everything, a scent that felt as much a part of this city as the cobblestone streets beneath our feet.

Damian was quiet beside me, a rare thing that set my nerves humming. His silence was heavier than the usual brand of stoic he liked to wrap himself in; it was sharp, calculating, the silence of a man with something on his mind he couldn't—or wouldn't—say out loud. And I didn't push him, not yet. Whatever weight he carried, I had the sense it was better left undisturbed, at least for the moment.

"Where to now, fearless leader?" I asked, my tone light, though my pulse was anything but. I couldn't shake the feeling that every step brought us closer to some invisible edge, a line we'd been skirting for too long. I wanted to turn back, to find somewhere hidden where we could catch our breath, but Damian had a different idea.

"We go to the night markets," he said finally, his voice barely a murmur. "There's someone I need to speak to."

I arched an eyebrow. "Someone who won't sell us out to the Guild the second they lay eyes on us?"

His mouth twisted into a smirk that didn't reach his eyes. "Not everyone has your sunny outlook on life."

He didn't wait for me to respond, slipping into the narrow streets that wound toward the market district. The night markets were infamous—a network of stalls and makeshift shops that appeared like clockwork every evening and vanished by dawn, leaving no trace. It was a place where loyalty was bought and sold as easily as old trinkets, where no one asked questions, and everyone had something to hide. It wasn't exactly the kind of place you went to find allies.

As we walked, I kept glancing over my shoulder, a prickling feeling on the back of my neck. Someone was watching us—I could feel it, like the brush of cold fingertips against my skin. I sped up, closing the gap between Damian and me, and nudged him with my shoulder.

"Are you sure about this?" I asked, keeping my voice low.

He gave a slight nod, his eyes fixed ahead. "There's a man I know, goes by Grayson. If anyone can tell us what the Guild's next move is, it's him."

I frowned. "And why would he help us? Last I checked, information isn't exactly free in these parts."

Damian hesitated, a flicker of something unreadable in his gaze. "He owes me," he said simply. But there was a tightness in his voice, a shadow of something darker. It wasn't like Damian to be evasive, at least not with me. And that made me wonder what kind of debt this Grayson fellow carried, and why it weighed so heavily on Damian.

The night market appeared around us in a blur of colors and noise, people moving in and out of shadows, their faces hidden beneath hoods or masks, their voices low and urgent. Every corner seemed to hold a secret, every flickering lantern a promise or a threat. Vendors called out to us, offering everything from rare spices to black-market tech, the sort of items that drew the Guild's attention in all the wrong ways.

We wove through the crowd, Damian leading us with a confidence that belied the tense set of his shoulders. Finally, we reached a stall tucked into the far corner of the market, the sign barely visible beneath layers of dust and neglect. A tall, lean man lounged behind the counter, his eyes glittering like chips of onyx as he spotted us.

"Well, well, if it isn't the prodigal son," he drawled, his voice thick with sarcasm. "Come to cash in that favor, have you?"

Damian didn't bother with pleasantries. "I need information, Grayson."

Grayson's eyes flicked to me, his lips curling into a smirk. "And who's this? You bringing in strays now, Damian?"

I felt a flare of irritation but bit my tongue, letting Damian do the talking. Grayson was the kind of man who thrived on getting under people's skin, on drawing out reactions. I wasn't about to give him the satisfaction.

"Enough, Grayson," Damian said, his voice laced with steel. "The Guild's been setting traps, forcing us to turn on each other. We need to know what they're planning next."

Grayson leaned back, crossing his arms as he gave Damian a long, assessing look. "You think the Guild's gonna just let you walk away? That's not how they operate, and you know it. They want you to run, to think you're safe. Then they'll close the net, when you're comfortable. It's a classic tactic. And by the looks of it, you two are doing exactly what they want."

The words settled over me like a cold weight, and I saw Damian's jaw tighten, his hands clenching at his sides. Grayson didn't seem to notice—or care—that his words had struck a nerve.

"You know how they work," Damian said, his voice calm but deadly. "But you also know what it's like to be hunted. So unless you want to find out what it feels like to be on the other side of that equation, I suggest you start talking."

For a moment, Grayson looked at Damian, his gaze as sharp as a knife, but then he sighed, his shoulders sagging slightly. "Fine," he muttered. "But this is the last time, Damian. Consider us even."

He leaned closer, his voice dropping to a conspiratorial whisper. "The Guild's after something big, something they've been planning for months. They call it 'The Clearing.' It's supposed to wipe out anyone who's crossed them in the last year, a purge to clean house. But they're being careful—too careful. That means they're not just cleaning out the rank and file. They're after high-value targets, and that includes anyone who might've gotten too close to their secrets."

Damian's face darkened, his eyes narrowing. "And they think we know something?"

Grayson shrugged. "The Guild doesn't care what you know. It's what they think you might know that matters. And if they even suspect you're holding out on them, they'll come after you with everything they've got."

The words hung heavy between us, and I felt a shiver run down my spine. This wasn't just about survival anymore. It was about staying one step ahead, staying alive long enough to figure out what the Guild wanted so badly they'd risk hunting us down like animals.

Damian took a step back, nodding once, and I followed his lead, my thoughts racing. As we turned to leave, Grayson's voice stopped us, laced with something dark and ominous.

"Oh, and Damian?" he called out, his tone almost mocking. "Watch your back. Not all the traps the Guild sets are meant to be obvious."

We stepped back into the night, the city stretching out before us in a maze of alleys and empty promises. Damian's face was unreadable, but I knew one thing: whatever the Guild was planning, we'd be lucky to get out of this alive. And as we walked, every shadow seemed to close in tighter, every whisper taunting us, daring us to make one wrong move.

And then, from behind us, a sharp sound—a footstep, closer than it should have been. I spun, heart pounding, but the darkness was empty.

Chapter 16: A Kiss in the Shadows

The stone beneath my fingertips is cold, worn smooth from centuries of hands much holier than mine. Ancient whispers seem to rise from the shadows, voices lost to time but echoing now, swirling around us like old ghosts. I can feel Damian's gaze, unwavering and intense, and despite the lingering chill of our hasty retreat, there's a warmth in his eyes that ignites something in me I've kept buried. It's an inconvenient fire—one I would have snuffed out if I could.

"Let me see it," he says, voice barely a murmur, like anything louder might shatter the fragile peace between us. His hand reaches out, fingertips hovering just above my cheek, and the absurdity of it hits me—Damian, who could wield a dagger with an elegance that bordered on art, was afraid to touch me too roughly, as if I might break under the weight of his care. I almost laugh but stop myself, unwilling to let sarcasm ruin this moment.

"You're staring," I reply instead, a teasing note in my tone. It's meant to be lighthearted, a deflection. But he doesn't take the bait. His hand lingers in that unspoken space between us, his eyes tracing the scar along my cheek, the one that runs down to my jaw, a jagged reminder of battles fought and nearly lost.

"It suits you," he murmurs, his voice somehow more vulnerable than before. It's a strange thing to say, and even stranger to hear it without the sarcasm he usually favors. I raise an eyebrow, and for once, he looks away, his bravado slipping. "What I mean is, it shows that you're... stronger than anyone else I know."

That warmth in his gaze, as foreign as it is, makes me uneasy. I've been trained to take any display of affection as a trick, a weakness, or—at best—a temporary convenience. And Damian, my self-appointed protector and ever-sarcastic thorn in my side, isn't supposed to look at me this way. This is the same man who once sneered at my clumsiness in combat and called me "reckless." Now, he's looking at me like I'm something delicate. It's infuriating, and it's confusing, and I hate how much I don't actually hate it.

"Spare me the compliments, Damian," I say, rolling my eyes, though a hint of a smile betrays me. "You know I'm not here for praise."

His smirk returns, and it's a relief, like the snap back of a taut rubber band. Familiar and easy to brace against. He crosses his arms and leans back, studying me with a renewed sense of mischief. "Maybe not, but I think you secretly enjoy it," he says, his tone light. "I've seen the way you smile when no one's looking. It's like you're waiting for the world to give you a reason to laugh."

My heart does an odd twist at that. I keep my expression impassive, shrugging as though I haven't been caught off guard. "Maybe the world needs to try harder," I reply, letting the words hang between us.

The silence stretches, thick with unspoken things, and then, almost without realizing it, I take a step closer, drawn to the warmth in his voice, the softness I'd never expected to find in him. It's ridiculous, but here we are, two wounded souls hiding out in a cathedral with shattered windows and cracked walls. We're a far cry from saints. But right now, in this half-light, with the shadows swirling around us like forgotten prayers, it almost feels like absolution.

"Tell me something real," I say before I can stop myself. It's a foolish request, a slip of vulnerability that I might regret. Damian raises an eyebrow, a slow grin tugging at the corner of his mouth.

"You want something real?" he asks, his voice low, daring.

"Yes." My voice is barely more than a whisper, but it echoes through the cathedral, louder than I intend. I swallow, bracing myself. I know him too well to think he'll make this easy.

"Fine." He steps even closer, and the warmth of him is overwhelming, a stark contrast to the cool stone around us. I can see the faint scar above his eyebrow, a line from a fight we'd both barely escaped. He'd been the first to pull me out, despite my protests, his face set with grim determination. Now, his eyes hold that same resolve, but it's softened by something else. Something I almost recognize, but can't bring myself to name.

He reaches out, fingers brushing my chin, tilting my face up so that I'm forced to look him in the eye. "I've hated every second of this," he says, his voice barely a murmur, filled with a raw honesty that hits me like a punch. "Every second of watching you throw yourself into danger, fighting battles I can't always save you from. Every scar, every close call. It terrifies me more than I'd care to admit."

I blink, caught off guard by the vulnerability in his voice. It's like he's stripped away every wall he's ever put up, leaving himself bare, exposed. And I realize, with a jolt of clarity, that he's not just talking about fear. He's talking about something deeper, something I've spent so long ignoring that it feels foreign to acknowledge it now.

"Damian..." I don't know what to say, words slipping through my fingers like sand. He watches me, his expression unreadable, and for a moment, I think he's going to pull away, retreat into the familiar armor of sarcasm and indifference. But he doesn't.

Instead, he leans down, closing the distance between us, his breath warm against my cheek. His lips are barely an inch away, and I can feel my heart pounding, a reckless rhythm that matches the intensity in his gaze. And just as I'm about to lean in, drawn by an invisible force I can't explain, he stops, his eyes searching mine.

"If you don't want this, say it now," he murmurs, his voice low and rough. It's a challenge, but there's an unmistakable tenderness there too, a gentleness that I never expected from him. And in that moment, I realize that the choice is mine, that he's offering me something precious, something fragile and rare.

I take a breath, my voice steady despite the storm raging inside me. "I want this," I say, my words barely more than a whisper, but they feel like a confession, a leap of faith into the unknown.

And then, without another word, he closes the distance, his lips meeting mine in a kiss that's both fierce and gentle, a delicate balance of fire and restraint. It's like nothing I've ever felt before, a whirlwind of emotions that leaves me breathless, reeling. The world fades away, and for a few precious moments, there's only us, two souls tangled together in the shadows, finding solace in each other amidst the ruins.

The kiss lingers, neither of us daring to pull away, as if the slightest shift might unravel whatever fragile truce we've built here. His hand rests at the curve of my waist, the other tracing a slow path along my jaw, igniting a shiver that ripples through me like a whispered secret. I should step back, regain control, remind myself that I have no business letting him get this close. But the pull is magnetic, and here in this broken sanctuary, it's easier to forget all the rules I've spent years writing.

When we do finally break apart, it's like surfacing from underwater, the world rushing back with a vivid clarity that leaves me dizzy. I half-expect him to make a wry comment, to diffuse the tension with one of his usual quips. But Damian only stares, his expression solemn, as though he's just made some irrevocable decision.

"Now, that's one way to warm up," I say, a smile tugging at the corner of my lips, trying to inject a bit of levity into the moment. But my voice comes out softer than intended, a breath of laughter lost in the silence.

"Trust you to make a joke," he replies, but his voice lacks its usual edge. There's a gentleness there, a hesitation that feels foreign coming from him. I watch as he tilts his head, eyes tracing the faint patterns of stained glass on the stone floor, his expression pensive. "I know what you think of me," he says after a pause, his voice barely more than a murmur, as if he's confessing to the cathedral itself.

My pulse quickens, and I brace myself, wondering if he's going to ruin this with some sharp admission, an arrogant dismissal, the way he always does when we're too close for comfort. But he doesn't look at me; instead, he fixes his gaze on the darkened altar at the far end of the room, where shadows swallow up the ornate carvings like they're hiding secrets of their own.

"You think I'm reckless," he continues, his tone measured, as though he's piecing together words he's never said aloud. "And I am. I've done things... things I don't expect you to forgive or understand." He pauses, a muscle ticking in his jaw as he finally meets my gaze, and there's something raw and unguarded in his expression that pins me in place. "But for what it's worth, I don't take this lightly."

He lets the silence hang, heavy and tangible, before he drops his hand from my waist, taking a small step back. Instantly, I feel the cold air slip between us, filling the space where he'd just been, and it's as though some unspoken bond has frayed, leaving me adrift in its absence.

"Damian..." I start, but he shakes his head, offering a faint smile that doesn't reach his eyes.

"No speeches," he says, a flicker of his old bravado returning as he tucks his hands into his coat pockets, the faintest glint of humor rekindling in his gaze. "I know you've got a talent for them, but let's not ruin the moment."

I roll my eyes, grateful for the familiar bite of his sarcasm, even if it's just a mask. "And here I thought you liked my speeches," I say, managing a smirk, even though a part of me wants to reach out, to bring back that softness I'd glimpsed a moment ago.

"Oh, I enjoy them immensely," he replies, arching an eyebrow. "You're positively relentless. Terrifying, really."

For a moment, we stand there, the old dance of banter sparking between us, but there's an undercurrent now—a warmth, a hint of something that's more than just words. It's as if we're two actors suddenly aware of the stage, caught in a play that neither of us fully understands. I wonder if he feels it too, the strange weight of possibility hanging in the air.

Before I can untangle my own thoughts, a low rumble shakes the ground beneath us, sending a cascade of dust from the rafters. The sound is distant but unmistakable, a reminder of the world outside these walls, of the chaos we've managed to evade for the briefest of moments.

Damian's expression shifts instantly, his gaze sharpening as he moves toward the broken doorway, his every movement poised, alert. He's back in his element, the warrior ready for whatever danger waits beyond the stone walls. It's a relief, in a way, to see him slip so easily into his familiar armor. I follow, adjusting the strap of my pack, my fingers brushing against the hilt of the dagger tucked at my side.

The night outside is dark and heavy, the air thick with the scent of rain and smoke. We move swiftly, Damian's footsteps barely audible beside mine as we cut through the abandoned streets, weaving between crumbling buildings and shattered statues that loom like silent sentinels in the darkness. I can feel the adrenaline building again, the pulse of energy that always hits just before a fight, filling every inch of me with a razor-sharp clarity.

"Do you think they're still out there?" I ask, my voice low, as we slip into the shadows beneath a stone archway, the cold seeping through my jacket.

Damian nods, his gaze scanning the alleyway ahead, his eyes flickering with that familiar intensity. "They'll be looking for us," he replies, his tone matter-of-fact. "We left them with too many questions and not enough answers. People don't like that." He glances over at me, a wry smile tugging at his lips. "You're a bit of a mystery, you know."

"Coming from you, that's rich," I retort, but there's a spark of amusement in my voice, a welcome relief from the tension winding tight around us. I know he's right; we've left a trail, one that's bound to catch up with us sooner or later.

But as we move through the deserted streets, something else settles in me—a quiet resolve, a certainty that I hadn't felt before. Whatever happens next, I'm not backing down. We've come too far, faced too much, and I can't shake the feeling that this is exactly where I'm meant to be, dangerous as it is.

We pause beneath an old lamppost, its light flickering in the darkness like a wavering heartbeat. Damian turns to me, his gaze lingering just a moment too long, as though he's memorizing this instant, this fragile alliance we've built in the face of everything that's tried to tear us apart.

"What?" I ask, my voice softer than I intended, the question slipping out before I can stop it.

He shrugs, his expression unreadable as he holds my gaze. "Just making sure you're real," he says, a faint smile curving his lips. "It'd be a shame to find out you were just a figment of my imagination."

"Oh, I'm real," I reply, matching his smirk with one of my own. "And if you don't watch your back, I'll prove it."

His laugh is low, a rough sound that somehow makes my pulse quicken. And in that brief moment, under the flickering lamplight, with danger closing in from every side, I realize that, for all the uncertainty and fear, I wouldn't want to be anywhere else. The path ahead is treacherous, filled with risks I can't yet see, but there's a thrill in the unknown, a spark of exhilaration that I can't deny.

We slip back into the shadows, side by side, ready to face whatever waits in the dark.

The night presses in around us as we leave the cathedral, and I can feel the weight of it like a cloak. Damian's quiet beside me, his footsteps purposeful but silent, his gaze flickering to the shadows as if something might leap from them at any moment. The city is quiet, unnervingly so. I try to ignore the prickle of unease creeping up my spine, but the sense of being watched clings to us, thick and unshakable.

"Any idea where we're going?" I ask, keeping my tone casual, though I'm not sure I want the answer. The streets are a labyrinth of forgotten alleyways and twisting paths that seem to close in the further we go.

He glances at me, his expression unreadable. "Not a clue," he says with a grin that's far too smug for someone who might be getting us hopelessly lost. "But you'd get bored if I had a plan. I'm just keeping things interesting."

"Oh, right," I reply dryly, unable to help the faint smile that tugs at my lips. "Getting us both killed? Fascinating."

"Exactly." He laughs, but there's something strained in it, as if he's trying to convince himself as much as me. "Besides, you like a bit of danger. Admit it."

I roll my eyes, but I can't deny the truth in his words. There's a thrill in the unknown, in the sheer unpredictability of where this path is taking us. Yet the thrill is laced with fear, the kind that lurks in the back of your mind, nagging, pulling at the edges of your thoughts.

The flickering lamplight casts long shadows across his face, sharpening the angles of his jaw and the glint in his eyes. He looks like a creature forged from darkness and steel, like someone who's grown accustomed to living on the edge of the knife. I wonder, briefly, how long he's been running—if he's ever had a chance to simply be still.

"Stop staring," he says, though his tone is more amused than annoyed. "Or I'll start thinking you're falling for my charms."

"Please," I snort, but my heart betrays me with a skip. I'm not quite sure if he noticed, but he throws me a grin that seems to suggest he did. "Your charms," I add, "are about as subtle as a kick to the shins."

He laughs again, but it's softer this time, and something in it catches me off guard, like he's dropped the mask he wears so often. We walk in silence, each step bringing us deeper into the maze of abandoned buildings and forgotten streets. The air feels thick, each breath laced with the scent of damp stone and earth, like the city itself is holding its breath, waiting.

Then, ahead of us, there's a flash of movement—a figure disappearing around the corner, too quick to make out any details. My hand instinctively moves to my dagger, every nerve on high alert, but Damian's hand finds mine before I can draw it, holding me back with a warning glance.

"Wait," he whispers, his voice barely a breath. His grip on my hand is firm, grounding, and though my pulse pounds, I nod. We press ourselves against the wall, the cold stone digging into my back as we wait, listening to the silence. A faint rustle drifts toward us from the darkness, followed by a scrape of metal on stone.

He releases my hand and gestures for me to stay close. We creep forward, and as we reach the corner, I feel his fingers brush against mine—a brief, fleeting contact, but it's enough to steady me. We turn together, moving as one, and the narrow street opens up into a small courtyard. The figure stands at the center, cloaked in shadows, watching us with an air of unsettling calm.

"Going somewhere?" The voice is smooth, too smooth, and my stomach twists with a sharp jolt of recognition.

Standing before us is someone I haven't seen in years, someone I'd hoped to leave far behind. A smirk pulls at the corners of his mouth, and his gaze fixes on me with a predatory glint, as though he's been waiting for this exact moment.

"Elias," I say, the name tasting bitter on my tongue. My voice is steady, but I can feel the blood roaring in my ears, the adrenaline flooding my veins. Beside me, Damian tenses, his gaze flicking between us, sensing the shift in the air.

"It's been a while, hasn't it?" Elias says, his tone light, almost mocking. He takes a step closer, and I fight the urge to back away. "I was starting to think you'd forgotten about me."

"Trust me," I reply, forcing a smile. "I'd forget you in a heartbeat if I could."

Damian's gaze sharpens, and though he doesn't speak, I can feel the unspoken question hanging between us: Who is he?

Elias laughs, a low, dark sound that scrapes against the silence. "Still as sharp as ever, I see," he says, his eyes gleaming with something dangerous. "Though I'm disappointed to see you've picked up such questionable company." His gaze shifts to Damian, assessing, cold.

I step forward, placing myself between them, the weight of Elias's stare prickling across my skin. I'm painfully aware of Damian's presence behind me, of the tension radiating off him, and I know he's ready to fight if it comes to that. But this isn't his battle. This is mine.

"You don't get to be disappointed," I say, my voice low and firm, the anger simmering just beneath the surface. "You lost that right a long time ago."

For a heartbeat, something flickers in his expression, a glint of surprise, maybe even hurt, but it's gone as quickly as it appeared, replaced by a cool, calculating smile. He tilts his head, studying me with a look that makes my skin crawl.

"You're right," he says softly. "But I still have questions. So many questions."

Damian shifts beside me, his stance subtly defensive, and I know he's as tense as I am. The air between us crackles with the unspoken threat, and I feel my fingers itching to reach for my dagger, to put an end to this standoff before it spirals any further.

"Ask your questions," I say, my tone sharp. "But don't expect any answers."

He smiles, the expression slow and sinister, as though he's savoring some private joke. "Oh, I don't need answers from you," he replies, his gaze flicking to Damian, something sinister gleaming in his eyes. "I already know everything I need to know."

Before I can react, he raises a hand, and a blinding flash erupts from his fingertips, a brilliant arc of light slicing through the air. Instinctively, I throw myself to the side, grabbing Damian's arm and dragging him down as the light crashes into the wall behind us, sending a shower of stone and debris raining down.

We scramble to our feet, my heart pounding as the dust clears, but Elias is gone, his laughter echoing in the distance, leaving nothing but the faint scent of scorched stone. Damian turns to me, his face set with a hard, unspoken question, but I shake my head, a knot of dread tightening in my chest.

"Later," I manage to say, though my voice is barely steady. "We need to get out of here. Now."

Without another word, we slip back into the shadows, the danger of Elias's return hanging over us like a dark promise, our path suddenly more treacherous than before.

Chapter 17: The Path of Shadows

The cobbled streets were slick underfoot, the kind of wet that glistened darkly in the moonlight, like the world was made of obsidian and water. The air held a faint tang of salt and something else—like burnt sugar, thick and sweet, lingering from the alchemists' quarter. I felt Damian's presence beside me, his shoulder a steady line of warmth against the creeping chill that seemed to rise from the stones themselves. We walked in silence, each step muffled, as if even the night itself was conspiring to keep our path hidden. Or maybe it was simply the city's way—old, ancient as memory, and full of secrets it didn't want to share.

Damian didn't speak, but his silence said more than words could. He moved with a practiced grace, each step quiet, deliberate. For someone who was usually so cavalier, it was strange to see him this way, all tension and focus. I knew he was feeling it too, that thin line of doubt that wove between us, fragile and almost invisible, yet strong enough to hold us apart even as we walked side by side. Maybe it was the kiss—or maybe it was the simple fact that we were heading straight into danger, not for glory or gold, but for something far more complicated: trust.

We rounded a corner, and the narrow alleyway opened up into a courtyard, a forgotten slice of the city where time seemed to stand still. Ivy crawled up the cracked stone walls, and a single fountain bubbled faintly, its once grand statues eroded into soft, unrecognizable shapes. The scent of rosemary and mint wafted faintly from a neglected herb garden, its leaves shimmering with dew. Here, the city exhaled a quiet breath, undisturbed, almost sacred. Damian stopped, his eyes sweeping over the shadows that clung to the corners, his expression unreadable.

"Are you sure you're up for this?" His voice was low, barely louder than a whisper, but it cut through the stillness, grounding me.

I looked at him, his face half-hidden in the shadow of his hood, and felt the flicker of something I couldn't name. It was the kind of feeling that had teeth, sharp and hungry, a feeling that scared me almost as much as it thrilled me. "Are you?"

He gave a small, wry smile, one that didn't reach his eyes. "Depends on what 'this' is, doesn't it?"

I snorted, rolling my eyes. "Typical. Always dancing around the truth."

He leaned in, close enough that I could feel his breath against my cheek. "And what truth would that be?"

There was a challenge in his voice, a dare, and it pulled at something deep within me. I wanted to press forward, to ask him the questions that clawed at the back of my mind, but the words felt heavy, caught on the edge of a precipice I wasn't sure I wanted to fall into. So instead, I took a step back, slipping into the shadows.

"The truth," I said, my voice quieter now, almost thoughtful, "is that you're as terrified as I am. Of this. Of us. But you're too proud to admit it."

His expression didn't change, but I saw the flicker in his eyes, the brief moment of something raw and unguarded before he locked it away. He was quiet for a beat, then two, and I felt a pang of guilt for the words, sharp and unforgiving as they were.

But then, he laughed—a soft, almost reluctant chuckle that held no malice. "Maybe. Or maybe I'm just enjoying watching you squirm."

I rolled my eyes again, this time letting myself smile. "Ass."

The tension eased, just a little, replaced by the familiar banter that felt safer, easier. And yet, beneath it all, the uncertainty still lingered, a shadow that wouldn't quite disappear.

We moved through the courtyard, slipping past a crumbling archway that led to another alley, narrower and darker than the last. The walls here felt closer, pressing in, and I felt a shiver creep down my spine. There was something about this part of the city, something that felt different—watchful, almost alive. I glanced over at Damian, but his gaze was fixed ahead, his expression taut, unreadable.

Then, just as we reached the end of the alley, he stopped, holding out a hand to halt me. I felt my pulse quicken as I followed his gaze, and there, in the dim light, I saw it—a figure, cloaked and hooded, standing in the shadows just a few steps ahead. The figure was still, silent, and for a moment, I wondered if it was simply a trick of the light, a shadow cast by the flickering lantern hanging from the wall.

But then the figure shifted, a slight tilt of the head, and a voice, low and smooth, slid through the silence. "You're late."

Damian didn't move, didn't even flinch. "We weren't aware we had an appointment."

The figure chuckled, a soft, almost mocking sound that made my skin crawl. "Oh, but you did. The moment you decided to take something that wasn't yours, you made an appointment with me."

I felt a chill spread through me, and I instinctively took a step closer to Damian, my hand brushing against his. He glanced at me, a quick, reassuring look, and I felt a surge of defiance rise within me, cutting through the fear. I wouldn't let this stranger see my hesitation, wouldn't let them know how they unnerved me.

"What exactly do you want from us?" I asked, my voice steady despite the tremor in my chest.

The figure tilted their head, considering. "What I want," they said slowly, "is simple. A trade. What you took—for something far more valuable."

Damian raised an eyebrow, feigning disinterest. "And what makes you think we're interested in your trade?"

"Because," the figure replied, and though I couldn't see their face, I could feel the weight of their gaze, sharp and knowing, "you're in far deeper than you realize. And this path you're on? It only leads to ruin."

For a moment, the words hung in the air, heavy and ominous. I felt the weight of them settle over me, a cold, creeping dread that threatened to smother the flicker of resolve I'd been clinging to. But then, I caught a glimpse of Damian, his jaw set, his eyes hard with defiance, and the dread melted away, replaced by something fierce and unyielding.

I stepped forward, my chin raised, meeting the figure's shadowed gaze with one of my own. "Then I guess we'll just have to see about that, won't we?"

There was a beat of silence, and then, slowly, the figure nodded, a small, almost approving gesture. "Very well. But remember—every shadow has a cost. And some debts can never be repaid."

The stranger's words hung in the air, chilling as a winter wind slipping under a too-thin coat. Damian was the first to break the silence, his voice low and measured, carrying a touch of that infuriating calm he wore like armor. "Debts," he said, as if tasting the word, rolling it around like a wine he wasn't sure he liked. "An interesting choice of vocabulary for someone whose face we can't see."

The figure responded with nothing more than a slight incline of their head, as if granting us a magnanimous silence. Their hood slipped back just a fraction, enough to catch the gleam of eyes like molten silver, sharp and watchful. "I find," they replied, voice as soft as smoke, "that clarity can be overrated. Mystery... often works better."

I wasn't in the mood for cryptic nonsense, but Damian gave a slight nod, as if acknowledging some unspoken rule of engagement. He could be infuriatingly polite when the moment was least appropriate, as if bantering with shadowy figures in hidden alleyways was an ordinary Tuesday activity. And maybe for him, it was.

But I was done with riddles.

"Enough games," I said, stepping forward, feeling the cold press of anticipation coil in my stomach. "If you're so keen on this little 'trade,' let's see what you're offering. Show us what's so valuable."

A smile crept onto their lips, a soft, almost pitying curve, as if I were the one who'd missed some crucial part of this dance. They reached into the folds of their cloak, and I braced myself, expecting to see some small gleaming object, perhaps another artifact to tempt us. But instead, they drew out something surprising. It was a simple, folded piece of parchment, yellowed and curling at the edges.

I felt a surge of irritation. "A paper scrap?" I shot a glance at Damian, who met my gaze with a faint twitch of his eyebrow that seemed to say, Let's hear them out.

The figure, either unaware or utterly unbothered by my skepticism, held the parchment toward us. "There are things," they murmured, voice so soft I had to lean closer to catch the words, "that can only be understood when seen for yourself. Go on."

Damian took it, his fingers brushing against mine as he unfolded the parchment, the warmth of his hand a brief, disorienting contrast against the damp chill that settled over the courtyard. I leaned in to read, but the words themselves were strange—a series of symbols and looping script that made my head ache just to look at. But then, in the corner of my vision, something shifted. It was subtle, barely perceptible, but the words on the page began to dance, aligning themselves into phrases I could comprehend.

The instructions were as brief as they were cryptic: Follow the shadowed path where the twin rivers meet. There lies a key, hidden by those who guard it with silence.

My heart sank as I reread the words, realizing the figure's little "trade" wasn't much of an answer. It was just another question wrapped up in a riddle, and frustration built up, thick and bitter.

I exhaled, glancing up at Damian, who was studying the paper with an intensity that made it clear he was already working on solving the next step. The stranger observed us quietly, the faintest glimmer of satisfaction in their eyes, as if enjoying some private joke we'd yet to understand.

Damian finally lowered the parchment, folding it back carefully. "And what's your part in all of this? If we're to go on a wild chase after a 'key,' I'd at least like to know who's giving us directions."

The figure let out a low chuckle, almost affectionate. "Knowing would spoil the fun, wouldn't it?"

He scoffed, glancing at me with a bemused grin that was gone in a flash. "Maybe you're right," he muttered, then shot a last, narrowed look at the figure. "But you'd better hope we find what we're looking for. If not, this city might have one less mystery to worry about."

The figure's only response was a slight bow, before melting back into the shadows, their form blending with the night until they disappeared entirely. I waited, heart pounding, wondering if they'd reappear just as suddenly, but the silence settled back over the courtyard, thick and final.

Once they were gone, I turned to Damian, who was already focused on the task ahead, his expression more intense than I'd seen in days. "So... the place where the 'twin rivers meet.' Does that ring any bells?"

"Only one," he replied, tucking the parchment into his pocket. He gestured for me to follow him as we made our way through the winding alleys, his steps quick and purposeful. "There's a place on the city's east side. Locals call it the Veiled Crossing—where two old canals intersect. It's mostly abandoned now, save for a few... let's say less-than-friendly types."

I raised an eyebrow. "You mean the kind of people who might prefer to keep their secrets buried?"

"Exactly." His tone was grim, but there was a spark in his eyes that betrayed a hint of excitement. "If that key is anywhere, it'll be there."

We navigated the city streets, slipping through narrow alleys and crossing forgotten courtyards that seemed to whisper old secrets with every gust of wind. The silence between us was a comfortable one, our footsteps echoing softly on the stone. The path grew darker as we ventured east, the buildings looming taller, casting long shadows that twisted and stretched like fingers reaching out to grasp us.

Finally, we reached the edge of the Veiled Crossing, where two narrow canals met in a dark, murky swirl. The water was still, too still, and I felt a prickle of unease crawl up my spine as I peered down into its depths. Something about this place felt wrong, like the air itself was holding its breath, waiting.

I turned to Damian, who was surveying the area with that focused intensity, his eyes scanning every shadow. "So, do we just start digging? Or should we wait for the ghosts to give us a sign?"

He grinned, a quick flash of teeth. "I wouldn't put it past them. But if that parchment's right, then we need to look for a hidden entrance—something small, easily overlooked."

With that, we began our search, combing through the narrow bank beside the water, poking and prodding at loose stones and half-rotted wooden planks. But every stone seemed to lead us to another dead end, and the frustration grew like an itch I couldn't scratch.

Just as I was about to voice my impatience, Damian's fingers brushed against something cold and metallic, wedged between two stones at the water's edge. He knelt, examining it more closely, and I watched as he gently pried a small, rusted handle from the crevice. Slowly, he turned it, and with a low, grinding sound, a section of the stone bank shifted, revealing a narrow, dark passage leading down into the earth.

I glanced at him, my heart pounding. He gave a nod, the hint of a grin playing at his lips. "After you."

"Why do I feel like this is the start of something terrible?" I muttered, but stepped forward anyway, my pulse thrumming with a mix of fear and exhilaration.

As I descended into the darkness, with Damian close behind, I couldn't shake the feeling that we were plunging into something far deeper than we'd ever anticipated, something that would test every hidden fear and lingering doubt. But with each step, that thrill only grew sharper, slicing through the uncertainty with a heady, dangerous clarity.

The air in the narrow passage was stale, thick with the scent of damp earth and decay, like stepping into the lungs of something ancient and long forgotten. Each footstep echoed, the sound bouncing off the stone walls, reverberating back at us with an eerie hollowness. I held my breath, straining my ears for any sound beyond our own movements, anything to suggest we weren't alone down here.

Damian was a steady presence behind me, his hand occasionally brushing against my shoulder as we squeezed through the passage, which seemed to grow narrower the further we went. Despite the creeping unease, a thrill simmered beneath my fear, and I felt it was mutual. This wasn't just another alley or courtyard in the city; we were descending into the hidden heart of it, into layers most people never saw.

He muttered something under his breath as we approached a junction, where the tunnel branched off into three different directions. I glanced back at him, raising an eyebrow. "Care to share your brilliant insight, or are you planning to keep the ominous muttering to yourself?"

He smirked, that infuriatingly calm expression of his barely dimmed by the dim light. "It's called 'thinking,'" he replied dryly. "And if you're nice, maybe I'll even let you in on it."

I rolled my eyes. "I'm quaking with anticipation."

He leaned closer, glancing down the three tunnels with a calculating look. "If that parchment was right—and that's a mighty 'if'—then we're looking for the left passage. Old city records show it was part of a network for the original watchmen. Probably hasn't been used in years, but with a little luck..."

I didn't let him finish. "Luck? Oh, good. I'm glad we're basing our lives on that."

He chuckled softly, the sound bouncing off the walls, oddly comforting in the gloom. "Think of it as an adventure, then. Keeps the stakes interesting."

"Define 'interesting.'" I muttered, but I took the lead down the left passage anyway, moving forward into the darkness with a determined, if slightly shaky, resolve.

The air grew colder as we continued, prickling my skin in a way that felt less like temperature and more like a warning. Faint, unfamiliar markings appeared on the walls—strange symbols carved into the stone, some weathered and nearly erased with time. They reminded me of the symbols on the parchment, sharp lines and curves that twisted into impossible patterns. I felt a twinge of unease as we passed them, an instinctual discomfort, like my body recognized something my mind couldn't comprehend.

"Tell me, do you think we're getting closer, or are we just enthusiastically lost?" I glanced back, aiming for humor but betraying a bit of my nerves.

"Both, if we're being optimistic," he replied, the faintest hint of a smirk curling at his lips. "I'd say we're following the right signs, though. Those markings... they look like the ones on the artifact we found in the library archives."

I squinted at the nearest one, trying to match it to the intricate designs I'd studied earlier that day, but it was difficult in the low light. "Lovely," I said, with forced cheer. "So at least we're following creepy, ancient graffiti. I feel much better."

He chuckled, and that small bit of levity made it easier to push forward, step by cautious step. The tunnel twisted, leading us down a steep incline, and soon I heard it—a faint, rhythmic sound, like the whisper of water against stone. I held up a hand to signal for quiet, and we both listened, ears straining.

Water.

It flowed somewhere nearby, hidden beyond the walls, its sound both soothing and ominous. As we moved further, the noise grew louder, until we turned a final corner and found ourselves at the edge of an underground chamber, the source of the sound finally revealed.

A massive, subterranean river cut through the stone, its dark waters swirling and churning in relentless motion. It looked as though it had been running there for centuries, carving its own path through the rock. A narrow stone bridge spanned the river, its surface slick with moisture, leading to an alcove on the other side where a small, carved door was set into the wall. The door was plain but for one detail—a brass sigil in the shape of a coiled serpent, its eyes small emeralds that glittered even in the dim light.

"Do you think that's the keyhole?" I asked, pointing to the serpent.

Damian's eyes narrowed as he studied it, nodding slowly. "If not, it's a spectacular coincidence."

We exchanged a glance, a shared look of determination that required no words. He stepped onto the bridge first, moving with careful precision. I followed, every nerve on edge as my boots slipped slightly on the damp stones. Beneath us, the river surged, cold and powerful, as if waiting for any misstep to pull us under.

We made it to the other side without incident, and Damian stepped up to the door, examining the serpent closely. "There's an inscription," he murmured, his finger tracing the edge of the brass. "It says, 'Only the bearer of truth shall pass.'"

I couldn't help a sarcastic huff. "And what exactly is that supposed to mean? Do we give it a heartfelt confession, or what?"

Damian shook his head, but there was a glint in his eyes that told me he had a guess, one he wasn't fully comfortable with. "There's something... specific about this. I think it's a magical barrier of some kind, one that only lets someone through if they're sincere in their intent."

I raised an eyebrow. "So we just stroll up, declare we're here for completely noble reasons, and hope the door believes us?"

"Something like that," he muttered, frowning.

Taking a breath, I stepped forward, focusing on the door. "We're here for answers," I said softly, and as I spoke, I felt an odd warmth settle in my chest, as though the truth of my words anchored me to the ground. "We're here because we want to understand what lies beneath this city and what it's hiding from us."

The serpent's eyes flashed, and, to my surprise, the door shuddered slightly, as though considering my words. I glanced at Damian, who gave me a faint, approving nod, and I felt a surge of confidence rise within me.

Then he stepped forward, placing a hand on the door. "I'm here because I have nowhere else to be," he murmured, his voice almost too low to hear. "And because, for the first time, there's something I don't want to lose."

My heart did a strange, unexpected flutter, and I felt a flush rise to my cheeks as the serpent's eyes flared bright, bathing the small alcove in an eerie green glow. The door gave a low, rumbling groan, then slowly swung open, revealing a narrow staircase leading down into an abyss of darkness.

Damian looked at me, a wry smile barely disguising the tension on his face. "Ladies first?" he quipped, though I could see the flicker of unease in his eyes.

"Only if you promise not to stare at my back too hard," I shot back, masking my own nerves with a grin. But as I stepped onto the first stone stair, the smile faded, replaced by a prickling sense of dread and excitement that made my heart race.

The air grew colder, heavier, as we descended, and I could feel the weight of the city pressing down on us, layer upon ancient layer. Shadows stretched longer, twisting into shapes that seemed to shift just beyond the edges of my vision, and an oppressive silence settled around us, broken only by the faint drip of water echoing through the dark.

Finally, we reached the bottom of the staircase, and what we found there stole the breath from my lungs. A vast, cavernous room stretched before us, filled with towering statues and crumbling pillars, each one carved with intricate, unsettling faces frozen in expressions of anguish and fury. At the far end of the room, a pedestal gleamed, illuminated by a strange, pulsing light that seemed to come from nowhere.

Damian moved to my side, his gaze fixed on the pedestal. "That's it," he whispered, voice tinged with awe. "The artifact."

But before we could take a single step forward, a voice echoed from the shadows, low and mocking. "I wouldn't touch that if I were you."

Every muscle in my body went rigid as I whipped around, heart hammering, and there, emerging from the darkness, was a figure wrapped in shadow, eyes gleaming with dangerous intent.

Chapter 18: The Stone Guardian

I didn't expect the air to be warm down here. Not in the belly of the earth where the world is little more than slabs of stone overhead, arching low and close enough to make the bravest soul feel like they're suffocating. But as I breathe in, the atmosphere clings, sticky and thick, like molasses and melted candle wax.

Damian, naturally, is unaffected. I can see him, tall and stalwart as he scans the chamber, brows furrowed and lips pressed into a single, focused line. I'd been so sure that beneath the solemn facade, he was as human as the rest of us, with quirks and flaws hidden beneath his chiseled, intimidating features. But now, with his easy strength and unflinching gaze, I begin to wonder if there's something colder at the core. My fingers drift toward the hidden blade at my side—a silly habit, maybe, but comforting all the same.

"I don't like this," I mutter, more to myself than anyone else, but the echo betrays me, bouncing off the curved walls like I'd shouted. Damian's head turns in my direction, his dark eyes glinting, catching the faint glimmer of torchlight flickering off ancient sconces.

"Neither do I," he replies, low and even, with a careful edge that tells me he's weighing his words. A trace of discomfort? I almost laugh, picturing his controlled expression cracking at the edges.

The chamber stretches out around us in an intricate grid, the walls etched with sprawling symbols, winding and curling like vines, twisting into patterns that shimmer faintly as if lit from within. I can't read them—no one could, not without years spent poring over ancient texts, trying to piece together a language that no living scholar has fully understood. But there's a whisper, something tugging at the edge of my mind. A quiet knowledge, or maybe just dread. I shiver, fingers tightening on my blade, knowing that whatever lies within those markings wasn't written for my eyes.

Damian steps forward, just a hair's breadth away from the arcane lines on the ground, then glances back at me with a look I've come to recognize: cautious, controlled, and silently asking if I'm sure I want to go further. The truth is, I'm not, and I'm pretty sure he knows it. But it's too late to turn back now. We're closer to our goal than we've ever been, closer than anyone's been in centuries. And maybe—just maybe—closer than we should be.

As we press on, the temperature rises. Every breath tastes thicker, tinged with an earthy bitterness. The floor begins to slope, a subtle descent that forces us to lean forward, to tread lightly as if the stone beneath our feet might splinter and shatter at any moment. I reach out to steady myself against the wall and pull my hand back immediately—the surface is hot, pulsing with a heat that feels alive, as if the rock itself is drawing breath.

And then I see it—the outline of a door, a massive, hulking slab of stone embedded within the wall, framed by a faint, shimmering light. My pulse quickens. This is it. This is what we came for.

But Damian's hand snaps out, catching my wrist in a firm but careful grip before I can move another inch. I open my mouth to protest, but he shakes his head, eyes flicking toward the shadows pooling in the far corner of the room. At first, I don't see anything—just darkness, thick and unmoving, blending into the cavern's natural gloom. But then, slowly, the shadows begin to shift, and a figure emerges. Stone-grey and hulking, it steps into the faint light, and I catch my breath, instinctively shrinking back as I take in the creature before us.

It stands well over seven feet, its body molded from rock, and yet it moves with an eerie, almost liquid grace. Its eyes are empty, hollow, and somehow all the more terrifying for it. There's an intelligence lurking in the way it stands, the way it cocks its head, watching us with an unnerving stillness. And then it speaks—a voice that is less sound and more vibration, rolling through the chamber in waves, making the stone beneath us tremble.

"You do not belong here."

The words are plain, devoid of malice, but heavy with purpose. It's a warning, a final chance to turn back. I can feel Damian's grip on my wrist tighten, just for a moment, as if reminding me that he's there, but I barely register it. All I can think is that this is it—the creature that stands between us and the artifact we've risked everything for.

I should be scared, and in a way, I am. But there's something else, too—an itch, a burning curiosity that refuses to back down. Maybe it's the madness of the journey, the countless nights spent chasing shadows and whispers, the sheer hunger to understand what lies beyond. Or maybe I'm just a fool. Either way, I pull my wrist from Damian's grasp and step forward.

"Step aside," I say, my voice sharper than I intend. My fingers brush the hilt of my blade, though I doubt steel would do much good against living rock. "We've come too far to stop now."

The creature's empty gaze fixes on me, and for a moment, I swear I see something flicker in those hollow eyes—a glimmer of amusement, or pity, I can't tell. It says nothing, simply watches as I draw my blade, though the gesture feels pitiful in the face of such a formidable presence. My heart pounds, each beat a drum against my ribs as I brace myself, ready for the inevitable clash. Beside me, Damian falls into a stance, his movements smooth and practiced, a silent agreement to fight by my side.

The guardian moves with a swiftness that belies its stony form, lurching forward in a blur of stone and shadow. It strikes, one massive arm swinging toward us, and I barely manage to dodge, feeling the air whip past my face with the force of its attack. Damian deflects the blow with a blade that glows faintly in the dim light, and for a second, I feel the slightest hope that we might actually stand a chance.

But then I catch the look in Damian's eyes—an uncharacteristic flash of doubt, a hesitation that sends a chill down my spine. He's always been the steady one, the unbreakable force at my side. If even he doubts, then maybe this fight is truly beyond us.

A sharp crack echoes through the chamber as Damian's blade connects with the creature's arm, a spark of light flickering between stone and steel. The guardian doesn't falter; instead, it seems to absorb the blow, its eyes flickering with something akin to amusement. The unnerving calm in its gaze makes me grit my teeth. Damian and I are giving it everything we have, and this thing hasn't even broken a metaphorical sweat.

I dodge another swing, barely keeping my balance on the uneven ground. The air feels thicker, each breath tinged with that strange earthy scent. I'm half convinced the creature is breathing with us, inhaling and exhaling in sync, as if mocking our mortal need for air.

Damian glances at me, his face stony, unreadable. That's his thing—no matter the situation, he's always the picture of calm, as though he's got a backup plan stashed somewhere, waiting for just the right moment. But I know him too well. Beneath that quiet resolve, there's tension in his movements, a sliver of doubt that makes my stomach tighten. Whatever confidence he had when we entered this chamber is fading.

"Any bright ideas?" I ask, dodging the guardian's next strike with a less-than-graceful twist that sends me sprawling against the wall.

"Survive," he replies, without looking at me, his focus fixed on the creature.

"Helpful," I mutter, pushing myself back to my feet. I tighten my grip on the blade, cursing the fact that we don't have any ancient, mystical weapon capable of defeating this stone monstrosity. Just a couple of ordinary blades and whatever scraps of courage we can scrounge up.

I've fought plenty of battles, faced down dangers that would make most people lose their nerve. But this... this feels different. The creature isn't just strong—it's ancient, woven from the same magic as the artifact we came to retrieve. The realization settles heavily in my mind, like a stone dropped into dark water. If this guardian is part of the artifact, then maybe it's not guarding it so much as testing anyone who dares to come this close.

And yet, here we are, ill-prepared but stubborn enough to try.

Damian manages to get close, his blade slicing a faint crack along the creature's forearm, and for a second, I allow myself a flicker of hope. But then the guardian straightens, twisting its arm as if inspecting the damage. The crack seals itself, the rock melding back together like water healing over a cut. Damian takes a sharp step back, his jaw clenched.

"I think it likes you," I say, and despite the situation, I can't help the grin tugging at my lips.

"Great. I'll send it a thank-you note."

He shifts slightly, positioning himself between me and the creature. His gaze flickers, a quick, assessing glance that seems to measure my exhaustion and find me lacking. I almost snap at him, but I know he's only doing what he's always done—putting himself in harm's way to keep the people he cares about safe.

Except we can't keep doing this forever. Every second we spend here, the guardian seems to grow stronger, as if drawing power from the very air around us. It lunges forward, and Damian shoves me to the side, taking the brunt of the impact himself. He hits the ground hard, his body colliding with the stone floor with a sickening thud. I scramble to his side, grabbing his arm and pulling him up.

"You don't get to die in some underground dungeon," I say, my voice rough. "Not on my watch."

"And here I thought you enjoyed the thrill of the unknown," he replies, his smile faint but there.

The guardian stands motionless, as if waiting for us to make our move. I can feel its gaze boring into us, a silent judgment. It could crush us in seconds, and yet it holds back, as if testing our resolve. A thought occurs to me, something wild and ridiculous, and yet the only idea that makes sense. The creature is waiting for something—something that doesn't involve brute strength or sharp steel.

"Put the blade down," I say, not quite believing the words even as I say them.

Damian stares at me, a flicker of confusion in his eyes. "You want me to disarm myself in front of a rock monster?"

"Trust me," I reply, though it's unclear if I'm saying it to convince him or myself.

With a reluctant sigh, he lowers his weapon, letting it drop to the ground. The sound echoes, the blade clattering against stone, and I follow suit, letting go of my own weapon. The guardian's eyes narrow, its massive head tilting as if it hadn't expected this turn of events. The tension in the air shifts, subtle but undeniable. It takes a step back, watching us with what almost seems like curiosity.

Damian raises an eyebrow. "Well, that's... unexpected."

"I think it wants something else," I say, my mind racing. If this thing isn't here to kill us outright, then maybe there's a way to pass whatever twisted test it's putting us through.

The guardian moves toward us, each step sending vibrations through the floor. I resist the urge to back away, standing my ground as it looms over us. It raises one massive arm, and I brace myself, unsure if this is about to end in disaster. But instead of striking, it points toward a symbol on the wall behind us—a single, intricate marking that glows faintly, pulsing in time with the creature's movements.

"Do you see that?" I whisper, and Damian nods, his gaze fixed on the symbol.

Without a word, we move toward it, the guardian following at a careful distance. I can feel its gaze on us, watchful but no longer threatening. The symbol is unlike any I've seen before, swirling patterns twisting into shapes that seem to shift the longer you look at them. My fingers reach out, almost instinctively, drawn by the faint warmth emanating from the wall.

"Are you sure this is a good idea?" Damian asks, his voice low but tense.

"Not even a little bit," I reply, but I press my hand to the symbol anyway.

A surge of energy pulses through me, powerful and all-consuming, as if the very essence of the chamber has come alive in my veins. The guardian remains still, its hollow eyes watching as the symbol flares to life, casting a warm glow across the room. I feel something shift, a release, as though the air itself has sighed in relief.

When the light fades, the guardian steps back, its form softening, the rigid lines of stone giving way to something almost human. It nods once, a solemn gesture of acknowledgment, before stepping aside, revealing the path beyond.

"Looks like we passed," Damian says, his voice filled with a mixture of relief and awe.

I let out a shaky breath, feeling the weight of the moment settle over me.

The glow from the symbol fades, leaving us in near darkness again, save for the dim torchlight flickering against the walls. But the path before us is clear now, the guardian standing aside as if granting us passage. I don't dare look back at it, lest I accidentally offend whatever strange magic has granted us this uneasy truce. Damian's breath, slightly uneven, is the only sound that cuts through the thick silence, and for once, I'm grateful for his steadiness. I'm not sure if it's out of courage or some fatalistic sense of adventure, but together we move forward into the narrow passage that stretches beyond the guardian's lair.

The walls here are closer, the air cooler, with a strange dampness that clings to my skin. Each step we take echoes sharply, bouncing back and forth down the corridor until it fades into silence. It feels as if we're walking into the very heart of the earth, deeper and deeper, as if the weight of all the stone above presses down, eager to swallow us whole.

"Why is it that I get the feeling this isn't just a quick stroll to the artifact?" Damian's voice is low, and I can hear the thin thread of humor lacing his tone. The quip feels as much for my benefit as his own, an attempt to lighten the thick, creeping tension.

"Because every adventure that involves ancient magic and stone guardians usually ends with... well, more surprises." I keep my voice steady, though I can't help glancing over at him, half-expecting to see a grin pulling at the corner of his mouth.

"Ah, so it's the 'probably doomed but let's keep going' kind of surprise."

"The best kind," I reply, trying for a smile. It lands somewhere between confidence and grim determination, and he gives me an approving nod.

The corridor soon opens into another chamber, smaller and less grand than the one we left behind. Here, the walls are plain, devoid of the glowing symbols or intricate carvings that marked the guardian's lair. The only thing in this room is a pedestal at its center, unadorned and sturdy, with a faint shimmer above it—the artifact.

It's smaller than I'd imagined, a simple orb made of some glass-like material, suspended in the air, glinting softly in the dim light. There's nothing especially impressive about it; no radiant glow, no thrumming energy that suggests it holds untold power. Just a small, unassuming sphere that hovers a few inches above the pedestal, as if waiting for someone to take it.

"So... that's it?" Damian's voice breaks the silence, carrying the same undercurrent of doubt that I feel.

"Looks like it," I say, but I don't move. Something feels off, as if we're standing in the eye of a storm that hasn't yet hit. Every instinct I have is screaming at me to turn around and run, and yet I'm rooted to the spot, unable to tear my eyes away from the orb.

Damian steps forward, but I grab his arm, pulling him back. "Wait."

His eyes meet mine, questioning but trusting, and I try to steady my thoughts. I don't know what I'm afraid of, but the sense of foreboding is impossible to ignore. "What if this is another test?" I ask, my voice barely above a whisper. "What if taking it isn't as simple as it seems?"

He sighs, running a hand through his hair, and I can see the wheels turning in his mind. "We don't exactly have a lot of options," he says after a moment, his tone resigned. "We didn't come all this way to leave empty-handed."

I nod, reluctantly releasing his arm, though every fiber of my being wants to stop him. I can't shake the feeling that whatever happens next will change everything, in ways we can't possibly understand. He steps forward, extending a cautious hand toward the orb, his fingers just inches from its surface. The air around us seems to shift, a sudden rush of cold that prickles against my skin, raising the hairs on the back of my neck.

The moment he touches it, the chamber trembles, a low rumble that reverberates through the floor and walls. The orb pulses, a brief flash of light that blinds us both, and I stagger back, shielding my eyes. When I blink away the spots from my vision, I see Damian frozen in place, his hand still on the orb, but his face twisted in pain.

He's not moving, not even breathing, as if trapped in some invisible hold.

"Damian!" I shout, rushing forward, panic tightening my chest. I grab his arm, trying to pull him away, but he's rooted to the spot, unyielding. The cold seeps into my fingers, a biting chill that spreads up my arm, and I stumble back, gasping as the cold wraps around my heart, squeezing like a vice.

And then I hear it—a voice, soft and disembodied, echoing through the chamber. It's not speaking in any language I understand, but the words press into my mind, each syllable sharp and jagged, like shattered glass against my thoughts. It's an ancient, primal language, carrying the weight of centuries, and I can feel its intent as clearly as if it were shouting.

The voice demands something, a payment or sacrifice, though I can't understand the exact words. The only thing I know is that it wants something in return for the artifact, something we weren't prepared to give. I look back at Damian, still trapped, his eyes closed, his face pale and drawn.

I'm out of options. Desperation claws at me, and I press my hand to my chest, feeling the faint warmth of the locket hidden beneath my shirt. It's an old heirloom, something passed down through my family, rumored to hold protective magic. I'd never put much stock in it, but now, with Damian's life on the line, I have nothing left to lose.

Without thinking, I tear the locket from my neck, the chain snapping easily, and I hold it out toward the orb, my heart pounding in my chest. The chamber seems to respond, the cold easing just slightly, as if considering my offering. The voice quiets, a strange calm settling over the room, and I close my eyes, hoping, praying that this will be enough.

There's a sudden warmth, a soft, pulsing heat that spreads from the locket in my hand. I feel it resonate through the air, wrapping around me like a protective shield, pushing back the icy grip that had seized my heart. The light around the orb dims, the tension in the room easing as the voice fades into silence.

When I open my eyes, Damian is free, stumbling back, gasping for air. He looks at me, confusion and relief mingling on his face, and I can barely breathe, relief washing over me in waves.

But the orb is gone. The pedestal is empty, the shimmering light that had once surrounded it vanished. And in its place is a small, unfamiliar figure—a childlike shape, pale and translucent, standing quietly where the artifact had been, watching us with wide, curious eyes.

Before I can react, the figure speaks, its voice soft and hauntingly familiar, a voice I recognize but can't place. It tilts its head, staring at me, and the chamber around us begins to blur, the walls melting away, replaced by a swirling darkness that encircles us, pulling us deeper into the unknown.

Damian grabs my hand, his grip tight and reassuring, but it's the last thing I feel before the darkness swallows us whole.

Chapter 20: Shadows of Sacrifice

The chamber walls breathe with a silence that feels heavy, almost oppressive, the stillness settling around us like the remnants of a storm that left too much broken and not enough salvageable. My heartbeat is still pounding in my ears, too loud, too uneven, like it's trying to remind me of something I can't quite recall. Damian stands beside me, his breathing ragged, the flickering torchlight casting long shadows across his face, illuminating the conflict in his eyes. I don't ask why he hesitated during the fight, but the question pulses between us, unanswered, dense as the dark stone walls surrounding us.

He avoids my gaze, brushing a hand through his dark hair, looking anywhere but at me. It's as though he's willing himself to disappear, to dissolve into the silence before he has to speak whatever truth he's been hiding all this time. My stomach twists, the burn of doubt curling into something sharper, something that scratches at the surface of my certainty, threatening to pull it apart thread by fragile thread. But he's not going anywhere—not this time.

He lets out a low, mirthless laugh, more for himself than me, a sound so dry it could crumble. "I bet you'd laugh if I told you that this was the one place I swore I'd never come back to."

"Doesn't sound like much of a joke," I reply, crossing my arms, trying to hide the shake in my hands. "More like the setup to a tragic monologue."

"Oh, I promise it's more of a tragedy than anything you'd be prepared for." His voice is soft, like he's talking to the stones instead of me, as though speaking the words aloud would invite them to close in around him.

I wait, biting down on every question, every plea, because in this place, under the weight of secrets and sacrifices, I feel that whatever Damian's about to say might be the only truth he's ever told me.

"There was a deal," he starts, looking at his hands, clenching and unclenching his fists as if that would help him hold onto his words. "A deal I made before I ever met you. One that... well, let's just say it bound me to certain... obligations." He glances at me then, a brief, haunted look, his dark eyes swimming with something like regret, and I feel my pulse stutter.

"A deal?" I echo, and the words taste bitter, like the air in this cursed chamber. "And what does that have to do with me?"

His shoulders tense, and he laughs again, a humorless sound. "Everything."

The silence is thicker now, pressing against my chest, choking any semblance of calm. I can feel my heart pounding faster as he searches for the words, his mouth opening and closing as if the sentences are too jagged, too sharp to let out all at once.

"To get my freedom," he says, and there's something raw in his voice, something that makes my spine go cold. "I had to agree to deliver something to them. The artifact... and the person who could find it." He stumbles over the last words, and they hit me like stones, each one sinking in deeper than the last.

I don't breathe. I don't blink. I just stare, feeling the ground sway beneath me, my chest tightening with a pain that's both familiar and foreign, an ache that comes from seeing every inch of trust I've given him splinter into pieces that I'm not sure will ever fit back together.

"You're lying," I manage, though the words taste hollow, empty. "You... you wouldn't betray me. Not now. Not after..." My words trail off, unfinished, and I can't bear to look at him.

But he doesn't argue, doesn't try to convince me otherwise. He just watches me, his expression a battlefield of remorse and determination. It's that look that makes the truth unbearable. He isn't lying. He's been waiting for this, waiting to confess, like a man already condemned to the gallows.

"When I made the deal, I didn't know you," he says softly, his voice barely more than a whisper. "You were just... a name, a task. Something distant, unimportant. But when I met you, when I saw you..." He pauses, and his voice cracks, his hands clenching into fists as if he could somehow hold himself together through sheer willpower. "It stopped being that simple. I can't turn back now, but... I wish I could."

I wish I could hate him, wish I could yell, scream, or break something. But all I feel is a strange numbness, a hollow emptiness that settles deep in my bones, like this betrayal was always inevitable, like I should've seen it coming from the beginning. The warning signs had been there, the flickers of hesitation, the moments of silence, the half-truths that had felt off but never blatant enough to catch.

"You could have told me," I say, barely hearing my own voice over the crushing weight of disappointment. "You could have given me a choice."

His expression shifts, a flash of something like agony crossing his features. "And what would you have done? Run? Left me here to deal with this alone? Or tried to save me, even if it meant losing everything you've worked for?"

I don't answer, because I don't know. I don't want to know.

The chamber seems colder now, the shadows darker, like they're swallowing the space between us. I want to turn away, to leave him here with his regrets and broken promises, but I can't bring myself to move. Because, despite everything, a part of me still believes in him, in the version of him that's tried to protect me, fought beside me, laughed with me. It feels like clinging to smoke, but it's all I have left.

"So, what now?" I ask, my voice steady but empty, the words void of any expectation or hope.

He doesn't answer right away. His gaze drops, his expression shadowed, and for a moment, I think he's not going to say anything at all. But then he takes a slow breath, lifting his eyes to meet mine with a haunted resolve that chills me to my core.

"I don't know," he says finally, his voice barely more than a whisper. "But I do know that, for the first time, I don't want to follow the path that was set for me. Not if it means losing you."

Damian's words linger in the air between us, thick and unyielding, like the dust that settles heavy on forgotten things. It's strange how a single revelation can splinter through the foundation of a moment, leaving everything around it cracked and warped, like nothing could ever fit together the same way again. I try to breathe, but it feels as though the chamber itself is conspiring against me, stealing the air from my lungs as I struggle to reconcile the man before me with the stranger he's just admitted to being.

"So, that's it, then?" I say, my voice sharper than I'd intended. I can feel my own anger and betrayal simmering, a dangerous mix of heat and hurt I can barely keep contained. "After everything we've been through, after everything I've done, you're just going to... hand me over? Like I'm some pawn in whatever bargain you made?"

He doesn't flinch, but there's a subtle shift in his expression, a tightening around his mouth, the slightest drop of his gaze. For once, I think he might actually look ashamed. Good. Let him feel even a fraction of what I'm feeling, this poisonous cocktail of disbelief and disappointment that threatens to overwhelm every good thing I thought we'd built between us.

"Do you think it's that simple?" he says, his tone surprisingly soft, as though trying to temper the anger simmering between us. "Do you think I wanted this? That I wanted to lie to you, to betray you?"

"Yes," I snap, unwilling to give him even a sliver of grace. "Yes, because that's exactly what you're doing right now. You could have warned me. You could have told me, Damian, instead of letting me walk blindly into this... this trap you set up with whoever you made your deal with."

"It's not that simple," he repeats, but the words sound hollow, as if he's trying to convince himself as much as me. "They wouldn't have cared if you knew or not. The end result would be the same."

"But you would have cared," I say, stepping closer, not giving him room to look away, to avoid the weight of his choices. "If you had even a fraction of the loyalty I thought you did, you would have told me. You owed me that much."

For a long, excruciating moment, he says nothing. Just stands there, his expression a wretched mask of conflicting emotions, and I can't help but wonder if any of this was real, if he ever cared at all, or if I was just another bargaining chip to him, a means to an end. I open my mouth, ready to hurl something, anything, to puncture the silence between us, but he beats me to it, his voice barely more than a whisper.

"I wanted to protect you."

I scoff, the sound bitter and mirthless. "Protect me? By betraying me? That's your idea of protection?"

"Believe it or not, it is," he says, a hint of frustration edging into his voice. "If you knew the kind of people I was dealing with, the things they've done... I didn't want you anywhere near it. That's why I kept it from you. I thought I could handle it alone. I thought... maybe I could find a way out without dragging you into it."

"Newsflash, Damian, you're doing a terrible job," I say, anger sizzling in my chest, hot and unyielding. "I'm standing right in the middle of it. And guess who brought me here?"

He has the decency to look away then, and I almost feel a twinge of satisfaction, a vindication in his guilt. But it's short-lived, swallowed up by the yawning chasm of betrayal that stretches between us. I don't know how we get past this. I don't know if I even want to.

For a long moment, we just stand there, locked in a stalemate of unspoken accusations and fractured trust. The silence presses down on us, thick and oppressive, like the weight of everything we've left unsaid is finally coming home to roost.

Then, as if sensing that words will only worsen the wounds between us, he steps back, his gaze turning distant, a cold resolve hardening in his eyes. "Fine," he says quietly. "If you can't understand why I did this, if you can't forgive me... then let's end it here. Go. Take the artifact and leave. I'll deal with the consequences."

I can hardly believe what I'm hearing. "Just... like that?"

"Yes," he says, and there's a bitterness to his tone that almost matches my own. "Take it. Take it and leave, before I change my mind."

It's a strange thing, standing there on the edge of departure, with freedom so tantalizingly close, and yet feeling anchored in place, bound by the very thing that I should despise. Because as much as I want to run, to put as much distance between us as possible, a small, stubborn part of me doesn't want to leave him. Not like this.

"Why are you doing this?" I ask, the question slipping out before I can stop it. "If you wanted to hand me over, why let me go now? Why give me the artifact and risk everything?"

His jaw clenches, and he turns his head, avoiding my gaze. "Because... because it's not that simple," he says, his voice thick with something I can't quite place. "Maybe I don't want this to end like every other job I've ever done. Maybe... just maybe, you're worth more than that."

I don't know how to respond to that. I don't know if I even want to. So instead, I do the only thing I can think of—I reach for the artifact, pulling it free from its resting place, feeling the cold, unyielding weight of it in my hands. The light catches on its surface, casting strange, fractured shadows across the chamber walls, and I feel a surge of power thrumming beneath my fingertips, ancient and formidable.

Without another word, I turn, heading toward the passage that will lead me out, my steps heavy, each one a brutal reminder of the tangled mess we've made. I don't look back, don't give him the satisfaction of seeing whatever sorrow or doubt lingers in my gaze. He's made his choice, and so have I.

The air grows colder as I move down the passage, the darkness pressing in around me, as if sensing the weight of my thoughts, the fractured pieces of my loyalty, my trust, scattered like glass behind me. I try to push them away, to focus on the path ahead, but they cling to me, each memory, each word, carving into my mind with the same cruel clarity as a blade. And though I tell myself this is the end, that I can't afford to look back, a small, infuriating part of me knows it's not over. Not yet.

The passage stretches on, cold and unforgiving, as if the walls themselves are trying to press the air from my lungs. My footsteps echo in the silence, a hollow rhythm that only serves to amplify the feeling of being utterly, irrevocably alone. I keep my gaze fixed ahead, willing myself to keep moving, to focus on anything other than the knot of betrayal and anger that coils tighter with every step. Damian's words chase me, shadows I can't outrun, seeping into my mind like ink in water, darkening everything they touch.

But as I walk, a thought claws its way to the surface, an itch I can't shake. Damian had a chance to hand me over—he could have done it right then and there, fulfilled his obligation and washed his hands of me. And yet, he didn't. Instead, he offered me the artifact, gave me an out, as if he was daring me to take it and leave him to face whatever punishment awaited. It doesn't make sense. None of it does, and the more I think about it, the more I feel a rising dread, a sense that maybe I've missed something vital, something that could twist this whole mess into an entirely different shape.

A faint whisper of air stirs ahead, brushing against my face like a cold breath. I'm almost out. The exit looms just a few yards away, framed by a scattering of faint light that spills in from the open night sky beyond. And yet, instead of feeling relief, there's a prickling at the back of my neck, a tingling awareness that makes me hesitate. Something's wrong. I turn, glancing back into the shadows of the passage, half expecting Damian to be there, watching me leave. But the path is empty, silent, like he's already vanished from this place, from my life. And maybe he has.

Just as I turn back toward the exit, a low rumble begins to resonate beneath my feet, the ground trembling with a warning that sends my heart racing. Before I can react, a wall of dust and debris erupts from the far end of the passageway, blocking the way I came. The rumble grows louder, like the very bones of the earth are grinding against one another, and I stumble back, clutching the artifact tighter, my heart slamming against my ribs.

Then, out of the darkness, a figure emerges—hulking, cloaked in shadows, with a presence that feels more ancient and malevolent than anything we'd faced in the chamber. I feel the weight of its gaze settle on me, an oppressive force that makes my skin crawl, and a chill runs down my spine. It isn't Damian, and somehow, that realization fills me with an even deeper dread. This isn't someone I know; this is something far worse.

A voice slithers out of the dark, thick and oily, winding its way around me like a vice. "You thought you could just walk away with it, little thief?"

I swallow hard, forcing myself to stand taller, even as every instinct screams for me to turn and run. "I didn't know it belonged to anyone," I say, my voice steadier than I feel. "And I'm not looking for trouble."

"Trouble," the voice mocks, amusement coloring its edges. "You're carrying trouble, child. That artifact isn't just an ancient trinket. It's a key—my key."

The words hang heavy in the air, laced with a venomous promise, and my blood runs cold. I glance down at the artifact in my hands, its intricate patterns catching the dim light, and suddenly it feels as if the weight of it has doubled. A key. Damian never mentioned that. He'd said it was valuable, important, but this... this is something else.

"I don't care what it is," I manage, meeting the shadowed figure's gaze. "I'm leaving, and I'm taking it with me."

"Oh, I don't think so," it purrs, a glint of something malicious flashing in its dark, unseen eyes. "That artifact has been bound to me for centuries. And you—" it gestures with a skeletal, elongated hand, fingers like talons curling through the air "—are merely a vessel, a temporary steward. I will have it back, one way or another."

The weight of its presence presses against me, thick and suffocating, and I feel my grip on the artifact falter. But some stubborn spark flares to life within me, a refusal to give in to this shadowy, faceless creature, to let it undo everything we've fought for. I take a shaky step back, tightening my hold, and try to summon whatever courage I can muster.

"What do you even need it for?" I ask, trying to keep the creature talking, to buy myself a few precious moments to think. "You've been waiting for centuries, right? So why now?"

A soft, sinister laugh echoes through the passage, chilling in its ease. "Time is nothing to me. But it is everything to you, is it not? Humans are so bound by it, so easily worn down by it. And that little artifact? It can unlock doors you wouldn't dare imagine. Realities. Powers. But it only works in the hands of the one destined to wield it."

A sick realization dawns, a twisting knot forming in my stomach. The artifact, the binding, the endless chase—Damian's deal was never about me. I was never the target. It was the artifact all along, and he'd been set up as much as I had. This creature, whatever it is, had been pulling the strings from the start, and Damian... he'd known, somehow. Or maybe he hadn't. Either way, he'd been as trapped as I was.

And now I'm here, alone, with a creature that wants something I can't afford to give up.

"Look," I say, a desperate edge slipping into my voice. "I don't want any part of this. Just take the artifact and let me go. I won't look back, I won't tell anyone. You'll never see me again."

But it shakes its head slowly, a mockery of sympathy in its movements. "You misunderstand, child. The artifact chose you. It is bound to you now. You can't simply hand it over." It reaches out, its skeletal fingers extending, each one a promise of agony. "But don't worry. I will help you release it."

My body goes cold with dread as I realize what it means, as I realize that the only way to separate myself from this cursed object is to separate myself from life itself. I take another step back, nearly stumbling, my heart pounding wildly as the creature inches closer, its twisted, empty gaze fixed on me.

"Stay back," I warn, lifting the artifact as if I might somehow wield it as a weapon. "I swear, I'll use this if I have to."

Its laugh is low, mocking. "Do you even know how, little thief? That power is not yours to command."

I feel a pulse of something within the artifact, a flicker of energy that feels both foreign and strangely familiar, and suddenly, a surge of reckless courage courses through me. I lift it higher, summoning every ounce of strength, every spark of resistance within me.

And then, just as the creature lunges forward, I throw myself backward, shouting a single, desperate word that resonates in my mind like a command.

In an explosion of light and sound, the world goes white, and for one terrifying, blinding instant, I feel myself being ripped away from everything I know.

Chapter 21: The Binding Curse

The artifact sat on a pedestal of cold, dark stone, nestled in shadows that seemed to shift with the faintest breath of air. As Damian and I moved closer, its surface pulsed faintly, as if alive, casting a strange, otherworldly glow that flickered like candlelight against the vaulted, cavernous ceiling above us. Everything about this place seemed ancient and untouched, as if forgotten by the world outside. The walls bore carvings of creatures whose faces were twisted in snarls or smiles—depending on how the light hit them—while darkened veins of moss crawled down to meet the ground, blending with long-dried bloodstains that I refused to dwell on.

Damian's voice was low, almost reverent. "You know, this could be the answer to everything," he murmured, his gaze fixed on the artifact. His face was lit by the faint, pulsing glow, casting shadows that made his usually stoic expression look almost haunted.

"Or it could kill us both," I replied, doing my best to ignore the way his nearness made my pulse trip, something that had become alarmingly common in the last few weeks. I wasn't sure when that had happened—when he'd gone from merely tolerable to downright infuriating in the best kind of way. I chalked it up to the adrenaline of nearly getting ourselves killed every other day. Surely it was just that.

He rolled his eyes, the hint of a smirk betraying his amusement. "What's life without a little risk?"

I opened my mouth to retort when a shockwave of energy crackled between us, silencing any clever comeback I might've had. I felt a sharp tug, as if some invisible cord had hooked itself deep in my chest, yanking me forward. I staggered, and Damian's hand shot out to steady me. His fingers wrapped around my arm, firm and warm, grounding me just as the room spun wildly out of control. The air between us grew thick, almost tangible, vibrating with an energy that made the hairs on the back of my neck rise.

Then it hit—a rush of magic as raw and ancient as anything I'd ever felt, a potent wave that swirled around us, binding us in an invisible but unmistakable tether. My breath caught, and I knew instinctively that this wasn't just any ordinary spell. It was a curse, and a powerful one at that, ancient enough to make my fingers go numb where Damian's hand held me.

"You feel that too?" I managed, my voice unsteady, my bravado quickly fading.

His jaw clenched as he nodded, his hand tightening on my arm. "It's a binding curse. One that doesn't just go away with a few choice words and a flick of a wand."

"Brilliant," I muttered, unable to mask the sarcasm. "Bound by a curse to the one person I'd least like to be bound to."

He arched a brow, a glint of amusement despite the tension crackling between us. "I could say the same, you know. Don't flatter yourself."

"Trust me, I wasn't."

The curse's pull intensified, forcing us even closer, and suddenly, my heart pounded for reasons that had nothing to do with fear. His face was inches from mine, close enough that I could see the flecks of gold in his eyes, the faint scar just above his brow, and the way his breath hitched ever so slightly as our gazes locked. For a moment, everything else faded—the pulse of the artifact, the distant echoes of dripping water, the weight of the curse pressing down on us like a physical shackle. All I could feel was the heat of his hand on my arm, the tension simmering in the air between us.

But then he let go, and reality came crashing back in, more brutal than ever.

"So," I said, swallowing hard, trying to maintain some semblance of control. "This curse—how exactly does it...work?"

"It binds us in more ways than one," he replied, his tone clipped, as if he was choosing each word carefully. "Physically, emotionally. The stronger the magic, the stronger the bond. And this"—he gestured to the artifact, which continued to pulse ominously, almost as if it were watching us—"is as strong as they come."

I felt a chill run down my spine. "And what does it want? For us to—what, sacrifice each other?"

He shook his head, a grim smile tugging at his lips. "No. Worse. It wants us to choose between the power it holds and each other. It's a test, a cruel one. Either we stay bound forever, or we sever the curse by walking away from this artifact and the power it holds."

His words sank in slowly, and I felt my stomach twist. If we kept the artifact, we'd be bound together indefinitely. But if we chose to walk away, we'd be forfeiting the only thing that might save us from the dark forces hunting us. It was a twisted, impossible choice, a cruel trick of fate that demanded we lay our lives—and, apparently, our hearts—on the line.

"Great," I muttered, a bitter laugh escaping me despite the dread settling in my gut. "Just what I needed. A magical ultimatum."

Damian's eyes softened, just for a fraction of a second, before he looked away, his gaze hardening again. "This wasn't exactly on my wish list either, you know."

Silence fell between us, heavy and suffocating, and for a moment, neither of us moved. Somewhere deep in my chest, I could feel the curse settling in, sinking its claws deeper with every heartbeat, binding us tighter, as if relishing in our confusion, our reluctance, our fear. I wanted to hate him for it—for being here, for being the one person I was trapped with, for being the only person who somehow, against all odds, made this nightmare a little less terrifying.

But I didn't hate him. If anything, that was the problem.

With a resigned sigh, Damian crossed his arms, leaning against the stone pedestal with a calm that made me want to scream. "So, what's the plan, oh fearless leader?"

"Plan?" I shot him a look. "You're the one who dragged us into this mess."

"Me?" He raised an eyebrow, smirking. "If I recall, you were the one who insisted on touching the artifact."

"Oh, so now it's my fault? Fine. Next time, I'll just leave the cursed ancient relics for you to play with."

He chuckled, a low sound that did strange things to my already fragile nerves. "I'd prefer that, honestly."

And there it was again, that maddening, infuriating warmth in his eyes, a spark of something unspoken that made me wonder if maybe, just maybe, this curse was more than a twisted punishment. Maybe, in some inexplicable way, it was exactly what we'd both been avoiding for too long.

The glow from the artifact cast us in an ethereal light, its pulse slow and rhythmic, like a heartbeat. The weight of the curse settled on me, pressing against my chest until I felt like I could hardly breathe. And Damian? Well, he seemed just as conflicted as I was, though his expression remained an impassive mask, the kind I'd seen him wear a hundred times when facing down some malevolent creature or a stubborn council official. But this was different. This wasn't something he could stare down or outwit. We were well and truly trapped.

I lifted my hand tentatively, fingers tracing the strange tether that now connected us. It wasn't visible, exactly—more like a sensation that lingered between us, an unmistakable sense of presence, of closeness. Every time I moved, I felt an answering pull, like a magnet, compelling me closer to him. He stood just a foot away, his gaze fixed firmly on the artifact, refusing to meet my eyes.

"What are you thinking?" I asked, struggling to keep my tone light, though I was certain he could hear the tension buried in it.

"That we're in deep," he said flatly, jaw tight. "And that if I'd known this would happen, I would've... I don't know. Done something differently." He sighed, his shoulders sagging slightly, the weight of our situation clearly beginning to wear on him.

"You're acting like I dragged you in here at sword point. I don't remember you putting up much of a fight," I shot back, crossing my arms in defiance. There it was again—that instinctive need to challenge him, to push back against whatever control he thought he held over me.

He glanced down at my crossed arms, and despite everything, a wry smile tugged at the corners of his mouth. "No, you wouldn't remember. That would require you to actually notice someone other than yourself for a change."

The words stung, and he knew it. But I wasn't about to give him the satisfaction of a reaction. Instead, I raised an eyebrow, giving him my most unruffled look. "Funny, coming from the man who spends half his time brooding in dark corners and the other half convinced he's the universe's personal savior."

He scoffed, shaking his head. "You know, for someone who claims to hate me, you seem to spend a lot of time analyzing my every move. A little obsessed, are we?"

I felt a flush rise to my cheeks, and I struggled to maintain my composure. "Believe me, Damian, you're hardly the center of my universe."

The silence that followed was thick, crackling with all the things we weren't saying. This was the part where I would usually walk away, throw up a wall, and leave him to stew in his own arrogance. But there was no walking away now, no escaping this invisible chain that bound us together. Instead, I stayed rooted to the spot, hyper-aware of every shift of his stance, every flicker of emotion that crossed his face.

And then, suddenly, his gaze softened, just slightly, as if he was letting his guard down for the first time. "Look, I know you think I'm some...emotionless automaton or whatever," he said, his voice surprisingly gentle. "But this—this is serious. It's dangerous. And I don't like the idea of putting you at risk, not like this."

The admission caught me off guard. It wasn't the Damian I was used to, the one who reveled in sarcasm and cool detachment. This Damian was vulnerable, almost tender. And that was terrifying. Because it meant that maybe, just maybe, he actually cared.

"Well, thanks for the concern," I said, keeping my tone carefully neutral. "But I'm a big girl, Damian. I don't need you to protect me."

He met my gaze, his eyes searching mine, and for a moment, I felt the world tilt on its axis. The tether between us grew stronger, humming with an intensity that felt both thrilling and terrifying. I wanted to look away, to break whatever spell was weaving itself between us, but I couldn't. His gaze held me captive, and I was powerless to resist.

"We need to figure this out," he murmured, his voice so low it was almost a whisper. "Before this curse...does something we can't undo."

There was something in his tone, a thread of fear that I wasn't used to hearing from him, and it was enough to shake me out of whatever strange trance had taken hold. I forced myself to take a step back, putting a sliver of distance between us, though I could still feel the pull of the curse, dragging me back toward him like a relentless tide.

"Right," I said, clearing my throat. "So let's be practical. If this curse binds us together, there has to be a way to unbind it."

"Usually, yes," he replied, nodding slowly. "But this is...different. Older. It's not the kind of curse you can just dispel with a simple incantation."

"Of course it's not," I muttered, rolling my eyes. "Because why would anything ever be that easy?"

He smirked, and despite everything, I felt a reluctant smile tugging at my own lips. There it was again—that infuriating charm, the one that somehow managed to wriggle its way under my skin, no matter how hard I tried to resist.

"We'll figure it out," he said, his voice steady, confident in a way that made me almost believe him. Almost. "We always do, don't we?"

"Yeah," I said softly, a pang of uncertainty creeping into my voice. "But this feels different."

It was a quiet admission, one I hadn't meant to make, but there it was, hanging in the air between us. This curse wasn't just a magical trap or a deadly artifact. It was something deeper, something that forced us to confront the things we'd both been trying to ignore for so long.

He reached out, his fingers brushing my arm in a gesture so uncharacteristically gentle that it made my heart ache. "Then let's make a pact," he said, his gaze serious. "No matter what happens, we don't let this curse break us. We stick together."

The simplicity of his words was almost painful, a promise that held so much more than I was ready to admit. I wanted to scoff, to laugh it off and pretend like it didn't matter, but the look in his eyes told me that this was more than just a casual agreement. It was a vow, one that felt as binding as the curse itself.

"Fine," I said, my voice barely above a whisper. "We stick together."

For a long moment, we stood there, both of us bound by promises and curses and the strange, unspoken connection that seemed to grow stronger with every passing second. And then, almost reluctantly, he let his hand drop, the warmth of his touch lingering like a ghost on my skin.

"We should get moving," he said, his tone brisk, businesslike, as if he hadn't just opened up a part of himself I'd never seen before. "This curse isn't going to solve itself."

"Right," I replied, trying to match his sudden shift in tone, though my heart was still racing. "After you."

As we turned to face the path ahead, I felt the weight of the curse press down on us again, stronger this time, as if reminding us of the choices we'd have to make, the sacrifices that would inevitably come. But for now, at least, we had each other.

The tunnel stretched before us, dimly lit by the flickering glow of the artifact in Damian's hand, casting shadows that danced against the stone walls. The silence was thick, settling between us like an unspoken question neither of us dared to voice. Every so often, our arms would brush, a sharp reminder of the invisible tether binding us, a constant, pulsing presence that neither of us could shake.

Damian cleared his throat, his voice cutting through the quiet. "So, any grand ideas on how to break this thing, or are we just hoping it'll get bored and let us go?"

I sighed, feigning an ease I didn't feel. "I don't know, maybe we could annoy it to death. Between your endless brooding and my charming optimism, I'd say we stand a good chance."

He gave a half-smile, the kind that barely reached his eyes but softened his usual hard edges just a fraction. "Funny, but I'm not sure ancient magic is as susceptible to sarcasm as you are."

"Only one way to find out," I shot back, and he shook his head, though there was the faintest hint of a laugh beneath the tension.

We kept walking, every step a strange, awkward dance as we tried to keep a respectable distance but failed miserably, tugged together by the relentless pull of the curse. And as we walked, I began to feel it—the subtle but growing influence of the binding magic, weaving its way into my thoughts, amplifying my awareness of him in ways I didn't want to admit. It wasn't just his presence or the fact that I could feel the heat radiating from him whenever we brushed shoulders. It was something deeper, like a whisper at the edge of my mind, compelling me to look closer, to understand him in ways I had resisted for so long.

I turned to him abruptly, trying to shake off the creeping sense of vulnerability. "So, what's the plan, fearless leader?"

He raised an eyebrow, his gaze sharp. "I'm working on it. But let's be clear—you're as bound by this as I am. So maybe ease up on the attitude."

I snorted. "The day I ease up is the day you stop acting like you have the entire world resting on your shoulders. And let's be honest, Damian. That's never going to happen."

He opened his mouth to argue, then closed it, an odd look crossing his face. And for a fleeting second, I thought I saw a flash of something unguarded, something raw and uncertain. But just as quickly, it was gone, replaced by his usual stoicism.

"Fine," he said at last, his voice steady, almost weary. "If we're going to do this, let's at least try to do it without tearing each other apart."

The path narrowed, forcing us closer, and I felt his arm brush mine again, sending a shiver up my spine that I told myself was nothing more than the chill of the underground air. But my own resolve was slipping, every forced proximity and accidental touch making it harder to keep my usual defenses in place.

I swallowed, keeping my voice even. "Agreed. I'll try not to say anything too infuriating if you do the same."

We fell into a silence that felt heavier than before, the kind of silence where every unspoken word lingered, thickening the air. And then, just as I thought I might actually suffocate under the weight of it, the tunnel began to widen, opening into a vast underground chamber that took my breath away.

The room was massive, larger than any underground space had a right to be, its walls lined with intricate carvings that spiraled up toward a ceiling so high it was lost in shadow. And at the center of the room, set on a raised stone platform, was a pedestal that looked eerily familiar.

Damian stopped short, his eyes narrowing as he took in the sight before us. "This...looks a lot like the place we found the artifact."

I nodded, the hairs on the back of my neck standing on end. "Yeah. A little too similar."

He took a cautious step forward, his gaze flickering over the carvings on the walls. They were old, older than anything I'd ever seen, and the figures depicted seemed to writhe and shift in the dim light, their faces twisted in expressions of agony, ecstasy, or something else entirely. A cold shiver slid down my spine, and I had the unsettling feeling that we were being watched, though I knew we were alone.

"Do you think this is...a way out?" I ventured, though my voice sounded hollow even to my own ears.

"I don't know," he replied, his voice barely above a whisper. "But I have a feeling we're not here by accident."

He was right. There was a purpose to this chamber, a reason why we'd been led here. The air hummed with energy, the same ancient magic that had bound us together, but stronger, more concentrated. I felt it thrumming beneath my skin, a relentless pulse that matched the beating of my heart.

And then, as if in response to our presence, the pedestal began to glow, a faint, eerie light emanating from its base. I took a step back, instinctively grabbing Damian's arm, though I immediately let go, pretending I hadn't just clung to him like some terrified damsel.

But he didn't comment, his attention fixed on the light growing brighter with every passing second, illuminating the carvings around the room. And as the light intensified, I saw it—a figure, emerging from the shadows, tall and draped in dark, flowing robes, its face obscured by a hood. The figure's movements were fluid, almost graceful, and it glided toward us with a purpose that sent a jolt of terror through me.

"Damian," I whispered, my voice trembling. "Tell me I'm imagining that."

"You're not," he said, his voice tight. "Stay close."

He moved in front of me, his stance protective, and I felt an unexpected surge of gratitude, though I would've died before admitting it. The figure stopped a few feet away, its face hidden in shadow, though I could feel its gaze piercing through me, as cold and unyielding as the stone walls around us.

"Why have you come?" The voice was low, resonant, echoing through the chamber like a distant thunderclap. It wasn't human—not entirely. There was something ancient in its tone, something that hinted at knowledge beyond comprehension.

"We...we were looking for a way to lift the curse," Damian replied, his voice steady, though I could see the tension in his jaw, the way his hand had drifted to the hilt of his sword.

The figure inclined its head slightly, as if considering his words. "You seek freedom from what binds you," it intoned, a hint of amusement in its voice. "But freedom is not given. It must be earned."

I swallowed, forcing myself to speak, though my voice sounded small in the vastness of the chamber. "And how exactly do we 'earn' it?"

The figure's head tilted, and though I couldn't see its face, I felt a cruel smile in its tone. "By sacrifice," it said, its voice soft, almost gentle. "Only a life freely given can break the bonds that hold you."

A chill ran through me, freezing me to the spot. I glanced at Damian, and for once, his expression was unreadable. He was staring at the figure with a look that I couldn't decipher, something that lay just beyond the edges of fear.

"A life freely given?" he echoed, his voice barely a whisper. "You mean...one of us has to die?"

The figure nodded, as if amused by our shock. "That is the price. The only way to sever the curse is through the ultimate sacrifice. One of you must choose to give your life...for the other."

The words echoed in the silence, reverberating through my mind, each one landing like a stone. I looked at Damian, my heart pounding in my chest, and for the first time, I saw the depth of the choice laid out before us.

"Choose wisely," the figure said, before fading into the shadows, leaving us alone in the chamber, the weight of its words settling over us like a shroud.

Damian turned to me, his eyes dark and unreadable. And as he opened his mouth to speak, I realized, with a sinking dread, that this was a choice neither of us was prepared to make.

Chapter 22: The Enemy Within

The darkness crept over us, shrouding the mountainside in inky silence as the sun dipped below the horizon, taking any remaining warmth with it. The artifact was heavier than I'd expected, though not in the physical sense; it felt more like the weight of a hundred eyes watching from every shadow, a pulse of danger woven into every breath we took. Damian hadn't spoken for the last hour, and I was fine with that. But now, his voice broke the silence, low and almost apologetic.

"I need to tell you something."

I glanced over, gripping the artifact tighter, my fingers prickling as if I'd touched live wires. Damian's face was shadowed, unreadable in the dim light, but there was something different in his eyes, something uneasy. And that, more than anything, made my pulse skitter.

"This is about your people, isn't it?" I kept my voice steady, even though every word felt like it was dragging my heart over gravel.

He nodded, his mouth a tight line. "They've been watching us. Tracking us."

"Us?"

"Me." His gaze fell to the ground, and he dragged his hand through his hair, a gesture I'd come to know meant he was wrestling with something. "They think I've turned. They think... well, they don't know what to think. But they want the artifact, and they'll do anything to get it."

The words sat heavy in the air between us, twisting my stomach into a familiar knot. "And you didn't think to mention this sooner?"

His head snapped up, eyes fierce and guilty. "Do you think I wanted to? Do you think I enjoyed watching them inch closer, knowing they could ruin everything?"

He had a point, but I wasn't ready to admit that. Instead, I folded my arms and took a step back, feeling the rough stone of the mountain at my back. "So what are you saying? You want me to just hand it over? Trust you after everything?"

"No." His voice softened, and he took a hesitant step forward. "I want you to trust that I'm here, that I'm choosing to be here. With you."

It would've been easier to laugh, to brush him off and pretend that I didn't care, but there was something raw in his eyes, a kind of vulnerability that made it impossible. The hard truth was that I wanted to believe him. I wanted to believe that this wasn't just some elaborate scheme to get close, to take what we'd worked so hard for and disappear back to his side.

"How do I know?" My voice was barely a whisper, but it echoed around us, bouncing off the rock walls like a question that couldn't be ignored.

His hand twitched at his side as if he wanted to reach for me, but he didn't move closer. "I don't know if I can convince you. But I'm here because I want to be. Because I couldn't walk away."

The words hung there, both a promise and a warning, and I knew that either way, I was walking into something dangerous. Trusting him might save us. Or it might destroy me.

Before I could respond, a crackling sound echoed from above, shattering the tense silence. Damian's head snapped up, and I followed his gaze, catching sight of a silhouette moving along the ridge, barely visible in the fading light. My heart lurched, and I felt a surge of adrenaline, a desperate urge to run—or fight.

"We have to move," he said, grabbing my arm with a grip that was firm but gentle, as if he was still unsure if I'd bolt.

I nodded, biting back the instinct to pull away, and we scrambled down the rocky path, our breaths loud in the stillness. The artifact thumped against my side, a reminder of the stakes, of the danger we carried. Damian kept his hand on my arm, guiding me through the winding terrain as shadows stretched longer, swallowing the path ahead.

We slipped into the cover of a small alcove, breathing hard. My mind raced, trying to piece together a plan. If his people were tracking us, we were at a disadvantage. They knew the terrain; they had numbers, and who knew what else up their sleeves. But we had the artifact, the one thing they wanted above all.

"Do they know you're with me?" I asked, watching Damian's expression carefully. It was unreadable, a mask he'd perfected over the years. And for the first time, I wondered what he had to lose if he defied them.

"They know enough." His voice was strained, almost resigned. "And they're prepared to go to any lengths to get what they want."

A chill ran down my spine, colder than the mountain air. "Any lengths?"

"They won't kill me," he said with a forced grin, the kind of humor that came out in dire situations. "Not yet, anyway. But you…" He trailed off, his eyes darkening, and I saw a flicker of something I hadn't expected—fear. Real, honest fear.

"Great. So I'm the sacrificial lamb."

His jaw clenched. "Not if I can help it."

I hated the way that promise sounded so sweet, hated that it gave me hope when I should've been preparing for betrayal. But then, Damian had always had that effect, that maddening ability to make me want to believe him even when everything pointed to the contrary.

A rustle from behind sent both of us into silence, and I pressed myself against the rough stone, feeling its chill seep into my skin. Damian's gaze locked onto mine, a silent message passing between us. Whoever was out there was getting closer. And we didn't have much time.

I held my breath, waiting, listening as footsteps crunched over loose rocks, each one closer than the last. The weight of the artifact against my side felt like a ticking clock, each second counting down to some inevitable collision. Damian's hand found mine, a small, fleeting connection, but it steadied me. Reminded me that we were in this together, for better or worse.

And as the shadows shifted, revealing a face I hadn't seen in months—a face I thought I'd never see again—I felt that hope twist into something sharper, more dangerous. Because the last time I'd trusted this person, it had nearly cost me everything.

"Hello again," she said, her voice smooth and cold, her smile as sharp as the knife at her belt. "Miss me?"

I swallowed, feeling the weight of Damian's hand still on mine, grounding me, steadying me. But I couldn't shake the feeling that the real battle had only just begun. And this time, the enemy was closer than I'd ever imagined.

The tension was like an invisible cord between us, stretched taut, vibrating with every stolen glance, every question unasked. Damian's eyes flicked from the shadows ahead to the steady line of our tracks behind, his jaw set in a hard line that told me he was as wary of what lay ahead as I was of what he hadn't yet said. The wind had picked up, carrying with it the sharp scent of pine and the faintest hint of smoke, a reminder that we weren't alone up here.

"Don't suppose you've got any other confessions tucked away?" I asked, keeping my voice light, though my pulse hammered beneath my skin.

He shot me a look that might have been annoyance or amusement—I couldn't tell with him sometimes, and maybe that was part of the appeal. "No more surprises. I promise."

"Funny," I replied, matching his tone. "You don't really strike me as the trustworthy type."

The corners of his mouth quirked, the closest thing to a smile I'd seen since he'd dropped that particular bombshell. "Says the woman who just stole an artifact of untold power. Should I be worried about your loyalties?"

I rolled my eyes, though I felt the warmth of his gaze like a spark catching on dry tinder. "Please. If I was going to betray you, I'd have done it back in the city where there were more escape routes and fewer steep cliffs."

"A good point." He stopped, one hand raised, his head tilting as if he'd heard something. The breeze ruffled his hair, and for a heartbeat, he looked like someone from another time entirely—like he belonged to the wild mountains more than to the sleek cities where we'd first crossed paths.

I listened, too, but heard only the sighing of the trees and the distant whisper of water somewhere below. And yet, I didn't doubt him. We'd both learned that silence could hide more than it revealed, and right now, there was too much silence for my comfort.

"You still think they're close?" I asked, keeping my voice low.

His gaze didn't shift, his attention fixed somewhere in the trees. "I know they are. And they're waiting for us to get sloppy. This isn't just about the artifact anymore. They'll take you out to get to me, if that's what it takes."

"Well, then," I said, sliding the artifact into the inner pocket of my jacket and zipping it securely. "We'll just have to be a little less predictable, won't we?"

His grin was quick and unexpected, a flash of teeth and something reckless. "You make it sound easy."

"Nothing with you is easy."

Damian laughed, low and quick, and the sound was an anchor in the growing dark. For a moment, the tension eased, replaced by something almost light, almost normal. And maybe that was the scariest part of all—that we could find humor here, of all places, with shadows circling and enemies closer than I could see.

We moved in silence after that, each of us listening for the crackle of branches or the crunch of footsteps. The air was sharp with cold, biting at my cheeks, and I forced my mind to focus on the path ahead, on each careful step over stones and fallen branches. The artifact felt heavier now, a weight pulling me down, and I could feel its strange energy thrumming against my side, like a second heartbeat.

Damian's hand brushed against mine, steadying me as I slipped on a patch of loose gravel. I caught my breath, gripping his hand instinctively, and for a moment, I felt something pulse between us, something both terrifying and reassuring. It was absurd, really, the thought that I could feel anything other than wary, bitter distrust toward him, and yet here we were. Caught in something that neither of us could seem to name but both seemed reluctant to let go of.

"Careful," he murmured, his voice low and too close, wrapping around me like smoke. "Wouldn't want you to get hurt on my account."

"Too late for that," I muttered, letting go of his hand and focusing on the ground ahead.

Another laugh, softer this time, and I could feel his gaze lingering on me as we moved forward. I didn't dare look back.

The darkness thickened as we descended, the air growing colder, the silence stretching tighter. I could feel the weight of the artifact, yes, but something else, too—the undeniable sense that we were being watched, every step weighed and measured by eyes I couldn't see.

"Damian," I whispered, stopping short. He paused beside me, his body tense, his eyes scanning the trees.

"Yeah. I feel it too."

No sooner had the words left his mouth than a shape moved in the shadows to our left—a figure stepping into the faint moonlight, lean and confident, her gaze sharp as she regarded us with something dangerously close to amusement. She was dressed in dark clothes, her hair tied back in a way that made her look more like a weapon than a person, and in her hand, she held a blade that glinted faintly in the dim light.

"Well," she said, her voice smooth and familiar, a voice I'd last heard when I was certain she'd left me to rot. "You two certainly look cozy."

My heart thudded against my ribs, a mixture of shock and something like anger coursing through me. "You," I said, feeling Damian tense beside me. "What the hell are you doing here?"

She tilted her head, eyes gleaming with a smile that didn't quite reach her lips. "Funny, I was going to ask you the same thing. Running off with the enemy, stealing priceless artifacts—looks like you've been busy."

I clenched my fists, the anger simmering just beneath the surface. "I thought you were dead."

She laughed, the sound cold and sharp. "A little faith, that's all I asked for. But no, you left me behind. Figured I'd repay the favor."

Beside me, Damian shifted, and I could feel the tension radiating off him like heat. He didn't trust her any more than I did, and in that moment, it was probably the only thing holding us together.

"You're working with them, aren't you?" Damian asked, his voice steady but his gaze razor-sharp.

"Let's just say I'm working with whoever's got the best deal," she replied, her smile widening. "And right now, it looks like I'm on the winning side."

"Funny, I didn't realize betrayal was a competition," I shot back, feeling my own confidence spike. I could feel Damian watching me, his gaze weighing my reaction, but I didn't flinch. I wouldn't give her the satisfaction.

She only shrugged, that insufferable smirk still firmly in place. "I guess it depends on what you're willing to lose."

In that instant, I knew. This wasn't just a game to her. She was here to take the artifact, and she was more than willing to do whatever it took to get it. We were no longer allies, no longer friends—if we ever had been. She'd made her choice, and so had I.

Damian's hand brushed mine, a silent question, and I nodded, understanding his intention. Whatever happened next, we'd face it together.

The night was an ocean of dark whispers, the air thick with unspoken threats and barely contained tension. I held my ground, my gaze never wavering from the woman in front of me. She was watching us with the look of a predator who'd been waiting too long for the perfect moment to strike. Damian's hand brushed mine again, a flicker of warmth in the cold, reminding me he was here, and despite everything that had happened between us, we were in this together. For now, at least.

She tilted her head, that maddening smirk still painted across her face, and I had to resist the urge to wipe it off with a well-aimed punch. "You really thought you could outrun them?" she asked, her tone dripping with condescension. "Or did you forget what you're carrying?"

"Maybe I was hoping they'd forget what it's worth," I shot back, keeping my voice steady, though I knew she could probably hear the edge in it. "But I suppose that's just a little too much optimism for you, isn't it?"

She laughed, a cold, brittle sound that felt like broken glass scraping against my skin. "Oh, sweetheart, you always did have a soft spot for lost causes. And this?" She gestured to the artifact, glinting under the moonlight like a silent witness to all our bad decisions. "This is the biggest one yet."

Damian shifted beside me, his gaze locked on her, his expression as unreadable as stone. "You don't have to do this," he said, his voice softer than I'd expected. There was something vulnerable in it, something that made my chest tighten even though I knew better than to believe anything could sway her now. "There's still time to walk away."

Her smile faded, replaced by a hardness that cut through the night like a blade. "You don't get it, do you? I already made my choice."

For a heartbeat, the silence thickened, a pause heavy with history and regret. I felt a pang of something I didn't want to name—some faint, unwelcome sympathy for whatever had once connected them. But I'd learned long ago that regret didn't keep you safe. It didn't keep you alive.

I straightened, feeling the cold bite of metal under my jacket where I'd stashed the artifact. The weight was familiar now, a constant reminder of everything we stood to lose. "Then I guess we're done here," I said, my voice sharper than I intended. "Because whatever you think you're getting out of this? It's not going to be worth it."

Her gaze snapped back to me, the smirk gone, replaced by something colder, something deadly. "Oh, I think you're wrong about that."

Without warning, she lunged, her blade flashing in the moonlight as she moved with a speed that caught me off guard. Instinct took over, and I sidestepped, feeling the rush of air as the blade missed me by inches. Damian reacted instantly, grabbing her wrist before she could swing again, his grip iron-strong. She twisted, using his momentum against him, and he stumbled, just enough for her to wrench free, landing a sharp kick to his side.

Pain flashed across his face, but he held his ground, his gaze never leaving her. "You don't have to do this," he said, his voice strained but steady, a strange mixture of anger and desperation. "This isn't who you are."

Her laugh was a dagger, cold and merciless. "Oh, but it is. You just never wanted to see it."

She moved again, faster this time, her blade aimed straight at him. I reacted without thinking, stepping between them, grabbing for her arm. She twisted, and I felt the sharp sting of metal against my skin, a hot line of pain slicing across my forearm. I gritted my teeth, refusing to give her the satisfaction of seeing me flinch.

"Nice try," she whispered, her face inches from mine, her eyes gleaming with something dark, something hungry. "But it's not enough."

Damian was on her again, his grip unyielding as he forced her back, away from me. She struggled, her movements frantic and wild, like an animal caught in a trap, and for a moment, I saw the fear in her eyes—the realization that she'd underestimated us, that maybe she wasn't as invincible as she thought.

"Give it up," Damian said, his voice low, fierce. "This doesn't have to end this way."

But she only laughed, a desperate, hollow sound. "You think you've won? You think you're safe?" Her gaze shifted to me, a flash of triumph in her eyes that sent a chill down my spine. "They're coming. And when they find you, no amount of loyalty or love or foolish heroics will save you."

A strange, heavy silence settled over us, her words hanging in the air like a threat, like a curse. Damian's grip loosened, just enough for her to break free, and she took a step back, her eyes still locked on mine. There was a feral gleam in them, a hint of something unhinged, and I realized with a jolt that she wasn't bluffing. She really believed every twisted word she'd said.

"See you soon," she whispered, a promise laced with venom, before slipping into the shadows, her footsteps fading into the night.

I exhaled, feeling the adrenaline crash through me like a tidal wave, my knees weak, my mind reeling. Damian was beside me in an instant, his hand on my shoulder, his touch grounding me, steadying me in the aftermath of her presence.

"You okay?" he asked, his voice soft, his gaze searching my face for answers I wasn't sure I had.

I nodded, though I wasn't sure if it was true. The cut on my arm throbbed, but the pain was distant, overshadowed by the weight of her words, by the ominous certainty of what she'd left behind.

"We need to move," I said, my voice steadier than I felt. "If she's right, if they're really coming..." I trailed off, unable to finish the sentence, the implications too heavy to put into words.

Damian's jaw tightened, and he nodded, his gaze hardening, his expression resolute. "Then we'll be ready."

But even as he spoke, I could see the doubt flicker across his face, a shadow that mirrored the unease curling in my chest. We both knew that readiness wouldn't be enough—that whatever was coming, it was bigger than either of us, bigger than the choices we'd made, the lines we'd crossed.

We moved in silence, the night closing in around us, the path ahead shrouded in darkness and uncertainty. The artifact pulsed against my side, its strange energy humming through me, a reminder of the power we held—and the danger that came with it. I didn't know what lay ahead, didn't know if we'd make it out of this with our lives or our souls intact. But as the shadows deepened and the trees loomed closer, I felt a new resolve harden within me, a fierce, unrelenting will to survive, to fight, to prove her wrong.

And as we disappeared into the night, leaving behind the faint echo of her laughter, I couldn't shake the feeling that we were heading straight into the lion's den. That somewhere in the darkness, something was waiting for us, watching, biding its time.

I only hoped we'd be ready when it finally struck.

Chapter 23: Fire in the Night

The flames licked higher into the night, an uninvited chorus to the frantic symphony of clashing swords and shouts of rage. Each breath tasted of ash and sweat, thick on my tongue and sharper than any blade, though the sting of a near-miss had already kissed my cheek. I dodged, ducked, and threw my weight against the nearest attacker with every ounce of strength left in me. Damian's faction was relentless, a swarm of dark shadows converging on us with practiced brutality. I felt their eyes trained on us, watching each move, counting breaths and missteps, waiting to make that one, fatal strike.

A flash of steel whizzed past me, catching only the edge of my sleeve as I spun away, my heart thrumming wildly against my ribs. "Keep moving, don't let them pin you," Damian had said, his voice low and steady in the lead-up to this hellish dance. I'd thought, at the time, that it was a piece of obvious advice, something he threw out because he knew I didn't trust him, not yet. But now I could see why he'd drilled it into me, making sure I knew that if I stopped, even for a second, that would be it. They'd close in, like wolves, quick and silent. A flicker of panic rose up inside me, but I buried it, fueling each strike, each frantic evasion with the energy of that fear.

Damian, somewhere to my right, was a whirlwind of motion, every move precise, every swing of his blade calculated. His face was hidden under the shadows of his cloak, but I could feel his eyes on me, tracking my movements, making sure I wasn't lost in the chaos. And there was something about that knowledge—about knowing he was there, close enough to catch me if I stumbled, that made me fight harder. I hated it, that feeling of wanting someone's protection, that quiet thrill of trusting someone else to have my back. But here I was, battered and bruised, grateful for every second that I could lean on that borrowed strength.

The night stretched on, an eternity of blood and smoke. I couldn't tell who was friend or foe anymore; they were all shadows, faceless forms melting into the dark. The flames cast shifting patterns of light on the ground, and my eyes flickered, drawn to every movement, every glint of steel. A soldier lunged toward me, his sword swinging with brutal precision, and I blocked it just in time, feeling the shock rattle up my arm. I gritted my teeth and thrust back, catching him off guard. He stumbled, and I took my chance, pushing past him, not bothering to see if he would rise again.

My breath came in short, ragged gasps. I was tiring, the weight of each blow, each evasion pulling me down, like invisible hands were reaching up from the ground, trying to drag me under. I saw Damian then, his form silhouetted against the inferno behind him, striking down another assailant with a merciless swipe. There was something both terrifying and beautiful about the way he moved, an effortless grace that belied the violence in each swing. And I hated that I noticed, hated that in the midst of this madness, a part of me was awed by him.

A scream tore through the air, and I barely turned in time to see a figure rushing toward me, sword raised high, eyes wild with desperation. I braced myself, feeling the ache in my arms as I lifted my own weapon. But then, a shadow stepped in between us, moving with a fluid, deadly speed, and I realized it was Damian. He parried the blow, twisting his blade in a way that disarmed the attacker in a single movement. The man fell back, scrambling in the dirt, and Damian didn't give him a second glance. Instead, he turned to me, a smirk curving at the corner of his mouth, like he was enjoying himself.

"Try not to die on me, will you?" His voice was low, almost amused, and in any other moment, I might have snapped back, told him to worry about himself. But now, all I could do was nod, the words catching in my throat, swallowed by the heat and smoke that surrounded us.

Another soldier charged, and I blocked him, using the last dregs of strength left in me. I couldn't tell if it was sweat or blood that blurred my vision, but I blinked it away, refusing to give in. Damian stayed close, fending off attackers when they came too near, but never close enough to make me feel like I was being protected. No, he kept a distance, letting me fight my own battles, step in only when the odds turned too bleak. And for some reason, that was what made me trust him, more than any promise or oath he could have made. He didn't smother me; he didn't try to take over. He just... was there, when I needed him most.

Time slipped away, the minutes melding into one endless blur of violence and fire. I was dimly aware of the battle winding down, the shouts growing quieter, the clanging of swords fading into the distance. The bodies of the fallen littered the ground, their faces frozen in expressions of fear and pain, and I couldn't bring myself to look at them for too long. It was over, I realized, the tension seeping out of my muscles as I lowered my sword, my arms trembling with the effort.

But just as I let my guard drop, a figure rose out of the shadows, a blade flashing in the dim light. I barely had time to register the danger before Damian was there, his arm wrapping around me, his body shielding me as he took the blow meant for me. I heard the sickening crunch of metal meeting flesh, felt the warm, sticky wetness of his blood against my skin, and for a moment, I was frozen, paralyzed by the sheer shock of it.

Damian staggered back, his hand clutching his side, but his eyes found mine, steady and unflinching. He gave me a small, pained smile, the kind that said he didn't regret it, not one bit. And in that instant, everything shifted.

The fire is everywhere, licking up the night sky with a hunger that seems insatiable. Each flame twists like a dancer, casting our faces in a vivid, flickering light that speaks of danger and whispered promises alike. I'm barely breathing, each step carefully measured, every swing of my weapon calculated and sharp. I glimpse Damian in the midst of the chaos—his eyes trained on the enemy with a resolve so intense it's almost frightening. Around him, his men fight with brutal precision, a well-oiled machine that's accustomed to the frenzy of battle. This is their life, their skill honed in countless skirmishes. And yet, here they are, risking it all not just for him, but somehow for me too.

There's a moment when my back is unprotected, an opening that any skilled fighter would see and exploit without hesitation. I barely have time to brace myself, feeling the chill of death's brush against my neck, when Damian appears in a blur, his blade flashing as he deflects the blow meant for me. The move is clean, effortless, and in the heartbeat it takes him to pivot back to his own opponent, I see it—that fierce, unyielding loyalty. For a second, my chest tightens, words caught somewhere between gratitude and the frightening realization that he'd risked himself for me.

But there's no time to dwell on the sentiment, not now, not with the fire crackling closer, and the night filled with shouts and the harsh clash of steel. "Get a grip," I mutter to myself, forcing my focus back as I dodge a strike aimed at my shoulder. I counter with a quick jab, catching my attacker off guard, and he stumbles back, his eyes wide with surprise before he collapses to the ground. For an instant, everything goes quiet, the heat from the flames pressing in on me, suffocating, until I hear Damian call out—a sound laced with warning and urgency.

Before I can respond, an explosion rips through the camp, throwing me off balance. I'm on my knees, palms digging into the rough ground, dazed, my ears ringing from the blast. Out of the smoke, a figure emerges—a man whose eyes gleam with a wild, almost gleeful madness. He raises his weapon, his face twisting with a dark, ugly satisfaction that sends a shiver down my spine. But before he can strike, Damian's there again, a wall between me and the danger. His movements are a dance of precision, each motion smooth as he parries the attacker's blows, his own face a mask of calm intensity.

The fight between them is swift and brutal, Damian's strength overpowering the other man in a matter of seconds. He stands over the fallen figure, chest heaving, then turns to me, his expression unreadable in the flickering light. "You all right?" His voice is steady, even if his gaze searches mine with a flicker of concern.

I nod, managing to find my feet. "You didn't have to—"

"Don't start with the gratitude speech now," he interrupts, his lips curving into that wry, familiar smile. "Save it for after we survive the night." There's a hint of something warmer in his tone, something that tightens the air between us, if only for a moment. And then he's back in motion, shouting orders to his men, guiding them through the chaos with a clarity that steadies them all.

As we continue the fight, the tide begins to turn, the enemy's forces thinning. But victory, I've learned, always comes at a price. The losses are mounting on both sides, each life a weight pressing down on the night. When the last of Damian's enemies retreats into the darkness, leaving behind the wounded and the dead, there's an unsettling silence that follows, punctuated only by the distant crackle of flames.

Damian is leaning against a tree, his breathing heavy, blood smeared across his cheek—not his own, I realize with a sick sort of relief. He's quiet, his gaze turned upward to the stars, as if he's seeing something far beyond this battlefield, something more peaceful, something that doesn't involve bloodshed and betrayal.

"Why?" The question slips out before I can stop it, raw and unguarded. "Why risk yourself for me like that?"

He looks at me, his expression unreadable but softened around the edges. "Because, as much as it pains me to admit it, you're worth fighting for," he says, his tone casual but the words striking like a flare in the dark. "And because, strange as it is, I trust you."

I swallow, unsure how to respond, the weight of his words settling heavily between us. The warmth in his gaze, the vulnerability hidden beneath that bravado—it's more disarming than any enemy we'd faced tonight. But before I can untangle the surge of emotions, he's already brushing it off with a faint, lopsided grin. "Besides," he adds with a wink, "I couldn't have you thinking I'm the sort of man who just lets a lady fend for herself in a situation like that."

I roll my eyes, relieved by the familiar sarcasm but feeling the pulse of something deeper, something unspoken yet lingering in the air. "You're impossible," I reply, my voice carrying a grudging smile.

"And yet, here you are, alive and kicking because of it." His grin widens, and for once, in the dim light of the dying fire, I feel a strange sense of comfort—like we're two sides of the same coin, bound by shared danger and reluctant loyalty.

The fire dwindles, its glow casting long shadows over the wreckage of what was once a battleground. There's a weariness settling over us now, a kind of shared exhaustion that's almost comforting in its familiarity. As Damian's men begin to gather around, tending to wounds, murmuring quietly among themselves, I catch his gaze once more.

He doesn't say anything, but there's a quiet promise in his eyes, one that speaks of battles yet to come and perhaps, just maybe, a trust that runs deeper than either of us expected.

The fire dwindles to a slow, simmering glow, but the tension still hums like a live wire between us, taut and thrumming in the air. Damian's men move about, cleaning weapons, binding wounds, speaking in low voices that slip away into the night. But here, under the vast, star-scattered sky, it feels like there's no one else but the two of us, still locked in the silent conversation we began in the heart of battle.

Damian's gaze flickers over to me, his expression half-hidden in the shadows. He has that look—steady, assessing, as though weighing something unseen and dangerous. It's unnerving, knowing that the man who only hours ago faced down an entire force with the strength and ferocity of a storm is now studying me, like I'm the one puzzle he still can't solve.

"Well," I say, breaking the silence with a nonchalance I don't feel, "I suppose I should thank you, but I know how much you hate those." I flash him a smile that feels a little too forced, hoping to lighten the tension that lingers like smoke.

He doesn't respond immediately, only continues watching me, his eyes a sharp, searching green in the dim light. "You could," he says finally, a slow smirk curving one corner of his mouth, "or you could save it for a time when I actually need rescuing. It seems only fair."

"Only fair?" I arch an eyebrow, crossing my arms. "I'd like to see you try, Damian. I don't imagine you've ever needed anyone's help in your entire life."

His gaze sharpens, something dark and unguarded flashing in his expression. "You'd be surprised," he says quietly, his voice like gravel smoothed by rain, soft and edged with something old, something raw.

For a moment, I forget how to breathe. It's a strange, unnerving intimacy, like we're standing on the precipice of something vast and uncharted. Before I can think of a response, one of his men approaches, murmuring something urgent in his ear. Damian straightens, his demeanor shifting back to that of the calculating leader I'm used to, the brief glimpse into his guarded soul vanishing as quickly as it appeared.

"We have to keep moving," he says, all business now. "There's a chance they'll regroup and come after us. This is far from over."

He gives me a look that speaks of shared understanding—a kind of unspoken agreement that whatever had just passed between us would be locked away, filed under things best left unexamined. And so, I nod, falling in step beside him as we gather the remaining men, the remnants of the battle slipping into the dark as we move onward.

The terrain is rough, treacherous in places, with gnarled roots that seem to twist and claw at our boots, slowing our progress. But Damian's pace never falters, and I match him step for step, each silent minute stretching into something that feels like an unbreakable thread binding us closer, even if neither of us dares to acknowledge it.

Eventually, we reach a clearing, a space mercifully devoid of flames or corpses. Here, the air is fresher, tinged with the scent of wet earth and moss. Damian signals for his men to make camp, and I sink onto a fallen log, my muscles aching with the weariness of both the fight and the strange intensity that had lingered in its wake.

"Long day?" Damian's voice cuts through my thoughts, and I look up to find him standing across from me, a slight grin tugging at his lips.

"Understatement of the year," I reply, forcing a laugh that comes out more tired than I intended. "But I'll live."

He chuckles, his gaze softening just a fraction. "Good to know you're resilient."

Silence settles between us, not quite comfortable, but no longer the prickling kind of tension that it was before. And yet, in the stillness, I can feel the question lurking on my tongue, stubborn and insistent. Perhaps it's the exhaustion loosening my grip on caution, or maybe it's that strange, inexplicable pull that seems to tighten each time we're thrust into danger. Whatever it is, I can't hold back.

"Damian." I say his name like an accusation, and he raises an eyebrow, clearly surprised by the edge in my voice. "Why are you doing this? Fighting a war that isn't even yours?"

He studies me for a long moment, his jaw tightening. For a heartbeat, I think he's going to dismiss me, to throw up that wall of indifferent charm he wears like armor. But instead, he sighs, running a hand through his hair in a rare display of frustration.

"Maybe it isn't," he says slowly, "but I made a choice, one that I intend to see through. Whatever the cost."

There's a finality in his tone, a kind of self-imposed doom that sends a chill through me. I want to ask what he means, to press him until he reveals the secrets that seem to haunt him, but his eyes have already gone distant, closed off. I bite back my questions, feeling the ache of words left unspoken settling into my bones.

Before I can say anything else, a scream tears through the night, sharp and piercing, slicing through the quiet like a blade. Instantly, we're on our feet, the comfortable lull shattered. Damian's men are scrambling, drawing weapons, their eyes darting around, searching for the source.

Damian gives me a look—a fleeting, intense glance that seems to convey a thousand warnings. "Stay close," he mutters, his voice low and urgent.

The scream comes again, closer this time, echoing through the trees. My heart hammers in my chest, adrenaline surging as Damian and I move forward, our steps careful, silent. Shadows twist and dance around us, cast by the feeble moonlight filtering through the trees, and every crunch of a branch or rustle of leaves seems amplified, a harbinger of the unknown.

And then, we see it—a figure stumbling out from the shadows, clutching their side, their clothing dark with blood. It's one of our scouts, his face pale and eyes wide with terror. He collapses at

Damian's feet, gasping, his words a tangled mess of fear and desperation.

"...they're coming," he manages to choke out, clutching Damian's arm as if it's the only thing anchoring him to the world. "They're coming, and there's no stopping them."

Damian's expression hardens, and a chill sweeps over me as I realize that whatever we'd just fought—whatever horrors we thought we'd left behind—were nothing compared to what was still coming.

Chapter 24: Broken Chains

The night presses in around us, heavy and full of secrets. The fire crackles nearby, flickering shadows onto the walls of what remains of our encampment, our hastily assembled sanctuary in the aftermath. The scent of charred wood lingers, blending with the faint iron tang of dried blood, and as Damian sits down across from me, I see a glint of something in his eyes—a hint of vulnerability, exposed like a thin crack in armor.

He stares into the flames, his profile sharp against the shifting light. For once, his expression is unguarded, as if the weight of all we've been through has finally breached whatever defenses he's built around himself. I lean back, hugging my knees, careful not to break the fragile silence between us.

"It wasn't always like this, you know," he says, his voice soft, almost swallowed by the night. "I was... different once." He glances at me, searching, as if checking to see if I'm willing to listen. I don't move, afraid that any motion might shatter this rare moment of openness. Damian rarely speaks of his past. It's as though he believes that, by not acknowledging it, he can erase it from existence.

"My family," he begins, pausing to draw a shaky breath, "they weren't like me." There's a bitterness lacing his tone, a hardened edge to his words. "They wanted power—no, they craved it. Every choice, every decision was a calculated move toward domination, control. And I... I wanted no part of it."

I nod slowly, encouraging him to continue. I can't help but feel a pang of understanding, a familiarity in his words. I know what it's like to carry the weight of expectations that don't match the desires of your own heart. He rubs his hands together, fingers trembling slightly, and I realize he's more human than I ever imagined.

"They trained me for one thing—to follow in their footsteps, to be ruthless, to abandon any notion of mercy or compassion. But that isn't me. It was never me," he says, almost a whisper, as if admitting this out loud will make him vulnerable in a way he's never allowed himself to be. "So I left. I ran, hoping that putting distance between us would make me... different. But they found me, pulled me back, again and again."

His words resonate in the air between us, carrying a weight I feel in my own chest. I reach over, placing my hand on his, a silent offering of support. Damian glances at me, his gaze locking onto mine. His eyes, usually so guarded and intense, soften, revealing a depth of emotion that catches me off guard.

"You know," I say, my voice barely more than a murmur, "I understand what it's like to feel trapped by the expectations of others." I take a shaky breath, my fingers tightening around his. "My father was... let's just say, he wanted someone who would carry on his legacy of deception and manipulation. Someone strong enough to wield the family's influence like a weapon. But I was never ruthless enough for him. He taught me everything I know, but I never had the heart to use it the way he intended. And when I finally left, when I thought I was free..." I trail off, feeling the memories tighten around me like a noose.

"Did he come after you?" Damian asks, his voice low, almost protective.

I nod, feeling a familiar bitterness rising in my throat. "He did. And I've been running ever since."

Silence stretches between us, thick with shared pain and unspoken words. I can feel Damian's gaze on me, a warmth that seeps past my defenses. I've spent so long trying to outrun my own past, burying it beneath layers of sarcasm and indifference, but here, in this quiet, there's no place to hide.

"We're more alike than I realized," he says softly, his fingers threading through mine. His hand is warm, steadying, as if he's offering me an anchor in this storm we're both caught in.

There's a long pause, and in that silence, something shifts between us. The walls we've both kept up, the shields we've carried, crack and crumble, leaving us raw, vulnerable. His thumb brushes against my knuckles, a soft, barely-there touch that sends a shiver down my spine.

"We don't have to be what they wanted us to be," he murmurs, his voice filled with an intensity that makes my heart race. "We can be something else. Someone else."

It's a simple statement, but the weight of it wraps around me, a promise and a challenge all at once. I don't know who I am without the shadow of my past looming over me, and I can see in Damian's eyes that he feels the same. But in this moment, holding his hand, I feel a spark of hope, a glimmer of possibility that I've long thought impossible.

"Maybe," I whisper, feeling the truth of the words as they leave my lips. "Maybe we can."

We sit in the stillness, neither of us moving, as if afraid that breaking this connection will somehow return us to the lives we've fought so hard to escape. The fire crackles softly, casting a warm glow over us, and I allow myself to feel, truly feel, the weight lifting, the chains loosening, if only for tonight.

In that moment, I realize that Damian isn't just another fighter in this war, nor just another ally. He's something more, someone who understands the darkness I carry because he's borne it himself. And together, perhaps, we can face what lies ahead with something stronger than just survival.

Damian's hand lingers in mine, a reassuring weight I didn't realize I needed. The firelight flickers, casting shadows over his face, softening his sharp edges and making him look almost peaceful, vulnerable in a way I've never seen. A knot in my chest loosens, one I've carried so long it had almost become part of me. I've been hardened, too, by choices and betrayals, by a world that seemed to carve us both into warriors whether we wanted it or not. But tonight, amid the stillness of the camp, it's easier to imagine we're just two people finding refuge from the storm.

Damian shifts beside me, his thumb brushing over my knuckles, and I feel a surge of something close to warmth—not the blazing fire of a lover's embrace, but a slow, quiet flame, something patient and steady, something that could last.

"You ever think," he murmurs, eyes still on the fire, "about what you would have been like if things had been different?"

The question catches me off guard, and I find myself fumbling for an answer. It's strange, thinking about the version of myself who never had to dodge shadows or lie just to survive. There's a faint memory, hazy and distant, of a girl with a heart that wasn't so guarded, a girl who believed in goodness for goodness' sake. But that version feels like a ghost, something I can barely recognize as part of me.

"Maybe," I say after a moment, my voice sounding small. "Sometimes, I think about it. But then I remember everything that brought me here, and it feels... impossible." I laugh softly, more bitter than I intend. "I mean, look at us now. We're barely holding together as it is."

Damian raises an eyebrow, a glint of wry amusement flashing in his eyes. "Speak for yourself. I'm holding together just fine," he teases, though the faint twitch of his lips betrays him. There's a hint of boyish charm beneath his usual stoicism, a hint that maybe, just maybe, he wasn't always this hardened either.

"Oh, sure," I counter, rolling my eyes. "The man who insists he's never slept a full night since he was thirteen is perfectly well-adjusted. Got it." I give him a pointed look, unable to resist the playful jab.

He chuckles, a low sound that seems to melt away some of the tension lingering between us. "Touché. But I'm still here, aren't I?

Battle scars and all. And you are too, which means we've got a bit more grit than the world gave us credit for."

I nod, feeling an odd pride swelling in my chest. It's true—we've survived things that would have crushed others, things that probably should have broken us. And yet, here we are, sharing quiet confessions by a dwindling fire. If nothing else, it's proof that we're both too stubborn to give up.

There's a beat of silence, and then, almost impulsively, Damian speaks again. "You know," he begins, his voice softer, "I think I'd have liked that version of you. The one who wasn't hardened by all this." He glances over, a slight vulnerability in his gaze. "But... I think I like this version more."

The words sink in slowly, and I feel my cheeks warming, caught off guard by his quiet honesty. I'm used to sharp banter, sarcasm laced with undertones, but this sincerity is something new. It's disarming in a way I didn't expect, leaving me flustered, almost uncertain of how to respond.

"You're not so bad yourself," I reply, aiming for lightness but missing, my voice betraying something deeper. "Though I have to admit, I like this version of you too. The one that's not constantly trying to run off and play the lone wolf."

Damian's smile is small but genuine, and it feels like a rare treasure, something I want to tuck away and keep safe. "Guess it's a good thing we found each other, then," he murmurs, his fingers tightening briefly around mine. The warmth of his hand grounds me, a reminder that, for tonight at least, we're not alone.

But just as quickly as the moment settles, a distant sound breaks the spell—a sharp snap, the crack of a twig in the darkness beyond the camp. Instinctively, we both tense, our bodies shifting from soft vulnerability to readiness in an instant. My fingers slip from Damian's, reaching for the knife at my belt as he does the same, his gaze hardening as he scans the shadows.

For a heartbeat, everything is silent. Then, another sound—a faint rustle, a whisper of movement. Whoever it is, they're trying to be quiet, but not quiet enough.

I rise slowly, my knife glinting in the faint firelight. Damian moves with me, his posture tense, his eyes sharp as he locks onto the direction of the sound. Whoever thought they could sneak up on us is about to get a rude awakening.

"Friend or foe?" I call out, my voice steady, betraying none of the adrenaline surging through my veins.

The rustling stops, and a figure steps out from the shadows, hands raised in surrender. It's a man, thin and wiry, his face pale and drawn in the dim light. He's dressed in ragged clothes, his expression wary as he stares at us, clearly assessing whether we're friend or foe as well.

"Just passing through," he says, his voice shaky, though there's a hint of defiance in his eyes. "Didn't mean to intrude."

I exchange a quick glance with Damian, our silent communication honed by weeks of fighting side by side. The man looks harmless enough, but we've both learned not to trust appearances. I keep my knife steady, ready to spring if he tries anything.

"Who are you?" Damian demands, his tone hard, unyielding. There's a warning in his voice that brooks no argument.

The stranger swallows, his gaze flicking nervously between us. "Just a traveler," he replies. "Trying to stay out of trouble, same as everyone else." His gaze lands on me, and his eyes narrow slightly. "Though, I'd say you two look like you know trouble a bit better than most."

Damian's jaw clenches, but he doesn't respond, letting the silence stretch as he sizes the man up. I can see the calculations in his eyes, the careful weighing of risk and trust, and for a moment, I wonder what he'll decide.

Finally, Damian steps forward, his voice low and steady. "If you're lying, you won't make it out of here," he warns. "But if you're telling the truth, you're welcome to share our fire. Just don't try anything stupid."

The man nods, his expression guarded but grateful as he edges closer to the fire. Damian and I exchange a look, a silent agreement to keep our guard up, even as we offer him a place at our side.

The firelight throws eerie shadows over our new visitor, making his sharp features appear hollow and ghostly. He sits just beyond the warmth of the flames, as if afraid to come any closer, his eyes flicking between Damian and me with a mix of caution and curiosity. He's younger than I first thought, though the lines around his eyes speak of weariness that comes from living on the edges of survival, a state I know all too well.

Damian settles back into his seat but keeps his knife balanced on his knee, a subtle reminder that we are still in control here. I can sense his tension, a barely restrained coil of energy, ready to snap at the first hint of danger. I grip my own blade, my thumb tracing its worn handle, comforted by the familiar weight. Survival, it seems, is a language we both speak fluently.

"So," I begin, trying to inject a casualness into my voice I don't quite feel. "What brings you out here, lurking in the shadows?"

The man glances at me, eyes narrowing, as if measuring his response. "Same as you, I imagine," he replies. "Trying to find somewhere safe. Somewhere that isn't..." His voice trails off, and he gestures vaguely toward the darkness beyond the camp. "This."

His vagueness only heightens my suspicion. "Forgive me if I don't take you at your word just yet," I say, tilting my head, a slight challenge in my tone. "People with nothing to hide usually aren't skulking around after dark."

A glint of amusement flashes in his eyes, gone almost as quickly as it appears. "Fair enough," he concedes, his gaze lingering on the fire. "But there's not much else to say. Just a wanderer, trying to avoid the mess of it all. People like us... we don't exactly fit in."

There it is—a flicker of something unspoken, a hint that maybe he's not as harmless as he wants us to think. Damian catches it too, his fingers tightening around his knife, and for a moment, I wonder if we should just send him on his way. But then, the man's expression softens, something vulnerable slipping through the cracks in his guarded façade.

"You don't have to trust me," he adds quietly. "But the truth is, I don't have anywhere else to go. Not anymore."

A pang of recognition stabs through me, unbidden. I know that feeling—the hollow ache of having nowhere and no one, of drifting through a world that's all too willing to turn its back on you. I exchange a glance with Damian, catching the faintest hint of something soft in his expression. The look is gone in an instant, replaced by his usual wary intensity, but it's enough. He sees it too. We're all caught between trust and suspicion, forced into a strange sort of camaraderie by circumstance.

"What's your name?" Damian asks, his tone softened but still edged with caution.

The man hesitates, as if weighing the consequences of sharing this small piece of himself. "Ezra," he says finally. His voice holds a note of relief, as if the simple act of giving a name grants him a shred of humanity he thought he'd lost.

"Alright, Ezra," I say, leaning forward, my gaze steady. "If you're staying, you play by our rules. No disappearing acts, no sneaking around. We have enough enemies out there without adding mystery guests to the list."

Ezra gives a small nod, his face lit by the flickering firelight. "Understood."

Satisfied for now, I settle back, though I keep a close watch on him from the corner of my eye. The fire crackles and pops, filling the silence, and for a while, we just sit, three strangers bound by a tenuous thread of trust. Damian shifts beside me, his hand resting close enough to mine that I feel a faint warmth, a silent reassurance.

"So," Ezra says suddenly, breaking the silence. "What about you two? How long have you been running?"

The question catches me off guard, and I laugh, a bitter sound that echoes in the stillness. "Long enough," I reply, my gaze drifting to the stars, bright pinpricks against the night sky. "Feels like forever, sometimes."

Ezra nods, a hint of sympathy in his eyes. "I used to think there was a way out," he says softly, almost to himself. "That if I ran far enough, fast enough... maybe I could start over. But the past has a way of catching up, doesn't it?"

The weight of his words settles over us, thick and suffocating. I know that feeling too well—the futile hope that distance could somehow erase everything we've done, everything we've lost. But we carry our ghosts with us, shadows that cling no matter how far we flee.

Damian shifts, his expression hardening. "Running only gets you so far," he says, his tone grim. "Eventually, you have to turn and face what's chasing you. Otherwise, you're just a prisoner to it."

Ezra's gaze meets Damian's, something unreadable passing between them, and I can feel the air thickening with unspoken memories, wounds that haven't quite healed. But before I can speak, a faint sound reaches my ears—a low, distant rumble, like thunder rolling in from the horizon. My heart skips, and I glance toward the darkness, straining to see beyond the campfire's glow.

Damian's head snaps up, his eyes narrowing. "Did you hear that?"

Ezra tenses, his gaze darting to the shadows. "Sounds like... horses."

A cold dread slithers down my spine. Horses at this hour, in this desolate place, can only mean one thing: we've been found. I grip my knife tighter, every muscle in my body coiled and ready. Beside me, Damian rises to his feet, his posture tense, a feral light flickering in his eyes.

"Stay low," he whispers, his voice barely audible, and we move as one, slipping into the darkness beyond the fire's reach. Ezra follows, his footsteps silent, his face set in grim determination. We crouch together, hidden in the shadows, our breaths shallow, eyes straining to pierce the night.

The rumbling grows louder, and soon I can see the faint outlines of riders in the distance, their figures silhouetted against the starlit sky. There are at least half a dozen of them, cloaked in shadows, their movements too calculated, too precise. They're hunting—no, they're tracking, closing in with the ruthless efficiency of predators who've found their prey.

Damian's hand brushes mine, a silent question. I nod, my heart pounding, and we begin to edge backward, each step careful, measured. But Ezra lingers, his gaze fixed on the approaching riders, his expression tight with something between fear and anger.

"They're looking for me," he murmurs, his voice strained. "They won't stop until they find me."

Damian's eyes narrow, suspicion flickering across his face. "What did you do?" he asks, his tone sharp, the words laced with accusation.

Ezra's jaw clenches, his face shadowed, unreadable. "I did what I had to," he says, his voice barely a whisper. "But they won't understand that."

The riders draw closer, their shadows looming larger, and I feel a surge of panic rising, the instinct to flee battling against the need to know the truth. Damian grabs my arm, his grip firm, his gaze intense.

"Time to go," he whispers urgently.

But Ezra stands rooted to the spot, his face etched with defiance, as if he's finally found something worth standing up for. And in that moment, as the riders close in, I realize with a sickening dread that he's not going to follow us—that he's going to face them alone.

"Ezra, don't—" I start, but my words are drowned out by the thundering hooves, the night swallowing us whole as the riders descend, swift and merciless.

Chapter 25: The Rising Storm

The artifact feels alive, pulsing with a sinister warmth that seeps through my fingers and snakes up my arm, curling tendrils of energy prickling beneath my skin. My breath hitches, each inhale and exhale an uneven, trembling thing. It's a strange kind of weight, that which both draws you in and repels you, a tug-of-war I can feel in my very bones. Damian stands close by, tense and unreadable, his eyes holding that same steely resolve I've come to depend on, though today, there's something else, too—a wary, flickering uncertainty.

My fingers twitch, and the artifact seems to shudder in response, as if attuned to every ripple of my thoughts. It's always been this way, unpredictable and tempestuous, a power that responds more to feeling than to reason. I've learned that trying to rationalize it only makes things worse; it's like coaxing a wild animal that can sense every nuance of hesitation. I tighten my grip, feeling the artifact's weight, hoping—perhaps foolishly—that it might help ground me, but the pulsing warmth only intensifies, spiraling into something deeper, darker, as if it's feeding off every shadow I've ever known.

Damian's hand finds my shoulder, grounding, steady. "You don't have to do this alone," he says, his voice low and sure, each word an anchor pulling me back from the edge of whatever abyss this thing is opening.

I glance up at him, a wry smile tugging at the corners of my mouth despite the tension coiling around us. "Tell that to the artifact," I mutter, forcing a steadiness into my voice I don't feel. The artifact doesn't care about companionship or loyalty. It's ruthless, thriving on the hidden parts of us, the secrets we bury, the fears we deny. And I've buried enough to fuel an army.

His eyes soften just a fraction. "Then tell it to me," he says. "Whatever it is you think you're hiding." There's an invitation in his words, one laced with that rare kind of vulnerability that almost,

almost makes me want to give in. But I know better than that. Vulnerability is an indulgence neither of us can afford right now.

I feel the pulse again, sharper this time, like a heartbeat growing wild with anticipation, and I realize it's no longer just feeding on me—it's spreading. Damian's face tightens, his fingers digging into my shoulder as a ripple of the artifact's energy snakes toward him, winding itself around us, binding us to its chaotic rhythm. His jaw clenches, but he doesn't let go.

"You have to fight it," he says, his voice a low growl. "Whatever this darkness is, don't let it own you."

Easier said than done. The darkness feels infinite, a heavy expanse of every doubt, every regret I've tried to leave behind. It presses against my chest, pulling me down, like quicksand I'm only just beginning to realize I've been standing in all along. I close my eyes, fighting for a breath that doesn't feel like a gasp, for thoughts that don't spiral, unspooling into a web of half-remembered mistakes and fears that have lived in the shadows, quiet but deadly.

When I open my eyes, Damian's gaze is still on me, unyielding, fierce. His fingers slip down to entwine with mine, holding them around the artifact. It's a simple gesture, and yet it feels monumental, grounding me in a way I hadn't anticipated.

The storm of energy lessens, the artifact's pulsing rhythm slowing as if lulled, tamed by our touch. For the briefest of moments, I almost believe it's over, that maybe Damian's presence is enough to tether it. But then I feel it—the power shifting, coiling with a calculated precision that's far more terrifying than any wild energy. It's waiting, sensing, and somewhere in the pit of my stomach, I understand that it's biding its time, feeding off our doubts, waiting for a weakness.

I don't realize I'm squeezing Damian's hand until his thumb brushes against my knuckles, a gentle reminder that he's still there, still holding on, still refusing to let the darkness win. "You're stronger than this," he murmurs, almost as if he's trying to remind himself as much as me.

A laugh bubbles up, half-mad and wholly unhinged. "You have far too much faith in me, Damian."

"I don't think I have enough," he replies, and there's something in his tone that pulls me back to him, to this moment, grounding me in a way that feels like a lifeline. The storm within me quiets, just a fraction, enough to breathe.

I don't tell him that this darkness isn't just mine—it's something deeper, more ancient, woven into my very bones. But maybe that doesn't matter. Maybe it's not about facing the darkness alone, but finding someone willing to stand beside you, even when the shadows grow long. The artifact pulses, but its rhythm is slower now, like a creature lulled by the presence of something stronger, something unbreakable.

Damian's eyes lock on mine, a question in his gaze. "Are you with me?" he asks, his voice a steady thrum that resonates with something deep inside me, a warmth that's been absent for so long I'd almost forgotten it existed.

I squeeze his hand back, feeling a strange, tentative confidence growing, not because I know we'll win, but because for the first time, I'm willing to face the darkness with someone by my side. "Always," I reply, and the word feels like a promise, binding and irrevocable.

The artifact shudders once more, but this time, I feel the energy bend, yielding, as if acknowledging the strength in our unity. I don't know what lies ahead or if we'll make it through the storm. But with Damian beside me, the darkness feels a little less daunting, a little less consuming. It's not gone, not by a long shot, but it's quiet—for now.

And as we stand there, holding the artifact together, I can't help but think that maybe, just maybe, this is enough.

The artifact's pulsing heat has settled, but the silence between Damian and me is anything but calm. His eyes hold me, steady, unyielding, like he's willing me to let down every last guard, to let him see the things I've kept buried so long I'm no longer sure where they end and I begin. Part of me wants to shake him, tell him to walk away, to leave me and this cursed artifact and all the tangled mess that's my past. But that's not Damian. And, against all my better judgment, I can't bear the thought of him leaving. Not now.

The first rays of sunlight creep in through the dusty window, casting sharp lines across the worn wooden floorboards. They slice through the tension, illuminating his face in a way that softens the hard lines of worry etched across his brow. I wonder, fleetingly, what he sees when he looks at me, this woman clinging to an artifact that's as unpredictable as she is. There's no room to ask, though. Not with the way the artifact's magic hums, a low growl beneath our feet, as if it's drawing power from every hesitation, every secret we're trying to hide from each other.

I feel a pang of frustration prickling beneath my skin, an urge to break the quiet and lash out, to do anything to relieve the pressure building between us. But the artifact tightens its grip, binding me to the silence. Damian's fingers brush against mine, a steadying weight, and his gaze sharpens, slicing through the quiet with a soft, biting insistence.

"You look like you're about to implode," he murmurs, his lips quirking in that half-smile that somehow manages to disarm me even now. "If you want to scream, go ahead. Might do us both some good."

I glare at him, partly because he's right and partly because I'd rather do anything than admit it. "And what if I want to throw something?" My voice is sharper than I intend, but he just raises an eyebrow, unfazed.

"Then throw it." He nods to the empty room around us, a little too calm, like he's daring me. "If breaking something makes you feel better, by all means, go for it. Or, you know, we could start with the actual problem and go from there." His gaze flickers to the artifact, and then back to me, his expression steady and infuriatingly patient.

I let out a heavy sigh, feeling the weight of everything pressing in, a storm brewing just beneath the surface. The artifact's power throbs in my grip, a mocking echo of every dark thought swirling through me. But there's no turning back now. Not when we're so close to... well, to whatever it is we're supposed to be facing here.

"I don't think it's as simple as throwing things, Damian," I say, forcing a calm I don't feel. "This isn't something you can just punch or yell at until it behaves."

He grins, that infuriating, charming smirk I've come to know too well. "Who says? Sometimes all you need is a little forceful persuasion." But there's an edge to his voice, a softness underneath that tells me he's not really joking. He's afraid, too. Afraid of whatever this power is, whatever it's doing to us.

For a moment, I'm struck by the absurdity of it all—the two of us standing here, holding hands like we're grounding each other, like we're fighting off some unseen darkness. It would be almost funny if it weren't so painfully real, if I didn't feel the artifact's pull, dragging me into places I'd rather not revisit.

"What if it's too late?" The words slip out before I can stop them, a quiet whisper of a fear I've been trying to ignore.

Damian's grip tightens, a small reassurance. "I don't believe in 'too late,'" he says, his voice steady, as if it's the simplest truth in the world. "Not for you. Not for us."

I look up at him, and for a moment, I almost believe him. The artifact's power pulses again, but this time, there's a hint of something else beneath the darkness—a flicker of warmth, almost gentle, like it's responding to his certainty, his stubborn belief in me.

But that moment is shattered when the artifact's pulse grows, shifting from a gentle warmth to a searing heat that makes me flinch, a sharp reminder of the darkness still lurking beneath. Damian's fingers slip from mine, and for a second, I feel the weight of it all, the crushing realization that maybe this power is too much, too dangerous, even for us.

But then he's there again, his hands steady, his gaze unwavering. "You don't get to give up on me now," he says, a fierce determination in his voice that pulls me back, anchors me to this moment. "We're doing this together, whether you like it or not."

There's a defiance in his tone, a challenge that sparks something inside me, something that makes me want to fight, to push back against the darkness with every ounce of strength I have left. I feel the artifact's pulse steady, its rhythm slowing as if responding to the fire burning within me, matching its intensity.

Without thinking, I tighten my grip, feeling the artifact's power surge through me, a wild, untamed force that I can barely control. But this time, I don't resist. I let it in, let it flood through me, facing the darkness head-on, feeling every fear, every regret, every doubt rise to the surface.

And then, slowly, I feel a shift. The darkness softens, the edges blurring as if it's no longer a threat but a part of me, something I can control, something I can face without fear. Damian's hand finds mine, a steadying presence that reminds me I'm not alone in this, that I don't have to face this darkness by myself.

The artifact's power hums, a low, steady beat that feels almost comforting, like a reminder of everything we've been through, every challenge we've faced. I look up at Damian, feeling a surge of gratitude, of something deeper, something I can't quite put into words.

"Thank you," I whisper, my voice barely audible, but I know he hears me.

He just nods, a small smile tugging at the corners of his mouth. "Anytime," he says, his voice soft but filled with a quiet strength that makes me believe, if only for a moment, that maybe we can get through this, that maybe, just maybe, we can find a way to control this power, to face the darkness together.

The artifact's pulse slows, its energy settling, and for the first time, I feel a glimmer of hope, a small spark of light piercing through the shadows. We're not out of the woods yet, not by a long shot, but with Damian by my side, I feel a strength I didn't know I had, a determination to face whatever comes next, no matter how dark or dangerous it may be.

For now, that's enough.

The air around us crackles, alive with the artifact's simmering energy, and I feel its pulse synchronizing with my heartbeat—a steady rhythm that feels both intimate and intrusive, like it knows every hidden part of me I'd rather keep buried. Damian's hand remains wrapped around mine, grounding me, his thumb brushing in slow circles against my skin, a silent reminder that he's still here. It's absurd, really, how his touch alone feels like the one thing tethering me to reality, even as the magic digs in, demanding more, pulling me toward something I can't quite understand.

I close my eyes, trying to drown out the hum of the artifact, trying to separate my own thoughts from its insistent tug. The darkness within it is endless, vast, and hungry, whispering in tones I don't want to understand. I feel a coldness slip into my bones, a creeping chill that spreads from my fingers to my chest, as if every hidden fear, every regret, is resurfacing, clawing its way back to the forefront. Memories flash before my closed eyes—mistakes, losses, moments I'd rather forget but can't seem to escape.

I shake my head, fighting the urge to let the memories pull me under, but the artifact's magic is relentless, seeping into every corner of my mind. And beneath the swirl of guilt and doubt, I catch glimpses of something darker—a shadowy figure, watching, waiting, its face obscured yet unmistakably familiar. My heart races as I try to focus, to see it clearly, but every time I get close, the image slips away, replaced by another, darker memory, a fragment of a past I've tried so hard to bury.

"Hey," Damian's voice cuts through the fog, gentle but insistent. His hand tightens around mine, pulling me back to him. "Whatever you're seeing, it's not real. It's just the artifact's magic, trying to mess with your head."

I open my eyes, meeting his gaze. He's so close, his face etched with worry and determination, and suddenly, I feel the urge to laugh—partly out of relief, partly because I realize how absurd it all is, the two of us standing here, trying to wrestle with a power neither of us fully understands.

"It's doing a pretty good job," I admit, my voice barely a whisper. "I can't seem to separate myself from it."

His eyes narrow, a spark of that familiar stubbornness flaring to life. "Then don't. If this thing wants to show you darkness, show it yours. You don't have to fight it—you can own it."

It's a strange, reckless idea, and yet something about it resonates, a deep, primal part of me responding to his words. I don't have to fight the darkness. I don't have to be afraid of it, not when it's already a part of me, a part I've carried all along. I feel a surge of defiance rise within me, a fierce, stubborn strength that's always been there, buried beneath layers of fear and regret.

Without hesitating, I turn my focus inward, letting the darkness wash over me, feeling it seep into every hidden crevice, every shadowed corner of my mind. Memories flood back—mistakes, betrayals, things I'd rather forget. But instead of fighting them, I let them flow, a torrent of emotions and images that I finally allow myself to feel, to own. The artifact's pulse shifts, almost as if it's confused, uncertain, and I can feel its power bending, adapting to me, rather than the other way around.

And then, just as suddenly as it began, the darkness subsides, replaced by a strange, quiet clarity. The artifact's pulse slows, its energy settling, and for the first time, I feel a sense of control, a steadiness that wasn't there before. Damian's eyes are still locked on mine, a mix of relief and awe flickering across his face.

"You did it," he says, his voice barely above a whisper. "You took control."

I let out a shaky breath, feeling the weight of it all, the sheer enormity of what just happened. But before I can respond, a sharp, shattering sound fills the air, like glass breaking, and a sudden wave of cold crashes over us, the artifact's power twisting and writhing in my grip.

Damian's hand flies to his side, reaching for the dagger strapped to his belt, his eyes scanning the room as if searching for something—or someone. I feel the artifact tremble, its power surging wildly, as if reacting to a new presence, a foreign energy that's suddenly filled the room. A chill runs down my spine, and I can sense it, a dark, looming presence watching us, its gaze piercing, intense.

A figure emerges from the shadows, stepping into the slant of dawn's light. Tall, with an air of quiet menace, his face is partially hidden beneath a dark hood, but there's no mistaking the power radiating from him, an aura that's both alluring and terrifying. He lifts his head, and I catch a glimpse of his eyes—cold, sharp, and unnervingly familiar.

"Well," he drawls, his voice a low, mocking purr. "It seems I arrived just in time for the show." His gaze flickers to the artifact, and a slow, cruel smile spreads across his face. "You've done well, better than I expected, in fact."

My grip tightens on the artifact, every instinct screaming at me to protect it, to keep it from him, whoever he is. Damian steps in front of me, his stance tense, ready, but the man just laughs, a cold, mirthless sound that sends a shiver down my spine.

"Oh, don't worry," he says, his tone dripping with disdain. "I'm not here to take it from you. Not yet, anyway." His gaze shifts to me, and there's a strange, unsettling familiarity in his eyes, as if he knows me, knows every secret, every fear I've ever had. "I'm simply here to watch. To see how much darkness you can really handle."

The air thickens, the weight of his presence pressing down on us, suffocating, and I feel the artifact's power surge, reacting to his challenge, as if it, too, recognizes him. My heart races, every instinct urging me to run, to escape, but I force myself to stand my ground, to meet his gaze without flinching.

"What do you want?" I ask, my voice stronger than I feel, the words laced with a defiance I didn't know I had.

His smile widens, a cruel, mocking expression that makes my skin crawl. "Oh, I think you know," he replies, his tone smooth, calculated. "After all, you've been carrying it with you all along. A little darkness, a little power. Isn't that why you're here?"

Damian's hand finds mine, a steadying presence that gives me the strength to hold my ground. "Whatever you think you know about us, you're wrong," he says, his voice low and fierce. "We're not afraid of you."

The man laughs again, a hollow, empty sound. "You should be." He takes a step closer, and I feel the artifact pulse, its power twisting in my grip, as if caught between me and him, torn by a pull it can't resist.

And then, with a final, mocking smile, he fades back into the shadows, leaving a silence so thick I can barely breathe, the artifact trembling in my hands as if it, too, senses the threat lurking just beyond our reach.

I turn to Damian, my heart pounding, every nerve on edge. But before I can speak, the artifact's power flares again, a sharp, searing pulse that fills me with a sudden, bone-deep certainty—whatever darkness we've faced so far is nothing compared to what lies ahead. And as the weight of that realization settles over me, I feel the world shift, the ground beneath us trembling, as if the very fabric of reality is beginning to unravel.

Chapter 26: The Final Choice

The streets were a maze of slick cobblestone and shadow, the night draped over us like a weighty velvet. Each step echoed, bouncing off the narrow alleys and walls crowded with centuries-old memories. The heart of the city pulsed around us, vibrating with an unseen power, and my skin prickled with the kind of tension that felt both electric and unsettling. It was the artifact; I could feel it even through the thick leather of the satchel against my hip, like a heartbeat out of rhythm with my own. Damian was at my side, his silhouette a dark, unmoving sentinel against the approaching storm. His hand brushed against mine, just enough to remind me that I wasn't alone in this madness.

We'd known that getting this far meant more than half the city's underworld was now trailing us, eager to take the artifact and with it, the power they believed it promised. The kind of power that would mean control, dominance. A sort of insatiable greed floated in the air, as palpable as the thick fog that coiled around our ankles. I didn't dare to let my hand slip from the dagger at my side. Damian was the same, his gaze steely and unyielding as he scanned the darkness.

It wasn't supposed to end like this—at least, not in my head. But I'd learned that nothing about this journey had gone according to plan. It was almost ironic, really, how we'd once joked about a simple heist, a quick score, before riding off to celebrate. Now, we were little more than targets, hunted by a dangerous blend of mercenaries, relic thieves, and old-world mystics who'd crawl from their graves for a shot at this prize. I wanted to laugh, if only to relieve the pressure building in my chest, but I doubted that would go over well.

Damian finally glanced my way, his face half-lit by the distant glow of the streetlamps. "So," he said, his voice rough around the edges, but warm in a way that made it sound like a dare, "what's the plan?"

I didn't miss the smirk he wore, that aggravating hint of amusement as if we weren't standing at the very edge of disaster. "Don't tell me you're suddenly interested in a plan," I shot back, quirking an eyebrow. "Last time I checked, you liked winging it."

He chuckled, low and rich, and despite everything, it was impossible not to feel a twinge of comfort in it. Damian was the type of man who could make facing certain doom seem like a grand adventure. "Just trying to give you a chance to impress me," he said, and then he took a step closer, his gaze sharpening. "But I've got a feeling you'll do that anyway."

I rolled my eyes, but my fingers tightened around the satchel's strap. "Look, I know you think we can fight our way out of anything, but this..." I paused, glancing toward the end of the alley, where the shadows seemed to writhe and shudder as if alive. "This might be different."

Damian's jaw clenched, but he didn't look away. "You're saying we destroy it."

It wasn't a question. His eyes met mine, unwavering, as he took in the weight of my silence. And in that moment, I saw something flicker across his face—something raw, stripped down. He understood the stakes, as much as he hated admitting it. This wasn't just about the artifact or its power. It was about the blood-soaked history that had followed it, the people who'd died or worse in its shadow. If we wanted to end this—really end it—then there was only one choice.

"Yes." The word slipped from my lips with a finality that surprised even me. "We destroy it, and the curse along with it. We take away their reason to hunt us, even if it means losing everything we've fought for."

A cold wind sliced through the alley, making me shiver, but Damian's hand found mine, grounding me. "Guess we're in it together, then," he murmured, a flash of his usual bravado softened by something... real. For once, there was no joke, no sly smirk. Just him, standing with me on the edge of a decision that could unravel everything.

The sudden clatter of footsteps sent us both spinning, back-to-back in an instant, poised and ready. The faint glint of steel caught the streetlamp's dim light, and our enemies slinked from the shadows, a slow and deliberate encirclement. They were an unsavory mix of rogues, their expressions twisted with a greedy kind of hunger that left no doubt about their intentions.

"Hand it over," a voice called out, thick and venomous, cutting through the tension. The man stepped forward, his smile a cold, crooked slash against the darkness. "You can walk away. Just give us what we came for."

I shot a glance at Damian, and he responded with a look that practically dared them to try. "Sorry," I said, my voice as steady as I could make it. "But that's not in the cards."

The man sneered, a nasty gleam in his eyes. "You'll regret that."

The fight that erupted was chaos—quick, brutal, a flurry of strikes, dodges, and desperate attempts to keep hold of the artifact. Damian's blade flashed, a brutal rhythm that held them at bay, while I focused on moving, weaving in and out of reach, using the narrow space to our advantage. But there were too many, their shadows multiplying, pressing in with relentless force. I could feel my strength waning, and with each step, the satchel weighed heavier, as if the artifact sensed the danger and was pulling me under.

I didn't realize my breathing had gone ragged until Damian shouted my name, his voice cracking through the chaos. "Now, do it now!" he yelled, his eyes blazing with an intensity I'd rarely seen.

With a trembling hand, I reached into the satchel, gripping the artifact's cold, smooth surface. It vibrated under my fingers, almost like it was alive, resisting my hold. Closing my eyes, I focused, summoning every ounce of courage, of conviction I had left. I didn't know what would happen when I released its power, but I knew it was our only chance.

A sudden warmth spread from Damian's hand to mine as he closed his fingers over mine, grounding me in the storm of magic and danger. I opened my eyes, finding his gaze unwavering. "Together," he murmured, his voice so low only I could hear.

And so we did.

A rush of blinding light seared through every inch of my skin, pouring from the artifact in brilliant waves, rolling outward, until I thought it might tear me apart. The pressure built and twisted, rising and rising until I couldn't tell if it was the artifact's energy or my own heart about to burst. And then, just as quickly as it had started, the light shattered. Fragments of glowing dust filled the air, dissolving around us in a gentle shimmer, drifting like the first snowfall of winter.

For a heartbeat, there was silence—utter, perfect silence. My ears rang, and I staggered, blinking against the sudden calm, half-expecting the ground to fall out from under me. But Damian's hand stayed clasped in mine, steady, grounding, as though he knew that was the only thing keeping me upright. His grip was warm, rough, an anchor amidst the dizzying aftermath.

Then I felt it—the unmistakable emptiness where the artifact's energy had once burned. The weight of its power, the endless, magnetic pull that had thrummed against my skin since we first found it, was gone. Just like that. And in its place, a strange sense of relief, like breathing fresh air after days of suffocating in a smoke-filled room.

"Did we...?" My voice came out thin, barely a whisper. It felt strange to speak aloud in the fragile quiet.

Damian's eyes met mine, something like disbelief sparking in them, and for once, he looked almost as shaken as I felt. "I think we did," he said, his words laced with an edge of surprise. "You always know how to make an exit, don't you?"

Despite everything, I laughed, the sound rough but real. I could still feel a tingling in my fingers, the lingering trace of the artifact's energy, but it was fading, like the afterglow of a dream slipping away with the first light of dawn. And that's when I noticed the city around us, the silence giving way to murmurs, footsteps, distant voices—normal sounds, like the world was slowly stirring back to life.

But before I could process it all, the ground trembled beneath us, a shudder that reverberated up through my boots. A ripple spread outward from the spot where the artifact had unleashed its final burst, sending the last remnants of its magic out in a shockwave. Windows rattled, loose stones clattered in the alley, and I heard the distant yells of people reacting, like a ripple of waking panic.

Damian's hand tightened in mine, and I glanced up, catching the shift in his expression. It was subtle—a tightening of his jaw, a flicker of something darker in his eyes, as if he'd seen this part coming before I had. "You realize," he said, his voice low, "they're not going to give up just because the artifact's gone."

"Let them try," I muttered, though even as I said it, I felt a flicker of doubt. The truth was, the artifact might be gone, but that didn't erase the memories of those who'd killed and schemed to possess it. A power vacuum didn't mean peace; it just meant more desperation, more hunger.

But Damian's smirk was back, an almost comforting sight amid the chaos. "That's the spirit. Nothing like a bit of reckless defiance to keep things interesting."

"You're terrible, you know that?" I shot back, but there was a warmth behind my words. I knew him too well by now, knew the way he used humor like armor, the way he'd throw himself headlong into danger without a second thought, and it wasn't lost on me that he'd done it all for this—whatever this was between us.

We slipped out of the alley, merging into the winding streets of the city, each step a careful calculation as we skirted away from prying eyes and curious onlookers. The morning sun was rising, casting long shadows across the cobblestone and gilding the edges of the old, crumbling buildings. It felt strange, surreal, like walking into a new world, one where the artifact's curse no longer loomed over us. Yet my muscles were still coiled, my senses sharp, because if there was one thing I'd learned in all of this, it was that danger never really disappeared—it just found new ways to manifest.

We cut down a narrow side street, one of those quiet corners that seemed to exist just outside the city's pulse, and finally, we paused. Damian leaned against the wall, catching his breath, his gaze settling on me with a new kind of intensity.

"So," he drawled, his voice smooth but his eyes sharp, "what's next for our fearless artifact-destroying duo?"

I raised an eyebrow, crossing my arms in an attempt to look as unbothered as he did. "You're acting like I had some grand plan for after this."

He gave a low chuckle, his eyes dancing with that maddening mix of challenge and admiration that he seemed to reserve only for me. "No plan at all? I'm shocked."

"Oh, please," I scoffed, a smile tugging at my lips despite myself. "You were the one who dragged me into this mess, remember?"

"Details, details." He waved a hand, brushing off my words like they were no more than an idle complaint. But I could see the glimmer of something softer beneath the smirk, a quiet gratitude that he'd probably never voice.

A silence settled between us, and I found myself looking out toward the distant skyline, where the rooftops melded into the horizon, bathed in morning light. Without the artifact's pull, the city felt smaller, less ominous, like it had lost some of its weight.

Damian's voice broke the quiet, low and thoughtful. "I think... maybe we should get out of here. Just for a while."

It wasn't what I'd expected him to say, and I blinked, taken aback. "You're suggesting we run? Not very heroic of you."

"I'm suggesting we be smart," he corrected, though the teasing note in his voice was still there. "We've got enough people wanting us dead without sticking around to add to the list."

I opened my mouth to argue, but the truth was, he had a point. With the artifact gone, there was nothing left to fight for, nothing worth staying for—at least not in this city. The thought was both freeing and terrifying, a clean slate tinged with uncertainty.

"Fine," I said, exhaling. "But only if you promise not to get us in more trouble wherever we end up."

Damian laughed, a deep, genuine sound that I hadn't heard in a long time. "Now, where would be the fun in that?"

Shaking my head, I couldn't stop the smile that spread across my face. He was impossible, infuriating, and yet there was no one else I'd rather face the unknown with. As the city faded behind us, the thrill of a new beginning stirred within me, sparking like a match struck in the dark.

I felt his hand brush against mine, warm and solid, as we stepped forward, leaving the shadows of our past behind. It wasn't much—a simple touch, a silent promise—but in that fleeting moment, I knew we were heading toward something that was ours to define, to shape, free of curses or artifacts, and for the first time in a long time, that felt like enough.

The road stretched before us, a thin, winding ribbon cutting through the fields that lay just outside the city's boundaries. Tall grasses swayed in the morning breeze, still damp with dew and shimmering under the light. It felt surreal to be here, breathing air free of the city's weight, with no artifact pulling us in a thousand different directions. For once, the future stretched out in front of me like a blank canvas—a thought that was both exhilarating and more than a little terrifying.

Damian walked beside me, hands in his pockets, whistling a tune so carefree I almost wanted to punch him. How he could switch so easily from near-catastrophe to this casual saunter was beyond me. I envied it. The adrenaline was still coursing through me, my body on high alert, waiting for something—anything—to jump out from the roadside and remind us we weren't actually free yet.

"What are you so happy about?" I asked, squinting up at him, half-annoyed, half-intrigued.

He flashed me a grin, that infuriatingly charming one that suggested he knew far more than he let on. "It's a beautiful day, we're alive, and the world is suddenly full of possibilities. Why wouldn't I be happy?"

I snorted. "Yeah, because we're totally out of the woods. No one's going to come after us, and there's definitely not a single bounty on our heads."

His grin only widened. "Maybe. But for now, we're free. And who knows? We might even find ourselves a nice little beach town, get a taste of the good life."

"A beach town?" I raised an eyebrow, trying to picture Damian, the city-dweller and chronic trouble-magnet, lounging on a beach. "I'd give that about five minutes before you're bored out of your mind and off to stir up some new catastrophe."

"Is that a challenge?" He looked down at me with mock seriousness, one brow raised.

"It's a prediction," I shot back, but I couldn't help the smile tugging at the corners of my mouth. "And let's be real, if there's one thing you know how to do well, it's finding trouble."

"Ah, but you like that about me." He winked, and I rolled my eyes, though I couldn't deny that he had a point. As maddening as Damian was, I'd grown used to his chaos, to the way he threw himself headfirst into danger with that reckless confidence that somehow, against all odds, usually saw him through.

But even as we bantered, a shadow nagged at the back of my mind, a sense of unfinished business that refused to be ignored. Every few steps, I found myself glancing over my shoulder, scanning the fields, the road, half-expecting someone or something to materialize out of the morning mist. Freedom was a fragile thing; it felt too thin, too temporary, like it could shatter at any second.

And maybe Damian sensed it, too, because after a while, his usual lightheartedness faded, replaced by a quiet intensity I knew well. He fell silent, his gaze focused ahead, his steps purposeful. It was in these rare, silent moments that I saw a different side of him—the part he kept hidden behind jokes and grins, the part that understood the weight of what we'd done, of what we still had left to do.

"You know," he said finally, his voice low, "we don't have to run forever. We could... I don't know, actually stop somewhere."

The suggestion caught me off guard, and I felt my steps falter. "Since when are you the one suggesting we settle down?" I tried to keep my tone light, but the thought hung in the air between us, heavier than I'd anticipated.

He shrugged, not meeting my gaze. "Maybe I'm getting tired of running." He let out a half-hearted chuckle. "Or maybe I just like the idea of having somewhere to go back to that isn't just the next job."

The honesty in his words took me aback. Damian wasn't one for serious conversations, preferring to mask his thoughts with wit and mischief, but I could see that this time, he meant it. And though I wanted to brush it off, to laugh and turn his suggestion into just another joke, a part of me felt that same ache for a place to belong, a place that wasn't always slipping through my fingers like sand.

But before I could answer, the sound of hoofbeats broke the stillness, the steady rhythm growing louder with each passing second. I froze, instincts kicking in, and Damian's hand shot to his side, where his blade hung, ready and waiting.

Three riders emerged over the hill, silhouettes dark against the morning sky. They moved with a deliberate, unsettling calm, as if they already knew where we were going to run before we even decided. Their faces were obscured, but I didn't need to see them to understand what they represented. The city's reach was longer than we'd anticipated, its fingers stretching out to drag us back before we'd even had a chance to taste freedom.

"Friends of yours?" I asked, my voice steady, though my heart raced.

He shot me a sidelong glance, his mouth set in a grim line. "Guess that's the price of being unforgettable."

The riders slowed as they approached, their figures sharp against the golden light, cloaks trailing like shadows. One of them, a tall, broad-shouldered man with a scar slashing across his cheek, lifted a gloved hand in a mocking salute. His voice carried over the quiet morning, deep and laced with an unmistakable threat. "Thought you could slip away that easily?"

Damian's hand brushed mine, a quick, reassuring touch. "Not the warmest welcome party I've seen," he muttered, eyes fixed on the riders.

The man with the scar dismounted, his movements slow and measured, like a lion circling its prey. He tilted his head, studying us with a look that made my skin crawl. "The city doesn't take kindly to thieves and deserters," he drawled, his voice smooth as silk but with an edge that hinted at violence waiting just below the surface. "Hand over the artifact, and maybe we'll consider letting you live."

Damian let out a low chuckle, crossing his arms with a nonchalance that was almost impressive given the situation. "Funny thing about that artifact," he said, feigning casualness. "It's a little... unavailable at the moment."

The man's smile didn't reach his eyes. "Pity," he replied, taking a step closer. "Then I suppose you'll have to answer for its loss."

My mind raced, weighing options, calculating angles. There was no easy escape here, no convenient alley to slip down, no dense crowd to disappear into. The open road stretched behind us, and ahead, the riders were closing in, blocking any chance of retreat. For the first time in a long while, I felt the sharp edge of fear prickling at my composure.

The man's hand moved, almost too fast to see, and suddenly there was a blade in his grip, glinting in the morning sun. Damian tensed beside me, his fingers itching toward his own weapon, but I could see the realization in his eyes—this wasn't a fight we could win.

And then, with a suddenness that stole my breath, Damian moved, his hand gripping mine tightly as he whispered, "Run."

Before I could react, he was pulling me backward, away from the riders, his footsteps pounding in time with my own. The men shouted, their voices harsh against the morning quiet, but I didn't look back. All I could hear was the rush of blood in my ears, all I could feel was Damian's hand in mine, leading me into the unknown.

But as we rounded a bend, the ground trembled beneath us, and I stumbled, catching myself just as I looked up and saw what lay ahead. Standing there, blocking our path, was another figure—a familiar face twisted in an expression I never thought I'd see.

My heart stopped. Damian's grip faltered. And as we stared into the face of our latest betrayer, I realized with sickening clarity that this wasn't just about escape anymore. It was personal.